Also by Tim Susman:

Breaking the Ice: Tales from New Tibet (editor)
Shadows in Snow: More Stories of New Tibet (editor)
Common and Precious

THE TOWER AND THE FOX

Book One of The Calatians

by Tim Susman

Argyll Productions
Dallas, Texas

The Tower and the Fox
Production copyright Argyll Productions © 2017

Copyright © Tim Susman 2017

Cover and interior artwork © Laura Garabedian 2017
http://www.FairyTalesWithTails.com

Published by Argyll Productions
Dallas, Texas
www.argyllproductions.com

ISBN 978-1-61450-385-9

First Edition Trade Paperback July 2017

CONTENTS

To Mark and Jack
for making this possible

PROLOGUE: JOHN ADAMS WRITINGS

Excerpt from "Letter of Response to the Abolitionist and anti-Abolitionist Movements," by John Adams, published in the Boston Herald, 1802

It seems to me that there is another People to which we may turn for guidance on the subject of Abolition of the repugnant practice of Slavery: the Calatians which live among us. In number they are so few that it is possible for a man to pass his life without seeing one, should he avoid the large cities of the British Empire and the towns surrounding the two Colleges of Sorcery in the Colonies, so it behooves those of us who have seen their diligence and example to communicate such to those who have not experienced the pleasure of their company.

Prior to the Council of Birk's declaration that these animal-people are possessed of souls just as humans are, their lot was not a happy one; in London there was no penalty for the killing of a Calatian until 1623, five years after that Council. Even now in many quarters they are considered lower than man, despite their every efforts to prove themselves equal. And yet no Southern landowner has come forward to attempt to bind them into slavery as they have freely done with the African and West Indian Blacks.

The Calatians, I believe, we regard in some fashion as our children. One of our number, for reasons of his own, created them by magic, and left them to us as our responsibility. The West Indian and African people who have been taken into slavery are more like our brothers, and as any man with both brothers and children may attest, he feels more love for the latter than the former, especially when the brother may have grown apart since their early days. In the same way, we can see that the Crown treats these American colonies, populated by its own children, with greater accommodation than the colonies of the West Indies.

But sons and brothers are still our family, and we owe them the same courtesy and respect. The Calatians have shown how a different race may live among us peacefully, industriously, and to the benefit of all.

CHAPTER 1: THE FOX

Kip grasped the wrought-iron bars of the school's gates with his black-furred fingers and pushed his fox's nose through the gap, staring at the large limestone tower that rose from the center of the well-trimmed lawn a hundred yards away. In bright daylight the White Tower earned its name, but today's cloud cover darkened the ancient stones and showed the moss and the cracks. It might well be a Roman ruin if not for the still-complete walls and crenellation around the roof. To the left stood a large canvas pavilion, with another barely visible behind it. A stone path cut through the grassy lawn, and beyond those was a small orchard, all of it safe behind the barred gate.

The fox's eyes dropped to the figure standing two feet behind the gate, an olive-skinned young man with short hair as coal-black as his eyes. "You have to let us in!" he cried.

The young man folded his arms over his tan cotton tunic and looked back at Kip with a half-smile that might have held regret or amusement, or both. "I was told to admit any young men who wished to apply for admission to Prince George's College of Sorcery," he said. "And while I am sure it would cause the sorcerers great consternation were I to open the gates to admit a fox-Calatian," he gestured to Kip, and then dipped his slender hand toward Kip's companion, "and an otter-Calatian, neither of you is technically a 'man.' I am sadly bound by the direct order I was given."

"We are men," Kip protested.

"Aye," Coppy, the otter, said from behind Kip. Where Kip talked with a Massachusetts brogue, Coppy's accent betrayed his London birthplace. "Should you like, we can pull our trousers down and prove it."

The young man's smile did not falter. "There's no need to expose what's under the clothes when the proof of your in-humanity swings freely outside of them."

Kip turned and looked back at his father. His tail, a long russet brush with a white tip, swept from side to side with his agitation. "You said Master Vendis approved me."

"So he did." Max Penfold, Kip's father, stepped up to the gate. Only in the past two years had Kip caught up to his father's height, but his father stood broader across the shoulders, and where Kip's large triangular ears were a pure coal black, his father's were edged with grey. "Please summon Master Vendis, and he will order us admitted."

"Summon him yourself," the young man said. "My orders are only to open the gates and show applicants to the Master of Admissions."

"Just go back into the tower for five minutes." Kip smacked the heel of his paw against the iron, but not hard. Though he had four fingers and a thumb, his fingers were tipped with claws rather than fingernails, and the heel was covered with a thick leather pad, not fur nor the soft skin of a human hand.

His father placed a paw over his. "He doesn't need to go inside," he said. "Look at his feet, Kip."

The bare feet of the young man hovered two inches above the neatly trimmed damp grass. The young fox's breath caught. "He's under a spell?"

"He's a demon," Max said.

Kip stared. He breathed in, trying to catch any scent, but the slight breeze blew from him toward the demon. His nose did tickle as if he were smelling peppermint oil, but without the mint, just a cold tingle in the tips of his nostrils.

The young man inclined his head to the older fox. "Then you understand that I am bound by my order."

"Yes," Max said. "And you understand that Master Patris will be quite put out by my son's application."

The demon smiled, showing preternaturally white teeth. "As enticing as that prospect is, your Master Vendis will also likely be pleased by it, balancing out the annoyance."

"I would wager that more sorcerers will be put out..." Max exhaled as the young man shook his head. "Let us try another tack. One moment."

"God's wounds!" Kip swore, and smacked the gate again. "But Master Vendis promised!"

"Easy to promise, hard to deliver." Coppy looked up at the taller foxes.

"Calm down." Max raised a paw, emerging from his brief study, and addressed the young man. "Tell me, were you given any other orders in your duty at the gate?"

"I see no reason to share my orders with you." But the young man's smile grew. "Certainly a clever fox such as you can figure them out. Think of the college as a chicken coop you wish to burgle."

"You foul-mouthed—" Kip stopped himself before going any further. He breathed in until the fur on his shoulders and tail settled down.

"That's not fair," Coppy said, stepping forward. "Kip here hasn't been in a coop for years, ain't that right?"

"It's not a joke," Kip muttered, but he drew comfort from his father's calm. They are only words, he told himself. "What if we wait until another candidate comes up and then come in with them?"

"There's another on the way," Coppy observed.

The demon shook his head. "I would be obliged to prevent you."

Kip turned to look down Founders Hill. Among the gold-tinged maple trees, a figure made its way up the muddy road. In the light rain, he could not make out any details, and the wind brought him no scent. He looked past the figure, down to the Founders Rest Inn at the base of the hill, the black shingled roofs and limestone church steeple of the town of New Cambridge, and the vast expanse of fields and gentle hills beyond. It was as beautiful and peaceful as the cemetery it would feel like if Kip had to return there without entering the College. Maybe he would go to the quarry where he'd practiced lifting rocks with self-taught magic and smash them into each other like stone gladiators.

A horse-drawn cart rumbled by on the street below: the local dairy with their roan gelding. Would the cart mount the hill? Did the College have milk delivered? Did the sorcerers use magic to bring milk directly from the farms? Did they create their own milk by magic? He turned, the need to know burning in him, at his father's voice.

"Tell me," Max said. "What precautions have been put in place to protect my son, should he be admitted to the College? We can see behind you the devastation left by the attack—"

"We were here!" Kip pushed his nose through the bars again. Small pieces of brick and wood timber stuck out around the fringes of the large canvas tents, the remains of the grand buildings that had comprised over half the college as of five months ago. "We helped!"

"—and I am most anxious to know that such an event will not be repeated."

The young man's smile broadened. He bowed. "I can certainly understand such a concern. Sadly, I am not in a position to answer that question."

"Please relay my inquiry to a sorcerer who might be able to reassure me," Max said, with a crisp authority to his voice. "Preferably Master Vendis."

"I will inquire as to which sorcerer is available." The demon vanished.

Kip stared at the empty space, then turned to his father. "How did you get him to do that?"

"Demons are bound with very specific orders," Max said, leaning against the iron of the gates. He reached up to rub his whiskers. "If you can find a way around those orders, you oblige them to seek clarification from their masters. Often they will prefer to do that, as it disturbs the sorcerer, although some demons are much more willing servants."

"Like the fire elementals."

"Phosphorus, yes." Max corrected his son gently. "Although the sorcerers do not speak of the elementals as demons."

Behind them, Coppy said, "Oh, hallo."

The two foxes turned. Coming up the path, feet plastered with mud, shoes in one hand and a large bag over the other shoulder, was a young woman with long light brown hair sticking damply to her skin and dress. She showed no surprise at seeing the three Calatians, only laughed and said, "I would wager that those fellows expected a more respectable crowd when they encouraged 'all those desirous of acquiring an education in the magical arts' to come to their gates. Is there nobody there yet?"

"They wouldn't let us in," Kip said. "And the demon said he was only to admit 'young men,' so likely you'll be no more welcome."

"Oh, I expected that." She brushed damp locks away from her eyes. "Their advertisement said specifically 'any Colonist of magical inclination and ability may apply.' I memorized it and brought a copy along. I haven't come all the way from Boston to be turned away."

"Did you come by yourself?" Max asked.

The young woman drew herself up. She had high cheekbones and flashing grey eyes, and even bedraggled with the rain, she looked dignified. "I did. Mother refused to accompany me, and the sorcerer I learned a little magic from was taken ill." She glared around at them. "But I made it here safely, and my journey is not over yet."

"Nor is ours," Kip said. He extended a paw. "Kip Penfold."

"Emily Carswell." She grasped his paw firmly and without hesitation. "Where have you come from?"

He gestured down the hill as Max introduced himself to Emily. "Just the town."

"Oh." Her eyes widened. "You live here? Then you were here when it happened?"

"Yes," Kip began, but was interrupted by movement from behind the gates.

He turned with his father and saw the demon leading back a young man in a long black robe fastened at the neck with a bright silver pin: Not Master Vendis, who was older and had light brown hair. Kip glanced at his father and saw from the upraised ears and smile that the older fox remained hopeful, so Kip smiled as well. This, here, was his first contact with a sorcerer as a candidate for admission, and he would show them he was worthy.

The young man was pleasant enough, his puzzled expression clearing for a smile. "I'm Master Argent," he said. "Are you…?" He turned to the demon. "Corimea, you told me there were candidates here."

"So there are."

"Then why did you not open the gates for them?"

The demon's voice changed, became older and gruff. "Stand at the gates and open them for any young man who wishes to apply for admission to Prince George's College of Sorcery, and his family."

"Young *man*." Master Argent shook his head. "You may open the gates for any *person* wishing to apply for admission. Is that clear?"

"You do not hold the keys to my binding," the demon said.

Argent kept his smile, but made a small hissing noise of exasperation. "I will have Patris amend your orders later."

The demon Corimea bowed. "As you wish."

Master Argent gestured at the gates. They parted outward, pushing the Calatians and Emily to retreat several steps. Kip and Emily picked up their bags and suitcases with alacrity and led Max and Coppy forward, into the grounds.

"Now," the sorcerer said, "here is an unusual group of applicants."

"We're as good as any man who might apply." Emily stepped to the front.

"We shall see about that, I suppose." Argent smiled. "All four of you wish to apply?"

"I am Master Vendis's calyx," Max said. "This is my son, who wishes to apply, and our friend Coppy, who will not."

"Highly unusual," Master Argent said, but he rubbed his hands together as though relishing the prospect. "Come inside and we will discuss whether the College can accommodate you." He turned and walked along a stone-lined path to the nearest of the two large tents.

"Discuss?" Emily followed at his side as the three Calatians walked behind. "We are here to apply to the College. What needs to be discussed?"

"Come now." The sorcerer turned so that Kip could see his smile. "A woman intelligent enough to apply to Prince George's is certainly intelligent enough to know the difficulties involved."

"Women can learn sorcery if given a chance. There is no reason a woman should be treated differently." Emily put her shoes down on the stone, wiped her feet on the grass, and stepped into them.

"Nor a Calatian," Kip added as he lifted his cloth suitcase. He glanced up as a raven flew over their heads, and then another. The first returned to the tower, while the other circled above them.

After the terrible noise and thunder of the attack back in May, the ravens had been the first signal that there were survivors on the hill. Kip had not seen more than one since that night; his father's sorcerer, Vendis, now sent his raven down when Max was needed, rather than coming in person as he had previously.

When they arrived at the entrance of the tent, Master Argent held the tent flap aside. Before any of them could step through, a black shape flew past, skimming the edges of the cloth. Master Argent ignored it. "The problems are not insurmountable," he said, "but they must nonetheless be addressed. How fortunate I am to be the first sorcerer presented with a Calatian candidate and a female candidate."

His smile was fixed enough that Kip could not tell whether he was being sarcastic. Before he could decide, the fox's attention was caught by a bit of glistening white in the debris around the edge of the canvas. For a moment, he was convinced it was a bone, and the chill of that suspicion followed him into the spacious tent.

Inside, the grey light of morning and the smell of damp remained, but the air that brushed Kip's whiskers held unexpected warmth. A stately desk stood in the center of the tent, burnished mahogany or cherry—Kip was not very clear on his woods—with loose sheets of rough paper atop it. To the left, a high perch stood that allowed the raven upon it to look down at all of them, and to the right of the desk, a large copper brazier on foot-tall legs and a thick stone base radiated soft light and heat in rippling waves. Inside the open bowl of the brazier, Kip saw a familiar pattern, like blackened pieces of wood bark lying atop a fire, so that bright orange shone through in jagged lines. As they entered, the pattern shifted, and a triangular reptilian head, eyes glowing, opened its mouth to reveal a steaming pink tongue.

"First of the new lot, is it?" it said in a thickly English accent. "Ooh, they're an unlikely looking bunch."

"This is Geoffrey," Argent said, gesturing to the steaming lizard. "He's a phosphorus elemental."

Geoffrey sat up straighter, opened his mouth, and hissed. Kip, who had seen phosphorus elementals, bowed. "Pleasure to make your acquaintance," he said.

"Can you breathe fire?" Emily asked, staring.

The lizard's smile grew. "Course I can! Set me down in the biggest fire an' I'll breathe happily away. Prefer it to this cold dead air, anyway."

"No, I mean—can you breathe fire *out*?"

It tilted its head. "What'choo mean? Out where?"

Master Argent cleared his throat. "If you are admitted to the College," he said, "you will have ample time to debate philosophy and semantics with our elementals. Geoffrey here is by no means the only one."

"But I'm the hottest, eh? You said so."

"Quite right." The young sorcerer smiled tolerantly and seated himself behind his desk. Kip and Emily set down their bags and came forward; Coppy stared at the lizard a moment. Max remained behind them with Coppy, a bulwark against which Kip could set his back.

Master Argent had brought out two sheets of paper and taken down their names, his words somehow appearing on the paper without any visible pen or motion on his part, when a loud, angry voice called his name at the opening of the tent, and the ruffle of chilly air from the flap opening and closing turned everyone's head.

A sorcerer with a short white beard, fiery brown eyes, and a mane of white hair that remained thick and full despite the rain strode around to the side of the tent, storming towards the desk from the raven's side. The raven edged toward Argent on its perch, eyes on the new arrival as he bellowed, "What is the meaning of this?"

Argent remained seated, a small smile meeting the fury of the other. "These are our first applicants to the College."

The furious master flung his hand out toward the four, and for Kip, the room went silent. The fox tried to turn his ears and then his head through the thick, syrupy air. His breathing was unaffected, but no sound reached him. To his right, Emily appeared to be trying to shout. The silence unnerved him; to his large fox's ears, the world was an unending bustle of chatter: people talking and walking, birds singing, mice in the walls of buildings. To have all the sound taken away made his fur crawl. He looked back at his father and saw the older fox's ears flattened against his head, but he remained calm, so Kip tried his best to do the same.

In front of them, the two sorcerers engaged in a heated dialogue, to judge from the expressions on the older one. Master Argent remained placid and smiling throughout. After about thirty seconds, the older man pointed a finger at the younger, gestured toward Kip and Emily, and then turned on his heel and stomped out of the tent.

The air returned to normal around Kip's ears in time for him to hear the older sorcerer say, "I will be happy to conduct matriculation interviews with legitimate candidates."

"Excuse me!" Emily said loudly, but the man had already disappeared through the tent flap.

She turned to Master Argent. "Who was that?"

He had been staring past the four of them, toward the outside of the tent, and now turned to her with an attentive smile. "Master Patris, the Head of the College, has some objections to my liberal standards, it seems. But the responsibility for reviewing candidates has been placed in my hands, so—Miss Carswell!"

Argent stood, both hands on the desk, as Emily rose from her chair and whirled. She paid him no mind, but hurried out to the front of the tent, and after a glance at his father, Kip followed.

"Master Patris," she called as she and Kip emerged into the misty rain. The older sorcerer was halfway back to the Tower, and did not turn as she called his name.

"Perhaps we'd best let him go," Kip said.

Emily paid him no more mind than she had Argent. "If you allow someone to treat you the way they think they can, they're going to keep doing it. We have to show him that we will not stand for it."

"But he's the Head." Kip hurried alongside her. He glanced behind, but neither Coppy nor his father had followed. "If you antagonize him, we might not be allowed in at all. Wouldn't it be better to get in first, and then establish the rules by which you want to be treated?"

"Well," she said. "You're a good one with words. Better educated than most men I know our age."

"Thank you."

"And don't you think that education deserves respect?" They had closed the distance between themselves and the retreating sorcerer, near the point in the path where it curved around the corner of the tower. "Master Patris!"

A raven wheeled over them, and the older sorcerer turned, finally. "Candidates are not allowed in the Tower until they have been accepted," he said, and began to turn again, as though that were the end of the discussion.

"We will not be treated the way you have just treated us." Emily folded her arms and glared.

He stopped, and straightened. His voice chilled Kip more than the rain. "And how have I treated you?"

"Silencing us without asking. Talking about us behind our backs right in front of us. It's disrespectful and condescending and we deserve better."

His eyes narrowed. "Your feet are rather bare to be a bluestocking."

"I would be proud to be called such. Education and outspokenness are no shame for any person, man or woman." She did not look over at Kip, but added, "Nor Calatian," after a second's pause.

"Education is quite worthy," Patris said tightly, "and here is a small measure to add to your store. I am the Head of this College, and if I have matters to discuss out of your hearing, then I will remove your hearing. Should you by some fantastical chance meet the requirements to matriculate as a student of this College, you will accept that my authority over you is supreme. If I wish to render you blind, deaf, and dumb—and believe me when I say that the latter is growing more appealing by the minute—then you will trust that I have excellent reason for doing so and you will submit to my authority."

"And let me assure you," Emily said, "that if you treated any student the way you have treated us—"

Kip put a paw on her arm. "It was inconsiderate, surely, not to warn us," he said, and then looked at Master Patris. "But all we ask is the same treatment you would extend to any other student seeking education at your College."

"When you have proven yourselves worthy of equal treatment," Patris said with a sneer, "then you may expect to receive it."

He turned on his heel. Emily shouted after him, "Why do we have to prove ourselves?" but he did not respond, nor turn, and this time she did not pursue him.

Kip felt a sinking feeling in his chest, watching the sorcerer walk away. "Because we always have to prove ourselves," he said. "Because of how we look."

"Rubbish," Emily said. "We're living in the age of enlightenment, for God's sake. There's no reason a woman can't be a sorcerer. Nor a Calatian, for that matter."

"I hope not." Kip rubbed his paws together. "But none has, not ever."

"Because of people like him." She didn't have to specify whom she meant. "Because of people who think men are the only capable creatures God made. Only men can own property or have a voice in government. Can you own property?"

"My father owns a shop," Kip said. "But he rents the building—well, not the building, but the land. I think he owns the shop itself, but—" He stopped. "It's all rather complicated."

"Why should it be? Why can't he own his shop?"

"We've had this argument before."

She tilted her head. "You and he?"

"Me and Coppy."

"Oh. The otter."

Kip nodded. "He came from London, where the Calatians all live in a sort of slum, I believe. And he thinks we are blessed here, where we live alongside the humans and can own businesses and live more or less undisturbed."

"That 'more or less' is worrying," Emily said grimly. "And you have odd marriage requirements, don't you?"

"We have to marry in our species." Kip nodded toward the gates and the town below. "I'm already promised to a fourteen-year-old girl. Alice Cartwright."

"What does she think of you becoming a sorcerer? You know that no sorcerers are married?"

Kip held up one paw to her, showing the fox's pads and claws. "Our wedding is three years off, so Alice doesn't concern herself with my affairs yet. And there are a few married sorcerers. Their wives don't live near here and they don't announce their husbands for fear of being made targets, Father says."

"Fair enough. In my case, I was told one day," she screwed up her mouth and mimicked a stiff, matronly tone, "'Put on your nice frock, Emily, you're to meet your fiancé today.'"

"Your husband let you come apply to the College?"

Then she laughed, and he saw real joy in her face for the first time. "Heavens, no. I managed to get divorced."

Despite himself, Kip must have shown his shock. "Oh, don't look like that," Emily said. "I know two other women who have been divorced." She laughed again, but more subdued. "We met on alternate Wednesdays. We called ourselves the 'Old Wives' Club.'"

It took Kip a moment to reconcile the abstract image in his head of a Divorced Woman—there were none in New Cambridge—with the patient, smiling Emily. "Did your husband take up with other women?"

"Oh, let's go back out of the rain if we're to talk about Thomas," she said. "The subject's quite dampening enough."

He turned with her and then stopped, staring at the grey-white limestone wall of the Tower, just fifteen feet from them. "Wait," he said. If Patris got his way, Kip might never get another chance to be this close to the Tower.

The great building rose some eighty feet in the air, each block the size of his chest. Here at the corner, the stonework was more even and meticulous, alternating long and short blocks rising in a neat right angle, but as the wall extended away from the corner, pits and grooves, the natural peaks and valleys of the stone, made themselves known. From afar, Kip had never seen these, and he felt now as though he were about to shake the hand or paw of a person he'd admired for years, though in fact there was no person save his parents he had admired for as long as he had looked up Founders Hill to the White Tower of the College.

"You want to touch it?" Emily asked.

"I—" He hadn't even been thinking it, but he did, very much.

"Go." She pushed him off the path, and his feet landed in damp, soft grass. The blocks of the tower rose closer now. High above him, regular indentations in the wall showed where the windows were, and at the very top—was that a raven? A black shape, indistinct at this distance, stood on the edge.

What was the harm? If he were rejected as an applicant, at least he would have stood this close and touched the stone of the Tower. And that same fascination he'd felt as a small cub, as a teenaged student, as a furtive student of magic with the book his father had taken for him, that fascination rose in him, extending his paw toward the wall.

He took another step and then looked around the grounds. The large admissions tent remained still, the demon at the gate faced away from them, and only Emily watched him. "Go on," she said. "I won't tell. I'll turn away if you want."

Kip flattened his ears. "I've never been this close."

"It's a big old building," Emily said.

"Can't you feel it?" he asked, and she shook her head. But he could feel it now that he quieted himself and focused. Around and below him, the presence of magic like the pressure of a thunderstorm, registering in the hollows below his ears and in the fur from the back of his paws up his arms, that power that lay in the earth for sorcerers to take as they needed, that power that Kip had tasted a spoonful of, lay here in great quantities. It wouldn't be the Tower itself, but the presence of so many sorcerers and demons within it, the magical essence brought out of the earth and into the air, that he felt.

His tongue flicked the edge of his lips. He stepped closer, and now the Tower filled his vision, the white veins running through the grey stone, the patterns forming characters of a language he did not yet understand. An insect crawled along one of the stones; a patch of ivy crawled up the side. He followed the tracery of white through the grey, across mortared boundaries to new maps and characters, until Emily said, "Go ahead with it. I'm getting terribly wet."

Kip leaned forward and delicately pressed three fingertips to the Tower. For a moment he felt only the rough, cold stone. Then his awareness of magic exploded tenfold, a hundredfold.

CHAPTER 2: THE TOWER

Kip had summoned magic from the earth, up in his room in his father's house, and had grown more adept at it with practice. Still, it required concentration and focus. Here, magic was not deep in the earth but right at his fingers, an immense reservoir of it.

And there was something else, a deep tuneless sound like the distant rumble of thunder that echoed through his bones and then, unexpectedly, resolved into a word, as clear in his head as his own thoughts.

Fox?

Before he could register the word or question its origin, the pressure of the magic surrounding him intensified, sharpened, and then it was surging into him, a giddy rush that quickly set his head spinning. He staggered back, fingers leaving the wall, but the magic remained in him, pulsing below his fur.

"Your hands," Emily gasped, and Kip couldn't spare the concentration to correct her. His paws were covered in an intense purple glow, like radiant gloves, the proof of his trespass made plain for anyone to see.

He turned toward the admission tent in time to see Max, Coppy, and Master Argent come out. Whirling to hide his paws, his ears caught footsteps on the path coming from the Tower. If Master Patris was coming back, if they caught him—

"How do I get rid of the magic?" he pleaded with Emily.

Her eyes were wide. "I don't know. I barely know how to gather it. I never had anything that strong."

It burned now, demanding to be used and released. He only knew a small number of spells, and as the desperate seconds ticked by, he could only think of one that he was certain would be safe. He spoke a short series of syllables under his breath and lowered his paws, pads flat down and facing the grass.

The last time he had tried this spell, he'd lifted himself slowly into the air, levitating five feet and then stopping. Now his body shot up alongside the tower, past rows and rows of windows, and he was nearly to the top before he regained control. He rose more slowly after that until he reached the roof, and because he did not dare look below, he looked across at the nearest blocky parapet.

A raven looked back, its feathers sprinkled with rain, eyes gleaming in the brightening morning light.

Kip swallowed. "Brightbeak?"

The raven opened its beak. "How unexpected," it said in a hoarse croak.

"I didn't mean to," Kip said. "It was the Tower. I—"

"We may have much to talk about," the raven said. "Should you remain, you may find me here. But for now, I think it would be prudent for you to descend."

Kip gulped. The framework of the spell around him seemed to be draining the magic; at least, he felt no more pressure to use it up. But what if he tried to lower himself and smashed into the ground? "I would very much like to."

With a clack of its beak, the raven hopped from one crenellation to the next, nearer to him. "I believe Patris will be managing your descent in a moment, if you feel unable."

"Oh, no." Kip did look down then, and cupped his ears downward as well. Though the shapes were some eighty feet below, the black-robed figure with the mane of white hair currently pointing up at him was as unmistakable as the fury in the indistinct words he was shouting. "Not Patris."

The raven croaked a laugh. "Patris is a bad enemy to have in the College."

Force seized Kip, none too gently, and dragged him down through the air, fighting his spell. "I know," he said miserably.

"But," the raven said as Kip was pulled down below its line of sight, "he was never going to be a friend to you." It hopped off the roof and soared away and then back to him. "You may end your spell. You'll be quite safe now."

And then it was gone. Kip closed his eyes and hesitated—he was still a good ways up—but he could feel the force around him, and he found that he trusted the raven. He loosed the spell.

His descent speeded up, more than he would have liked, but he did not strike the ground so hard that he could not remain on his feet. More threatening to his stability was the red-faced Patris's shouts the moment he landed, six inches from his muzzle.

"Explain yourself! Unauthorized, unsupervised use of magic is highly dangerous and if you thought to impress us by this ridiculous display then I am very pleased to tell you that you have achieved exactly the opposite effect. What have you to say for yourself? Well? Is there no explanation?"

Kip opened his mouth to reply after each question, only to have Patris cut him off every time. It was not until Master Argent rested a hand on Kip's shoulder and drew him back a step that Master Patris stopped to take a breath. "I'm sorry, sir," Kip said, taking advantage of the pause. "I didn't mean to! I touched the tower and then there was magic all around. I didn't know it would do that!"

"Do what? Speak intelligibly, not in your animal noises."

Behind him, Emily widened her eyes. But Master Argent held up one calm hand and said, "Patris, you know that overeager apprentices have difficulty on occasion with the gathering of magic. Let Penfold explain himself."

Kip gulped. Patris's words were too familiar to injure him. "I didn't mean to gather magic," he said. "It was just there. And—" Should he tell them about the voice? He was not certain now that he had not simply imagined it. "And I didn't know how to get rid of it. The only thing I could think to do was send myself into the air. I knew that wouldn't harm anyone else."

"Ridiculous," Patris said. "Not know how to get rid of magic? You were able to summon it and not dismiss it?"

Argent interposed himself. "It sounds completely reasonable to me," he said. "Penfold, come back and finish your application, and let's hear no more about this."

"Reasonable?" Patris's voice rose again, this time directed at Argent. "If you think I will have this unpredictable danger in my College—"

"Sir," Argent said, "May I remind you that not ten minutes ago you informed me that I would bear full responsibility for the applications of these candidates? I choose to continue the process."

"Waste of your time," Patris said, but his voice lowered. "Someone who can't dismiss magic? Who can't control a basic levitation spell?"

"Yes." Argent's smile grew just a little. "And who has learned that spell on his own. Would you not say that that is someone most in need of our instruction?"

He met Patris's glare, held it until the older man said, "It is your time to waste." And then Patris drew himself up and his voice lowered, became iron-rigid as he turned his glare on Kip. "He will never be a sorcerer in this college."

Kip started forward, but Emily held onto his arm. He wanted to complain, to tell Patris how unfair this was, but he kept his muzzle shut. Though his father remained silent, he recalled the older fox's frequently spoken advice: let actions speak more than words. Very well. He would prove Patris wrong.

The Head seemed to be daring Kip to challenge him, and when the fox remained quiet, sneered and turned back to Argent. "When Adamson gets here, send Blacktalon to me. I will greet him myself."

Argent bowed, and as Patris left, the younger sorcerer beckoned Kip and Emily. Coppy and Max waited a little way along the path for them.

"What was that little display about?" Max's ears were back and there was a low growl in his voice. "You worked hard to prepare and then jeopardized it all in a moment?"

"I didn't mean to," Kip said in a low voice, Patris's comment still ringing in his ears. "The Tower—something happened when I touched it."

"Why touch it at all?"

"To be fair," Coppy said, "Who'd think harm could come from touching the stone of the tower? An' Kip has been in love with it for months."

Kip rounded on the otter, but before he could comment, the words had the intended effect on his father. "Years, actually." The older fox's expression softened. "I don't suppose you could have thought any harm would come from it. So what did happen?"

Without mentioning the voice, Kip told the story again. He hesitated before mentioning the raven at the top, worried what Master Argent might think, but the young sorcerer was deep in conversation with Emily a few feet ahead of them, and he did not have a fox's ears. So Kip added the conversation he'd had with the raven. "I thought it might be Brightbeak—Master Vendis's."

"Perhaps." His father rubbed his whiskers. "I don't know why Master Vendis would be watching and not come down."

"Being a calyx is different from being a student," Coppy said. "Maybe that's it."

Max's ears folded down. "Yes," he said. "It is different."

He met Kip's eyes, and Kip wanted to say something about how it was equally important, but his father forestalled him. "There are many calyxes and no Calatian sorcerers," he said. "You have a chance to change that. Remember the words of Mr. Adams."

"Which ones?" Coppy interposed himself. "You two are always going on about that fellow."

Kip raised his ears. "'That the only limits on anyone's ambition should be those of their God-given talents, not those imposed by any accident of birth.'"

"He said that about Calatians?" The otter's eyes widened.

"He was talking about men born in the Colonies not being able to hold offices in England." Kip saw his father's smile and went on. "But Adams writes very carefully. Those words were surely meant not only for Colonial men, but also for Calatians and even, we believe, slaves in the South. He has to talk carefully because of all those who don't believe in allowing people that kind of opportunity. Many of whom are here," he added with a look at the tent into which Patris had disappeared.

Before his father could reply, Coppy laughed. "Ah, folks are always worried 'bout change. Some of the fellas back on the Isle, they didn't want me to come to America. 'Runnin' away,' they said, 'why not stay here where you know what your life is?' 'Well,' I told them, 'it's because I know what my life is.' And look at me now. Got a chance to become a friend to the first Calatian sorcerer."

"You could be a sorcerer too." Kip put a paw on his friend's broad shoulder. Coppy was solid where he was light, thick muscle and bone where the fox was spindly and fragile.

"Got no talent for it. Not like you. Never set accidental fires or learned to throw rocks."

"Saul didn't show a talent either, but he was accepted and learned a little magic." Now that he had a chance to relax, Kip found it hard not to think about his old friend who'd been an apprentice here.

His father and Coppy looked away from his eyes, but the otter looked up again after a moment. "It might be possible, true. But yer father needs help at the store, and you won't need me up here." His large paw reached out to hold Kip's wrist, fingers circling it easily. "Nobody up here going to break your arm."

"I think Patris might have a go at them." Kip patted Coppy's paw. "Anyway, I'll miss you."

The otter released Kip's arm as they approached the tent, his thick tail swinging from side to side. "You can come see me weekends, and don't worry about Patris. You survived a whole childhood with Farley. Worst Patris can do is throw you out."

He said this as they walked into the tent behind Argent and Emily, and Master Argent did hear that remark. "You may be speaking facetiously, but in fact, Master Patris could not deny you admission by himself. All thirteen Masters will vote on the candidates."

"Surely the Head of the College bears additional weight?" Max stood to one side of the tent, letting the three candidates approach the desk.

"As does the Head of Admissions." Master Argent smiled. "You candidates will be tested by myself and two other Masters over the next three days. Our reports will be presented the following day, and that night we will vote on which candidates to admit."

"On Saturday, then?" Emily asked, and only then did Kip notice that she was fiddling with the front of her blouse.

"Yes." Master Argent sat and looked up at them. "Now, shall we complete these forms?"

Kip wanted badly to ask him what spell it was that allowed the ink to flow through the paper without pen or inkwell, but he felt he had used up what leeway he had, so he spoke only to answer the questions Argent asked, and while Emily answered her questions, he let his mind race back to the incident at the Tower.

One, the voice. Two, the magic. Had he really heard a voice in his head? It seemed unlikely. His father had been a calyx for years, for as long as Kip could remember, and he had never spoken of sorcerers putting words directly into his head. Master Vendis and the other sorcerers had come down the hill to the town in person, at least until the attacks. Thereafter, they had sent ravens. If they could talk directly into the heads of their calyxes, would that not be a more efficient means of summoning?

Perhaps it worked only when they were close by. But no, then Master Patris would simply have spoken into Master Argent's head. He would have had no need to still the air around Kip and the others.

Then could it have been a demon? A spirit unbound? His ignorance of the possibilities of the world weighed on him like iron chains which rattled with his frustration.

And the flood of magic, what of that? Kip had called magic into himself enough times to be practiced at it, but it did not yet come instinctively, much less unbidden. It reminded him of his first dive into the deep water of the quarry, falling through air and then plunging through water, deeper and deeper. The feeling had been terrifying, but also seductively thrilling.

That, too, might be a known phenomenon. He had to learn more.

Beside those two mysteries, the meeting with the raven on the roof felt pedestrian. A sorcerer spoke through his raven; someone had been watching him and wanted to talk and could be found in the tower. Kip could explain that easily and therefore felt less urgency in pursuing it. If he were admitted, he would have time to explore all these questions, and so that was where he needed to focus his attention now.

When Master Argent had finished the papers, he stood. "If you'll take your bags, Blacktalon will show you to the candidates' quarters on the other side of the Tower. When he returns," he added, for the raven had left his perch during the application and flown out a sheltered gap at the top of the tent. "The large tent next along the path here is the dining tent, and testing will take place there, here, and in the practice tent beside your quarters. I will see you tomorrow morning here for the beginning of the tests."

"Why are they all tents?" Emily asked. "Are you going to replace the buildings?"

Master Argent's smile tightened for the first time since he'd met them. "This year we hope to. But the Tower is large enough for seventeen Masters, with room to spare, and as we are still investigating the attacks, Master Patris feels it would be imprudent to erect any permanent structures until our investigations have concluded."

The raven returned then, perched at the gap in the roof. When it croaked, Argent said, "Blacktalon, please show Miss Carswell and Penfold to tents one and two."

"Sir," Coppy said. "May I stay with Kip a few hours?"

"Of course." Argent bent his head over his papers.

They exited the tent in time to see the raven wheeling and diving through the air in front of them, water drops spraying from its wings. As they did, Kip's father touched his arm and pointed at the debris showing around the base of the tent. "They still have not excavated it all," he said quietly. "New buildings would require a new foundation."

Kip nodded, staring at the thin gap between grass and tent, and the broken brick and splintered wood. Behind all the mysteries of that day, there lurked the larger one: what had demolished four sturdy buildings and killed over a hundred people in the space of a thunderclap?

CHAPTER 3: VICTOR ADAMSON

Master Argent's raven led them to a row of tiny tents, where they dropped their luggage before following the raven through the drizzling rain back to the large dining tent. They hurried through the tent flap, and while Kip brushed rain from his tail, Emily took possession of the table closest to the entrance in the warm, empty tent. She swept her skirt beneath her legs, sat on the long wooden bench, and rested her arms on the table, palms out to invite the others to sit. Kip took a seat opposite her, sweeping his tail to the side much as she'd managed her skirt, and as Max and Coppy joined them, Emily extended a hand to Kip. "So that we may be properly introduced, my name is Emily Carswell, of Boston," she said. "It's a pleasure to make your acquaintance."

"Kip Penfold, of New Cambridge." Max and Coppy introduced themselves as well, and Emily shook each proffered paw gravely.

"So you were living here during the attack," she said.

Kip's eyes flicked down to the floor. He forced them back up to the brazier over Emily's shoulder where one of the phosphorus elementals lay with only the tip of its tail visible. "Perhaps we could save those stories for a time not so close to a meal."

"My apologies." Emily transitioned smoothly into another topic. "It must be terrible keeping your fur dry when it rains," she said, producing a handkerchief from an inner pocket. "I am only wiping my hand dry of moisture, not of having touched you lovely people," she announced as she dabbed the droplets from her skin. Her hands, Kip noticed, were not a bright, pale white, nor yet the tanned farmer's wife's hands he'd seen around New Cambridge so often, but a dusty pink color, like the hands of the schoolteacher he'd watched from the front row of his schoolhouse for so many years.

"It is challenging," Max said, "but we learn to adapt and not to worry overmuch about the state of our fur from day to day. It can remain damp beneath the clothes, but if we keep the clothes clean and treat them with oils, they do not grow mildew any more than your clothes would if they remained damp for days on end."

"Which seems likely." Emily looked up at the trickles of water running down the tent roof. Like the admissions tent, the dining tent was warm and even a little stuffy from the heat of two braziers, the one behind Emily and the other in the right corner at the back. Both stood well away from the canvas, though as wet as the canvas was, steam still curled in small billows from the walls nearest the heat. Between the braziers, three tall poles supported the roof, and a wooden dowel ran between the three of them. Whether intended for this purpose or not, that was currently serving as the perch for Master Argent's raven as it shook its feathers clear of water and preened.

"Tell me," Kip said, "how are you so comfortable with Calatians? I had not thought there were many in Boston."

"There are enough," Emily said. "Thomas's law firm employed a dormouse to do odd jobs, and he and I spoke several times. Then Thomas fired him because he'd been talking to me, and I insisted he hire him back." Her smile broadened.

"And did he?" Coppy asked.

"Oh, of course." She laughed. "Thomas gave me anything I asked, eventually."

"Including a divorce," Kip said.

"Indeed." Her eyes sparkled. "By that time, although he never would have said it aloud, I believe he was happy to be rid of me."

"How did you procure a divorce?" Max leaned across the table and lowered his voice.

Emily pushed a sodden hair back from her face and leaned in as well. Kip and Coppy followed suit as she spoke. "It was difficult. Thomas did not particularly care for spending time with his wife, but he did very much care for the status of having one. And he was very busy with his law firm and did not wish to spend another six months in courtship." She looked around at the three of them. "So I found a young woman who wanted nothing more than to be a lawyer's wife, to look pretty at parties and say the right things to the right people, to fetch her husband's newspaper in the morning and mind the servants, and I introduced them."

"And then he divorced you?" Kip asked.

"No…" Emily drew the word out thoughtfully, took the wet strand of hair, and twirled it between her fingers. "He slept with her, and then *I* divorced *him*."

"What a cad!" Kip exclaimed.

Emily's smile was appreciative, but also slightly condescending. "I could never have gotten my divorce otherwise. But it was not as easy as I made it sound. My Calatian friend helped."

"Helped?" Coppy's eyes sparkled with amusement. "Brought the two of 'em together in a romantic spot?"

"Well, passed forged notes proclaiming their passions for each other, but yes. And then let me in on the day they made their assignation so that I might 'discover' them. And caught me when I pretended to faint."

Kip gaped. "You tricked him into infidelity?"

"Oh, don't give me that look. He never would have divorced me otherwise, and we're both much happier now, I assure you. My reputation did him no favors, except to excuse his cheating as understandable, and while he did buy me the finest dresses…" She wrung out the sleeve of her dress, dripping water to the wooden floor. "You can see how much I care for that. But enough about me and my past." She fixed Kip with a demanding gaze. "Tell me how a Calatian comes to apply to the College of Sorcery."

Kip glanced at his father, unsure how much he could talk about the book, but his father waved a paw. "It's your story," he said.

"It starts with you." Kip looked from him to Emily. "Father's a calyx—a Calatian who helps sorcerers in their rituals."

"How do you help?"

Before Max could answer Emily's query, Coppy laughed. "Best of luck gettin' him to answer that question. 'Not allowed to talk about it,' he says."

"That's quite right." Max smiled placidly. "The condition of our help is that we not reveal any of the particulars of it."

"Are you paid?"

Max glanced at Coppy. "Not in coin," he said softly.

"There's plenty of places where we ain't exactly welcome," the otter said. "And in London 'specially, we remember the Blackstone. But it's good having sorcerers need you around, you know?"

"What's the Blackstone?"

"Old bakery," Kip said before Coppy could answer. "About two hundred years ago a bunch of Calatians were trapped inside and burned to death."

"We put up a small marker on the site." The otter's smile had faltered, and now came back, a sad memory. "Not me, I mean. Us. The Isle Calatians, fifty years ago. Been there lots of times, some when I was too young to understand it."

"I never learned that history." Emily twirled her hair in her fingers again.

"Come to the next Feast of Calatus," Max urged her. "The celebration in New Cambridge is the largest in the New World."

"It must be nice having grown up just here." She looked around at the three of them. "I mean, it'd be like me having grown up with Abigail Adams and Elizabeth Seton and Phyllis Wheatley all in the same neighborhood."

"There were challenges," Kip said.

"Oh? What sort of challenges?"

Kip took a breath.

He had just turned ten years old and was walking with Adam, a nine-year-old mouse-Calatian, around the back of the school. They had been discussing the war against Napoleon going on in Europe; many of the New Cantabrigians had gone over to Europe to fight—but none of the Calatians had. Their teacher, Miss Partridge, had explained that the Calatians were helping the war effort by remaining home to help the sorcerers in their magical attacks and the defense of the Colonies.

That morning, a sorcerer had come down from the College (Kip did not remember whom) to tell Amelia Broadside that her husband had been killed in the war, and her twelve-year-old son Farley, who sat at the back of the classroom and usually spent his time flicking pebbles at the backs of the Calatians' heads when Miss Partridge was writing at the chalkboard, had demanded to know why the Empire was fighting Napoleon. Michael Warner, a year younger, also had a father overseas, though his was still alive as far as anyone knew.

"Why don't we just breed lots of the Callies and throw them at Napoleon if he ain't got any?" Farley wanted to know, and Miss Partridge had spent a long time explaining that in fact the Empire had very few Calatians and that they were very valuable to the sorcerers. She had spent so much time on it that Kip and the other Calatian cubs in the front had grown quiet, unused to the attention and uncomfortable with it. Only Adam, whose father was a calyx like Kip's, had spoken often about how brave his father was.

That was what Kip was talking to the mouse about as they walked their usual shortcut, through the weeds behind the school. "We don't even know what our fathers do up there. You shouldn't say so much about it."

"Our fathers do as much as theirs," Adam insisted stubbornly. "My dad looks terrible when he comes down. He won't play with me at all. And he does that even when we're fighting."

"But he won't die," Kip said. If he were not so absorbed in the argument with Adam, in the need he couldn't articulate to be more sensitive to the humans, he would have acted on the scent of oil when it reached his nose. Instead, he walked two more steps.

"He might," Adam said, and then, "I am glad he doesn't have to—"

There was a hard pressure under Kip's bare foot, and then a click.

"—go away—"

Kip jerked his foot up, but not in time. A loud snap, a crunch of fragile bone, a searing pain around his foot.

Adam's breath quickened, his eyes already darting about. "What happened?" But even as he said it, he saw the iron jaws of the rabbit trap clamped around Kip's black-furred foot, the blood dripping onto the dry summer grass.

"Go...get help..." Kip whined through clenched teeth, his eyes filling with tears. He sat heavily in the grass, fiery pain, unimaginable pain, lancing from his foot up his leg. Would he ever walk normally again? He tried to lean forward to pull at the trap, but even that motion caught at his foot and he stopped, stomach roiling, his vision wobbly.

"Are you—"

A high-pitched triumphant shout interrupted them. "Mike! We caught one!"

It was the worst voice Kip could have heard in that moment. "Go!" he hissed at Adam. "Get out of here!"

But Adam remained frozen, uncertain, and the voices and shadows resolved into Farley Broadside and Michael Warner, and then Adam ran, then, when it was too late. "Stop 'im, Mike," Farley said lazily, and Michael, who was two years older and nearly a foot taller, sprang after the mouse. Kip did not want to hear the thud and the squeak, but his ears, even folded down, betrayed him.

"Leave him!" he yelled, and thick, muscled Farley stepped forward in a fluid motion, his fist like a rock smacking the side of Kip's muzzle.

"Thought we'd play French and English," he said. "You petts can be the French."

"Ow," Mike said from a little ways away, but it wasn't urgent, just mild discomfort. "Stop scratching, beast."

"French beast!" Farley reminded Mike loudly with a laugh. He turned back to Kip, who was holding his sore muzzle as pain surged through it. He didn't think that was broken, at least, and he couldn't taste or smell blood. So he kept silent as Farley went on. "Think we should torture 'em to find out what they know?"

"About what?" Mike called.

Kip wriggled his foot, but the teeth of the trap had bitten hard, digging into the pad and the bridge of the foot, and every movement stabbed him with pain. He would need to reach down and open the jaws himself, but Farley would never let him do that. So he watched the other boy warily as Farley brought one meaty hand to his chin and his small watery blue eyes watched Kip.

"About the sorcerers," Farley said finally. "Where the French sorcerers are and what they're planning."

"Right," Mike called, and then, "Tell me what you know, French scum!" Kip heard Adam's half-squeak, half-sob, and then the sound of an impact that could *have been a fist hitting a face, or a head hitting the ground, and Mike's, "Don't cry, little baby! Tell me where the sorcerers are!"*

Adam weighed little more than half what Mike did. Kip acted without thinking, the need to save Adam burning away the pain. He lunged at Farley and bit him hard on the arm, long canine teeth sinking into the unprotected skin.

Farley screamed, and tried to club Kip on the face again, but in close quarters, his punch was less effective, and Kip knew better than to keep his jaws sunk in Farley's arm. He drew back and punched the older boy in the gut, and then swiped at his side, but Farley had jumped back by this time. Blood trickled down his arm and now Kip could taste it in his mouth. He collected it and spit it on the ground. "Leave us alone," he said again.

"Mike!" Farley yelled.

"Right," Kip jeered, even though it was what he'd wanted Farley to do. "Call for help, cowardly—cowardly English! We French will defeat you." The thought flickered across his mind that he could say something about Farley's father, but even in this circumstance, the thought of his own father, both his disapproval and the thought of him dying on a French field, held the fox's tongue.

And then big Michael Warner was on the other side of him and he dragged himself back through the grass, the heavy iron trap on his foot, trying to keep them both in view. "Having trouble with this Froggy chap?" Mike said. "You think he knows something valuable?"

Farley had a hand pressed over the bite on his arm. "Give me your knife," he said.

"My—" Mike's hand went to his waist, and he looked at Kip. "My dad told me never to—"

"Give it!" Farley held his hand out, and Mike, looking much less comfortable, unsheathed his knife.

"We're not going to..." He trailed off as he walked around Kip to hand the knife over. Kip could have outrun them both, but not with the trap on his foot, and now not even if it were removed. His whole leg was cramping up and his foot throbbed in agony. He shut it out of his mind as best he could.

"I just want a trophy," Farley snarled. "Hold him down."

Kip couldn't hear if Adam was moving; Mike was tromping through the grass toward him and all his attention was focused on that. "Watch the mouth," Farley added.

"I know how to hold an animal," Mike said, and he approached Kip with none of the reckless emotion Farley had. He judged the fox and lunged, and when Kip moved to block the lunge, Mike revealed it to be a feint, already dodging to jump on Kip's chest and pin him to the ground.

"Not like that," Farley snapped. "The other way."

There followed some verbal struggles as Mike tried to understand what Farley meant, while Kip struggled against the physical weight on him. Finally,

Farley's meaning came through, and Mike said, "I ain't turning him over. You can get at it that way too."

"Well, hold the free leg, anyway." And Mike, who wrestled when he could find anyone to wrestle him, twisted and caught Kip's untrapped leg behind the knee, pulling it easily toward the fox's chest while keeping his weight there. Kip lashed his tail, but couldn't do anything else, and even with the burst of strength borne of terror, he couldn't shift Mike.

Farley knelt behind him and grabbed his tail, yanked it straight. Compared to the pain in his foot, the jolt to his spine was minor, as was the sharp pain of biting his tongue. Kip's mind raced, but there was nothing he could do, no way out, he was going to go home with a bloody stump where his tail had been and even the sorcerers couldn't grow one of those back, he was going to be like Matthias and Delilah who had had their tails cut off by bullies and God he couldn't breathe—

A whoosh and rush of heat. Farley jumped away with a yell as the dry grasses around him exploded into flame.

The weight of Michael Warner, the painful pressure on his leg, all vanished in a moment. The two boys yelled, "Fire! Fire!" and ran.

Kip pried open the trap with difficulty, as quickly as he could. Heat licked at his face and ears, and his pants leg caught fire, but he put it out with a hurried patting of his paw. He limped on one foot to where Adam lay in the grass, on his back.

The mouse was breathing, but very quickly and shallowly. Kip looked down into his staring eyes and saw no recognition. When he lifted Adam's head, he saw the jagged rock below it, and smelled the blood.

He held his friend until the Watch arrived.

"Good Lord," Emily breathed. "What happened to Adam?"

Kip exhaled. "He lived for a few more years. He never talked much after that, and he suffered from seizures. One in his sleep killed him."

Emily dropped the strands of hair she'd been twirling and put her hand to her mouth. "What happened to the bullies?"

"Nothing, then." Kip glanced at his father. "Nor any time."

"Aye," Max said tiredly. "That was the most extreme, but Kip here had more broken arms and legs than I can count."

"We have lighter bones." Kip straightened his back. "I can outrun any of the boys in town."

"And I can outfight 'em." Coppy curled one paw into a fist. "Kip's had no bones broke since I came to town."

Kip smiled. "Coppy came seeking his fortune in Boston, but he and I got to talking and he decided to stay in New Cambridge."

"Felt time was about right for a change. A town where Calatians can live in separate houses, where they live alongside humans and share the town? I grew up in the Isle of Dogs and there wasn't much to love about being a Calatian there 'cepting other Calatians."

Emily nodded thoughtfully. "I will miss Boston, but there is something to be said for air that doesn't smell of salt or fish."

"It does some days." Kip stuck his tongue out.

"To you." Coppy tapped his nose, looking at Emily. "If you was just thinking about a fish dinner, his sniffer could pick it up."

Kip laughed. "Not quite."

Emily rested her elbows on the table, turned toward Kip. "Extra-sensitive nose and ears. You'll be a good friend to have. Can you spot a fly at a mile away as well?"

"Actually, I'm not so good at seeing distances."

"But better seeing at night," Coppy put in.

"Marginally."

Emily shook her head. "I suppose it's a fair trade for having to wear that fur all the time. And you can cast fire spells?"

Kip shook his head. "Not consciously, but that's why Father got me the spell book."

"He'd wanted to do magic since he was old enough to talk," Max said. "And the fire was an extreme example, but there'd been other fires. And sometimes he would seem to be listening to things, or concentrating hard. Once or twice things wouldn't be where we'd left them and we couldn't figure out why."

"Oh, that happened to me all the time." Emily grinned at Kip. "That's plain absent-mindedness."

"Well, by 'not where we left them' I mean he would get vials of perfume from closed drawers over his head, things like that. Things that the sorcerers say are signs of a strong affinity for magic."

"But aren't you all magic anyway?" Emily looked around. "That's what my sorcerer told me—yes, did I mention I worked with a sorcerer as well?—that the reason you're used as calyxes is because of your magical nature?"

"That is true." Max nodded. "But being magical and using magic are different things entire."

Kip was about to add something when the tent flap opened. Argent's raven fluttered its wings and shifted on the perch, and Max and Coppy turned to see the newcomer.

He was a tall boy, slender and immaculately groomed, with neat pale hair and ice-blue eyes, and he strode into the tent ahead of an older man whose nose and eyes were so similar that Kip knew immediately he was the boy's father. Both wore finely tailored white shirts under formal black jackets, with cravats knotted at the front—blue for the boy, steel-grey for his father—and identical trousers and gleaming black leather shoes. The faint perfume of orange blossom met Kip's nose.

The boy surveyed the tent with a slight sneer, and then his eyes widened as he spotted the foursome at the table. "Look, Father," he said. "We're to be assigned calyxes from the beginning. And…" His gaze lingered on Emily. "Oh, they may not be done setting up the tent. Really, there will be time for gossip when the work is done."

Master Patris pushed his way into the tent behind the boy and his father. "The accommodations are rather rough, but we are still rebuilding from— what are you doing here?"

His tone grew sharp as he followed the boy's gaze. Emily rose. "Master Argent said we might sit here and talk," she said. "And for your information, sir, we are candidates for admission just as I imagine you yourself are."

Kip stood beside her. "Both of us," he said, anticipating the boy's question.

Light blue eyes measured him, and disbelief melted into smooth courtesy. "My apologies," he said, and executed a stiff bow. The orange-blossom smell deepened. "My name is Victor Adamson. This is my father Josiah."

The elder Adamson regarded the foursome with bored indifference. Though his eyes shared a color with his son's, age had dulled their brightness. Out of courtesy, Kip gestured to his father, who was also standing. "I'm Philip Penfold—Kip. My father, Max," he said.

Victor bowed again but did not extend a hand. His father turned to Patris and whispered in a voice that was clear to Kip's large ears, "What the devil is this, Patris?"

Emily and Coppy introduced themselves as well, and though Victor's eyes flickered to Emily's dress, he returned his gaze quickly to Kip. He said something, but the fox had his ears focused on Patris's whispered reply about the liberal interpretation of the rules and the testing process making sure that only the most qualified applicants would be admitted. Kip only became aware of the conversation when his father replied to Victor's question.

"I have experience as a calyx," Max said, "but Kip is a candidate, and we hope he is talented enough to gain admission to the College."

"There have been no Calatian sorcerers, have there?" Victor rubbed his chin. "It might be possible, had a Calatian deserted to the Spanish army, or the French, ten years ago. But I have not heard of it. Which means that if you succeed, you two will be the first."

"Oh, I'm not applying," Coppy said. "Just escorting our candidate here." He gestured to Kip.

"And I'll be the first female sorcerer," Emily spoke up.

"Indeed." Victor looked from Kip to Coppy and back again. Behind him, his father and Patris had retreated to the corner of the tent away from the brazier, and between that and the conversation, Kip could no longer hear what they were saying. He supposed that Patris, at least, might have experience with the hearing of foxes. "Well," Victor continued, coming up to their table, "as we are all candidates, perhaps we should join forces."

He sat between Max and Coppy, but the others remained standing. Then, slowly, Kip lowered himself to the bench. "How do you propose we join forces?" he asked, while the others followed.

"Share information," Victor said promptly. "I applied for candidacy two years ago and was not admitted—obviously," he drawled, "but I cannot imagine their tests have changed overmuch."

Kip met Coppy's eyes. They had talked so many times about not knowing what the tests consisted of, wondering if they would be tested on magic or simply on knowledge, and here the answers had dropped in their lap. "What can we offer you?"

Here, for the first time, Victor hesitated. "I…" He looked down at the wood grain of the table and traced it with a fingernail. "I admit that despite having studied magic extensively, I still have not managed to manifest it to my satisfaction. I presume that if you—you two, my apologies, Miss Carswell—are confident enough to apply to the school, that you have attained at least some level of familiarity with the magical arts."

The three of them looked at each other, and then Emily said loudly, with a wicked eye back at Patris, "Kip flew to the top of the tower by himself. It was dashed impressive, if you ask me."

Victor did not turn, but Patris looked up from his conversation to glower at them. Kip sighed and nodded to Victor's scrutiny. "I've worked with magic, and I believe Emily has studied as well."

She waved a hand. "I've learned to gather magic and simple lifting spells. Master Hobstone said I should not learn more without more instruction than he could give."

They talked about the practice of gathering magic, but Victor knew the theory; he was more interested in what it felt like. Their conversation only lasted a few minutes before Victor's father approached and pulled him away to have a word outside the tent.

Two more candidates walked in as Master Patris was leaving, a short red-headed boy, younger than Kip and obviously from a farming family given his weathered skin and plump physique, and a tall, pale youth whose skin looked stretched over his face, his clothes patched with the same fabric in an attempt to make the patches inconspicuous. They, too, were taken aback by the presence of the Calatians and Emily, but politely introduced themselves. When they moved on, they clung together in the way two strangers will create a bond to see them through their first days alone in a new community, the chance of meeting first sealing this temporary friendship. At their own table, they talked in low voices about the rubble of demolished buildings below their feet. Kip focused his ears away from them after the first few words.

Three more candidates came in, by which time Kip and Emily, at least, were getting tired of the same startled reaction. "It's as though they can't even conceive that we might be candidates," Emily said, eyeing the last boy to walk in, but she was half-smiling, looking smug about it.

"Reasonably," Coppy responded, "I don't know as I could conceive of either of you as a candidate. Still can't."

"Get used to it." Kip put a paw to his stomach. "I wonder if they'll feed us."

At that moment, Master Argent's raven clacked its beak against the perch with a loud rapping noise and then croaked. Conversation stopped as everyone looked up at the large black bird.

"Luncheon will be served in this tent shortly," it said in a croaking rendition of Argent's voice.

The three newest candidates gaped up. Kip noticed and grinned at Coppy. "Calatian candidates and now talking ravens! What next?"

Coppy laughed. "Welcome to Sorcerer's College."

A moment later, Victor returned to the tent in the company of Master Patris, whose large arm rested around the boy's shoulder and whose white-maned face spoke low into his ear. Victor nodded, said, "Thank you, sir," and then looked around the tent before walking back to Kip. "May I join you?"

He addressed the question to Kip, but it was Emily who answered. "You may as well," she said. "You're the only one not startled by our presence."

"The others will grow accustomed to you in time." Victor smiled as he sat. "Calatians are well-known here in New Cambridge and in Boston— we had several working in our shipyards. The mice particularly were quite cunning at getting into places the larger workers could not, and were more reliable than children."

"You employed children?" Max's deep voice cut across the conversation. Kip glanced his way. His father had been silent for a good portion of the morning, his only contribution being smiles during the interplay between the others.

Victor paused, his composure wavering. "It is perfectly legal," he said, "but as I said, the mice were more reliable and better at getting into small spaces in the ships. Sometimes families send their children to us because they need the money, and what should we do? Send them home hungry? We give them ropes to wind and jobs suited to their age."

"I read an editorial," Emily interposed, "by John Q. Adams, in which he bemoaned the state of an empire that allows children to be exposed to the dangers of the industrial workplace."

"If more sorcery was available to businesses," Victor replied, so quickly that Kip could tell he'd had this discussion before, "then we would not have to rely on every available source of labor. And," he said, composing himself, "some families who are not fortunate enough to have a guaranteed income would go hungry."

"My parents worked for their income," Emily said.

"And you never had to, did you?"

She shook her head. Victor leaned forward. "I have met the parents of the children who worked in our shipyards—often they work for us as well. They watch their children earn extra money for the family and learn the value of honest work, and in some cases the children may learn a trade. So it is not all as despicable as Mister John Q. Adams would have you believe."

Had Victor ever worked at some of those jobs, Kip wondered, but he kept his long muzzle closed. The boy was making an effort to reach out to them where most of the other candidates were sitting at tables occasionally looking over at them with curious glances. At least the glances weren't openly hostile.

"But their bodies are not—" Emily's heated rejoinder was cut off by the arrival of several floating platters of bread, cheese and fruit.

All the conversation in the tent died down as the platters were brought to each table, even the empty ones, and deposited in the center. Several of the other candidates stared with wide eyes, and even Coppy and Emily drew back as a platter approached their table.

The bread and cheese were familiar by both sight and smell. Kip knew the Oldman's Bakery well, as it was just two doors down from his father's shop, and Mr. Scort's loaves of thick wheat bread had been a staple of his meals ever since childhood. Likewise, two of the three cheeses on the plate were a Cheddar and a Cheshire from the Piermont Dairy, one of three in the New Cambridge area, and a farm Kip had visited many times in younger days because they had great hills upon which the Piermonts allowed the children to sled, even Calatians.

The third cheese was a sharp white cheese with veins of blue running through it, which Emily identified as a Stilton Blue, more common in England and Boston than in the rural colonies. And surrounding those cheeses were apples of a uniformly beautiful red with speckles of yellow, exuding a sweet-tart scent that made Kip's mouth water. His nose tingled again with that peppermint-oil feeling. Was it the smell of magic?

"Will they see fit to give us plates?" Emily murmured, just as half a dozen tin plates materialized seemingly out of nowhere and clattered to the table.

"There's yer plates," said a disembodied voice.

Emily started, staring toward the voice. Max chuckled and picked up a plate to hand to her. "Demons," he said. "They do much of the sorcerers' work."

"Well." She took the plate. Max passed other plates around the table, while Coppy picked up the knife and cut slices of the bread. "There you go then, Mister Adamson. Why don't you simply have demons work in your shipyards?"

"Had we the power to bind them, we would," he said pleasantly. "Thank you, sir," he added as Coppy dropped a slice of bread onto the plate. "That is one reason my father wishes me to study sorcery, so that I may benefit our company."

"Surely sorcerers are restricted from private employ?" Max took an apple, as Kip did, while waiting for Coppy to cut more of the bread.

"They are." Victor shaved off a slice of cheddar. "But one of our rivals in New York has benefited from association with a sorcerer, and sadly, New York being closer to the Road, there are more sorcerers there than in Boston. I would stay in Boston, once my education is complete."

A young round-faced man with jet-black hair and green eyes had walked past their table as Victor spoke, and he stopped with a smile. "Did I hear someone speak ill of the greatest city in the world?" he said with a soft Irish lilt.

"No," Emily said, looking up. "We have nothing but love for Boston."

His face broke into a wide smile and he laughed, which brought a smile to Kip's face as well. "Ah," the young man said, "'Tis true what my mother said, then, that beauty is in the eye of the beholder."

"Not at all," Emily replied. "For I've seen New York with my own eyes, and there was no beauty there."

"Ah, but you've not seen it through the eyes of one who loves her streets and ports, her rivers and bridges and the life that courses through her day and night."

"Some of us prefer to rest at night." But Emily, too, wore a smile now.

"Oh aye, and some prefer to rest during the heat of the day, especially in Boston when the fishing-boats have come in." The young man had a ruddy complexion and a scar down the left side of his face, and he wore a simple green shirt with what Kip now saw was a small piece of cloth, folded over to resemble a four-leafed clover, pinned to the breast pocket. "My name's Malcolm O'Brien," he said, and held up a hand. "I know, I know. 'O'Brien,' you may say, 'but surely the lad speaks with a tongue that betrays nothing of Ireland at all!' Well, a childhood on the streets of New York has beaten much of the Irish out of me, much to me dear mother's shame." He touched the cloth clover on his chest.

"Not all of it," Kip said. "You're a candidate here?"

"I hope to be." He smiled at Kip without any reservation. "I've signed a paper and told them why I wish to study sorcery, and now I've nothing to do but wait for it. Good heavens, my good fellow, did you know you have eyes like a cat?"

Kip blinked, and then looked steadily back as Malcolm's green eyes examined his own. "I've had encounters with a mirror once or twice, aye."

"What a thing! May I join you?" Without waiting for an answer, he sat on the bench next to Kip. "I've visited the Bronx, you know, there's a

Calatian town there, but I'd never encountered a fox. Sure, I mean no offense by it, for I see now how you come by them." He waved across at Max. "They're marvelous eyes, truly, the color of a lovely piece of amber, and it just took me by surprise."

"I had only seen taxidermied foxes in our museum," Victor said, "our grand Museum of Natural History in Boston, that is. But I did not see the need to make a spectacle of it."

"I'm sure your museum is quite fine," Malcolm said, helping himself to a plate and an apple. "But why not bring attention to it? Those eyes are on display for the world to see, much as the lovely storm-grey eyes across from him are, and why not remark on them? Me father says there's no shame in speaking your mind, and the only folk who hide things are swindlers and lawyers. And," he took a bite of his apple and kept talking, gesturing with the apple as he did, "there's scant difference between them, in his eyes. Begging the pardon of any of you who happen to be swindlers."

Kip laughed, along with Coppy, and Max and Emily smiled. The latter said, "I can vouch for the lawyer part of that. Thomas almost never spoke his mind."

Victor, though, chewed his bread and cheese thoughtfully, and said, "To speak your mind at every turn is to leave yourself vulnerable to those who would abuse you."

He looked rather meaningfully at Kip as he said that, which made Kip wonder what he'd said to Victor that the young man might be referring to. Or perhaps he was simply referring to the general abuse of Calatians. Kip's ears flicked to Emily, already expecting the fiery woman to respond, and saw that she was struggling to swallow a mouthful so that she might speak.

His father's thoughts had followed his lines, but he spoke where Kip had not. "Do the Calatians who work for you speak their minds too often, then?"

Victor frowned, thinking. "I simply meant that by speaking your mind, you allow others to know of your plans and formulate plans against them."

"By speaking your mind," Emily put in, having finally swallowed her bite, "you allow others to know that certain behaviors will not be tolerated."

Victor held up his hands and smiled smoothly. "I am outnumbered," he said. "Let us agree that there may be circumstances in which being outspoken may be a better course of action. And," he added, "I will agree that the eyes of the Penfolds are quite striking."

The compliment sat less well with Kip than Malcolm's had, perhaps because it felt more calculated, but he said, "Thank you," and then Coppy said that he didn't really notice it anymore and he was sure that after a few days they would all be used to it as well, and Emily claimed she already was, although a few times after that, Kip caught her looking at his eyes or his father's.

"So," Malcolm said into the ensuing silence. "Who do you all believe attacked the College?"

Emily opened her mouth, but Victor jumped in first. "I hadn't thought there was much doubt about the 'whom.' It was the Spanish, of course. The question is 'how?'"

"A demon, of course," Malcolm said, "but would the Spanish be so bold? Why haven't they attacked again?"

"Because the attack failed, obviously," Victor retorted, "and the colleges are warded against demons."

"Failed?" Malcolm arched an eyebrow. "There's four buildings gone and a hundred dead in your 'failure.'"

"Ahem." Emily cleared her throat. "We were trying to avoid the topic during our meal."

Victor and Malcolm fell silent, and then Malcolm said, "Sorry," and went back to talking about New York.

When they'd all eaten, Kip pushed his plate aside and said to Victor, in a low voice, "You were going to tell us about the test?"

"Perhaps not here." The young man looked around the tent. "Is that large tent on the other side of the Tower available?"

"I think Master Argent called it the practice tent," Emily said. "Let me see. Hello! Raven! Oh, what was its name? Blacktalon?"

At the name, the raven perked up its head and flew down to their table, landing with a clatter among the used plates. It eyed the remaining cheese, but paid attention to Emily. "May we use the large practice tent on the other side of the Tower?"

"Yes," it responded, though it was sidling closer to the cheese now and appeared to be distracted. "You may not enter the Tower, nor the Admissions tent today, but all other tents are available to you."

"Thank you." Emily reached for a piece of cheese and held it out.

"Please do not give me cheese," the raven said, but before Emily could retract her hand, it had lunged forward and snapped up the cheese in its beak. It croaked, and Kip could swear it grinned at her as it pushed off from the table and returned to its perch atop the tent.

"Shall we go, before someone else has the same idea?" Victor had brought out a handkerchief to wipe his mouth, and now returned it to a pocket of his jacket before standing.

"Glad to." Malcolm stood with Kip and Emily. "We're talking about the test, is it?"

Victor stopped. "As it happens," he said with cool courtesy, "we were going to exchange information. These three have practiced magic; I have taken the admissions test. What have you to contribute?"

Kip turned to Malcolm before he realized that everyone else was also turning toward the Irishman, subjecting him to their scrutiny. To his credit, the young man smiled. "I've my wits and my experience, and the cultural sophistication of a New Yorker that seems to be rather lacking in this circle."

Victor looked down at his jacket cuff and straightened it. "As charming as that is," he said, "I can assure you that neither experience nor New York cultural life are subjects of the examination. I think we would all prefer it if we were allowed to study by ourselves."

Kip, for one, would not prefer it, and in the glance he exchanged with Coppy, he thought the otter agreed with him. "I wouldn't mind," he said.

"Oh, well," Victor said. "If you would prefer to study with the Irishman, by all means. I'm sure there are other candidates with whom I can consult." He affected a look around the tent.

"All right," Malcolm said, and patted Kip on the shoulder. "Looks like you fellows need the help more. I can tell when I'm not wanted. I'll go find someone with more appreciation for the New York life, then, shall I?" And without waiting for an answer, he strode off toward one of the other tables.

Kip bit his lip, and Coppy did not look altogether at ease. Emily, too, stared after Malcolm, but only for a moment before saying brightly, "Let's be off, then."

As they walked back out into the rain, which seemed to be letting up, Max pulled Kip back. "I don't like people who exclude others," he said.

"I tried," Kip began, and his father interrupted.

"I know you did, and it was well done. I'm only saying that you should be cautious."

"I will," Kip said, inwardly irritated because he wanted to have done more, but he couldn't figure out a way. Malcolm had been friendly, and he hated to lose that; Victor had left him no option.

So he remained silent until they entered the practice tent, which was set up very similarly to the dining tent, though its two braziers sat empty and cold. "No matter," Victor said, sitting at one of the benches. "One of our magicians can warm us."

He looked expectantly at Kip and Emily, and both shook their heads. "Physical magic is all I've practiced," Kip said, and Emily nodded.

"All right, never mind." Victor smiled. "That's what we're here to learn."

The first thing they discussed was the attack. Victor asserted again that the Spanish must have been responsible, and Kip, who knew Max had told him that it was more frightening that the sorcerers did not know, kept silent. Emily had heard rumors that the Indians had gathered several tribes together and woven the spell as revenge for unfulfilled promises after the war with France. Victor told her that she knew nothing about Indians and that the tribes had not even worked together during the war; they'd had to be put in separate regiments.

The discussion threatened to get more strident at that point, so Kip stepped in and suggested they focus on the test they were about to take. Victor asked him if he'd been in town the night of the attack, and Emily said that she didn't want to hear about it, and that was the last time the attack was mentioned that day.

They talked about magic and about the test for an hour, while Max and Coppy sat nearby and watched (though Coppy, who had accompanied Kip on most of his practices, put in a word or two). Kip felt proud to be showing off his skills in front of his father, while he also felt awkwardly babied by having his father nearby. Whenever the desire crept into his mind that his father should leave him alone, he remembered the book that sat in his bag, the one his father had gotten for him, and the pride with which he'd watched Kip teach himself magic. He has the right to stay as long as he wants, Kip told himself firmly. If Coppy or Emily had family—well, Victor's father had come to see him off, too, and hadn't shown much interest in staying around.

Max watched them all with keen eyes and perked ears, remaining politely silent as they all talked about their experiences. Emily had succeeded in moving small objects around. Only Kip could levitate himself, or levitate multiple objects. But Victor was more interested in the feeling of gathering magic, and to that, they could all speak, even Coppy, who had tried it with Kip.

When it came time for Victor to discuss the tests, he told what he knew, and what he had been studying in the previous months. Kip was pleased to find that the education he'd gotten in the New Cambridge schoolhouse would serve him well: knowing French would be an asset, and he had diligently read through the classic works of the ancient world. He was also well acquainted with the history of sorcery, to which Victor said the exams paid particular attention.

At least, he thought he was, until Victor mentioned the discovery of demons. "It was in 1480," he said, "and it allowed the House of Lancaster to triumph in the War of the Roses. Calatians were instrumental in the discovery."

This piqued Kip's curiosity. "How?" He turned to his father. "Did you know?"

Max shook his head. They all turned back to Victor, who looked put out at the attention. "I couldn't find any more information on it," he admitted. "I know that sorcerers began agitating for protection of Calatians in the 1500s," he said. "And of course you would know well that you were first created in 1402."

"We celebrate it every year." Max did speak up then.

"Quite. I would guess that the discovery of demons coincided with the movement to protect Calatians, but I have not researched it thoroughly."

"What else do you know?" Kip asked, leaning in, and Victor spent most of the next hour talking about the other tests: math and philosophy and grammar.

"Grammar is frightfully important, because you must speak the spells clearly and well, even if only in your head." The boy looked at Coppy.

"We're all accomplished at that, given how well we all speak," Emily said.

"Cor, not 'arf, guv." Coppy exaggerated his accent. "I'm right precise wi' me speech, I is indeed."

Kip stifled a giggle. "Good thing you're not applying."

Adamson did not look amused. But they never heard what he would have said next, because Kip's ears perked up then, and a moment later he got up and ran to the flap of the tent.

That voice; that high-pitched laugh. What would he be doing here? Kip didn't want to open the tent flap, because if it was him, and Kip saw him, it would be real. And he was holding desperately on to these last few moments in which it was not.

CHAPTER 4: BROADSIDED

"What is it?" Emily asked.

Max, too, had risen. Coppy had not quite heard it yet, but he knew Kip, and even Adamson and Emily felt the tension in the tent. "It's not...?" Coppy asked.

"He may be up here with the Watch," Max said, coming to the tent.

"Why would the Watch be up here?"

"Who?" Emily stood now, her tone more worried.

"Remember the story I told you?" Kip spoke in a tight, low tone. "Well, Farley Broadside graduated with us this spring."

"I thought you said he was two years older."

"So he is." Max had his eyes locked on Kip's.

"And," Kip said, "he went and joined the Watch."

"To protect the town from miscreants like himself," Coppy put in. His thick tail smacked a table leg, making Adamson jump.

Understanding dawned on Emily's face. "And you think he may be up here to be a candidate."

Kip laughed, a short, humorless bark. "Only if obtuseness is a discipline of sorcery."

"Who is this person?" Adamson rose, surveying all of them

"In your shipyards," Coppy said, "with the mice and all, did you have fellows who went out of their way to step on tails? To make jokes about setting the cats on them? To crush paws, shove bodies, make life difficult?"

"Yes." The boy's eyes narrowed.

"Imagine all the worst ones rolled up into one, with bad breath the least of his offenses." Coppy pointed outside. "That'd be him."

From the way Adamson's hand went to his collar, Kip saw the importance he placed on personal grooming, but his voice remained measured. "It is of course possible to change one's opinion," he said.

"Surely you've read the Boston papers." Emily's eyebrows arched. "There are more than a few who would have the Calatians live with the sorcerers permanently so that 'good, honest humans' need never be troubled by them."

Kip had heard that too. "The good, honest ones aren't the ones with the trouble. It's easy enough to live with them," he said. And yet Calatians went missing, not as often in New Cambridge as in London, true, but still it happened. The night of the attack, a calyx had been killed, and yet Abraham Lapelli was listed in none of the accounts of the slain. And there was Adam, who'd suffered most at a human bully's hands—that Kip knew of. A younger squirrel kit had disappeared two years ago, and though Farley knew better than to brag or even mention it, the fact that it had happened just after Mike Warner's family had to leave New Cambridge had linked the disappearance to Farley in Kip's mind.

"Best to come back and sit down," Kip's father said to him. "There's no use in searching for trouble that hasn't found you yet."

Kip moved away from the entrance, stomach tight. He was sure of the voice, and yet he hadn't smelled or seen Farley yet, and there might be someone from Boston or New York or Philadelphia who sounded like him. Part of him wanted it not to be true, but a hot white flame inside him wanted Farley to be here, up away from the laws of the town, where Kip would be on a more even footing with him. He flexed his fingers, feeling the tingle of magic all around. If he felt a surge of magic again, even half as strong as the one he'd felt at the Tower, he could toss Farley in the air like a rag doll and let him fall.

Only he never would, he knew. Such a fantasy was best left to be a fantasy. He would be no better than Farley then, and yet the knowledge frustrated him, that by being the better person, by adhering to laws and respecting others, he was putting himself at risk—and not just himself, but any other Calatians Farley might come in contact with. His eyes swept the tent, covering his father and Coppy. At least Coppy would still be able to protect his father and the shop. Farley had tried several times to break windows or otherwise vandalize Calatian homes.

Once he'd sat down, they resumed their conversation, but it was not for very long. A disturbance at the entrance turned all their heads, and when a pair of hands wrestled with the tent flap, the tension in Kip's stomach tightened. A moment later, the smell reached him, and then there was no longer any doubt whose leering face he would see when the hands finally found the rope latch holding the tent flap closed.

"Ah, there it is," Farley Broadside said. "Knew I smelled some shitting pelts around here somewhere."

The stout boy had grown into a stout young man, though the pockmarks of youth still dotted his cheeks and forehead. His thick neck was easy to miss even when his shoulders were down as his chin seemed to disappear behind the high collar of the wool jacket of the Watch. His small eyes had not grown with the rest of him; they looked out from behind bulwarks of flesh and strands of wet hair at the five people in the tent. "You," he pointed at Kip, "you're to get your things. You're leaving."

Max stood. "By what authority?"

Kip stood too, and so did Coppy and Emily. After a moment, Victor got fluidly to his feet to join them. Farley faced them, a flush rising in his cheeks. He tapped the symbol of the Watch sewn onto his jacket and spoke in a loud, slow voice. "This here means I have aw-thor-eye-tee in the town."

"Not in the College," Kip said.

"We'll see about that, won't we?" A grin spread on his face, and it was not a pleasant grin. Kip did not think Farley capable of grinning a pleasant grin.

"I've been accepted as a candidate, and there's nothing you can do about it," the fox said quietly.

"Oh, Sheriff Winters might have a thing or two t'say about that. But you stay if you like." His hand went to his waist, grasped the handle of a solid wooden club. "I'd be happy enough to take you down by force."

"You won't take anyone anywhere," Coppy said, but Max acted while the otter spoke, walking toward Farley with such determination that the young man stumbled back two steps, crying out, and fell against the tent entrance. It gave way, leaving him flailing outside to regain his balance as Max strode by him, all with at least a foot of space between Farley and the older fox.

Kip hurried after his father, and the others followed him. Max stalked around the Tower, tail curled around his leg, ears flat, as angry as Kip could remember seeing him. This time, he barely even noticed the Tower's arched entrance; he did not look away from his father's back.

Emily caught up to him. "What's he going to do?"

"I don't know." Kip stared ahead. "I don't want him to get in trouble for me."

"If the sorcerers admitted you, the Watch can't make you leave. Can they?"

That was what Kip had been asking himself, and although the sensible part of his mind thought the answer would be no, the bruised part that had catalogued the grievances against his kind over the years whispered that of course they could, they could do anything they wanted, that Calatians might be people in the eye of the Church, but they weren't *real* people, were they?

They rounded the corner of the Tower. Three figures stood near the path by the Admission tent. Kip recognized Master Patris by his white mane, Master Argent by his face, and Sheriff Winters by his buckskin vest and the rifle slung over his shoulder. Winters, facing away from them, said something Kip didn't hear, and then Patris boomed out, "And what, may I ask, does that have to do with my College?"

Max halted just beyond the dining tent. Kip and Emily caught up with him, and he held up a paw to stop their progress. Master Argent turned briefly toward them, and though he did not move or nod, his acknowledgment gave them at least a small reassurance.

Coppy and Victor hurried up. "What's going on?" Coppy asked in a low voice.

"Not sure," Kip hissed back. "But Patris isn't pleased."

"You'd think he'd be pleased enough to be gettin' rid of us."

"Aye," Kip said, and then shushed the otter, for Argent was speaking.

"The College has always operated with the town's best interests in mind," the young sorcerer said, "and has expected that the town would do the same. Never do we make unreasonable demands of New Cambridge, not even in our hour of need—"

Winters interrupted him then, too low for even Kip to hear, and Argent nodded. "The gesture was understood and welcomed. But this demand from the town—"

Again, an interruption. Again, an acknowledging nod, but curter. "No, it comes phrased as a request but it is unquestionably a demand. We understand that these are important matters to be weighed, and you may trust that the College is aware of the decision it faces."

"And we need no help from farmers and carpenters," Patris snapped.

Farley had come up behind them, and laughed harshly. "Pelt-lovin' sorcerers might not be too happy, but the law is the law."

Victor turned. "I believe in this case you may be mistaken," he said in a soft voice.

"You a pelt-lover too?" Farley sneered.

"I'm a believer in taking advantage of opportunities," Victor said. "And this antagonism is an oversight on your part."

"Oh, you don't half talk fancy. Go back to your pelts, you love 'em so much."

"Listen," Victor said, and then Kip lost that conversation as they moved away and Patris raised his voice.

"You may go back and tell the town that we will accept whatever candidates we deem worthy, and that if they wish a voice in our selections, they must procure for themselves an education in the magical arts, come and join the college as sorcerers, and apply themselves to our admissions process. Failing that, they may go about their lives quite contentedly at the bottom of the hill, and I shall not be sorry if I hear no more from them while I continue to be the sole authority at this College."

Kip and his father both strained their ears forward into the silence, and now Sheriff Winters' reply came audibly to them. "I thank you for your time," he said, "and I'll be on my way, then, as soon as I recover my associate."

It might have been Kip's imagination, but the Sheriff did not sound disappointed in the least. He turned, and Patris with him, and they saw the small knot of watchers for the first time. Even at the distance of fifty feet or so, Kip saw Patris's face twist, a moment before the sorcerer turned and stomped toward the gates of the College. It had clearly been difficult for him, turning down a chance to evict the Calatian from his grounds, but something more precious to him must have been at stake.

Winters raised a hand in greeting and came their way. Max's ears remained down, but he greeted the Sheriff cordially. "Marshall."

"Max." He turned and nodded to the others, and tipped his hat. "Boys. Ma'am."

They regarded each other, and then Kip's father broke the silence. "What is all this, Marshall?"

The Sheriff shook his head. "Best not to stir up more trouble. I was asked to come here and make a request of the College, and—"

"Asked by whom?" Max demanded.

"Never mind that. I've made it and can return with my reply." He looked past them. "Broadside!" he called. "Come on, we're going."

Farley and Victor were deep in conversation. At Winters' shout, Farley turned and grinned, though he was looking at Kip when he did. "You go on, Sheriff," he said. "I'm gonna stay here an' apply."

Kip had been feeling relief, even gratitude toward the sheriff, who had long been friendly to his family. The relief evaporated in a breath, and he clenched his fists against the roiling in his gut. "He can't," he barked before thinking.

"Oh, I can." Farley looked cheerful. "If an animal and a girl can, then surely there's room for an honest man of the Watch."

"There is," Kip said, "but I don't see one here."

"I could've been a carpenter, not stuck on some filthy farm—"

"I had nothing to do with his family losing their store," Kip told Victor. "Nor did any Calatian. His father died in the war."

"And the town put the store up to auction, and who bought it? Was it humans, who had always owned that store?"

Kip shook his head and turned to the sheriff. "Can't you—"

Farley stepped toward them, and Kip recoiled. "Sheriff," Farley said. "When I'm admitted, I'll have to relinquish my duties."

This, too, did not seem to upset Winters. "Good luck to you," he said, and raised a hand. "But you'll tell your mother yourself. I'm not knocking on her door with this news."

Farley blew a raspberry, though whether at the sheriff or at his absent mother Kip could not tell. They stood aside as the boy followed Master Argent into the admissions tent, and then the sheriff made to leave.

"You have to stop him." Kip grabbed the sheriff's sleeve and hissed at him in a low voice.

The sheriff's weathered face remained impassive. "Now, I was just told I can't stop you from applying here. How am I to stop him?"

"He reports to you! You could...or his mother could..."

Kip let go of the sleeve, desperation ebbing in the face of the sheriff's stolid demeanor. "All right," he said, lowering his voice. "But you imagine him with sorcerous powers and then tell me how you'll sleep at night."

At that, Winters did grin briefly. "Next to my wife," he said, tipping his hat. And he lowered his voice as well. "If you ask me, Broadside's got about as much magical talent as that pile of rocks there. He may be a candidate, might even be accepted as a student, but he won't be flinging rocks with aught but his arm."

Kip was not reassured by the sheriff comparing Farley to the Tower. "That's bad enough."

"Aye, perhaps, but he's your problem now. No, put those ears up. He'll be back at his mother's farm before you know it, and she perhaps not even the wiser for it, if he fails quickly."

"Your lips to God's ear." Kip stepped back. "Good day, Sheriff."

"Kip, Max." He tipped his hat again, and adjusted the rifle. "And the rest of you. Best of luck."

"Luck." Kip watched his back as he retreated, unwilling to turn around and see Farley's smirk. "We'll need that, all right."

On their way back to the practice tent, they questioned Victor about what he'd said to Farley, and he protested that he'd only told the boy that Kip seemed quite dedicated to pursuing sorcery, and that perhaps Farley should reconsider his assessment of him.

"There's where you went wrong," Coppy said. "Words over three syllables. He probably thought you meant he should join up too."

"It was all his idea," Adamson insisted. "After the antipathy you demonstrated toward him, why would I encourage him to remain?"

"It doesn't matter." Kip had been feeling queasy ever since Farley's announcement. "He's not magical. He'll be gone soon."

"Speaking of being gone soon," Max said as they passed the great wooden doors of the tower, "We should also take our leave, Coppy."

"This soon?" Kip squinted into the afternoon sun.

"You've your new friends to talk to, and we've a perfume store to return to." Kip's father grinned wryly. "I only hope young Johnny hasn't broken half the stock, or sold it for a handful of beans."

"Ah, a perfume store." Emily smiled. "That explains why Kip was retrieving vials, and why you all smell so pleasant. I suppose that your nature gives you an advantage in your work."

"They're dabs at the scent business," Coppy said. "Even got their own words for some of the smells. My favorite's '<storf>.'"

"Coppy." Kip folded his ears down, trying to sound reproving.

The otter spread his paws with a smile. "It sounds so cheerful."

"'Storf'?" Emily's pronunciation was not bad, for a human. "What's it mean?"

Max and Kip looked at each other. "Er," Max said, "It's rather unpleasant."

"I lived with a lawyer for years," Emily said. "I've heard most of life's unpleasantries."

Kip coughed into a paw. "It's the smell of a newly-dead person."

Emily frowned. "That has its own smell?"

"I'm pleased to say I've had little occasion to use it," Max said, "except for the times we were asked to cover it."

"People like myrrh for that," Kip said. "But cinnamon is less expensive and works better."

"It's not as solemn," his father added. "But you didn't ask for a lecture on funereal perfumes. We should take our leave now."

Emily extended her hand to Max. "It's been a pleasure to meet you, sir. I may send Kip with orders for some of your stock betimes."

"You're welcome to it. I'm delighted you'll be studying alongside my son." Max shook her hand.

When he turned to Coppy, though, the otter clasped his paws before him, kneading his fingers. "I was thinking, sir…if Broadside is to be up here, then perhaps I ought to apply as well. I would worry about Kip otherwise."

Kip's heart leapt. He wanted to tell Coppy that he would be able to take care of himself, but he also badly wanted the otter's company. "An' it might make things easier on Kip, you know, not being the only Calatian. I'm not born to magic like he is but I know a little, and I reckon I can last as long as Broadside can. If they send me home it'll be no great loss."

The older fox considered Coppy and then nodded, turning his muzzle toward Kip. "I'd be glad to know Kip had more company up here," he said. "I doubt I'll be able to have more than a few words a week with him."

"Will the store be all right?" Kip asked.

Max laughed. "The store will be fine, Kip. Don't act like you don't want your friend to stay."

"Lovely!" Emily clapped her hands together and took Coppy's paw. "Let's go tell Master Argent and leave these two to say their goodbyes." She looked meaningfully at Victor.

He took her hint and bowed. "Farewell, sir. I look forward to getting to know your son."

Coppy pulled free from Emily long enough to throw his arms around Max. "Thank you, sir," he said. "I'll look after Kip."

"Don't forget to look after yourself as well." Max embraced him back.

Kip watched Coppy's thick tail, Emily's dress, Victor's starched coat as they rounded the corner of the tower. Then he and his father were alone on the path, rain tickling the tips of his ears. If he turned them back, he could hear Farley's loud bray through the canvas wall of the admissions tent, so he kept them forward, toward his father, but he couldn't think of what to say.

"You'll do well here," his father said gently, and lifted a paw. Kip grasped it, and his father pulled him into a hug. "But whatever happens, for you to have come this far…I am very proud of you."

"But I haven't done anything yet." Kip's voice was muffled against his father's cheek fur.

"You have dared. You have raised your head up and said, 'I wish to do this,' and you have forced them to pay attention. If they send you home, then the next Calatian to attempt it will have an easier time."

"I don't care about him," Kip said, and then thought of Emily. "Or her. I want to be a sorcerer."

"You will." Max released him from the embrace. "If it is not here, then we will find another place."

"Where? Prince Phillip's is gone. I'd never get into the King's College in London. Where would I go? Spain?"

His father smiled. "Let us worry about that when the time comes. It may be that you will become a sorcerer in these very walls. I hope that comes to pass."

"Thank you," Kip said. "I don't know if I could have come up here alone."

"That, too, you will learn." His father leaned forward until their noses touched. "Now, go study. I will see you soon, whatever happens. I am up here with Master Vendis every other week, these days."

"All right." Kip stood up straight and smiled. "I still feel all…<coomek>."

Coppy had reminded him of their scent-words, and so the word for a superficial scent, one that didn't belong to the thing it was on, came easily to him. His father smiled and rubbed his shoulder. "Give it time, Kip. And remember that no matter what else you are, you are a Calatian. That scent will never leave you."

"Yes, sir." Kip didn't know why his father thought he would ever forget that, but it was not the time to argue.

His father looked him in the eye, the goodbye unspoken. Then the older fox nodded briefly and walked past Kip toward the gates.

CHAPTER 5: TESTING

Coppy's application went smoothly, so he left with Max to pack a bag to bring back up. In the meantime, Victor asked Kip to demonstrate some magic for them, pointing out that the designated practice tent remained empty of the other applicants. Kip had been thinking that after his scare that morning with the Tower, he wanted to practice on his own before doing it in front of a Master, if that was indeed part of the test, so he readily agreed.

Sitting cross-legged on the canvas floor, he closed his eyes and reached out into the earth with his mind. He hardly needed the relaxing chant anymore, but just to be safe, he recited the nonsense syllables to himself. The power beneath him opened up as it always had, no stronger up here than it had been down in his little attic room above the shop. He might feel the White Tower and all its sorcerers and demons (and inexplicable voice) outside their tent, but the power in the earth was constant. It flowed into him, manageable, controllable, and when he opened his eyes, his paws were lit with a soft purple glow.

Emily's eyes were closed too, and her hands flickered with lavender light. "Yet the Masters, when they cast spells, do not evince this glow." Victor leaned close to Emily's hands, and as Kip was wondering if he had any ulterior motive in getting so close to her, the boy leaned over and inspected Kip's paws as well.

"My father says that none of the advanced sorcerers show that glow, but

Master Vendis says that all apprentices do. It takes a good deal of work to learn to suppress it." Kip turned his paws over, but the light clung to them as though it were part of his fur.

"I see." Victor leaned back. "All right, what spells can you do? All physical, you said."

"Yes." Lifting small objects was easy for Kip now, and that he felt confident he could do in front of the sorcerers. Here he wanted to try something a little more impressive, so he spoke the syllables to activate the spell and then envisioned it around himself, spreading space between himself and the ground. But as he lifted, the tent flap came into his vision, sparking the memory of Farley's thick fingers prising it apart. Distracted, he lost sight of the spell, and magic crumbled around him. The purple glow around his paws flickered and faded, and he fell to the ground with a thud.

"It was a good effort," Victor said to Kip. "I know that lifting yourself is more difficult than lifting even the heaviest of objects."

"I can do it." Kip glared at the tent flap. "And that's very good and steady, Emily."

Emily had found a small pebble and was holding it off the ground. "Kip shot himself to the top of the tower this morning," she said, as her stone dropped to the canvas floor.

"So you said." Victor steepled his fingers together. "And what was different about that time and this?"

"I didn't know Farley was a candidate then." Kip wanted to avoid talking about his experience that morning as much as he possibly could, at least until he understood it better. He believed he could trust Emily, but his father's warning about Victor remained in the back of his mind, and he could not forget the image of the elegant boy talking to the crude Farley. What could he have had to say to him, if not talking him into applying?

"He's only a candidate," Victor said, "not yet a student, nor even an apprentice."

Emily wanted to know the difference between the three, and Victor explained that they were candidates until they passed the test, then they would be students for a year. Those with the highest aptitude for sorcery would be selected to continue on as apprentices for three more years, while those who did not make that grade would be assigned to practice magic for the Public Works (roads and building, at the lowest level) or the Royal Army (the higher level).

"The road-builders came through to improve the New Cambridge road two years ago." Kip talked while he decided whether he wanted to try lifting himself again. "They didn't go up to the College at all, and none of the sorcerers came down to see them." They had been loud, swaggering men who'd made a game of lifting the large rock slabs and dropping them in the road as if they were playing horseshoes. Kip had watched because he rarely got to see magic up close, and their arms had glowed, he remembered now. They'd brandished the glows and called each other filthy names, and they'd taken cider from Mrs. Worrington and told her to send the bill to Boston (she had; nobody had paid).

"We've seen the road-builders too," Emily said. "Never the military, though."

"I've seen the military," Victor said. "In the Boston parade after Napoleon was defeated. You didn't go?"

This was to Emily, who scowled. "Mother worried about young girls in large crowds."

"It was quite a sight." The young man gestured with his slender hands. "They made fireworks like you've never seen, huge glowing frigates and exploding smoke-demons and sea monsters diving through the clouds. It was a sight."

The parade in New Cambridge had been more modest and had mostly consisted of reading the names of the New Cantabrigians killed in the war, which had been an excuse for Farley to seek out Kip after the parade and attempt to take out his frustration on the fox again. Emily asked Victor how many sorcerers marched with the army, and while he answered, Kip closed his eyes and gathered magic again.

The conversation died down as power and its associated tension coalesced inside him. He opened his eyes to look down at his paws and spoke the words of the spell again. This time, he lifted himself two feet into the air. His tail hung behind him; he tried to extend the spell to lift it, wobbled, and decided to leave that for another time. He could do this. Damn Farley to Hades anyway.

At the thought of Farley, his concentration lapsed again and he listed to one side. He tried to shore up the spell, but dropped almost to the ground before he regained control, slamming one paw down to the canvas in anticipation of the fall that never came.

"That was much better." Victor said it kindly, but with an edge of condescension that prickled Kip's fur. He kept his teeth together and lowered himself slowly, letting the spell go completely when he sat on the ground.

Emily came to sit beside him. "Farley again? Why does it bother you so?"

Kip searched his memory. "It's like…it's like reaching the kingdom of Heaven, you know? And then finding out that all the wrongs and ills of the world followed you up."

"That seems a lot to put on the shoulders of one young man," Victor said.

"He's got big shoulders," Kip replied.

Emily leaned forward. "Why does he hate you?"

"It's not just me." Kip sighed. "Or maybe it is. I have trouble keeping my mouth shut sometimes. His father died in the war and his mother had to sell the store to pay their bills." The British army hadn't paid more than a pittance, his father had told him, but one of the farming families had allowed the Broadside widow and her son some land. "A Calatian family bought it, the Porters. So he started picking on the Calatian kids in school. And a bunch of the other kids liked him for it."

"Look," Victor said. "I'm willing to talk to him, to try to get him to moderate his views of Calatians. Nobody who's talked to either of you can deny what intelligent, worthy people you are. But you will also have to give him a chance to reform. If you persist in treating him like a scourge, he will instinctively behave as one."

"I will leave him alone if he leaves me alone," Kip said. "Aside from that, he can go to the Devil for all I care."

"I suppose that's a place to start." Victor smiled a thin smile. "You know, I suffered from bullying as a child as well."

"Did you indeed?" Kip stopped himself and moderated the tone of his voice; of course the young man wouldn't know anything of being a fox-Calatian, of feeling your bones snap, of feeling rough hands on your tail and panic at the gleam of the knife, of knowing there would be no justice no matter what happened. His friends had not sometimes disappeared, or turned up crippled, or been turned out of their homes and sent to Boston or New York when their businesses failed while humans with struggling farms or shops received charity. "I'm sorry to hear that."

"Yes, there are those even in private schools who look down on the students who prefer books to swords." He sighed.

"I imagine your father's money made school somewhat easier for you." Emily leaned back with arms folded, making less of an attempt to hide her feelings than Kip was.

Victor smiled evenly at her. "There is a limit even to the powers of money. It can punish, but it cannot force sympathy or collaboration."

"Why are you so invested in seeing everyone get along?" Emily asked, with some intensity.

Victor spread his hands. "Should I not be? Why would it not be in my best interests to make sure that all of us students—for I feel sure we will be studying together—can work in harmony? I have watched my father keep peace on the shipyards and have learned that a building crew that can work together is more productive than one that is constantly at odds."

"But we're not going to work together." Kip curled his tail around his side. "Some of us will go off to build roads, some of us to the army, and some to learn more of the secrets of sorcery."

"I can tell which appeals to you," Victor said, raising an eyebrow. "Nonetheless, we will all learn faster if we learn together."

A scuffling sound came from the top of the tent, and a moment later, as they all looked up, a raven dropped in.

"Dinner is served," it said. "During the dinner, Master Patris will address all the candidates."

"About time." Victor stood. "I'm famished. Tell me, do they traditionally wait until sunset to serve supper here in New Cambridge, or is it a sorcerer's custom?"

"We usually ate right after closing the shop," Kip said. "I don't know when other people had supper." He looked up and asked the raven, "Have all the candidates arrived? Is Coppy back already?"

The raven clacked its beak, croaked once, and climbed back out the flap at the top of the tent without answering.

"I suppose they must." Emily got to her feet. "The announcement clearly said applicants would be accepted today only."

"Usually down at the Founders Rest there are thirty of them staying the day before admissions." Kip stood as well, still holding a stone in his paw. He uncurled his fingers and let it fall to the ground.

"There were only twenty tents," Victor said.

He was closer to the tent flap but did not move in that direction, so Kip strode forward and pulled the canvas aside, holding it for the others. "I don't think they intend for us to stay in them very long." He wondered whether Coppy would get his own tent.

The rain had stopped, though in the twilight the clouds still massed overhead and the air smelled damp. "Three days." Emily turned and met Kip's eyes. "Then we go into the Tower or go home."

The fox looked up at the stone walls of the Tower. From this side it looked identical to the side he'd touched, austere and grand. In there the earth elementals that had destroyed Fort Duquesne had been summoned; from there the new world that stretched out to the west was being explored; within these walls, the Great Road had been researched. "I'm not going home," he said tightly. "No matter what Patris says."

"Nor I," she said.

Victor, who had walked on ahead, turned with a half-smile on his thin lips. "I don't believe any of us wishes to go home, but it isn't up to us, is it?"

Other candidates emerged from the tents as they passed, and Kip saw the raven flying back around the tower ahead of them. Emily, spotting the others, hurried ahead, and by the time Kip arrived, she had established herself at their table, sitting upright with a fierce smile. Otherwise, the tent was empty save for two ravens sitting on the long perch, facing in opposite directions.

Kip sat next to her, eyeing the space where Coppy would have sat. Victor stopped at their table and set one hand down on it. "If you don't mind," he said, "I'm going to continue to talk to the other candidates. Several of them probably have the same prejudices."

Indeed, as other candidates walked in and looked around the tent, though they were dressed in garments ranging from farmers' tunics to lawyers' shirts and coats, the one thing they all had in common was the startled look they had when passing the Calatians at the front of the tent. Sometimes they noticed Emily first, and the startled look became a smile, only to vanish as their eyes slid over to the tall black ears on the furred head of the fox sitting beside her. Only the red-headed boy they'd met earlier did not gape, but smiled and nodded, and he did not sit with them. The six tables in the dining room, with benches that would allow three Kips or two Farleys to a side, had ample other room for them.

Platters appeared, bringing with them the tingle to Kip's nose. They were now laden with fresh bread, whole roast fowls, carving knives, and steaming bowls of potatoes cooked with onions. Forks and plates clattered to the wood table beside the food, and then the tingle was gone.

"Potatoes and onions," Emily said, making a face as she scooped them onto a plate. "Thomas adored onions."

While Kip served himself, Emily looked around the tent. "I make it seventeen, counting us and Coppy," she said.

"Aye." Kip counted again: at six tables there were three, three, two, four, three, and two people. Adamson and Farley had been joined by a plump boy in a formal white shirt and black jacket whose sour expression didn't even lighten when he laughed at something Adamson said.

The tent flap burst open. "Sorry!" Malcolm gasped, staggering through. "Had a bit of a nap." Everyone turned to stare at him, and he returned the looks cheerfully. "Food's got here, I see," he said, and paused at Kip's table, looking down. "Mister Coppy's gone home?"

"Only to get his things." Kip couldn't keep from looking at Farley. "He's decided to apply along with us."

"Splendid!" Malcolm followed Kip's gaze. "Well, since Master Adamson has chosen other company, is this seat available to us lowly rabble with naught to contribute?"

"Please sit down," Kip said, and turned to Emily with a smile. "So, eighteen."

She nodded as Malcolm sat and reached for the carving knife. "May I?"

Conversation slowed as the applicants ate, save for Farley, who had little compunction about combining the two activities. "Ma brought it up to me," he told Adamson and the others as he chewed. "If we still had the land what was rightfully ours, of course I'd be managing a store right now 'stead of sitting here smellin' a stinking pelt with my dinner." Someone at his table, perhaps Adamson, murmured that that wasn't the appropriate word, and Farley laughed. "What's 'appropriate' mean? I call 'em what they are, not dressed up with fancy names and fancy titles. The mayor, the teacher, they all go outta their way to give the animals whatever they want to pretend they're human, and meanwhile my dad's dead in France and there's a shitting family of vermin working his land."

Emily put a hand on Kip's paw. "Most of us don't think that way," she said.

"Aye," Malcolm said cheerfully between bites. "If you'd call that thinking, that is. Sounds t'me more like a lot of blather coverin' up a lack of education and good manners."

"Not covering it all that well." Kip tried to match the Irishman's good humor. "I've heard that story a hundred times besides. The Porters did buy his store, but his mother gave it up for auction. Nobody forced her to. She's living rather well. Buys perfumes in our shop."

Before Malcolm could respond, chilly air blew past them as the tent flap was pushed open. Masters Patris and Argent strode through and in, flanked by another sorcerer, his face narrowing to the point of his goatee. Patris and Argent did not bother to look around the tent, save one quick look Argent gave Emily, but the third sorcerer made a lazy arc from his right to his left, dark eyes looking bored until he reached Kip's table. There the dark eyes lingered, and the lines around them became more pronounced. But a moment later he was facing forward again, as expressionless as before.

"Greetings, candidates," Master Patris said. "I am the Head of this College, Master Patris, and behind me are Masters Argent and Windsor. The three of us will be administering your entrance exams over the next three days. These examinations will be oral, and will cover languages, history, mathematics, and sorcery. As there are eighteen of you, you will be divided into three groups of six, and each group will be tested individually by one of us over the next three days. On Friday, we will announce our decisions, and those candidates admitted to the College will be shown to their quarters in the Tower. Master Argent will assign your groups now."

With that, the white-haired sorcerer turned and strode out of the tent, and Master Windsor followed. Master Argent cleared his throat. "Why don't we assign the groups by tables? Those two tables make up a group of six." He indicated Kip's table and the one adjacent. "Then those two in the back, and these two here." He took out a paper from his robe and spoke quickly. "Group one, Miss Carswell, Penfold, O'Brien, Smith, Cobb, and let's add Lutris to that group. Group two, Forester, Davies, Wormwood, Adamson, Broadside, Carmichael. Group three, Chesterton, Quarrel, Cooper, Middleton, Potterfield, Plant. Group one will see Master Windsor tomorrow, group two will see Master Patris, and group three will see me. You will be examined in alphabetical order by last name, and yes, determining the correct order is part of your exam." This last remark was accompanied by a smile, as the paper returned to the pocket of his robe. "Does anyone have questions about the examinations?"

"What's on them?" Malcolm called out, and nervous laughter skittered around the tent.

"You'll find out." Argent smiled, and then nodded to a young man timidly raising his hand at the back of the tent.

"Who's covering which subjects?"

"I will test you on sorcery. Windsor will test you on history and languages. Master Patris will test you on mathematics."

So Victor hadn't been misleading them about the contents of the test. Kip exhaled. Much as he dreaded spending any time in a room with Patris, at least mathematics had right and wrong answers, and Patris wouldn't be able to overlook the right answer if he gave it. He hoped Master Windsor would be a fair examiner as well. Then he might have a chance.

As soon as the masters left, Cobb and Smith pushed their table next to Kip, Malcolm, and Emily. "John Cobb of Philadelphia city," Cobb's brown hair, cropped short, framed a plain, square face with a pleasant smile as he extended a hand.

"Mark Smith of Charleston." Smith wore a brown cap over unruly blond hair and a handsome face with bright blue eyes. He didn't smile, and only extended a hand when Kip, Emily, and Malcolm had shaken Cobb's and looked at him expectantly. "Begging your pardon, but what do you hope to learn here?"

Kip opened his mouth to reply, but Smith was looking past him at Emily. "Are there spells to mend clothing? To boil water?"

"She's here for the same—"

Emily cut him off. "No doubt there are," she said tartly, "even as there are no doubt spells that can render you culturally sophisticated. But I wish to explore this continent. There is a vast swath of land won from Napoleon that lies out there to the west, and I intend to be one of the sorcerers tasked with exploring it."

"By yourself?" Smith said, eyes wide. "What will your husband think of that?"

"Should I perchance acquire a husband in the next four years, I shall be certain that he is of a similar mind, so I have no doubt that he will accompany me, or else he will be content to wait until I return."

Smith looked about to say more, but Malcolm waved him silent. "Unless you've a mind to add courting Miss Carswell to your studies, I'd recommend leaving this argument for her eventual suitors. Am I right in thinking Miss Carswell will be first in the testing by virtue of the spelling of her lovely name?"

Emily was not terribly upset about going first, but Kip chafed at his next-to-last placement. He wanted to show what he could do and then be done with the test. As other students arose and filed out of the tent, Kip attempted to smooth over the tension that still lingered from Smith's statements. "Would you like to study together tonight?" he asked.

Before Cobb or Smith could answer, Malcolm spoke up. "I suppose Mister Adamson would have something to say about what I could *contribute*.

So I should prefer to avoid that conversation." He stood and walked out. A moment later, Smith and Cobb joined him, with uneasy glances at each other.

"Say what you will about Adamson; at least he's polite," Emily muttered. "I suppose it's just the two of us then."

"And Coppy," Kip reminded her, hoping the otter would return soon. "And maybe Adamson—or perhaps not," he finished, as Adamson was exiting the tent ahead of Farley.

Coppy returned not too long after with his satchel and a straw pallet to move into Kip's tent. Officially he hadn't been assigned a tent at all, and even though there should be at least three empty ones, he said he preferred to stay close by. "If you don't mind," he said as Kip made room. "You never know what mischief Farley might get up to late at night, aye?"

"I'll be glad of the company." Kip moved his bag to the head of his pallet. If he piled the clothes on top of the spell book and perfume bottles, it would make quite an acceptable pillow.

Since they were both in that tent anyway, Emily joined them, all of them sitting cross-legged on the beds to discuss the subjects of the tests. Languages might be the weakest point for all of them, and none of them had books close at hand to study. History of magic and sorcery, though, they felt much more confident in. Emily assured them that their knowledge would be the only factor in their admission decision, "and judging by the quality of the other candidates, I don't see we've much competition."

"It wouldn't be a competition anyway," Kip said. "Did you see their advertisement? They're desperate."

"Good lookout for me, then." Coppy tapped the side of his head. "I may not know magic or languages, but I wager I know more than Farley. If they let him in, they'll let me in, and if they keep me out, they'll keep him out as well, I hope."

"And you know more history of sorcery than either of us."

"Sorcerers over in the King's College of Sorcery would feel obliged to remind us poor Calatians living down below how much we owe to sorcery, from time to time," Coppy said. "Had little theater shows for those who weren't lettered. Best entertainment we got."

"It must be delightful having a captive audience to brag about your accomplishments to." Emily brushed a lock of her hair back. "Were you also forced to tell them how handsome they looked?"

"Only on holidays." Coppy rested his thick arms on his knees. "Wasn't like it is here, where the sorcerers come down to be part of the community."

"Used to," Kip reminded him.

"Aye. Well, the Thames lies between the College and the Isle, so it's easy enough for them to look past us out over London if they've a mind."

Coppy didn't like to talk about the conditions of the Calatians in

London, but Kip had gotten a few stories out of him over the year they'd known each other. He knew, for example, that foxes there more commonly lacked tails than possessed them, because scalpers raided the Isle looking for tails from four-to-six year old cubs, tails that could pass for wild fox tails and be sold among the nobility. He knew that the sorcerers in London rarely bothered to help the Isle with disease or injury save when an epidemic struck. He knew that while the police made public spectacles of the punishment of people who came to rob or murder the Calatians, to discourage such behavior among the ruffians and villains of London, they only punished the ones easily caught.

He thought about those things lying on his straw pallet that night with his bag under his head as Coppy lay snoring lightly beside him. Around him in the night, his ears caught the snores of a few other young men, and their smells drifted to him on the night breeze. He had a packet of herbs in his bag that he could sleep with if the smells of the night became too distressing; his father had given it to him when Coppy had first moved in, but though the otter's scent was strong, it had never been objectionable and now Kip found it comforting. Would this be how their housing would be, should he be admitted? Would they all be sleeping together in one large room? Saul had been housed in a small room with only one other student, but those buildings were gone now.

Thoughts of Saul brought a dull, throbbing ache that he let sit in his chest.

"Of course I'll stay here. I'm going to study sorcery at the College, and I'll live right up the hill. I'll come down like Master Etton does and I'll repair shops and heal broken legs." Saul had rested his fingers on Kip's forearm, recently healed. They'd been lying in the summer sun late one evening in July over the rise from the quarry.

Even at seventeen, Kip had known that healing and brickwork repair were the responsibilities of two different sorcerers, but he didn't say anything. "I'll come up and be your calyx when I can."

Saul had tapped his fingers on the border between the reddish-brown fur of Kip's upper arm and the black fur that extended from mid-forearm up to his paws, like a glove. "Your dad won't like it."

"Your dad doesn't like you spending time with me, but you do it anyway."

The boy had smiled and said, "When I'm a sorcerer, Dad won't order me around." He'd wrapped his fingers around Kip's arm. "When I'm a sorcerer, I'll take care of all of you."

The summer grass had felt good under Kip's wagging tail. Even when he'd had to leave Saul a few minutes later because Nellie Porter arrived, he'd taken his time wandering back through the sun, excited at the promise that he would be part of some sorcery in the only way he was then allowed.

And now Saul's promises were dead and buried, but that tragedy had opened a door for Kip that he'd never expected. Ever since he'c gotten the spell book from his father, he'd dreamed of one day being able to command the fire that had driven Farley away, to be in charge of his own life. He'd seen himself returning from the war with Spain a decorated hero, his magical flame the ruin of the new Spanish fleet; he'd pictured himself living down in New Cambridge among the Calatians, not up in the Tower with the other sorcerers; he'd work with his father so his father could stay down in the town as well. In his more extreme flights of fancy, he'd imagined himself unlocking mysteries that normal humans couldn't, that his magical origin would be a blessing and that other sorcerers would come seek his advice. And of course, his life would be crowned by a Great Feat, something that would leave a permanent mark on the world.

From a young age he had always asked 'how?' How did perfumes smell so different? How did sorcerers fly? How did fire come about? He had once run up Founders Hill after his father and had been turned away at the gate, but not before meeting a phosphorus elemental, a lizard of fire, and the creature had seared itself into his imagination. How did they come to this world? How did they burn? Already his first full day atop Founders Hill had been frighteningly eventful, adding one new question to his mind: how had the stones of the Tower forced magic into him? How had a voice spoken into his head? The prospect of knowing those answers and solving them for others warmed him like few other visions his mind could conjure.

And to be the person who could answer the question of how the Colleges in the New World had been attacked and nearly destroyed, and by whom— well, that was the dream of everyone in New Cambridge, and probably in the American colonies and a good portion of the Empire, for that matter. Kip would settle for being one of those who would exact vengeance on the perpetrators. And so he fell asleep thinking once again of Saul.

Tendrils of mist lay on the ground the next morning, but the air had cleared, leaving the College bright and chilly. Despite the lack of heat in their small tent, Kip and Coppy had been perfectly warm under the thick blankets they'd brought and their coats of fur. Emily had not been quite so comfortable. "My nose is freezing," she complained the next morning, when the students all gathered outside the tents. Kip noticed many of the other students looking at Emily, but only Malcolm approached while she was talking to the Calatians, though Cobb stood nearby, obviously listening.

"Kip's is cold all the time." Coppy grinned at her.

"Yes, well, it's meant to be, isn't it?" Emily rubbed her reddened nose. "Thomas had a hound dog, and its nose was cold all the time, except when it was sick. Oh, dear." Her cheeks turned as bright red as her nose. "Oh, Kip,

I'm sorry. What a terrible thing to say. I'm tired, and not thinking clearly."

The words stung, a little. He could see it in Coppy's eyes as well. "We've heard it many times," he said, because Emily did look wretched, and that too was unnerving. "I know you didn't mean it."

Cobb did speak up at this point. "I don't see why you should be sorry," he said. "Acknowledging they came from human and animal both, well, it's a fact, isn't it?"

"They're not—" Emily stopped herself. "No matter where we came from, we're all people."

"But we were created by God. They were created by a man."

"Out of God's creation. They have the same divine spark."

"I don't see why it's offensive to acknowledge the differences."

"Aye," Malcolm said, "sure, it's a difference, but there's differences between all of us, and how would you be feeling if Kip and Emily here were to say to each other, 'Oh, that John Cobb, he's a good enough fellow, and I hear those Pennsylvanians are just as much people as you and I, no matter what strange customs they have there'?"

"What customs?" Cobb turned on Malcolm.

"Ah," the Irishman replied cheerfully, "it was an example made up on the moment, but if you insist, what about the custom of living in Pennsylvania, to start with, when there are such delightful places as New York and Boston in easy reach along the King's Road?"

"Pennsylvania is a beautiful land!"

"I hear the land is as beautiful as the women in Pennsylvania, and that's why the men drink from sunrise to sunset."

Cobb started toward him and raised a hand. "*We* tell that joke about New Jersey!"

"And we tell it about you, and nobody tells it about us, and what does that tell you?" Malcolm gestured back toward Emily and Kip. "Now, let's not be forgetting how this conversation started. Our friends are our friends, and let's not be worrying about where their ancestors were born, be it the noble heritage of a fox's earth or the 'lovely' hills of Pennsylvania."

"Pennsylvania is—"

"For the love of Jesus, Mary, and Joseph, my friend, it was a joke!" Malcolm set a hand on Cobb's shoulder, and though the other made to shrug it off, the Irishman persisted. "'Protest an insult once for honor, protest an insult twice, it's on yer,' my da used to say. None of us thinks ill of Pennsylvania, but the louder you cry her praises, the louder our doubts. So quiet down and put a smile on that Pennsylvania face and let's all go about our studying, shall we?"

Later, while Emily was off at her test and Cobb was waiting to follow her, Kip took Malcolm aside. "Thank you," he said.

"Ah, 'tis nothing I've not done before." Malcolm smiled and punched

Kip in the arm, lightly. "And I know you meant well yesterday with that Adamson fellow."

Kip nodded. "He's off studying with his group today, or at least he hasn't come to see us at all. Would you like to talk sorcery?"

Malcolm's green eyes gleamed. "I'd welcome it, aye."

It turned out that neither Malcolm nor Smith had any practice in sorcery, although both of them had felt an affinity for it. Smith had been rejected as an applicant in the past, but was hoping he could enroll now that the College was desperate. Malcolm's parents had not let him apply previously because, they said, the College would never take an Irish student.

"My da says the College wanted to become more American, to have Colonial-born students, and even that they were taking some Wampanog or Mashpee to try to learn their magic." He spread his hands. "But I thought that if they were desperate enough, they might take an Irish-born who happens to love these Colonies."

"Their advertisement sounded desperate indeed." Smith drew in his breath. "I'd applied to Prince Philip's before it was destroyed and the masters said I had encouraging potential but that they had enough students."

"If they take me, they'll certainly take you," Kip said, more to Malcolm than to Smith, and Coppy nodded his agreement.

"The Irish in London had a bad time of it, while I was there," the otter said. "Most Calatian families at least had their own houses and clothing. Many of the Irish all lived together in shacks on the Thames."

"Course, there are fewer of you." Malcolm's brow lowered. "What's more, you've got a piece of paper from King James himself says you're to be treated as human beings." He paused, looking between Kip and Coppy. "We Irish got no such thing."

In the silence that followed that remark, Kip said, "You do here," and Malcolm's smile came warmly back, making Kip wish that he'd insisted even harder that the Irishman accompany them the previous day.

Master Argent's raven flew by to summon the next student before Emily had returned, so Coppy walked off, and when it came cawing Malcolm's name, he and Kip guessed that the students, once tested, were not allowed to rejoin their fellows. They wondered whether they would be allowed to talk to the other groups once the day was complete.

Alone with Smith, Kip asked more about his previous test, but Smith gave short, clipped answers, and finally said, "Look, I'm sure you're a fine fellow. We had Calatians come in and help the slaves with the harvest, and almost none of them stole. But you don't belong here any more than that woman does."

"I'm here nonetheless," Kip said.

Smith looked away, and Kip, forcing himself to relax, stared past the Tower and longed for the raven to return so he could leave.

When it did, he followed it around to the Admissions tent, where it alit above the tent flap and regarded him with what he swore was a smirk. He bowed to it and entered the tent.

Master Windsor spoke the King's English more dryly and properly than anyone Kip had ever heard. His deep voice filled the tent. "Be seated," he said, and Kip obeyed. "Penfold. I understand that certain people upon this hill are of the opinion that you should be treated differently from the other candidates. I will tell you what I told Miss Carswell and Lutris: you need not seek any special favor from me."

He was making it sound far better than it was. "No, sir," Kip said. "I don't want any."

"What is of importance to me is your suitability for matriculation into this school, and should you satisfy me on that count, your ability to learn and do this school credit upon your departure from it. Now. Why do you wish to become a sorcerer?"

"To protect and serve the Empire to the best—"

"Not that formulaic drivel you wrote on your application." The sorcerer leaned forward. "You, Phillip Penfold, why do you want to become a sorcerer?"

Kip struggled to find the words. "To learn to cast magic—to know how it works—"

Master Windsor raised his voice, a barked command that cut through Kip's thoughts. "*Why?*"

"I want to cast a Great Feat!" Kip blurted out.

His ears went back immediately, and he looked down at the desk where the sorcerer's elbows rested, waiting for the laughter. Silence. He looked up. Master Windsor leaned back and surveyed Kip with steady dark eyes. His voice lowered, smoother. "Why?"

Kip squinted. "Why? I mean—doesn't everyone? Don't you, sir?"

"What I wish is of no consequence here." Master Windsor reached up, ran fingers through his hair. "But it is significant that you wish to learn sorcery for the sake of sorcery itself, rather than for revenge or personal gain. Your specific goal may be misguided, however. A Great Feat is an action shaped by history. It is a response rather than an achievement. Tell me of the Great Feats you know, and why they were worked."

The exam had started. At least Kip felt comfortable enough here to bring his ears upright as he spoke. "The Rolling Rocks of Alesia were cast to defeat a horde of Gauls. The Queen's Road was built to bring more British citizens from London to New York so that we could occupy lands the French wanted. And I don't know very much about the Statues of China, except they were supposed to have stopped an uprising, I think?" He tapped his teeth together. "I don't know why the Calatians were created either, sir."

"Nor does anyone else." Master Windsor gave no indication of how good Kip's answer had been, but on the paper in front of him ink flowed into indecipherable (to Kip) characters. The sorcerer went on to the next question, about the Punic Wars and how the Roman sorcerers had broken Carthage's famous Siege of Fire. Kip struggled with some questions, but all in all he did well in his history, only failing at one question, about the writings of Hecataeus.

"I suppose there was no reason to expect you to be any more educated than anyone else in this benighted colony," the dour sorcerer said, as though the long-dead Hecataeus had been a personal friend of his. "Now, let us cover your languages."

Kip demonstrated his excellent French and his capable Latin. He knew only the alphabet of the Greek language, and a few words of Spanish. After about fifteen minutes of recitals, Windsor cut him off. The ink continued to form strange words on the paper and then stopped. "You may proceed to the back of the tent," the sorcerer said, pointing behind him.

There, Kip found Emily and Coppy sitting together on the grass, and Cobb and Malcolm sitting a little ways off, not speaking much. He hurried over to Emily and Coppy and sat with them, discussing the questions Windsor had asked. "Old Sourpuss, he is," Coppy said. "Puts me in mind of this sorcerer used to come down to the Isle and pick up his calyx like we was a prostitute's underthings."

"He said we weren't to get special treatment." Kip was the only one who had thought that encouraging. Both Emily and Coppy thought that Windsor had been over-reacting to their difference and might single them out for punishment to prove that he was even-handed. Kip could not convince them otherwise, and he didn't himself know why he believed the sorcerer genuinely meant what he said.

"We both did rather well on the history part, anyway," Emily said. "Oddest history exam I've ever sat for, though. He was all interested in the causes of things, not when they happened."

"Good job we studied together." Coppy patted Kip's leg. "I remembered quite a lot."

"You learned most of that yourself in London." The fox turned to Emily. "Coppy's mum took books from the trash behind schoolhouses and brought them home so her cubs could have a good education."

"She swatted our backsides if we didn't learn." Coppy grinned and slapped his tail against the grass. "And we weren't allowed to scavenge the Thames if we failed a lesson."

"Was she a teacher?"

The otter slowed his tail. "Aye. She taught lots of us, but others said they didn't understand why a Calatian would need an education, when we'd be bound to be calyxes if we were lucky, and shipworkers or rope-walkers otherwise, and in any case there'd be no call for reading or learning."

"Rather short-sighted, I'd say." Emily folded her arms. "Of course,

Boston society women say the same thing about young girls. 'You'll be married or working a loom, and neither one of those requires you to read.' It's ridiculous. Abigail Adams is one of the best writers I know, and if she'd not gotten an education, I'd never have been able to read her work."

"Father would've never allowed me not to go to school." Kip had tried once or twice to quit, intimidated by the crowd of large human boys. Max had said that an education was worth one or two broken arms, and Kip supposed he'd been right even if the number of broken bones had risen so much that he could no longer pinpoint it exactly.

"Good for all of us, then." Coppy looked around and grinned. "Suppose we get Math tomorrow, or Magic?"

It was to be math, they learned at dinner, where they also learned the answer to Kip and Malcolm's speculation about the disposition of the groups. Everyone sat at the same tables, but could only hear the conversation within their group. Even Kip's ears, fully perked, caught nothing but silence from anywhere else in the tent. Adamson had approached them and attempted to talk, but whatever barrier had been placed between the groups had also been placed around their members, and all Kip saw was the young man's mouth moving. Adamson tried to make signs with his hands, and then a very peculiar expression came over his face and he stopped immediately.

After Adamson walked back over to his group, Kip watched Farley to see if he looked in any way discouraged by the exams. It had taken him three years to pass the examination to graduate from school, but he did not seem particularly worried; he smiled and laughed with the plump boy in the black jacket, while Adamson kept his smooth, glassy smile throughout. They paid little attention to the other groups.

Within the group, though, they could talk and compare notes. Smith and Cobb sat a little ways apart, and although Malcolm initially joined them, he moved over to sit with Kip, Coppy, and Emily before too long.

"So pleased you could join us," Emily said.

"Ah, that lot's rather boring. After a while you know what they're going to say next. Me ma used to say a conversation should be like a spring breeze, flying wherever the mood takes it, or else where's the point in talking? Those two talk with all the excitement of a spilled inkwell."

"I'm glad you find us so diverting." She turned back to Coppy and asked him another mathematics question.

Malcolm raised his eyebrows at Kip, but the fox had no answer for him. "How's your math?" he asked quietly. "Emily's worried because she wanted to learn, but no school would teach her, so she only has what lessons she learned herself."

"Never much cared for numbers." Malcolm lost his slight worry and the now-familiar broad smile returned. "What you reckon they'll ask us about?"

So Kip discussed geometry and algebra, trigonometry and triangulation, but within an hour, Malcolm had shaken his head. "It's too much for me to absorb in one night," he said, stretching his arms. "If I know it, I know it, and if I'm meant to pass, the Good Lord will guide me through."

"That's a fine attitude." Emily turned toward them. "I'd rather trust in my own intelligence."

"Which the Lord gave you."

"If you insist." She turned back to Coppy.

"Anyway," Malcolm said to Kip, though loudly enough for Emily to hear, "I'd rather work on sorcery. Since that is what we're here to learn, after all."

"I can show you what I've been able to do," Kip offered, and they walked over to the practice tent, which Master Argent had vacated, to work on magic for the rest of the night.

The following day passed much like the first. Kip's examination with Master Patris came in the afternoon, and the old Master spoke as little as possible. He sat behind a plain wooden desk in the dining tent with his raven (Kip assumed) watching from above.

"Recite the Pythagorean Theorem," Patris said.

"The sum of the squares of the shorter sides of a right triangle is equal to the square of the longest side," Kip recited.

"It is actually the sum of the squares of the sides that form the right angle that is equal to the square of the side opposite the angle." Patris, like Master Windsor, did not make marks on his paper, but they appeared there nonetheless.

Kip wanted to say that it came to the same thing, that of course the sides that formed the right angle would be the shortest, but he pressed his lips together. The rest of the exam proceeded much like that; when Kip gave the correct answer, Patris said nothing. When he gave a correct answer that could be better worded, or was slightly incomplete, Patris corrected him with a slight sneer of condescension.

Forty-five minutes into the examination, Patris said curtly, "You are done." He made two more marks on Kip's paper and then shuffled it aside. He didn't even look up to meet Kip's eyes.

Kip walked out the back without a word, but had to walk back and forth to work off his anger before he could sit down with the others. Coppy had been treated much the same, but it didn't bother him. "Least he listened to me," he said.

Emily, though, was still furious. "Whenever I didn't know something, he would say, 'as I expected,' or he would just smile, and once I was so angry that I said, 'If people would take the time to teach mathematics to women, they would find many willing to learn,' and he said, 'women do not have the proper parts of their brains to learn mathematics.' Aren't they supposed to be intelligent here? I expected him to start measuring my skull with calipers to see how in balance my humors were! It's completely laughable."

"She's rather upset," Coppy told Kip.

Malcolm did not have any such trouble, nor, as far as they could tell, did Cobb or Smith. And at dinner, most of the students seemed untroubled. Emily finally calmed down with some talk from Kip and Coppy. "Patris is going to be a thorn in all our sides," Kip pointed out, "and if you take your anger into tomorrow's exam you may well give him what he wants."

Kip wanted to talk to Victor again, to find out if he were having any success in his mission to change minds. It was true that Farley had barely paid attention to Kip during the last two days, but there was magic keeping them apart, and even his slow-acting brain might have figured there would be nothing he could do at the moment. That didn't mean he wasn't planning some mischief for later. And yet, for all the time Kip watched him, the stout bully only glanced the fox's way once, and he actually left the dining tent early. Perhaps he was worried after all and going to study.

Thursday morning, it was Malcolm's turn to be nervous, though he showed it by laughing more than usual and talking nearly non-stop, so much so that he drove Smith away to "find a corner of this hill with some quiet." Kip attempted to teach the Irishman the tricks of summoning magic while Emily, Cobb, and Coppy were tested in the practice tent, and by the time Master Argent's raven came to call him, Malcolm had at least managed to produce a flicker of orange light around his fingers.

"It shows aptitude," Kip said.

"Let's hope that'll be what they're looking for," the Irishman said, getting up and waving as he walked to the tent.

When Kip's turn came, he found the tent set up with a small wooden floor and a chair on either side of it. Master Argent sat in one of the chairs, and waved Kip to the other, a plain wooden chair shiny with varnish. What made Kip pause, though, was the array of ravens on the perch high above the floor. Ten of them he counted, watching him step carefully to the chair and take a seat, sweeping his tail around to one side. Not one of them made a sound. Not one of them moved, other than to turn their heads to follow his progress. Ten pairs of gleaming black eyes—and presumably, ten pairs of human eyes elsewhere—watched him sit straight, fold his paws in his lap, and stare at Master Argent.

The young sorcerer took no notice of the ravens. "Hello, Penfold," he said. "I believe we have already established that you have some command of at least one spell. However, I hope you will bear with me as we take you through the established examination protocol."

Kip sat quietly until it was clear the sorcerer was waiting for his answer. "Yes, sir," he said.

"Very well. Please demonstrate for me the gathering of magic."

So Kip breathed out and closed his eyes, and breathed in and pulled magic to him. It came easily, comfortably, the feeling of power, the awareness of more below him and around him. He knew his paws were glowing before he opened his eyes to check, looking right to Master Argent's smile and the reflections of his paws' purple glow in the sorcerer's eyes. "Well done," Argent said.

"Do you wish me to cast a spell?" Kip asked.

"If you like." On the desk before the sorcerer, six round marbles lay in a wooden tray. "Lift as many of these as you can."

Kip focused. He had lifted up to four objects, although three was easier, and he resisted the urge to try for all six. Three marbles rose unsteadily but about the same distance into the air, and then descended too quickly, clattering back into the tray. The glow around his paws vanished.

"Very well done. Shall we try another?"

Argent ran Kip through some less familiar physical magic spells; the fox made a game attempt at them and succeeded in one. "Have you studied any other areas?" the young sorcerer asked when they were done.

Kip shook his head. Master Argent nodded and brought out two books. "I am going to show you the most basic spells in the disciplines of translocational and alchemical magic, and I would like you to study them and attempt them."

"What about spiritual magic?" Kip leaned forward as Master Argent opened the first book.

"If you continue on at the College into your fourth year, you may yet learn it. But it is too dangerous for anyone to attempt prior to that level of experience. The manipulation of the human spirit affords very little room for error." He pushed the book toward Kip.

A rustling above made Kip's ears flick back, but he stared down at the book, not up at the ravens. The spell was "Basic Translocation," and the explanation was straightforward: he would recite the syllables, hold the target object as if it were a physical spell, and visualize the destination. The magic would push the object through a non-visible plane to appear elsewhere instantaneously.

But when he attempted the spell, the marble he was staring at did not move. He tried three times, and then Argent took the book back. "It is not easy," he said. "Try the alchemical."

Kip leaned over to the second book, in which the spell was to condense water out of the air. Here he had a little more success; the marble acquired a damp sheen, though not the puddle he had hoped for.

"Excellent work." Argent took that book back and closed it. Above, feathers rustled again.

There followed fifteen minutes of questions about magical theory and famous sorcerers, to which Kip mostly knew the answers. Then he was dismissed without any indication of his performance other than Master

Argent's smile.

He looked up as he left the tent. A single raven remained on the perch, its dark eyes following him as he left.

The sense of accomplishment and relief at being finished with the testing kept his tail high and his smile fixed when he rejoined his friends. Emily and Coppy looked similarly relaxed, and Malcolm had at least done better than he'd thought he would. All of them reported that multiple ravens had watched their progress, but only Coppy thought he'd seen as many as ten. "Naturally they'd be more interested in us," Kip said.

"I wonder if you're more proficient because you're made of magic." Malcolm extended his hands toward Kip. "Anyone ever try drawing magic out of you?"

"I don't feel I was very proficient," Coppy said. "But Master Argent said that summoning magic was quite good for an applicant at this level."

"You've heard the Church of God Sorcerer, haven't you?" Emily gestured above her. "They go about in these big tents preaching that God created humans by sorcery as well, that we're all magical beings."

"Tripe and nonsense," Malcolm retorted. "God is God. He created man out of Nothing."

"Just because someone thinks something different does not mean you should dismiss them out of hand." Emily's voice dropped several degrees, though Kip had thought her of similar mind, from her tone.

"If humans were magical, though," Kip said, "why would the sorcerers need Calatians to help them with their rituals?"

She nodded slowly, her manner thawing. "I don't know the answer to that. But I've found that one can rarely ask people logical questions about their religion."

"Personally," Coppy spoke up, "I always believed in a God who made man, and a man who made Calatians, but it's all of the same stuff, innit? I mean, we're made of whatever God made man of, and magic on top of that."

"Humans don't hold much with that." Malcolm grinned at him. "You'll give us a complex, you will, or turn us all into fanatical tent-dwelling cultists."

"You mean men don't hold with it." Emily sat up straighter. "The Bible says Eve was made from the rib of Adam. So when you get right down to it," she went on over Malcolm's beginning objection, "it isn't so different from the Calatians, except that it was that mage Calatus rather than God."

"And he mixed man with animal," Coppy pointed out.

Malcolm seemed confused, not by the argument, but by Emily's vehemence. "I never meant offense," he said. "And you made that comment about his nose just the other day."

"And I apologized for it directly." Emily looked down her nose at the Irishman, which was difficult as they were all sitting cross-legged on the grass, but she managed it nonetheless.

"I'll say this," Malcolm said. "At this moment I feel more akin to the

Calatians than I do to women. At the least I understand them better."

Kip thought Emily might have a chilly retort to this as well, but she let it go and talked instead about the other students, wondering how much sorcery they were able to perform. "Maybe we'll be allowed to talk to the other groups now," Kip said as a raven flew over croaking that dinner was served.

Smith hadn't come out to join them yet, but they got up from the grass and walked over to the dining tent, leaving Cobb to wait for him. On the way, they got their answer, as Adamson joined them.

"Good evening," he said, glancing behind him. "Ah, they've lifted the silence."

"So it would seem." Kip was not sure how he felt about Adamson now. The boy was friendly, but had also spent three days in the company of Farley, and Farley had not hit him. In Kip's experience, Farley divided the world into "people who needed a beating" and "people who helped administer beatings," and that Adamson was not in the first category meant he was likely in the second. It was possible, though, that someone as smart as he was could navigate the treacherous shoals of Farley without foundering.

"How do you feel you fared in the examinations?"

"Reasonably well." Kip indicated his companions. "We all do."

"I'm pleased to hear it." Adamson linked his hands behind his back as he walked. "I too feel that I have made some significant impression on the examining masters."

"I'm certain you must have."

As soon as he said it, Kip felt bad, but Adamson didn't pick up on any double meaning he might have read into the fox's words. He inclined his head and said, "You're very kind."

"How did you do in the sorcery test?" Kip wanted badly to know if someone who could not call on magic at all would be admitted to the college.

Adamson walked two steps before drawing in a breath to answer. "I feel that I covered the basics of sorcery and the necessary knowledge to explore the foundations of a magical education."

Behind him, Malcolm snickered and quickly covered up the sound. Kip felt guilty at his own rush of pleasure that the privileged boy would not be able to force his way into a college. If he'd demonstrated no aptitude for sorcery, how could they admit him? And yet, the college was desperate. Perhaps they would see in him a project, someone who might be trained to learn magic. Still, in the past several years he had presumably tried and failed to gather it himself.

And yet, even as Kip said, "I'm sure they will give you a chance," he envisioned a scenario in which Adamson with his human face was admitted, while Kip and Coppy were sent home despite being well able to cast spells.

He nearly missed what Adamson said after that, something about Farley, even though his ears were perked toward the other. He kept listening, and when Adamson said, "Therefore I believe that his admission will depend on his grasp of history," Kip deduced that Farley had done well enough on the magic portion.

"He never had any magic in him when I knew him growing up," Kip replied. "Farley has a great command of the physical without any magic necessary."

"You might not have heard about the incidents. It seems his mother did not approve of sorcerers and might have hidden any indication of his magical talent." Adamson stared fixedly ahead, his jaw set. Was he jealous?

"His mother shops in our store." She was a large, loud woman who did not mind giving her money to Calatian businesses, but who made it known that she thought they had made a "devil's bargain" with those sorcerers up the hill. She blamed the sorcerers and the French for her husband's death, but blamed nobody but him for the failure of his business.

"I presume he doesn't get his views of your people from her, then." They were approaching the dining tent, and Adamson slowed his steps. "He won't talk much about his father."

Kip told him shortly how the elder Broadside had died in the war, which story brought them to the tent flap. "Thank you," Adamson said. "That will be most helpful in tempering his views."

"Will you eat with us tonight?" Kip's other friends walked in behind him and took up seats at their customary table.

Adamson watched Emily and Coppy, and then his eyes slid to the back corner from which Farley and Carmichael watched him. "I suppose I could," he said. He moved toward their table with Kip.

Malcolm, who'd sat at the end of their table, got up when he saw Adamson approach. "Ah, seems I've sat at the wrong place. I'll just slide over here, shall I?" And he set himself next to Smith, across from Cobb, at the adjacent table.

"You can sit here." Kip indicated the seat beside him, but Malcolm affected not to hear him, and the fox didn't want to press the issue. He enjoyed the dinner less, though; he, Emily, and Coppy all felt an unspoken reluctance to share too much with Adamson, not only because of his association with Farley, but because he hadn't been a part of their group for the last three days and hadn't gone through the examinations with them. Emily in particular spoke little and often looked distracted.

After the meal, Adamson stood and walked quickly over to Farley as the thick-set boy was leaving. Kip heard Farley say, "pelt-lover," and Adamson say, "you know better" curtly in return. He wanted to listen further, but Emily pulled him aside.

"I have to talk to you," she said, "and quickly."

He followed her around the side of the dining tent, walking through the damp short grass away from the babble of the candidates leaving dinner, down to the long, thick shadows of the oak trees in the dying light. "What's the matter?" Kip asked as Emily slowed and looked around her.

"Was that something moving?" She peered into the shadows, down along the line of trees.

Kip followed her gaze to where a small orchard grew, whose apple trees he could distinguish from the wild oaks of the forest by their uniform height and regular rows. He heard rustling, but saw nothing amid the shadows. "I won't see better than you until after sundown," he said. "There's something moving there, but it might be an animal."

"All right." She turned back to face him, and her eyes traveled over his shoulder, rising to the tower behind him. "This is what I was thinking. You should levitate yourself to the top floor of the Tower on this side and listen in on the Masters discussing the candidates tonight."

She said it so calmly and reasonably that Kip nodded for a moment before he stopped. "Uh, no. That sounds like a terrible idea."

"It'll be fine. They won't expect you to be there, so they won't be looking for you. And anyway, they'll all be in the meeting."

"They have ravens." As if to illustrate his point, two ravens that had been perching in the dining tent flew away from it. "I'm sure they will be watching out."

"They won't expect it," Emily said again.

"Master Argent knows I can levitate. Most of them do, by now. Why wouldn't they expect it?"

"Because…" She sighed. "They just won't. I mean, they probably don't think you can control it properly."

"Anyway," Kip said, "why should I? We'll hear the results tomorrow morning no matter what. What's the use of hearing them early?"

"I'm not interested in the results," Emily shot back. "I'm interested in the discussions, and we won't ever hear that unless we listen in."

"Unless I listen in, you mean." Kip folded his arms, his tail switching from side to side.

"Yes."

"How do you know where it is?"

She tossed her head. "Argent told me. I asked if I might happen across him and the other masters deciding our fates, and he laughed and said 'not unless you're taking a walk around the top floor of the Tower.' I laughed too. I don't think he really thinks we'll do anything about it."

Kip didn't share her confidence, but he wasn't going to sway her; he knew that already. "What's so important about their discussions?"

Her grey eyes met his. "I think we're both reasonably qualified, probably moreso than most candidates they get in a normal year. I think you think so, too." He nodded. "So if they tell you tomorrow morning, 'thank you very much but go on home and don't bother with those dreams of being a sorcerer,' wouldn't that upset you?"

"Yes," Kip said, "but—"

"And," she pushed on, "wouldn't you want to know whether it was because you're not fit to be a sorcerer, or…"

He read her meaning before she said it, but she went on anyway. "Or because you have a tail?"

CHAPTER 6: ADMISSIONS

"I don't have a black cloak," Emily said, "but this grey one might match the Tower's stone."

Kip eyed the cloth she was holding out. "If they spot me, they'll spot me. I don't think any camouflage is going to make a difference."

"I don't suppose it'd hurt." Coppy took the cloak from Emily and draped it around Kip's shoulders. They'd told the otter about the plan on Kip's insistence that he would prefer two lookouts to warn him if anyone were approaching. The real reason was that he wanted Coppy to be included; only as they were walking toward the Tower's south side in the dim twilight did he realize that included also meant implicated, assuring that the otter would be expelled with him and Emily if they were caught.

But Coppy had been quite happy to help, and likely would have followed Kip to the Tower anyway. So here they were at the base of the Tower facing the empty dining and admissions tents, and Kip turned his head to look up the rough stone wall behind him.

He didn't want to touch the Tower again in case the same rush of magic overwhelmed him and was somehow perceptible to the sorcerers inside. But he told himself it was better to touch it here on the ground than accidentally seven stories up, and so he'd reached out and touched his fingertips to the stone, now chilly in shadow.

Nothing had happened. He'd left his fingertips there, then pressed his whole paw to the wall, and still nothing. No voice, no rush of magic; the blocks of stone remained solid, unmoving, unmagical.

He regarded the stone with the same sense of vague disappointment now, a few moments later, as Coppy settled the grey cloak around him. No ravens flew overhead that they could see, no movement interrupted the evening here. Kip could still, very faintly, hear the conversations carrying through the humid air from the candidates on the other side of the Tower, and he could smell the remnants of dinner from the dining tent.

"Go on," Emily said.

"You'll make the whippoorwill call if you see something?"

"Yes, yes." She motioned impatiently.

"All right." He took a breath, reached out, and gathered magic into himself.

There came the familiar tension, crackling in his fur, the purple glow around his paws. He spoke the spell confidently and then filled it with magic and pushed. His feet left the ground, tail dangling behind him as he rose through the air.

He stayed close to the wall, one paw out for caution. But he kept himself steady and his paw remained half a foot from the rough stone as he rose past one floor, then another, and another. He passed dark window after dark window, rising toward the top floor even though none of those windows were lit either. As he passed the sixth floor, he heard voices to his right, and he pushed himself in that direction until they grew louder.

Just outside the window where the voices were loudest, he stopped. Curtains inside blocked most of the light and muffled the sound, but he could make out Patris's distinct growl, Master Argent's milder voice, and Master Windsor's gruff tone. They were discussing one of the candidates he didn't know, a boy named Davies.

Kip crossed his legs in the air and floated next to the window, out of sight of the people inside. Probably nobody was peeking out through the curtains, and the evening had grown dark enough that they likely wouldn't notice him there even if they did, but he could hear well enough and did not want to take the chance.

After Davies, they went on to Forester, Middleton, Plant, Smith, and then Wormwood. Each boy's merits were discussed in similar tones, Master Patris giving about the same assessment of each, Master Windsor describing their knowledge of history in colorful negative adjectives from "execrable" to "depressingly average," and Master Argent kindly saying that some were "teachable" while others "displayed the spark of connection to magic." Each of the boys was grudgingly admitted by the group, in a chorus of yeas mixed with one or two nays from a high-pitched reedy voice and a clipped, sharp bark of a voice. Only Potterfield was denied entry, largely (Kip thought) because Master Argent said, "He has no magical spark whatsoever." Even then, one of the other masters asked if they could afford to refuse anyone interested.

"Now," Patris said finally, "we come to the unusual candidates. In alphabetical order, Miss Carswell first."

Kip leaned in close. The tips of his ears were cold, but otherwise he was well-insulated from the night-time chill. Patris's voice came clearly to him. "Her grasp of mathematics and science is tenuous at best, as one would expect from a woman."

"She evinces a surprisingly well-rounded grasp of history." Master Windsor's endorsement provoked surprised mutters that even Kip could hear.

"Her magical talent is beyond dispute," Master Argent said. "She is the third most talented of the candidates we review tonight, and more talented than the average candidate admitted to the College."

"In your five vast years of experience," Patris said.

"I hardly think his experience is relevant here, Patris," rumbled an unfamiliar voice. "Question is whether a woman can be a sorcerer."

"Surprised she can do magic at all."

"The Indians have witches who can do magic."

"Not proper magic."

"Master Ousamequin would have objected to that."

A silence followed here. It took Kip a moment to deduce that Master Ousamequin must have been one of the sorcerers killed in the attacks. The voices resumed a moment later. "But does she have the discipline to follow it through?"

"Don't want to train her for a year and then have her go off to take up quilting." This was the same voice that had been surprised she could do magic. Kip badly wanted to tell them that Emily was about as likely to take up sewing as she was to turn into a Calatian.

"I doubt she will." This was Argent again. "Her dedication to learning is admirable."

"What if she's taken with her monthlies and takes out her frustrations with sorcery?"

"Most women manage them with little complaint, but do tell, is that why you only go see your wife certain times of the month?"

General laughter, and then, "What about dissension in the candidates? Won't it distract the students to have a girl in their midst?"

"If they're that easily distracted," Master Patris said, "then they won't become sorcerers anyway."

"So you favor her admission?"

"I did not say that," he said.

"Patris is saving his objection for the Calatians." This was the high-pitched, reedy voice.

"We are not discussing them yet," Patris said stiffly, but Kip could tell from his tone that the reedy voice was right.

"Well, then, any objections to Miss Carswell's admittance?" This was Argent, pushing the matter forward.

The chorus of yeas was weaker, the nays more plentiful, but there was no question which carried the day.

"And now," Master Patris said, "the question of Coppy Lutris."

"Why not consider both together?" Master Argent said. "Unless the difference in their math or history is enough to separate them. No?"

There must have been non-verbal agreement, because Master Patris said, "Very well. Lutris and Penfold."

Kip strained to hear any words, but for several seconds, nobody spoke. Then Master Argent said, "Prejudices aside, Penfold has a strong grasp of sorcery. You all saw what he was able to do, and that untaught. Lutris shows potential as well, easily enough to qualify a human student."

"And yet," an unfamiliar voice said, "we cannot simply dismiss out of hand the differences between these candidates and the human ones. Vendis, the fox is the son of your calyx. What say you? Were you aware of his talent?"

Master Vendis had a soft, high voice that Kip had to strain to hear. "The father told me, of course, but I had not seen any evidence before yesterday."

"Is the father of good character?"

"Most excellent," Vendis replied. "The son is perhaps a trifle hasty, but I have confidence in the family."

"And the otter? What know you of him?"

Master Patris's voice cut through the argument. Kip braced himself, folding his ears down. "The question is not of the individual character of the Calatians. The question is of the policy of this College. If we admit these two, others will surely follow. I have spoken to Master Roylston at the King's College, and he warns strongly against admitting them."

"Did he forbid it?" Master Windsor's deep voice.

A pause, during which Kip thought his heart might not have beat at all. "No," Patris said finally. "He advised us to use our judgment."

"Then in my judgement as Master of Admissions," Argent said, "it would be a mistake to deny admission to these two candidates."

"And in my judgment," Patris responded, "it would be a greater mistake to admit them. My primary concern is the safety of this college and the remaining sorcerers, and allowing them to enter the college will create strife and tension. It could distract us from our vigilance and open us up to another attack. We are the only defense of these colonies, and as Master Roylston reminded me, any enemy wishing to strike at the Empire might well do so through her most prosperous—and now least defended—colonies."

"For God's sake, Patris," Windsor said. "Do not stoop to fearmongering. It has been months since we were attacked. Do you not think the Spaniards cunning enough to strike when we were at our weakest?"

"Exactly. Admitting them will weaken us, not strengthen us."

Argent raised his voice. "They are talented, they are learning sorcery, and if we do not educate them, I do not think I need remind you of the danger we may be exposing ourselves to."

The reedy voice said, "We can forbid them to practice sorcery. Set a demon to watch them."

"Would we truly benefit by such an effort? Shall we assign a demon to every renegade sorcerer as they arise?" This was the other deep voice that had occasionally added a "nay" to the reedy voice's. "I like it no more than you, but it seems to me we are between Scylla and Charybdis here."

"I see no dilemma," another voice cut in. "The calyxes are crucial to our fight against the Spanish. If Calatians are permitted to study sorcery, what will come of our calyxes? Will they permit themselves to be used in the same fashion? Or will they demand education, equality? This step we take may cripple the empire."

"Should we forbid the Calatians," Master Argent said, "the calyxes may revolt as well."

"Save your drama for the theater. This is a serious issue!"

"The class is small enough as it is without excluding two of the best students," Argent retorted.

It warmed Kip to hear himself and Coppy thus described. But then Master Patris said, "Roylston offered to send us a half-dozen students from England."

This announcement was not made nor met with the enthusiasm Kip expected. "Be delighted to send us his dregs, he would."

"They're good students," Patris snapped, but he sounded as though he was being forced to defend them.

"Because the worst of London is better than the best here?"

"Rather home-grown Calatians than London humans."

"We're all subjects of the Crown; what's the difference?"

"You've been in your room too long if you need ask that question." This was Master Argent. "I sing 'God Save The King' as loud as anyone, but I'm a man of Massachusetts Bay should anyone ask, and Massachusetts Bay's best can match London's best, even though we lost so many in the attack."

"London's students come here to live would become Massachusetts Bay students, if that is of such paramount importance." Patris, again.

"London never approved of our Indian sorcerers." A voice Kip didn't know. "Perhaps they fear we will turn in that direction again to fill our numbers."

"Indians would be preferable to Calatians." The reedy voice rose again. "Even Negroes."

"For God's sake, Sharpe," Kip heard before a general clamor arose.

"If I may." Master Windsor broke in. "We are straying from the point at hand."

"Yes," Patris said. "Quite right. The Calatians. So we are agreed? They will not be admitted?"

A low voice responded, "I believe we must examine historical precedent here. Back in 1785, this college…"

At that moment a weight dropped onto one knee of Kip's crossed legs. He made a noise and dropped about five feet, but had enough presence of mind to keep his jaw shut as he stared at the raven folding its wings, sharp talons digging into the cloth of his pants and the fur below.

"The vote will be close," it croaked. "I wish to know, if you will permit, what motivates you to pursue sorcery."

He knew the air wasn't dry because his fur was matted, but his mouth felt as though he'd had no water in days. He licked his lips and tried to keep his voice low. "I wish to—"

With a snap, the raven clacked its beak, making him stop and wobble in the air again. "I wish to know from your mind. If you will permit. I promise to listen only to what you tell me. We do not have a great deal of time. Master Barrett is long-winded but not infinitely so."

"Yes, I—I agree," Kip said quickly, ears straining at the murmurs of conversation from the window above.

In his head, a clear voice: *why do you want to learn sorcery?*

And he told it, with words floating in clouds of images, of the fierce joy of driving Farley away with fire, of the fascination the fire held for him and the long nights he'd spent trying to summon it back, of the giddy joy he'd felt from the rush of his first successfully cast spell, of his hunger to know more, to know how and why these spells worked and to be able to cast more of them, of the many little distresses he could help in the Calatian community and the justices he could render, and—

Thank you.

It stared back at him and then cocked its head as though listening. Kip stared at it and slowly brought his ears back up, inclining his head as well. He lifted himself and the raven back to be level with the window. Master Barrett, if that was the sorcerer to whom the low voice belonged, continued to drone on.

"…we must not underestimate the duty of this college. Not all the calyxes demonstrate an affinity to magic, and many of them are too old anyway to enroll. The responsibility to regulate the use of magic and education of sorcery in the Colonies now rests entirely on our shoulders and we must approach it with all the gravity such a duty merits."

The next voice was Patris's. "I notice you have not cast your stone to one side or the other with that pretty speech."

Barrett replied, "Have I not? Perhaps I can make it clearer. We now bear the entire burden of sorceric education in these colonies. Here are two students in need of it. How much more clear do you think I need be?"

"This decision," Patris said, "may shape the course of history, and we should not simplify it in order to be more quickly done with it."

Kip could swear the raven rolled its eyes.

"History," Master Windsor said, "is not shaped by single men nor single decisions. This may be the first rumble of thunder, but plugging our ears to shut out the sound will not stop the storm." He raised his voice, and the raven on Kip's knee listened as attentively as the fox did. "To those who view the tides of history from above, the surprise is not that these candidates have emerged now, but that they have not emerged before now."

"I watch the tides of politics," Patris said, "and I have not seen any sign of this."

"Perhaps you should look more closely into your calyx's eyes when he visits," the shaky voice said.

This provoked some laughter, nervous and short. Kip looked questioningly at the raven, but it simply stared back blankly at him. He hoped the sorcerers would continue with some hint as to what the calyxes' duties were, but instead Master Windsor resumed speaking.

"In any event," he said, "admission to the College does not guarantee success as a sorcerer. It might very well be that the Calatians will be assigned to duty as physical sorcerers, in which case they will serve as examples to the rest of their race, yes, but a limited example, not something to exalt, but something to temper expectations."

Kip's fists clenched. Building roads or walls? He would never settle for that.

"Tell me, you who have examined the Calatians." This voice was another unfamiliar one, soft and wispy, and Kip had to strain to hear the words. "Why do they seek to learn sorcery?"

"They want power." Patris jumped in. "Of course."

Master Argent replied in a more even tone. "Lutris wants to be able to better protect his friends. Very straightforward. Penfold—well I believe he truly wants to learn sorcery for its own sake."

"Protection from what?" Patris overrode Argent. "From the rest of us? And how do we know Penfold's not simply regurgitating the answers we want? Have we not all heard the legends of Reynard the trickster?"

"Reynard is a legend, not a Calatian," someone put in.

"I believe that to be the truth of him, and I have asked in my own way," the soft voice responded, and that silenced the group for a moment.

The reedy voice chimed in. "Sorcery for its own sake? Dangerous, dangerous."

"No more than any other candidate." The soft voice. "And more worthy of our regard than most."

"Ah, there I do not agree." Windsor. "There are few other candidates—the woman, the Irishman, perhaps—who would use their power to attack society and attempt to effect change. The scale upon which the Calatians might work is greater than most other candidates." Patris made a satisfied noise, and Windsor went on. "However, that danger must be measured against the danger of allowing them to embark on this course without the supervision of this college."

"You make a pertinent point there. But what about the danger of—"

All sound was cut off from him. His control over his spell wavered for a moment, and then he steadied himself. The raven on his leg stared directly at him and then opened its beak.

"You should not hear the votes cast on your behalf," it said. "But be assured that you will be admitted."

"We will?" Kip's heart thudded against his ribs. "Really?"

"The tides of progress inch forward, though there are many who wish to hold them back."

"Who are you?" He asked it quickly, still giddy with the knowledge of their success.

It fluttered its wings. "Now is not the time for us to converse. Your friends will be waiting for their news."

"You're not going to punish me?"

It tilted its head one way and then another. "It is important that you know what you face. The path will be difficult and there is much at stake beyond what you know."

"Beyond…" Kip drew in a breath, the cool air chilling his lungs. "How am I supposed to cope with things I don't even know about?"

The raven spread its wings. "Do your best. That is all anyone can ask." With a powerful push down that sent Kip two feet lower and ruffled his whiskers, the raven launched itself into the air. He craned his neck to follow it, saw a shadow pass across the moon, and then it was gone.

Sounds returned as he lowered himself to the ground. Emily and Coppy ran up and asked in breathless whispers what he'd heard. "Well," he said, drawing the moment out, "there was a lot of arguing. Patris doesn't want us in. But Windsor and Argent spoke in our favor. And…" He hesitated over whether to tell them about the raven, but Coppy made the decision for him by speaking up, eyes wide.

"Windsor? That old sourpuss?"

Kip nodded. "Though—well, he said that we were the first rumblings of thunder and that there was a storm coming—something like that, anyway—and that even if we got admitted, we might end up being sent to build roads and walls."

"Oh, let them try," Emily said.

Kip forced a smile to cover the familiar sour feeling. The masters had needed to know truthfully what was in his head, a caution they'd not needed for any other candidate, and even then the vote had been "close." Close, for a student who could actually cast spells already. Even Emily, with their doubts about her commitment to sorcery, had passed with less scrutiny. "It was more directed at me and Coppy, but there was some debate over you as well."

"Did any of them say I might be useful in the kitchen?"

"No. Honestly," because she didn't seem to believe him. "They were mostly worried about whether you would stay with the college or go off to, I don't know, take up quilting or something."

"Quilting?" She stared and then laughed. "They may think what they like. If they are waiting for me to quit, they will be waiting a good long time."

"That's what I thought." Kip wished he could somehow channel Emily's self-confidence and poise. Even after some of the stories she'd told them about her forced marriage and the way women were held back, she still believed in herself with a fierce determination.

Coppy put a paw on his arm. "Are we really to enroll here?"

He looked down into the gleam of the otter's eyes in the moonlight, saw the twitch of his whiskers, and smiled. His sour feeling faded as Coppy's excitement reminded him that what was important was that they had made it to the next stage with a chance to prove themselves. And even if they ended up road layers or wall builders (they would not) then they would have gotten farther than any Calatians ever had. "We really are."

Coppy exhaled a long breath whose traces hung in the chill, humid air. "I wish my mum could see me now." He leaned against the wall of the Tower and closed his eyes.

"She would've wanted you to be a sorcerer?" Emily asked gently.

Coppy cracked one eye open and grinned. "Far from it," he said. "Sorcerers is why she wanted me to leave London. So many of us went down to the docks, watching the calyxes go up to the King's College, and we wanted to go as well, until we were old enough. Mum was happy to see me off along the Road, and she was none too happy I chose to stay here in the shadow of another College." He waggled a finger at Kip.

"Glad you did." Kip smiled.

"Then Kip told me he could do magic and that I could too. You know the first thing I thought?" Emily shook her head, and Coppy smiled. "I thought, 'I could take this back to London and show the folks on the Isle that we can have more.' I thought we could be more like New Cambridge, have some businesses humans would come to instead of being naught but calyxes and builders.'

Kip had heard this before, but he stayed quiet, his ears splayed to either side. Emily listened, rapt. "But that's foolishness, so I thought," Coppy went on. "I never thought we could learn enough sorcery to be useful. I struggled to keep up with Kip there. But that's how the world is, you know? You take what life gives you and you do your best with it. And up until a few minutes ago, I never really believed we'd be allowed in the school. Now..." He closed his eyes again. They waited, neither Kip nor Emily wanting to interrupt. "Now maybe even if I don't learn much, I can go back and repair walls, build roads...show the cubs there what they can be."

This was perhaps the storm to which Master Windsor had been referring. Calatians seeing one of their own wielding magic, more of them getting ideas, maybe some of them thinking about times in their lives when magic had erupted around them, like Kip's fire. More of them demanding to be taught at the Colleges, learning on their own if that was denied (as it sounded like it might be, in London).

What would be the end result? He could not guess, but any venture that allowed him and his people more power, that stemmed the tide of broken arms and severed tails and seizures and disappearances, that was a venture he wanted to pursue. "It sounds admirable," Emily said, and Kip agreed; he had told Coppy as much in the past. He wondered if this might be one of those things beyond him that the raven on his leg had spoken of.

"We'll do our best," he said, echoing the raven's words, "and then nobody can say any ill of us."

Coppy gave him a big, full, smile, and Kip's tail wagged as they walked back around the Tower to their tents.

Neither the wagging nor the smile lasted to the tent door. As they stood at Emily's tent, before Kip could even wish her good-night, the reek of blood and rank fox urine—wild fox, not a Calatian—came to him on the night breeze. His fur prickled, rising on his shoulders and tail enough so that Coppy noticed. "What is it?" the otter asked.

Kip lifted his nose. "Blood," he said, and that stilled the other two while he made sure the scent was coming from his and Coppy's tent. Jaw set, ears flat, he strode for the doorway, then paused with his paw on the canvas flap, not certain he wanted to pull it aside and see what was there. No sound came from within, but added to the blood and urine smells were the musk of a panicked wild fox and some feces. Coppy, beside him, made a gagging noise, and Kip's throat tightened as well.

He grasped the flap and then stopped. There was another smell, fainter. Kip brought his nose close, running it up and down the cloth, not only to delay the moment when he would have to confront what was in their tent, but also to make sure of what he'd suspected from the first: the scent on the canvas was Farley's.

"You might not want to look at this," he told Emily.

"I've as strong a stomach as either of you," she retorted. "And we're classmates, or going to be. I want to see what our other classmates think is an amusing prank."

"It's not to be amusing." Kip lifted the cloth slowly. "It's to drive us away."

The scene inside looked like something out of a nightmare. Blood spattered their bags and both beds, but the majority of the blood surrounded the small, ragged body on the dirt floor. The sense of violation that had grown from the first scent of blood in the tent faded temporarily, overwhelmed by Kip's sadness at the wasted life and the suffering it had undergone.

"God's wounds," Coppy swore as Kip took two steps forward, not even attempting the vain exercise of keeping his feet clear of any bloody patches.

It was a young fox, he thought as he looked down, a male—of course. Both hind feet had been clumsily severed, and then the poor animal's stomach had been opened. His gorge rose. "They crippled it so it couldn't run, then gutted it so it would thrash around and cover the tent in blood before it died."

"Sweet Lord." Emily's hand was over her mouth, her face white. She stepped quickly back outside the tent.

Coppy's paw was at his mouth too, but he remained inside. "This is one thing we never had on the Isle. Farley, you reckon?"

"I know. I can smell him on the door." Kip's paw went to his arm. He could almost feel Farley's weight, smell his breath, hear his snarled words and see the hate behind those small eyes.

"They won't take that as evidence, I'd wager."

"No." Kip looked around the room, everywhere but at the animal on the ground that had suffered and died a painful death for no reason other than that it shared a remote ancestor with him. The short, shallow breaths he was taking to avoid inhaling too much of the smell were making him lightheaded. "How much of our luggage can be saved?"

"Oh, most of it, I should think." Coppy picked his way across the room, also avoiding the body and the blood-soaked ground. "Blood's mostly on the outside of the bags, and the beds aren't ours. Don't move, I'll get yours."

"Thank you." Kip looked down again then, because he thought he ought to. The fox was beyond his help, beyond anything he might do for it, and to avenge the life of an animal was ridiculous. And yet, he felt more outraged that this innocent creature had suffered than he did at the viciousness of the message it had been used to send. He was being warned that he, too, would suffer; or maybe the message was not even that sophisticated. Maybe the message was simply, *look what I can do to your kin.*

Coppy retrieved both bags, and then he and Kip stepped outside. They walked a little ways away, to Emily's tent, but she was nowhere in evidence. "Gone to fetch a Master, probably," the otter said.

"Or to be sick," which was what Kip wanted to do. He gripped his bag awkwardly in one paw, muscles tight as he fought off nausea. At least in the night, the blood on it wasn't visible, although he could still smell it. "Where will we get water to wash this off?"

"Down at the Inn," Coppy said.

"If we're going down the hill, we might as well go home."

"But come back tomorrow." The otter's eyes shone, his brow creased.

"Of course." Kip found it easier to smile, to reassure the otter. "We're not letting this keep us away."

Coppy relaxed, and so did Kip, the visceral revulsion of the violation receding. He had allowed himself to be lulled, however briefly, into thinking that he could be accepted here, and Farley had wasted no time in reminding him that he never would, that every day would be a struggle.

Emily returned as the fox and otter were gathering their bags to walk down the hill, two black-robed figures in tow. With a sinking heart, Kip recognized Master Patris's stomping stride and glowering stare, and next to him was the slighter figure of Master Argent.

"Allow me to warn you," Patris growled as they approached, "that disturbing the Masters for trivial altercations does not have a positive effect on your candidacy."

"Have you not made your decisions yet?" Emily asked. Kip glared to try to silence her and she looked away, pretending not to have seen.

"You will address me as 'sir,' or 'Head,'" Patris growled.

Emily smiled. "So that means we've been accepted?"

The old Master glared at her and then stared down Kip. "What is this about?"

Kip told him, trying to keep to the facts. "A forest animal—a fox—was slaughtered in our tent. Everything's covered in blood."

Argent looked past Kip to his tent, but Patris continued to stare at the fox as though he'd spoken in a foreign language. "Blood? What nonsense is this?"

"See for yourself," Kip said as calmly as he was able.

Master Argent strode forward first, and Patris followed him, hurrying the twenty feet to Kip and Coppy's tent. "You see how much trouble they attract. It is already starting," the older master said in what Kip thought was supposed to be a low voice, inaudible to the Calatians. The fox's ears caught it clearly enough, and Kip closed his eyes, taking a breath.

"Everything all right?" Emily asked.

"Fine." Kip breathed in and out. "I just—I wish I didn't feel that they were blaming me for this."

"Blaming *you*?" Emily's voice rose. "Who is?"

The two sorcerers opened the flap to the tent and stood, looking in. Neither made a move to enter. Kip glanced back at them, and Emily followed his gaze. "Patris?" she whispered.

He nodded once. She glared. "Of all the pig-headed, prejudiced, idiotic—"

"Hush," Kip said, caught between alarm and amusement. "It doesn't matter what he thinks."

"Doesn't matter? He's the Head!"

"I mean—" He drew in a breath. "He's only one sorcerer, and he isn't going to expel us for something like this. He can't."

"It still matters what he thinks," she said, "and if he thinks this is your fault, then he'd better not say that in front of me, that's all."

"Why did you bring him, anyway?"

"I didn't mean to. I asked for Master Argent and he came along."

"Did you go inside the Tower?"

She shook her head. "I waited at the door. Some servant answered and I asked him to fetch Master Argent. They both came down."

The sorcerers had retreated from the tent and were now conferring with each other. Kip politely looked away while not-so-politely cupping his ears back to listen. He caught a tingle of peppermint oil in his nose again as a third voice joined the two older ones. After a moment, he recognized it as the voice of the demon from the gate.

"No person was being harmed," it said, "so I didn't stop it. I was under no orders to."

"Did he capture the fox on the college grounds?"

"Nay. Brought it up the hill."

"Did you see who was responsible?" Argent asked.

"Of course. Opened the gate for him."

"And who was it?"

"Now, listen—" Patris said, but the demon was already responding.

"The stout young fellow from the town below."

"Farley Broadside," Argent said.

"Aye, perhaps." The demon sounded bored now. "I've not had time to learn all their names. I know the fox and the otter and the girl, though. It was none of them."

"It hardly seems worth—" Patris said, but again he was interrupted.

"The young man in tent number fifteen," Argent said. "That was him?"

Kip heard a faint rush of air and felt movement against his whiskers. Then another movement, and the demon said, "Aye, that was him."

"You're dismissed," Patris said.

A moment later, Emily said, "They're coming back."

"They know it was Farley," Kip whispered, and cupped his ears forward.

The two sorcerers approached them. Patris cleared his throat. "While we attempt to determine who was responsible, we will provide you with another tent in which to sleep, if you would like."

"It was Farley Broadside," Kip said. "I smelled him on the tent flap."

Argent began to speak, but the older sorcerer talked over him. "I'm sure you understand why we cannot accept your word for that. In the meantime—"

"I don't understand it," Emily said. "Kip's not lying. What's more, I think you know that."

Patris jabbed a finger in her direction. "This is not your concern, and you will address me as 'sir' or 'Head' or you will be subject to discipline."

"It is my concern," Emily shot back, "because if something like this is allowed to happen without any punishment, then I am worried for my own safety, *sir*."

"I don't see why." Patris waved a dismissive hand. "You're not a Calatian."

Emily gaped at this, and in the silence, Coppy said, "We're goin' down to the town to clean up our things."

"But we would like another tent to sleep in." Kip fixed Patris's eyes. "We're coming back."

Emily walked down with them, saying she wanted to meet Kip's mother, but Kip wondered if she preferred not to be left alone among the other candidates. He knew better than to voice that question, though she herself half-answered it with a short tirade as they left the college gates. "Not a Calatian! Not a Calatian!" she fumed. "Not to brush over the suffering of your people, but I don't believe I can name a woman of my acquaintance who has not been berated, struck, or worse by a man over the course of her life, not to mention forced into undesirable marriages, ignored, pushed aside, taken advantage of…" She took a breath.

"Neither of us has ever done that," Kip said.

The young woman sighed. "You are lovely people and I like you both. But you told me you're engaged to a thirteen-year-old girl? Was that her choice?"

"She's fourteen, but—she's the only fox. It's not exactly my choice either."

"That doesn't make it any more right for her."

Kip shook his head. "But—"

Emily raised her hand and smiled. "I don't wish to fight, Kip. I am more sensitive to marriages. Several of my Boston friends were married against their wishes—well, not against their wishes precisely, but without being consulted. They did not feel put upon. 'It's the way of the world,' they'd say, 'and I have a husband and will have children, so what have I to complain about?' I know how the world works, and as I think about it, it's bad luck you and your betrothed are caught by circumstance in a situation where there are no other choices for you."

There were other male foxes of near-appropriate age in New Cambridge, but Kip thought he might save that information for a future time. Coppy took advantage of the break in the conversation to point down. "There's the town hall," he said, gesturing to the white wooden clock tower that gleamed in the moonlight. "And the church just ahead of us."

The church's steeple glowed pale against the dark night. "Our school was right behind the church," Kip said.

"Did the humans go to the same church and school?" Emily looked up in between watching where she put her feet. She had removed her shoes, the better to pick her way down the dark road. Kip and Coppy, though they had not walked the hill often, saw more clearly in the dim light and walked with more confidence.

"Yes," Kip said. "Church, not at the same time. You know about the school."

"Oh, of course. Your story." She exhaled and stepped forward, then glanced up again. "What's that dark patch?"

"To the left? It's where some of the Calatians live. We have good night vision and we don't need lamps set about all over." He pointed to the right, where smaller patches of dark spotted the streets. "We live over there, in the shops."

"Some of us see better at night than others," Coppy grumbled with a smile.

"It's still very much a farming town, isn't it?" They had descended far enough that the leafy maples now blocked the view of most of the town. In the day, the first yellow spots of fall would be visible, but now the trees were nothing but silver-limned shadows. "I mean, not that that's a terrible thing. Boston is so built up, there are more shops than you can imagine."

"And we have no lawyers," Coppy put in.

"Indeed," Emily said. "There's another benefit."

They reached the Founders Rest, the inn at the bottom of the hill, and walked in front of the plain stone church. Few people were about at this time of night and barely a breeze stirred the few leaves that had fallen onto the road. Kip could remember when he'd thought the church had been built for Calatians, before he understood that humans had separate services under the same roof. But he also remembered the moments of peace he'd found there, the sermons Father Gregory made to apply holy text to the Calatians and include them in the community.

Turning left onto the shop-lined Half-Moon Street, Kip pointed out their perfume shop, some six doors down. Like all of Half-Moon Street, it was quiet and dark, the glassy windows shimmering with moonlight. At the end of the street, a figure walked past, paused, and walked on; one of the Watch on his rounds. Kip felt pleased to be sure it was not Farley.

"You live above your shop?" Emily murmured as Kip led them to one side and around the back. She touched the wooden boards Kip had helped paint blue as a cub of twelve.

He pointed up. "I jumped out that window once. Twisted my ankle but didn't break anything. I was trying to get into the Brocks' backyard." He nodded to the small yard next door. "Harley Brock bet I couldn't."

"Did you?"

He grinned and nodded. "I knew I could."

He and Coppy left their bloodstained bags at the corner of the house before they approached the back door that led to their living quarters. It had only been five days since he'd seen the door, but he paused before it anyway, breathing in his family's scent. And before he could reach out, his mother opened it, surprise creasing her brow over her narrow muzzle and amber eyes. "Kip? Coppy? We didn't expect—oh, does this mean—?"

Behind her, Kip's father walked up, frowning. Kip shook his head quickly. "We haven't heard officially yet."

"But we like our chances," Coppy chirped.

"I wanted to bring Emily down to meet you," Kip said to his mother. "She's become a true friend in a short time, and she's helped us greatly."

"We're all finding the way more difficult due to our fortunes of birth," Emily said. "I'm Emily Carswell. It's a pleasure, Mrs. Penfold."

The two ladies shook, and then Kip's mother said, "Call me Ada. Come in, please, and do sit down."

The three of them crowded upstairs past the kitchen into the small living-room with Kip's parents, and Emily sat with Kip's mother on the small sofa while Kip's father took his armchair and Kip brought in two wooden chairs from the kitchen. Coppy sat down in one, but Kip stayed standing, his paws tight on the back of the chair. Urgency with all the news he had for his father thrummed in him, but courtesy restrained his tongue.

"If you don't mind my asking," Emily said, "only I've never been in the home of a Calatian."

"Of course," Max said.

"The backs of the chairs are cut out for your tails, I suppose. Do you have them made in town or is there somewhere that sells them?"

Max smiled. "The Morgans make furniture."

"And it smells delightful here. I suppose you use your own perfumes for the room?"

"Yes," Ada said. "Max allows me to choose the fragrance, and we apply the scent to cloths like these." She picked up a folded cloth from the bookshelf to her right.

The cloths also held the scent of the family members who handled them, but Kip didn't feel like explaining that right now. "Dad," he said, "can I talk to you about something in the back?"

His father nodded and rose without asking any questions. Coppy stayed behind as the two Penfolds walked out through the back door, and though Kip saw his mother's flicking ears, Emily asked another question and their conversation kept going as he shut the back door behind him.

The bags stood near the wall, and his father's eyes flicked to them, but they could wait. Kip took a breath. "Dad," he said, "I got in."

For a moment, his father's muzzle stayed perfectly still, and Kip could pick out each whisker's silver shine, the reflections of the stars and moon in the curve of the older fox's eyes. Then his father broke into a wide smile and reached out to hug Kip, pounding him on the back. "I knew you could do it," he said, softly against Kip's cheek fur. "I knew it."

"I didn't." Kip hugged back, and it had been a long time since he'd hugged his father this closely. When he stepped back, he worried that his father would reprimand him for the wagging motion of his tail—showing emotion so publicly—and then saw that his father's tail was moving quicker even than his own.

"All it takes is one master to be on your side." Max rubbed his eyes. "How do you know? Did Vendis—Master Vendis—tell you?"

Kip hesitated, but it was too late to conceal his spying. So he told his father about his adventure, leaving out the conversation with the raven, and Max nodded throughout. "If you'd been caught, you could easily have been thrown out simply for that," he said when Kip was done.

"Yes, I know." Kip searched for any sign of anger, and found none. "But I wanted to know." He clasped his paws together and rubbed his fingers against each other. "You're not mad?"

Max smiled. "You're grown," he said. "It was your decision to make, and had you been thrown out, the consequences would be yours to face. Though not completely alone. You might have gotten Coppy thrown out as well."

"I know. But he went along with it. He and Emily were lookouts." And, Kip said to himself, Coppy would've left if I'd been thrown out regardless.

"It's done, and no harm has yet come of it." Max lifted a paw to Kip's shoulder. "But use caution. All they need is one simple excuse to do what several of them, I'm sure, would like to."

As if he needed the reminder, so soon after listening to them debate his fate and whether he could be trusted simply because of his nature, Kip gestured back to where his and Coppy's bloodstained bags sat. "Not only the sorcerers," he said. "Farley's one of the candidates."

They crouched by the bags, and his father's eyes widened when he smelled the blood. "This isn't yours, is it? No. Smell's wrong."

"Farley slaughtered a wild fox in our tent."

His father stood, hissing breath through his teeth. "Do you wish me to talk to the sheriff?"

"Why would that make a difference?"

Max exhaled. "Now you're a student at the college. Or—well, tomorrow you will be, officially."

"And the sheriff was sent up to prevent me from enrolling. So someone powerful asked him to do that. He'll just tell me that I won't have any trouble if I come down." Kip's mind raced. "For all I know, he put Farley up to enrolling as well. He certainly didn't seem bothered to be quit of him."

"He might also simply have been grateful for the opportunity to rid himself of what was sure to be a troublesome sentry on the Watch." Max put a paw on Kip's shoulder. "There are people who don't want you to enroll there, but I doubt they used Farley as a tool to discourage you."

"Who doesn't want me to enroll? The Mayor, I suppose? Some of the council?"

Max shook his head, his ears half-down. "I don't know. I will try to find out, if anyone will talk to me about it. It's the way things are, that's all."

The way things are. If Kip had a sorcerer's power and robes, people wouldn't scheme behind his back. He could exact justice from Farley himself, without having to rely on prejudiced Patris. Even Argent hadn't seemed too motivated to punish the boy. "Maybe not forever."

"No, not forever. But change takes time." His father rested a paw on his shoulder. "These will take time, too, to dry once they're clean. Will you stay here tonight?"

"Yes." Kip paused. "If we can also house Emily. I don't want her to walk back up to the College alone."

His father smiled. "You could walk her up. It's not far."

"Then we might as well stay up there."

"Mmm. I think we can find a place for her." His father looked down again at the bags, and touched them. "We won't tell your mother. Come, I'll get the bucket. You pump the water."

They washed the outside of the bag with a cloth until Kip could only smell the traces of blood when he put his nose up close. "None of your clothes were ruined?" his father asked, holding it open but not sniffing inside.

There was a time when his father would have pushed his nose into whatever of Kip's he felt he needed to investigate. Kip shook his head. "The bags were closed. One of my shirts was out, but that's all."

"I'll have your mother make up another one, or we'll get one from the Brocks. Is the book all right?"

"Of course. It was in the bottom of the bag, so…" Kip paused. He hadn't checked for the sorcery book his father'd gotten him, but he'd left it packed in the bag. Only now he was thinking that his bag had perhaps felt a little bit lighter. He reached inside where the book should be, heart racing.

His fingers pushed aside cloth and more cloth, and touched the inside of the bag shell. He rummaged more frantically—it had to be in there—and then his fingers met the old binding, the worn pages inside. "It's safe," he said, relaxing. "It's still here."

"You'll get a new one soon." His father smiled.

"I know, but…" Kip let his fingers rest on the book. He'd read maybe twenty or thirty books, counting the school's texts, but this one had always felt special to him, weightier than the others or more real. Mathematics and history were interesting but remote. Sorcery had gotten inside him, touched him directly, and was about to change his life. The thrill when his father had handed it to him still echoed in him when he touched it, and he'd felt it every night he opened the book and stared down at its worn pages and fading lettering. "You gave me this one."

"I'll get you another book." His father looked down. "In fact, since you don't need it...would you like to keep it here?"

It might be safer here, Kip thought. His tail curled around his legs. "I'd like to keep it," he said softly. "If you think it wouldn't be dangerous."

"I can hardly think of a more likely place for an old spell book to be found than a sorcerer's college." Max's grey-touched paw patted Kip's arm. "If you want to keep it, then keep it."

Kip let the book go and closed up the bag. "Let's do Coppy's now," he said, just as the otter himself appeared at the back door.

"You two done yet?" he asked. "We're runnin' out of small talk."

Emily agreed to stay in the Penfolds' bedroom above the shop with Ada, while Max moved upstairs to sleep in the attic alongside Kip and Coppy. The three of them lay in the dark room after Max extinguished the lamp, but Kip could tell from the rhythms of breathing that none of them were sleeping. He was wondering if they'd made a mistake in staying here, if they would come up in the morning to find the demon at the gates politely smiling, refusing to open them. The prospect of the doors so nearly open to him slamming shut tightened his chest, made him pant, and sent him trying to push his thoughts in another direction. Spells and magic, how right it felt when he was doing it, how much it would change his life. His breathing eased. He wondered how many spells he would be able to learn in his first year. It had taken him six months to learn his first one, three more to levitate himself (and that one was shaky when he wasn't being fueled by a mysterious surge of power).

"You're lucky to have fallen in with Emily," Max said presently. "She's very quick and quite well-read."

"She'll make a good sorcerer," Kip said.

"Will you manage the store well without me?" Coppy asked. "I know we didn't plan for me to enroll as well."

"I'll be fine." Max's voice echoed from the rafters. "Johnny Lapelli can come in and help. He knows enough and will learn quickly."

"Not too quickly," Kip murmured.

"Stop it." His father's voice grew sterner. "He'll be fine."

"I learned it well enough." Coppy lay on his back next to Kip staring up at the ceiling. "I'm not the quickest."

"You're quicker than Johnny." Kip flicked his tail.

"The store will be fine," Max said. "You make sure you work hard at your studies and don't do anything to upset the masters there."

Kip's paw rested on his stomach and he pushed up the fur there and smoothed it down. Too late for that, he thought, unless I could turn myself human.

The sun had not yet come up when Kip opened his eyes, but the pink-shaded early morning sky told him dawn wasn't too far off. He'd woken in this bed nearly every morning of his life, and the last time he'd been abuzz with excitement about going up to the College. Now the excitement had a slightly different tone. Four days ago, he'd worked himself up to challenge a College he'd been sure would try to keep him out. Now he was part of it, and that belligerent challenge lingered in him, but at the same time he knew he had his chance. He couldn't charge into the College with his teeth out and his ears back; he would have to show them that he could thrive within their rules, that he could learn as well as any human student—better, even—and that he would be the kind of sorcerer they couldn't afford to ignore.

"Thinking about the College?" Coppy said softly beside him.

"Aren't you?"

"A bit. Thinking of home too."

"Going back as a sorcerer?"

Kip could see Coppy's smile perfectly well in the dim light, even though the otter didn't show any teeth. "The two of us, aye. Go back and mend walls and…" He laughed softly. "Set fires, I s'pose?"

"I'll learn more than that."

"You will indeed." Max's voice joined them. "And you'd best be on your way up the hill to begin that education. If I'm not mistaken, your mother's brewing tea."

Even through the perfumed air of the house, the scent of tea was impossible to miss. By the time they made their way down two flights of stairs, it was already steaming in a flowered china pot and five cups sat out on the small table in the parlor where they often took their meals. "I thought that before you returned to the college," Kip's mother said, pouring tea for all of them, "we might visit the Cartwrights."

"I don't know if we have time," Kip said, taking his cup and pressing his paws around its warmth. The thick, rich aroma of the tea rose with the steam and filled his nostrils without him having to put his nose close to the cup, as Emily was doing.

His mother filled the last cup and set the pot down on the table with a sharp knock against the wood. "You'll make time."

"If I hadn't come back down," Kip protested.

"But you did. And the Cartwrights will be expecting us, so drink your tea and we'll go over and then you can get on back up to your College."

Kip looked to his father for help, but Max would not meet his eye, only sipped his tea slowly and then, in the silence, said, "I suppose I should open the store soon enough. Would you be so kind as to stop over at Bess Lapelli's house and ask Johnny to come over today?"

"Of course," Ada said, sipping her own tea. "Emily, if you and Coppy would like to walk up to the College, you needn't wait for us."

"Oh, no," Emily said brightly. "I'd be delighted to meet the Cartwrights."

So Kip and his mother walked ahead of Emily and Coppy back up Half-Moon Street toward the church and inn, where many townsfolk, human and Calatian alike, had already begun going about their daily business. Many of them carried fresh-baked loaves of bread under their arms, and the smell as they passed the bright, busy baker's shop and saw white-aproned Mr. Scort behind his counter made Kip's mouth water and his steps slow, but his mother kept up her pace. They passed behind the church to the neighborhood beyond, where the small one-story clapboard houses spread out amidst vegetable gardens and low fences. Here lived most of the Calatians who worked out on fields or for human businesses in town, and the streets here were quieter, as most of them had left with the sunrise. But at the house where his mother knocked, which had a neatly painted sign over the door proclaiming it the residence of "The Cartwrights," the whole family had remained home: Thomas Cartwright, a fox a few years older than Kip's father; Laurel Cartwright, barely a decade older than Kip himself (Thomas's second wife); Alice; and Alice's younger brother Daniel, who proudly informed the visitors that he would begin attending school the following week.

"Welcome," Laurel said with a smile at the door. Her blue eyes sparkled when the sun caught them, and her dark brown ears had no hint of grey yet, unlike her husband's. She showed them into a small kitchen with a plain wooden table and four chairs around it, two of them occupied by Alice and Daniel. Thomas stood stiffly behind his daughter's chair, one paw on the chair back, leaning to one side as a result of an old leg injury that had never fully healed. Alice had grown half a foot in the last year, and her ears now reached Kip's chest, but she hadn't grown into her height yet, so her arms and legs appeared thin even though her fur shone and her eyes were bright and healthy. Laurel gestured to the two free chairs. "I'm sorry—we weren't expecting so many of you."

"We can't stay long," Kip said before his mother could accept any invitation. "I only wanted to come over and tell you…well, you all know I applied to study sorcery up at the College. We went through the tests—you know Coppy, and this is Emily, another one of the applicants."

His speech then waited for Emily's introductions to the Cartwrights, and vice versa. He smiled at Alice as everyone was clasping paws to hands and saying names, and she smiled back shyly. As usual, he felt an odd mix of imposed obligation and responsibility when looking at her; he hadn't asked to be her husband, but together they would be responsible for continuing the line of foxes in New Cambridge, and his job would be to keep her safe.

At least, he reflected, with Farley up on Founders Hill with him, he wouldn't have to worry about that.

The introductions finished, and the group returned their attention to him. "As I was saying," he went on, "we've all been tested, and…well, we feel very confident about our chances."

Laurel smiled, and Alice clapped her paws together in delight, but Thomas's ears flicked back and his rigidly polite demeanor did not change. "I understand that the sorcerers' wives don't reside at the College with them," he said.

"Master Loman's lived here in the town," Kip said, and then snapped his mouth shut. Master Loman had been one of those killed in the attack, and his widow had moved to Providence to live with relatives.

"What of the builder sorcerers who spend all their time traveling around the Empire? Or the military sorcerers who can't tell their families where they live?" Thomas kept his eyes on Kip.

"Are you all three going to be sorcerers?" Alice asked with wide eyes, and then turned to her father. "I want to be a sorcerer too."

"Absolutely not," he said.

"Marriage certainly is much more difficult for those sorcerers living at the College," Ada said. "Max tells me that the strenuous life they live allows for little in the way of family, and those few who are married have sent their wives away. But that is only a temporary measure until the current war is resolved."

Thomas shook his head. "When this war is resolved, there will be another, and another. We have only just defeated Napoleon, and were promised years of peace. Before Napoleon there were the Spanish again, and the French monarchy's colonists before that, and that is as long as I've been alive. London has her ancient rivalries and we cannot escape from them."

This felt uneasily like a column Kip had read from Boston advocating independence for the colonies, which Max and Kip and Coppy all thought was foolish, especially since the Colonies' magical resources had been effectively cut almost to nothing, not counting the builders nor the military, who owed a more direct allegiance to the Empire. In any war, Britain's superior forces, both physical and magical, would be nearly impossible to overcome. "Three years is a long time," Kip said, because nobody else seemed inclined to respond to Thomas's words. "I remain committed to providing a family for Alice."

Alice smiled up at him, her tail wagging where it hung below the chair. Emily stepped up beside Kip. "After all," she said, "if a Calatian and a woman may become sorcerers, then not all traditions are rooted in stone."

Thomas did not relax nor smile at this. "There may be reasons for Calatians and women not to be sorcerers," he said.

Emily straightened, and even after only a few days, Kip knew her well enough to think, *oh no.* He raised a paw quickly. "If that is the case, then we will certainly find out, I'm sure." He had no idea what Thomas was talking about, but he didn't want to give Emily the chance to say anything. "The sorcerers would not have admitted us if there were insurmountable barriers."

"I'm not speaking of what the sorcerers know." Thomas scowled, his ears going back and his lip twisting up to show some of his teeth. "I'm speaking of the people in this town..." He looked around at them. "None of you work next to humans every day."

"They shop at our store."

"But you do not work alongside them. You don't hear how they think of us."

"I know well how they think of us." Kip wanted to ask, *why are we arguing? We're both foxes, we're on the same side.* "You know that."

"Aye, I do." Thomas lowered his eyes a moment, and then raised them again to meet Kip's. "And I know you don't know everything. Listen."

"Thomas," Laure said. "Please."

He raised a paw. "I will keep it brief, I promise. We have grasshoppers here, you know? You have seen them?"

"Of course," Ada put in. "They are harmless."

Thomas shook his head impatiently. "Yes. But when they gather in swarms they may destroy farms. Then we call them locusts, and the sorcerers call demons to kill them by the thousands. You understand?"

"I...I don't know." Kip followed this train of logic and metaphor. "It's a different situation. There are but three of us and we hardly qualify as some kind of swarm of locusts."

The older fox nodded. "But you may inspire others."

"We hope to," Emily put in fiercely.

"To become a threat to the Empire?"

Kip held up a paw. This whole situation was nothing like what he'd been expecting, and though he didn't want to show it, it unsettled him that Thomas couldn't see fit to support him. He'd thought that only a few among the Calatians would not want one of their number to gain the knowledge and power of sorcery. How could anyone think it an evil? "I understand your concerns," he said, only partly lying. "But I promise you that I am not striving to create any disturbance. I am simply hoping that having a Calatian sorcerer—and a female one, too," he added, as Emily's scent was strong in his nostrils and he was aware of her presence, "will make all of our lives better."

Thomas kept his lips tightly shut, but he nodded. In the silence, Alice held out a paw to Kip. "I want to be a sorcerer too!" she said as Kip knelt in front of her and clasped her smaller paw in his.

"No," Thomas said. "I forbid it."

"You have to listen to your father," Kip told the little vixen, whose ears had flattened. "But I will do magic for you when I'm permitted."

She leaned forward to touch her muzzle to his, and whispered, "I only have to listen to him until we're married."

Kip's eyes flicked up to Thomas, but Alice's whisper had been so soft and breathy that even Thomas hadn't heard it. "Well," Kip said, standing, "we should be on our way up the hill. Mr. Cartwright, I will be pleased to keep you informed of my progress and continue these discussions, if you like."

The older fox inclined his head, but did not say yea or nay to it. And so the four of them took their leave, walking out with the rising sun at their backs.

"I'll fetch Johnny Lapelli," Ada said as they reached the back of the church. "He's down this street. But Kip, do think about what Thomas said. He reads the newspapers and he thinks about these things."

Kip nodded and hugged her. "You think it's all right for me to be a sorcerer, don't you?"

Ada kissed the side of his muzzle and pulled back to look into his eyes. "I don't want you to be hurt. That's what I worry about."

"We'll all take care of each other," Coppy said. "And we've got Emily to help now, too."

"Indeed." Emily embraced Ada and gave her a wide smile. "Though the rest of the College may be arrayed against us, I believe two Calatians and a woman who have gained entry to the College may accomplish anything else they set their minds to."

Her optimism, though Kip suspected it was put on for his mother's benefit, made him smile. "All right," Ada said. "You all be careful and give me regular news of your studies."

They promised to do that, and parted from her there. None of them spoke until they were past the church and the Founders Rest, and then Emily said, "That Mr. Cartwright had some interesting ideas."

"He reads newspapers," Coppy said, huffing as he pushed up the hill on his short legs. "Wonder if someone was once afraid of teaching Calatians to read."

"Were we not always taught to read?" Kip glanced back over his shoulder. At his side, Emily remained quiet. "The school here has always taught Calatians as far as I know."

"Oh," Coppy panted, "some schools in London are for humans only and there are debates about what use we'll make of our education and if it's worth wasting money on it. If there weren't a few teachers pulling schoolbooks from refuse piles on the Isle, nobody would bother teaching us beyond learning our alphabet."

"People can be idiots," Emily snapped.

They both quieted, and she turned to Kip. "Oh, I'm sure your future father-in-law is perfectly nice, but really? A 'reason' why women might not be sorcerers? It's because of tradition, no more and no less, and a tradition that started because men were afraid of giving women too much power. You know what a witch is? It's a woman who has magic and hasn't been allowed to study sorcery. There's a name for it and everything. So they know that some women have magic, and yet they keep them from the study of sorcery."

Kip didn't say anything to that, but wondered privately how many Calatians might have manifested magic over the years. There were far fewer Calatians than women in the world, so there might not be a word for it yet, but he wasn't fool enough to think he was the first. Resolve gripped him then, that he would show all the ones to come that they were as worthy of studying magic as any human—man or woman.

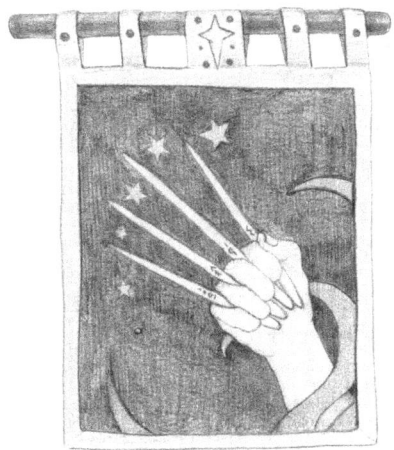

CHAPTER 7: EDUCATION

"**W**elcome to Prince George's College of Sorcery. You are the first students admitted to help rebuild this school to the prominence it once enjoyed. This privilege bears with it a great responsibility, to comport yourselves with the dignity and grace befitting a sorcerer."

A loud fart rang into the pause in Master Patris's speech. Though Kip was on the other side of the group of students standing outside the Tower in the chilly morning air, he recognized the perfect timing of Farley Broadside.

Kip had hoped that Farley would at least have failed the examination, if not been dismissed for the act of vandalism. But there he was, his nose and cheeks bright red with the cold, grinning. The only candidate to fail had been the Potterfield boy; seventeen students stood before the masters, listening to Patris's speech.

That Farley was still among them soured what was otherwise a perfect morning, bright and sunny with wisps of fog clinging to the dew-laden grass. The chill air did not bother Kip as much as it appeared to bother some of the students and even a few of the masters who stood before the Tower's grand doors; a florid red-haired Master sniffled and wiped his nose, and Master Argent kept his cloak tightly wrapped around him.

The Head had clearly seen and heard many classes in his day. Despite snickers from some of the students, he did not react at all to Farley's interjection. "In addition, a sorcerer must be possessed of sharp mind at all times, and to that end, there is to be no alcohol on the College grounds."

This elicited a groan from several students. Patris smiled, thin-lipped, before continuing. "You will be assigned to a dormitory room under the guidance of a Master. For the duration of your time at the College, this Master will bear the responsibility of guiding you through your studies. You will obey him and all the Masters of this College in whatever they may ask of you. We have been sorcerers for longer than you have been alive, in some cases." Here he glanced sideways at Argent, who kept staring straight ahead. "You will place trust in our judgment."

There followed a long-winded recitation of the history of the College: Lord Guileston's founding in 1624 and Master Johnson's creation of the Great Road in the name of Queen Mary in 1691 and Master Collins' heroics in the driving out of the French in 1698 and Master Woodward's defense of the College when it was besieged by the French in 1754.

By this time, several of the students were rubbing their arms or noses briskly, their breath white in the air. Malcolm, near Kip, muttered under his breath, "Did they have a master who thawed frozen students?"

The fox grinned, but Emily tsked and stood straighter, keeping her hands at her waist, though she'd complained about the cold previously. "Of course," Patris droned on, "we cannot speak of this College's history without speaking of the recent tragedy."

At this, complaints and hands dropped and red noses pushed eagerly forward. Kip and Coppy did not join the eager anticipation, but looked at each other, and Kip saw in Coppy's eyes the reflection of his own unease at the memories it stirred.

"You will all be part of the fight to avenge the losses," Patris said. He tried to give a stirring oration, and Kip was reminded of Mr. John Adams. He had come to New Cambridge some ten years before to speak out against the danger of the French and to urge the New Cantabrigians to contribute to the war effort. Many had enlisted following his speech (although Max had been thoughtful afterwards and Kip had overheard him telling Mr. Brock that much of Mr. Adams' rhetoric about 'a free people' had been cleverly constructed to have a dual meaning, which had puzzled the young fox because he was only just learning the single meanings of words). Kip remembered Adams' eloquence even if many of the words had escaped him at the time. Patris had none of the same gift of oration, with the result that what was likely intended to be a stirring call to arms left many of the students disappointed that they had not heard more details of the vicious attack.

Kip's thoughts wandered during Patris's speech once he realized he wasn't going to learn anything new. The night had been a terrible one, spent in fear and worry and choking dust outside the college's gates, jumping at every noise that might signal another attack or the onset of a full-on war. He hadn't slept properly for weeks afterwards, and even now if he let his mind wander out on the college grounds, he could picture the forms of the four red brick buildings like dusty ghosts.

Patris went on to talk about the destinations they might expect. "Some of you will become a part of the valuable work being done to make this country habitable, building roads and walls for our newest cities." He looked at the Calatians as he said this. "Others will participate in the defense of the Empire, against the ever-bolder Spanish incursions and the Oriental threat in India. And a select few will join the Masters of this college to explore and expand the world of magic as sorcerers with a direct commission from King George himself."

At this, he looked down at Victor Adamson. Kip couldn't see Adamson's face, but his back looked confident and smug.

He hadn't had a chance to talk to Adamson about Farley's violation of their tent. As he, Emily, and Coppy had approached the gates, they'd heard the calls of ravens shouting for the candidates to get up. They'd been admitted (despite their fears, the demon had recognized them and had opened the gate without being asked) into a general commotion, questions of whether they should leave their bags in the tent, where they should stand and whether they were all admitted or were going to be told the results of the examinations. Adamson had joined the rest as neatly pressed as always, standing beside Farley on the far side of the cluster of students. Kip had seen only his tight-lipped face and expression of concentration.

Adamson might yet learn sorcery. But Kip already knew how to do some spells, and they were all going to learn at the same pace.

Finally, finally, Master Patris concluded his remarks with, 'I think we had better introduce you to your Masters inside. Master Argent is looking rather chilly."

Argent simply exhaled deliberately so that they could see his white breath as he and the other masters entered the Tower. Patris remained outside until the last of the other sorcerers had entered, and then gestured the students inside.

Kip fairly sprang forward, all the tension of the morning releasing in quick steps that carried him to the front of the group. He and Adamson crossed the threshold at the same time, but Kip spared little attention to the other young man. He lifted his head and took in the sight and scent of the White Tower.

The room he'd stepped into filled the entire base of the tower, some eighty feet square. Four arches held up a ceiling twenty feet high at the apex, with fireplaces in the center of the walls to the right and left; the unlit fireplace on the left was a yawning black, cold cavity, while to the right, a great wide mouth spat sparks and heat into the room. Three lizards lay curled up in it, and flames wreathed their scaly forms.

The grand space, the carpet decorated in patterns of trees, the cold, safe embrace of stone: all these Kip had pictured. He had not expected the absence of books or other spellcasting materials. Upon the walls hung portraits of sorcerers, and in the room, a stage had been erected with seventeen chairs facing it. But no bookshelves lined the walls, no potions nor apothecary cabinets full of feathers and glass and sand and incense sat about anywhere.

Behind the stage, he saw as he stepped in and out of the way of the other students, a large Union Jack matching the one outside hung, high up on the wall, and below it, a flag with a symbol that Kip did not immediately recognize. In the still air of the hall, it hung limp, and only by coming up to the stage could he make out the design. It was four wooden wands spread in a fan formation held by a hand, with a different symbol on the body of each wand.

"Take your seats," Patris said before Kip could look more closely. He hurried back to sit with Coppy and Emily, near where Malcolm was sitting. As he took his seat, he wondered where Saul had sat a year ago, when he'd undergone this same ceremony. Had there been more apprentices? Had Patris been as solemn? Or had they felt only the confidence in their sorcery, the invulnerability that everyone assumed they had, not knowing how close they were to disaster?

The masters arrayed themselves on the stage as they had been outside the door, and Patris stepped forward. "I would like to take this occasion to welcome you officially to the White Tower as students of Prince George's College of Sorcery."

The sorcerers applauded briefly. Two or three students joined in and then stopped, abashed. The applause died down as the black-robed masters folded hands beneath their robes. "I will now assign you to your quarters, and the individual masters responsible for you will give you further information about your studies and your life here in the college. In Master Odden's quarters will be…"

He read off Farley Broadside's name and two others. When Patris went on to announce Master Argent's students, Kip sat up straighter, sure that he and Coppy would be assigned to the young sorcerer. But they were not, though Malcolm and Adamson both were. The next master was Campbell, who had Smith and Cook, and then Waldo, and then Sharpe, who had only two students—Sharpe was the sour, black-haired master who matched the reedy, obstreperous voice Kip had overheard the previous night.

Emily's name had not been called either. As the other fourteen students clustered around their assigned masters, Patris stepped down from the stage, followed by Master Windsor. Emily leaned in to Kip and said, "What do you think? Are they giving us Patris or Windsor?"

"I hope Windsor," Kip whispered back. "And you needn't whisper so loud. I can hear you quite well."

"You may stand," Patris said as the two sorcerers approached the students.

Kip, Coppy, and Emily obliged. "Your Master will be Master Windsor, who has graciously agreed to shepherd you through the school year even with all the difficulties your presence will create."

Emily started to say something, but Kip caught her motion and nudged her, and she fell silent. He flicked his tail back against his legs and felt the brush of Coppy's against his. Patris continued on. "In deference to the concerns raised by some of the sorcerers, you will not be housed with the other students on the second and third floors of the tower."

"What sorcerers were concerned about me?" Emily asked.

Patris ignored her. "Penfold and Lutris, there is a small room in the back of the basement that has been cleared for your use."

"The basement?" It was Kip's turn to be nudged, this time by Coppy.

"If you would prefer, you may use one of the outdoor tents." Patris appeared to be having difficulty restraining a smile. "The basement is not heated, but is at least sheltered from the wind and somewhat from the elements."

"Basement'll be lovely," Coppy said. "Hope it's somewhat damp. It'll feel just like home."

"Miss Carswell." Patris turned to her. "Given the impropriety of lodging you with any of our male students and the paucity of alternate accommodations, we have reserved a room for you at the Founders' Rest Inn. You will live there and come up to the College for classes."

Emily's mouth hung open for a moment before she recovered her voice. "You mean I must climb that hill every morning?"

"Vigorous daily exercise is highly beneficial," Patris said serenely.

"I'll be left out of everything!"

She had raised her voice enough to draw the attention of many nearby students. Patris glanced to one side at the silencing of conversation in the hall, but forged on. "You will be able to attend classes. The cost of the room, of course, you may repay to the college once you find employment with the education we will be providing."

"I'll stay in one of the tents." She folded her arms.

"You can stay with us," Kip said. He didn't have to look at Coppy to know that the otter was nodding.

"Penfold, I hardly think that is a solution. The propriety—"

"Thank you, Kip," Emily said. "I accept."

"Miss Carswell." Patris held up a hand in the now otherwise silent Great Hall. "I'm afraid I cannot allow—"

"She knows us," Kip said. "She stayed in my family's house last night."

"There you are." Emily smiled. "Besides, they're only allowed to marry their own kind. What would they want with a human woman?"

It wasn't want that kept the Calatians from the human women in New Cambridge, Kip reflected. He'd known a girl who'd kissed Luke Cooper, a dormouse a little older than he was, and Cooper had been attacked one night, leg and arm broken, several teeth knocked out, and one ear torn nearly off, by a bunch of men who'd told him to "leave humans alone." Johnny Lapelli had told Kip that two boys had forced themselves on his sister Letitia, but no punishment had been issued. Kip privately believed that one of the boys was Farley, but had not been able to find out even that much. So the proscription did not hold evenly for male and female Calatians. And then, of course, there'd been Saul.

But Patris, if he was aware of that at all, did not mention any of those incidents. "There will be talk," he said.

"Then we will give her the small room and we will stay in the basement proper." Kip had no idea what he was getting himself and Coppy into, but helping Emily—and getting to stay with her—was worth it.

Patris shook his head of white hair and then turned to Windsor for one final appeal. "They are in your charge," he said. "What say you?"

Windsor measured the three of them and rubbed his chin. "For the time they are here, if they are applying themselves, there will be no time for impropriety. And if they are not, they will not be here long enough for it to matter."

"You bear full responsibility for this arrangement," Patris told Windsor, and then the Head stalked off across the hall.

"All right." Emily smiled cheerfully, though Kip was bristling at the tone of Windsor's words. "It's settled, then. Where's this basement?"

The rest of the students were filing toward a staircase at the back left corner of the room, a cheerful doorway lit from smokeless sconces on either side. But Master Windsor led Emily, Kip, and Coppy to the opposite wall, to a dark doorway that smelled of earth and rot and made Kip's fingers itch with cold.

Windsor held a lantern to light their way down. They descended one flight of stairs to a landing, where a faintly-lit corridor led off to the right. When Windsor's light had descended farther, Kip peered down the corridor and heard nothing, though he smelled lye and felt a dampness in the air. He sniffed and then hurried to follow the others, down a dogleg to a stout wooden door.

Behind the door lay a room half the size of the hall above it, and here were the bookshelves Kip had dreamed of; here were the tomes and papers covered with archaic symbols. They littered the floor in careless piles, crammed full the shelves against every wall, and shelves were stacked against shelves. Mildew and dust filled the air, and things scuttled away below papers as Windsor, with a gesture, called magical light into being in the tarnished sconces on the walls.

Emily coughed. "It's not quite the Royal Crown," she said finally. "It'll take some fixing up."

"Your room, Miss Carswell, is in the back." Windsor pointed to a decrepit door hanging on one hinge, in the middle of the far wall. "Penfold and Lutris, you may move the beds currently there out into this space. I will have one brought down for Miss Carswell."

"Can we clean up a little?" Coppy said. "Only it's a little too much like home, if you take my meaning. I used to sleep on old papers the Londoners'd thrown out, but these look too valuable for sleeping."

"Do they?" Windsor picked up one of the papers from the ground gingerly between two fingers. He read from it, slowly. "Being an account of the expenses incurred by His Majesty's College in the month of April of the year seventeen hundred and fifty-one at the firm of Slauson and Hedges."

"There's a Slauson and Hedges in Boston," Emily said. "They sell cloth."

"Indeed." Master Windsor stared at the paper a moment longer, and then it tore itself into sixteen equal pieces. He let them flutter to the ground. "Do with the paper what you will." The sorcerer gestured again, and a path cleared through the mounds and piles, from the door to the back room. He gestured, and the Calatians and woman stepped down onto a stone floor. "The floor and walls are fireproof, and anything of value has been removed to the library long hence."

"Where is the library, sir?" Kip's tail twitched. There, at last, would be the reserve of information he craved.

"Third floor," the master said, "but it is off limits to students until you have completed one month of class. When you have been grounded in the basics of sorcery, you may explore what others have researched. We are already quite aware of what the three of you are able to accomplish with minimal guidance."

It was impossible to tell whether the look he gave them was approving or not. "And since the topic has come up, let me explain to you what that first month will consist of. Master Patris will educate you on the basics of sorcery and will begin to teach you physical magic. I am in charge of filling the enormous gaps in what passes for your knowledge of history, and will also be teaching the ethics of magic. Master Argent will introduce you to translocational magic, which you will begin studying in one month, and at that time, Master Odden will introduce you to the theory of alchemical magic, which you will not undertake until January, if you are selected to continue your studies here."

"When do we get spiritual magic?" Kip asked, and when Windsor glowered, he added hastily, "Sir."

"In your last year of apprenticeship, if at all. Spiritual magic is highly dangerous and only select sorcerers attempt it. But that assumes you will pass your examinations at the end of November."

"November?" Coppy had been looking around the basement and now snapped his head up to Windsor. "That's barely two months away."

"Indeed. The pressing need for apprentices has forced us to accelerate the testing schedule. Where once we could spend a year coaxing the best out of each student, now we must make swift determinations about the ability of each, and place them accordingly." The sorcerer's expression got even more sour, which Kip had not believed possible.

"It sounds like you don't approve of that," he said, trying to build a rapport.

"Whether I approve or not is immaterial." Windsor's tone was cold as a slap to Kip's figuratively outstretched paw. "It is what has been decided. So you will work as hard as possible over two months, because your success reflects on me as a mentor."

"Yes, sir," Kip said, and Coppy and Emily joined in.

Windsor's hard eyes surveyed them, his jaw set. "Allow me to say," he said, "that while you have accomplished tasks that some find impressive, you have not progressed any further than a student of average ability would here in three weeks. If your ambition is to serve as a builder of roads, well done. You are on your way. If you harbor higher hopes, then I strongly suggest you erase any sense of accomplishment from your minds as of this moment and apply yourselves to learning as much as you can in the two months you are allotted."

"Yes, sir." They chorused better this time, although Emily looked as resentful as Kip felt.

The sorcerer gestured around the basement. "As a rule, there will be no unsupervised practice of sorcery in the walls of the Tower. However, I will make an exception for today; if you wish to use sorcery to clean up, you may. I do not wish to be present as you do it, as your technique is undoubtedly so atrocious that it might cause me permanent damage to refrain from correcting it." He pointed up the stairs. "Meals will be served in the dining tent and announced once. You may leave the grounds of the College but you must be back in the Tower by midnight or you will serve a detention. If you need me for any reason, simply call my name and I will hear you."

"From just here, or from anywhere?" Coppy asked.

"From here only, Lutris. I am not your personal demon."

"Will we get personal demons?" Emily asked.

Windsor fixed her with a stare. "You may, when you feel confident enough to summon one, if—and I cannot stress this enough times—you succeed in remaining here long enough to be taught how."

They stared silently. He swept his gaze across the three faces. "Is there anything else?" They all shook their heads. "Then I will take my leave of you."

At the door, he paused to look back. "In your place, I would apply myself to find a way to heat the room. You Calatians may not be cold, but Miss Carswell will be."

"He's right," Emily said when he'd gone. "It's not bad now, but come winter, I'm going to need some heat."

"We will too." Coppy patted her shoulder. "Don't worry. We'll figure out something."

"Once we get into the library." Kip rubbed his paws together. Just a few weeks to wait.

"First things first." Emily turned around. "How shall we arrange this? I don't want to have you two sleeping in the open floor."

Coppy pointed to the shelves along one wall. "What if we pulled those out, arranged them to make sort of a room back in the other corner?"

"Clearing the papers away first, of course."

They looked at each other, and Emily smiled. "Thank you both for inviting me down here. It might have been warmer down at the inn, but I've no doubt this will be the better situation."

After an hour of work, Kip thought she might be reconsidering. They had shifted large stacks of paper to the front of the room, clearing away the back corner, and then Kip and Emily lifted the shelves while Coppy guided them into place. They tried stacking one on top of another, but the lower one creaked alarmingly and the top one listed forward, and Coppy said he wasn't sleeping beneath the Shelves of Damocles, so they settled for the four-foot-high wall around the space they would sleep in. Despite the disgusting nature of the work, Kip smiled throughout. He was building his living space in the White Tower, and he was going to be sleeping here in the heart of it.

Dust blanketed all three of them; Kip sneezed frequently and his eyes had been watering for the past hour. Emily, though determined not to show her disgust at the various insects whose homes they'd displaced, nonetheless refused to touch anything with her hands, and flinched whenever a stack of papers fell. Kip was sure he had spiders in his fur, and Coppy had bruised two fingers when he was trying to adjust a shelf and Kip had let go of his spell too early.

"Nobody said anything about where the baths are, did they?" Emily pulled spiderwebs from her sleeve.

"Nor about brooms or sweeping," Coppy said.

Kip dropped the second bedroll in the empty space. "I suppose they have demons to do the sweeping for them."

"It is curious," Emily said, "the lack of servants here. I mean, they have demons do some things, but why not have someone to do the cooking and cleaning? You don't need demons for that?"

"There used to be women who would come up and do the cleaning. Mrs. Bannister and her daughter, at least. But after the attack, the sorcerers dismissed them all."

"Terrified of any strangers in the College?"

Kip nodded. "They said it was because they had fewer buildings and could manage, but I don't know that I believe that. They wouldn't even let us in the Tower until we'd been accepted. "

"They've got women and Calatians doing their cleaning for them now." Emily looked around, holding her hands out in front of her, dirt and grime streaking her white skin.

"I don't think that's why they put us in the basement," Coppy said, brushing his paws together.

"No?"

"No." He grinned. "I think they put us in the basement to encourage us to leave of our own accord."

"That's probably right." Kip spotted a flash of red leather in one of the bookshelves, brighter than any of the surrounding worn leather and cloth. He reached idly for it with a claw.

"If they really want me to leave, they'll hide the baths." Emily picked up a towel from her bag and walked toward the door. "I'll find them and tell you where they are. Do you take baths? It must take ages to dry all that fur. Well, I suppose you don't mind so much…" She gestured to Coppy.

"We bathe," Kip said. "Not frequently, because it does take a bit to dry, and we smell strongly when wet." Emily opened her mouth and then shut it again, and he smiled. "Like a dog, yes."

"I wasn't going to say it. Well, yes, I was, but I stopped myself. I'm learning so much." She waved to them. "Wish me luck."

When she'd gone, Coppy said he wanted to try to find a demon to sweep the floor where their bedrolls were, or at least a broom, because the stone was thick with dust and cobwebs, and though they could use spells to pick up piles of paper and books, they could not as easily pick up thousands of minute particles. Kip had managed a small cobweb, but it would be easier to pick everything up with his fingers.

So Coppy walked off, and Kip, left alone, stared at the shelves and the mass of books and papers in them. Again, the little red leather book stood out among the others. Kip leaned closer, then teased at the top of the book with a claw, working it backwards and forwards. It came out easily, a slender volume only a bit larger than his paw, and no dust marred his fur as it fell onto his pads. Curious, he thought, that it should remain so clean. The cover bore no marking, so he opened it to read the first page.

> *Being the Journal of Peter Cadno, Apprentice to the King's College of Sorcery, London, England, 1614.*

He brought the small, cramped writing closer to the light to read it. The pages had browned, but not so much that he couldn't make out the letters with some effort. Nearly two hundred years old, and the book still felt firm and solid, not falling apart like many more recent ones. It wouldn't surprise Kip to learn that there was magic on it, he reflected, and that made him more eager still to read.

The first entry was dated October, 1614:

> *It seems to me a good idea to keep this journal, not only for my own records but to preserve my experience for those who might come after. I know not how long it may be until my fortune is duplicated. Perhaps never. But I owe my current position to my family, who supported my endeavours, and to Mister Jeremiah Wood, whose misfortune brought the books of spells to me with which I was able to prove my merits to the College and convince the Masters to allow me to enter their ranks.*

So this Peter Cadno had come to sorcery much as Kip had, by the unconventional procurement of a spell book. There were many disadvantaged in London who might not be welcome in the College unless they could demonstrate their ability, and perhaps, Kip thought, his situation was not so different from this Peter Cadno's.

He flipped the page, and then footsteps on the stairs made him stop and hide the book back in the shelf. The motion was instinctive, even though he knew it was likely just Coppy returning. His nose was clogged with dust and he couldn't catch any scents, even on the breeze flowing into the room from the open door.

"…but I wish to see for myself what you have done." Master Windsor's voice came to him, and a moment later the man stepped through the door into the basement, Coppy trailing behind him. The sorcerer surveyed the basement, his expression fixed, and then his eyes fell on Kip. "I have told Lutris that we will provide brooms for your cleaning, but that the demons of the Tower are not yours to command. When you have been allowed by Master Odden to summon your own demons, then you may put them to work as you like." His lip curled briefly and then flattened back into its usual straight line.

"Yes, sir." Kip stepped away from the shelf with the book. He felt obscurely that if Master Windsor knew he had discovered something useful in the room, the sorcerer might take it away from him.

"Where is Miss Carswell?"

"Gone to take a bath," Coppy said. "Was dirty work you set us to, sir."

If Kip had said those words, he would have filed them to a sharper point, but Coppy spoke so pleasantly that Windsor did not even turn the otter's way. "It will not be the last such task you will be set here. Count yourself lucky if at the end of your education, your worst experience is a coating of dust and insects." He took a breath. "I wished to speak to you both without Miss Carswell present, and now is as propitious a time as any.

"You are no doubt aware of your position in history. I will say that although your motivations may include the advancement of your race, neither of you showed evidence of that as your primary goal, which is a point in your favor. Not," he held up a hand, "because I do not believe in the advancement of your race. What I believe is immaterial. But because if your primary motivation is the attainment of skill in sorcery, you will make better sorcerers."

And, Kip thought, remembering Thomas Cartwright's words, because then we are not viewed as such a threat. But he simply nodded to Windsor, who was waiting for his acknowledgment before continuing. "There are many at this college who believe you will not succeed. This is a reality of your life here. There are some who may take it upon themselves to make it more difficult for you to succeed. You may be certain that I will defend you against any incident such as the one that occurred last night—a cowardly and ineffective attempt to frighten you. But you will face more than that."

"Will you help us, sir?" Kip asked.

"In my capacity as your mentor, I am bound to help you, because your progress through the college will reflect on me."

Coppy spoke, again so genially that the remark did not come off as sharp as Kip would have made it. "I doubt very much if Patris would hold our failures against you."

"Patris is a competent administrator and in many ways a brilliant sorcerer," Windsor said. "His esteem is not a large influence in my life. Yes, I will help you, and here is the first thing I will tell you, which you may also share with Miss Carswell: your continuing education here at the College depends on your ability to impress a Master enough that he wishes to work with you as his apprentice for three years. Otherwise, you will be sent to make roads or walls, and I consider that a failure."

"At least one of us can try to impress you, sir," Coppy said.

Now Windsor did turn to him. "I am extraordinarily difficult to impress," he said, and that made the otter's smile falter.

"How can we impress a Master?" Kip made an effort to keep his voice earnest, not desperate.

"That you will no doubt have to learn over the next two months."

Windsor turned to leave, but Coppy stopped him. "Sir? Do you believe we can succeed as sorcerers?"

The older man gazed levelly back. "As I have told you, it is immaterial what I believe."

And in the silence that followed that remark, he left.

Their books were brought down by a demon who looked like a small man with goat's horns and a goat's legs, who wore no clothing and acted completely unashamed of his nakedness. Knowing demons even as little as he did, Kip suspected that the guise was meant to discomfit them, and so where Coppy asked concernedly if the demon wanted pants or a robe, Kip simply ignored the state of dishabille as he did the tingle in his nose.

The demon did at least ask where they wanted the books, so they hurriedly cleared off the top of one of the shelves. When he had deposited the books, he simply vanished, taking the peppermint tingle in Kip's nose with him.

Emily returned as they were examining the titles, looking damp and very pleased with herself. "The baths are along that corridor," she said. "There were two tubs and robes hanging up, and one of the tubs was warm, so I got in and washed off, and it felt heavenly." She sighed, looking down at her feet. "And now I am back in the dust and grime. I wish we could burn all these papers, but where would the smoke go?"

"Up into the Great Hall." Kip grinned.

"At least it would be warm," she continued. "Have you figured out how we will heat this room when it gets colder?"

They hadn't asked Master Windsor about that at all. Kip exchanged a guilty look with Coppy. "Not yet," he said. "I suppose fire is out of the question."

"Do you know how to make fire?" Emily asked.

"No." Kip gestured to the books. "Fire is an alchemical spell and we don't have that book yet. We're stuck with tinder and flint, or a torch and a walk upstairs."

Emily made her way along the cleared path until she could reach her stack of books. "Nothing else about heat?"

"We haven't looked all the way through it." Coppy was turning pages of *Considerations of Ethics of Sorcery and Their Application in Historical Context.*

Kip picked up the new copy of *An Introduction to the Methodes and Practickal Applications of Sorcery.* His old copy sat safely in his bag, and while this one had the same text, the same spells, it did not feel as grand, especially not next to the other books full of spells and knowledge he hadn't yet acquired. This book he had earned; the old book in his bag had been a gift of faith, and all these other books grew from that one.

"We have Saturday and Sunday to read them," Kip said.

"Or to fix up this basement." Coppy patted Kip on the shoulder. "I know which one you'll rather be doing."

And that night, lying on his bedroll with Coppy snoring lightly next to him, Kip looked up at the bookshelf he'd cleared to put his schoolbooks on them. This first night would have felt like a dream but for the itching of the dust that had wormed itself into his fur, and the small scratching of insects (and perhaps mice) that his ears constantly flicked around to pick up. The smells of himself and Coppy were nearly lost, even up close, in the overwhelming stench of old paper, moldering cloth, decaying leather.

Still, he could not sleep this night, staring at the ceiling, hardly daring to believe that the stones below his back were the stones of the Tower, lain two hundred years ago, that above him lay all the sorcery of the Colonies, and that he was a part of it all. What he'd known since he'd seen the sorcerers floating up the hill, since seeing the great, ancient Tower watching over the town, was that he belonged here, that even though nobody thought a Calatian could become a sorcerer, he had the ability. Magic is in our blood, he thought, and even so, none of the other cubs he'd known had felt the same pull. He knew that he could do sorcery, and finally, in his nineteenth year, he was going to have the chance to prove it.

CHAPTER 8: PHYSICAL SORCERY

The first week of classes left much to be desired from Kip's point of view. They were instructed in theory he already knew, taught basic spell language he had already mastered, and forced to practice gathering magic, which he could already do. He itched to get a start on impressing one of the masters, more even than his fur itched from dust. He wanted to perform magic for his father's master, Vendis, but he was not allowed to talk to any of the other masters, he was not allowed in the library to do research, and he was not allowed to practice casting spells except under Master Windsor's supervision, which was notable all week for its absence. When Kip complained, after their History and Ethics class, Master Windsor said, "You have no studies that require you to cast spells, and therefore no need of my supervision in order to do so."

Kip fumed at this on Tuesday morning, pacing back and forth in the small clear space in the basement. "They're holding us back so they don't have to keep us on as students. They're going to teach us enough to build roads and walls and that's it."

"That'd still be plenty for me." Coppy got up from his bedroll to approach Kip. "More than any Calatian's done so far."

"And all the students have the same restriction." Emily held up the Introduction to Sorcery book. "Why don't you just teach yourself more spells from the book?"

Kip's breath hissed out between his teeth. "Because it took me six months to learn each of those spells and we only have two. And the first spells in the book, the ones they're going to teach everyone first, are the two I know. So I need to get ahead."

"It's our second day." Coppy set a paw on his arm. "There's plenty of time."

"And the other students are living with masters," Kip said. "I bet they get to talk to them in the evenings and they get extra help and lessons." His fists clenched and his ears flattened. He could impose on Master Vendis, prevail upon the relationship his father shared with the middle-aged sorcerer, but he didn't know where to find the masters who were not teaching and not hosting.

"All right." Emily held up her hands. "Why don't we ask Adamson to share what he's learning?"

Kip considered that, his ears coming up partway. He had gotten the chance to ask Adamson about the dead fox in his tent, but not to his satisfaction; Victor had evaded the question twice and finally had said that Farley had gone and done that without his knowledge, and he had expressed his disgust. Kip left the conversation uneasy, partly because Adamson, in this denial, had reminded Kip strongly of his dead friend Saul. Saul, too, had protested that he couldn't watch Farley all the time, after the bully had ambushed Kip with thrown rocks. But Saul, at least, had gotten in a blow back for Kip. Victor Adamson's methods were slower and less direct; he had merely promised to keep Farley in check. "Or Malcolm."

Emily's lips tightened and she looked down at that. "What?" Kip tilted his head. "I thought he was perfectly pleasant."

"He's very glib," she said. "I don't doubt he would say just what you wanted to hear."

"That's not…" Kip considered. "I think he was fairly straightforward."

"I liked his manner." Coppy smiled. "Quite friendly, he was. Most of the Irish I've known have been."

"Yes, he's very proud of his heritage," Emily said. "Ask him if you must, and maybe then I will ask Adamson."

"Let's go now, then. They're both in Master Argent's quarters."

Emily sighed. "It's almost time for class. We'll ask them afterwards, or at lunch."

That morning they had History and Ethics, which proved unexpectedly engaging. Master Windsor lost some of his sour tone when discussing the earliest known sorcerers, in the Mesopotamian basin. Their names had been lost to history, but their deeds lived on: the great floods that wiped out the cities of Ninevah and Ur, the earth swallowing the armies of Sumer, the vast dam on the Euphrates, the fire that devoured Halicarnassus. Kip had read of some of these events in his classics, but Windsor concentrated on the magical features of each. None of these were considered Great Feats, as none continued to the present day, but to the many questions, Master Windsor replied irritably that they would cover Great Feats in a future class.

They did not catch either Adamson or Malcolm on their way to lunch, but Malcolm sat with Smith and Cobb at the adjacent table to Emily, Coppy, and Kip. A number of the other students lingered by Emily, clearly wanting to talk to her but put off by the Calatians. Kip was about to lean over and ask Malcolm whether Master Argent was teaching him and the others after hours when pain burst at the back of his head with a sharp impact.

He clapped a paw to the stinging pain, registering the noise of something falling behind him and the snickers of Farley across the tent. He didn't have to turn to put two and two together, especially as Coppy, sitting across from him, got up immediately. "Don't," Kip said, rubbing his skull, but the otter ignored him, bending to pick up the rock. "The ravens," Kip reminded him, pointing up.

Two or three ravens perched above them, as they had at every meal (possibly the same ravens, possibly different), watching intently but remaining quiet. "What of 'em?" Coppy said. "They didn't care when he threw a rock."

By now the whole tent was quiet. Coppy brandished the rock at Farley and raised his voice. "You want to start throwing rocks?" Kip half-turned in his seat, tensed and ready to get up in case a fight broke out.

Adamson spoke up, his voice at once commanding and languid. "We don't want to turn lunch into a sort of toddler's version of the Battle of Trafalgar now, do we?"

Farley scowled, and for a moment Kip thought he might throw a punch at the pale young man sitting beside him. But amazingly, Adamson's words both pushed Farley back into his chair and got Coppy's arm to drop. "Tell Admiral Gravina, then," the otter said, "to hold his fire from now on."

A good insult, Kip thought. The otter was quicker on his toes than he gave himself credit for. Farley wasn't, but even he knew the name of the Spanish Admiral who'd fought under the French Navy and been defeated by Lord Nelson. "Oh, I'm Gravina, is it?" Farley sneered.

"Aye. It's nice you've finally found your Villeneuve." Coppy gestured to Adamson, and then lobbed the rock onto the table, where it smacked into Farley's soup bowl, splashing soup into his lap.

Farley tried to scoot back, but could barely shift the bench and almost toppled over. He grabbed the rock and threw it at Coppy before Adamson could get a hand up to stop him.

Coppy grabbed the rock out of the air. "Want to play catch?"

"Whorepelt," Farley snarled. "Fancy yourself Nelson's pets, then, do you?"

"Stop it." Adamson rose to his feet. "Otter—Lutris—drop that rock."

Somewhat to Kip's surprise, Coppy let his arm hang down and his fingers open, letting the rock thud to the wood floor. Adamson lifted one white hand. "We all have to study together here. We're going to have to leave all of our old rivalries behind. There's nothing to be gained from fighting amongst ourselves."

Kip kept his eyes on Farley until the round head lowered and the small eyes returned to his meal, and then he relaxed, tail hanging down behind the bench. Coppy, too, kept his eyes on Farley as he made his way back to the table. "Pretty speech," he murmured. "Don't worry, Kip. Got my eye on him now."

"From now on," Emily said in a low voice as Kip reluctantly turned his back on Farley, "Why don't the two of you sit with your backs to the tent, and I'll sit with my back to Admiral Gravina there."

"Wouldn't put it past him to throw a rock at you," Kip growled back.

"Whatever you think of Adamson, he was right." Emily looked between the two of them. "We've too much to do to waste energy on fighting."

"He didn't do much to stop Farley throwing that first rock." Kip rubbed the back of his head.

Emily reached out and put a hand on the paw Kip was resting on the table. "Don't give them," she inclined her head up toward the ravens, "any more reason to kick you out than they already have."

"I know." Kip stared down at his bowl of soup. "It's just one more thing."

"Farley won't stop," Coppy explained to Emily. "Not for some fellow's words, fine as they might be."

"For what it's worth." They all turned to the next table, where Malcolm leaned over to them. "I'm thinking I find myself quite happy to be over here on this side of the tent."

"Thanks." Kip's eyes traveled down to the rock sitting in the middle of the floor and then up to the ravens above it. "Say," he said, "Master Windsor said no unsupervised magic in the Tower, right? Did he say anything about the dining tent?"

Coppy smiled. "No. I don't believe he did."

So the next day, when Adamson's talk again failed to keep Farley from throwing the first stone, Kip was ready. He caught it and then called magic to him. The ravens still made no protest, and Adamson and Farley watched with their friends, tense and ready for action. So he cast the spell and sent the rock floating over their heads.

"Drop it on his head," Emily murmured, but Kip had years of practice with Farley, and knew that retaliation was less effective than a show of strength. But he couldn't resist letting the stone hover over Farley's head, while the boy kept his neck craned back and one hand raised like the shadow of the stone that floated there.

"My control's not that good," he said, loudly enough that Farley scrambled to get out of the way of the rock.

And then Kip moved it toward the front of the tent and out. It slipped from his spell's grasp as he lost sight of it—something he would endeavor to master soon, when they were allowed to practice. But that little display was effective enough to stop the stone throwing for the rest of the day, although it did not appear to please Adamson.

"You should not show off your power that way," he told Kip, lingering in the Great Hall after dinner that evening. "It makes my job more difficult."

"What am I to do?" Kip had felt rather proud of his success. "Allow stones to fall in my food and accept it meekly?"

"In the long run, that would be the better strategy." Adamson's brow had been furrowed, his manner cross, but now he relaxed and stared beyond Kip. "If he sees you as a colleague rather than a threat, I will be able to make peace all the sooner."

"He'll never see me as a colleague. Never."

"Not as long as you don't see him as one."

Kip flattened his ears, propriety be damned. "Do colleagues throw stones at each other? Slaughter animals in each other's beds?"

"Someone has to make the first step," Adamson said, distant and patient.

"That someone is him." Kip folded his arms and curled his tail around his leg. "You have no idea what I and my friends have endured."

"I had hoped your obvious intelligence would allow you to take the long view." Adamson sighed. "I shall continue my efforts regardless, and I hope that when you see the fruits of my labors, you may trust that they have been worthwhile."

Privately, Kip thought it much more likely that Farley would bend Adamson to his ways simply by dint of sheer stubbornness and malice. More than one human boy had been bullied into shunning Kip and his friends. Saul never had, and maybe Adamson was made of the same stuff. "I wish you luck," he said.

"Say." Adamson stopped Kip with a hand on the fox's shoulder. "What did you think of Patris's lecture?"

Kip shrugged. "Nothing we didn't know. Magic comes from the earth."

"Indeed. But he didn't touch on one question. Is magic exhaustible?"

Kip tilted his head to one side. "What do you mean?"

"Like gold, for instance. There are gold mines that yield no more gold. Do you think that we are all tapping into a magic mine that might someday run out of magic?"

"Actually…" Kip rubbed his paws together. "I wondered about that with Calatians. I mean, we're magic, but we're born to our parents naturally. There's no spell needed for a child to be born."

"Other than the romantic kind." Adamson gave a slight smile. "But go on."

"So where does the magic to make each Calatian come from? Is it from the original Great Feat? Or do we somehow draw magic up as a wick pulls oil into a lamp?"

The blond boy rubbed his chin. "I had thought it believed that the magic inherent in all Calatians is a part of them and passed on to their children. You don't eat magic food, do you? You might as well ask how an ordinary piece of cheese contributes health to a magical being."

"I…hadn't thought of that," Kip admitted.

"I doubt we here are equipped to solve that problem tonight. But it might be worth some study in the future." Adamson inclined his head. "Good night, Penfold."

"Good night." Kip paused a moment to think about Adamson's question, then said good-night to the phosphorus elementals in the fireplace as had become his custom, and walked downstairs to his basement room.

"We'd best all get as good as Kip," Malcolm said later that week, "if we're to have peaceful lunches or dinners."

"I don't understand why the sorcerers don't stop it," Emily said.

"The masters have better things to do than stop every fight in school." Malcolm was leaning back against one of the shelves that separated Kip and Coppy's living space from the rest of the basement. They had cleared out a circle to sit in some days before, and now that the insects had sought other shelter and the stone had lost its damp, Malcolm had joined them to sit there.

"But fights in this school are liable to be more deadly than in other schools." Emily's eyes slid to Kip, and she caught herself. "Most other schools, I suppose."

"Boy in my school lost a hand in a schoolyard fight. Right gruesome," Malcolm said. "Another almost lost an eye when a nasty bully sat on him and rubbed his face into the dirt. But he and his eye survived, though some of his good looks were sacrificed that day." He touched the skin around his eye, and Kip realized that what he'd thought were pockmarks were actually scars.

"We didn't have injuries in our school," Coppy said. "But some nights, if cubs wandered too far afield, they'd have their tails docked and sold to rich people who wanted to wear fur."

"Young children?" Emily stared.

"Well, if they take the tails of the grown-ups, they're too big." Coppy pulled Kip's tail out and held it up. "No passing that off as a regular fox."

Normally, Kip didn't mind Coppy touching his tail, but the mention of a 'regular fox' only made him think of the poor creature Farley had killed. He slid his tail free to rest on the chilly stone, and Coppy didn't seem to notice.

"It's horrible," Emily said. "There was nothing of that sort happening in Boston, I'm sure."

Kip was only certain that it didn't happen in New Cambridge, possibly because the woods around were filled with creatures more easily caught with less risk of punishment, here in the shadow of the Tower. He would not have been surprised to hear that in Boston, there was an illegal fur trade, and Malcolm said the same about New York.

"When Farley tried to cut off tails," Kip said, "it wasn't to sell. It was to maim, that's all."

"Well, he's horrible, isn't he?" Emily rolled her eyes. "Did I tell you what he said to me at dinner tonight? He invited me out behind the tent if I was through with 'wearing fur.'"

"Was he meaning to cast aspersions on your honor?" Malcolm leaned forward.

Emily simply looked irritated. "I don't think he thinks of it that way to begin with. I mean, I don't think he thinks that any ladies have honor to speak of. Come to it, I'm not certain he thinks at all. He may be some kind of incarnation of basic urges on legs."

"That describes him rather well." Kip had had only one encounter with Farley since the stone-throwing had stopped, and that had been leaving a class, when he'd unwisely walked past Farley's desk and nearly gotten his tail stomped on. Fortunately, his reflexes were quick enough to save all but a few hairs from the heavy boot.

"He invited me to do something I shan't repeat in front of a lady," Malcolm said. "Granted, it was after I suggested he might defeat the Spanish single-handed simply by exposing them to his odor."

"I appreciate that you take advantage of the baths," Emily told him. "These fellows here don't smell bad, but some of the other students make the class truly uncomfortable."

"Anything for a lady." Malcolm inclined his head graciously. "But I'm not certain that room you found is the bath. I believe it might be the laundry. That's what those robes hanging up mean, I wager."

Emily raised an eyebrow. "Then where did you bathe? For I m certain you did."

"Oh, I bathed there." Malcolm's grin widened. "I only meant to caution you in case someone wanders in to have a robe laundered while you're laundering yourself."

"It occurs to me," she said, "that perhaps one of the first spells I should be interested in learning would be one that could seal a door shut."

"Before a heating spell?" Kip indicated the sweater she had wrapped around her shoulders. The air in the basement felt comfortable to him, but when he breathed he could feel the chill, enough to know that Emily and Malcolm were uncomfortable, though the latter bore it without complaint.

"Second, then," she said with a smile.

"The rate we're going," Malcolm said, "we won't get to locking doors and heating rooms until spring, by which time we'll all have become so familiar with each other that there's no more need for either."

Emily arched an eyebrow. "You presume much."

He looked genuinely stricken. "I didn't—it was a bit of humor—I mean—"

Into the awkward silence, Coppy spoke. "Where do the sorcerers bathe, if not there?"

"They certainly do bathe." Kip flared his nostrils. "Master Windsor smells of jasmine attar often."

"What on earth might that be?" The change of subject revitalized Malcolm. "I thought 'attar' was something you put on dead people."

"They may put perfume on dead people to mask the smell. But it's also a perfume. Jasmine is an exotic one; we only got it into the store once as it tends not to escape the rich people of London. I remembered it, though."

"Maybe London is where Master Windsor goes when he's not allowing us to practice magic." Emily reached out and pushed one of the piles of paper and then brushed her hands together briskly as though she'd forgotten the papers were dusty.

"Maybe it's where he goes to bathe," Coppy said, and they all laughed.

"Kip, what does Master Patris smell like?" Malcolm wanted to know. "I wager he's a 'plain soap' kind of fellow."

"Laundry soap," Kip said. "And—well, a little bit of fear, too."

"Fear? What's he got to be afraid of?" Coppy gestured around the circle. "Us?"

"Don't know." Kip shook his head. "And it's not all the time. It was strongest when he grabbed me after I levitated myself that first day."

"So he has someplace to wash off the stink as well." Emily turned to Kip. "Why don't you ask your father? Perhaps he's seen a bath on the upper floors?"

Kip lowered his head and ears. "I'm not sure when I'll see him. He doesn't come up on a schedule."

Two evenings later, a hard rapping sounded on their basement door as he and Coppy were going through their books with Emily. All three looked up; the rapping was not Malcolm's quick cadence, which they knew well, and in fact it did not even sound like human knuckles, but like a hard stick being tapped against the thick wood.

Kip got up, tail swinging behind him, and navigated the piles of paper easily, his bare paws used to the cold stone. He swung the door open and saw nobody there.

"Penfold," croaked a familiar voice from below his knees.

On the stoop, a raven looked up at him, eyes glinting in the dark basement stairwell. "Come," it said with Master Vendis's voice, and hopped up the stairs without waiting for him to acknowledge it.

"I need to go," he said, turning to the others, but they had already seen the raven and both of them nodded.

Once it reached the Great Hall, the raven hopped along the floor past the fireplace. The student desks had already been cleared away, by what agency Kip could only guess (demons), but the great glowing lizards remained in the fireplace, coiled around and over each other.

He'd spent so much time staring at their flickering forms over the past few days that he'd felt it rude not to talk to them, though more than one sorcerer had advised him not to waste his time on them. "Evening, fellows," he said as he passed.

"Oh, the fox."

"It's 'Penfold,' Robby. Use his name."

"Aye, you'd not like being called 'the fire-thing.'"

"Where you off to?"

Kip indicated the raven. "I've been summoned."

"Oh-ho."

"Hope you come back!"

"We all been summoned."

"He knows that, Chez."

"We got to stay here for years."

"It ain't years."

"Months."

"Days."

"Centuries."

"Who can tell?"

"If you count the times the stone cools down…"

The raven croaked again, impatient. "Sorry," Kip said, raising a paw. "I've got to go."

"Oh, aye."

"When you're summoned, you got to go."

"Don't mind us, Penfold."

They were usually not quite so garrulous; maybe the loneliness of evening and the chill of the sun's warmth fading made them restless. Kip made a note to come up and speak to them again in future evenings.

Outside, in the dim light, he worried that he would lose the raven when it took flight, but it remained on the ground, hopping agilely ahead. He followed it around the corner of the tower toward the dining tent and what had been the admissions tent, and then the breeze brought a familiar scent to him. He squinted ahead into the twilight and broke into a run.

"Dad!"

His father held out arms to welcome him, and Kip tumbled into his embrace. Max's fur smelled lightly of perfumes and of incense, but mostly of the older fox himself, familiar and steadying. "You're up here for Master Vendis?" Kip asked when they stepped apart.

Max nodded. One paw went to his left elbow while he talked, as though it were injured, but Kip smelled no blood and the arm appeared to be working well. "I asked if I might speak with you, and he sent Brightbeak to fetch you."

The raven clacked its beak. "Do not tarry long," it said, and then it did launch itself into the air. It flew once around them with a brush of wind that ruffled Kip's whiskers, and then disappeared into the night.

"How is the shop?" Kip asked.

His father smiled. "The shop runs well, but I would not waste the time we have speaking of it. What of your classes?"

"Boring." Kip told him briefly of their concentration exercises and of Farley's stone-throwing. "How do the people in town feel about me and Coppy being up here?"

"Coppy is not a New Cantabrigian," his father said, "and most people feel he may do what he likes, although they also feel he is following you more than his own mind."

"That's not true." Kip said the words heatedly, then relaxed; it wasn't his father he was angry at. "Not entirely. He wants to learn sorcery and go back to London."

His father held up a paw. "Be that as it may, the perception is that you are the instigator. I hear little enough about it, but I hear less these days than I used to."

Kip's stomach stirred with unease at the thought of making trouble for his father, or hurting his business. "From the Calatians as well as the humans?"

"The Calatians mostly. The humans are not the least bit concerned about your ambition. At least, they frequent my shop and make conversation as they always have. They are more worried about the coming winter or when the Spanish may attack again than about how you and Coppy will fare at the school."

"I'm not trying to make anyone else's life difficult," Kip said. "I want to make mine better."

"You cannot separate your life from theirs."

"Why not?" He curled his tail, then relaxed it and folded his arms. "What have they to do with me?"

"You're betrothed to Alice Cartwright, for one thing." His father's eyes held his, stern.

Kip lowered his ears. "I know. But I can be a sorcerer and have a wife.

And that's not what they are mad about."

"No. But this gate," one paw swept back toward the iron bars, "does not separate lives. You may pass through it freely. And the things you do here will be heard below and will be felt below, and you would do well to remember that."

"They would be pleased if I fail," Kip said bitterly.

"Some would. Not all." The paw that had indicated the gate returned to grasp his arm. "Breaking a new path is difficult when those behind you would rather use the old, worn one. It is your job to show them why your path is the true one."

"I don't see why they have to be on my path at all. Why can't they stay to theirs and leave me to mine?"

Max smiled. "Someday perhaps you will see more clearly."

The creak of the tower's front door caught both their ears. Kip's swiveled back toward his father as the older fox patted him on the shoulder. "I shouldn't tarry, as Master Vendis warned. Study hard and persevere. You'll make a sorcerer yet."

Kip smiled and embraced his father again. He stood in the chill night as the gates creaked open and let Max through, then closed again with a heavy clunk. The bobbing white tail tip moved down the hillside road and out of view, and only then did Kip turn back along the path to the tower.

He'd walked three steps before a low sound made him snap his head up. Two shapes stood on the path right at the corner of the tower, but he had only a moment to register that before something struck him hard on his chest below the shoulder.

He stumbled backwards, twisted and almost fell, but kept his balance. Alert now, he still failed to dodge the second rock, a fist-sized missile that caught him in the side. Footsteps sounded, loud on the stone path, and he whirled to look for the nearest cover. He'd only taken two steps toward the dining tent before they were on him.

One person crashed into him from behind and bore him to the ground; the other, upwind of Kip, hurried to join. Farley's rank scent and heavy footsteps sent Kip's tail between his legs, and he would have curled up into a ball if not for the lighter weight on his back. This other assailant was one of his fellow students—definitely not Farley. Even if he'd weighed fifty pounds more, Kip would have known it wasn't Farley because the boy hadn't grabbed his arms, pinned him down with one twisted behind his back. He was simply sitting on the fox, trusting his leverage to keep Kip pinned down. It worked for the moment, because even though he wasn't Farley's weight, he was heavy enough, and Kip had landed at an awkward angle. But at least he'd protected his tail and managed to get one arm over his head.

So that arm took the brunt of Farley's kick, a savage blow that struck Kip's shoulder. Another landed in the same place, and then one in his upper back that made him grit his teeth. "Go home, worthless vermin," Farley snarled.

"Easy," said whoever was sitting on Kip's back. Carmichael, he guessed. "Argent warned you…"

"Good thing about the animals is they don't bruise," Farley said. He kicked again, but Kip, squirming harder now, deflected the blow that had been aimed at his kidneys. "Hold 'im still, you corn shuck, and show me his belly."

Carmichael obediently tried to wrestle Kip around, but the fox fought him, taking advantage of the fact that Carmichael feared his teeth. Farley would have sent a fist to his muzzle by now. "Get…off!" Kip huffed. Of course they'd waited until he was away from Coppy to attack him, and had brought two to handle one scrawny fox.

"This's what happens to critters that come up to live among men," Carmichael sneered, getting a grip on Kip's paws and turning him over despite the fox's struggles. "G'wan, Farley, knock him into a cocked hat."

Kip struggled to free his paws, and then over the hulking shadow of Farley he saw the grey stones of the Tower glimmering against the night sky. The realization came to him that he wasn't helpless anymore. He began to gather magic, using some of the techniques Patris had been teaching them to focus—

Farley's boot came down on his stomach, the boy's weight behind it. For a moment, Kip's world narrowed to that feeling, the air driven out of his lungs, the waves of pain, the thick smells of Farley and Carmichael like a miasma around his head. When he emerged, Farley was drawing his leg back and Kip found to his surprise that he was still gathering magic, that his focus had only wavered, not broken. Purple flickered around his arms, growing stronger.

"Ho!" Carmichael released him and sprang away. Kip fell back onto his arms, the purple glow so bright now that it dimmed his perception of his attackers. But he could hear well enough.

"He won't do nothing," Farley said. "Can't do nothing to us."

"You can stay and find that out." Carmichael was halfway back to the Tower by the time he'd finished that sentence.

When Farley turned back, Kip had his arms behind his back so he could see the other more clearly. Their eyes met. "G'wan, then," Farley said. "Magic me. We'll see how long you stay up here."

The cramping in Kip's stomach made it hard for him to speak loudly, but he forced the words out. "Such…a shame," he said. "No idea…how Farley got up on the roof. But he sure came down in a hurry."

Farley squinted at him and backed up a step. "You can't."

"Right now…" Kip got one leg under him and pushed, slowly standing upright. "I am closer than I've ever been."

The stout bully stepped back again. Kip brought his arms out, the purple flickering and dancing like fire around his fur, and that was enough. "This ain't over," Farley said, turning on his heel. "You don't belong here and I'll run you off soon." Despite his bravado, his steps as he made his way back to the Tower were faster than the casual walk his pose affected.

Only then did Kip exhale and sink to the ground. His arm, back, and stomach still hurt, and he had gathered magic that he still didn't know how to dispel. As much as he wanted to go inside and lie down, he had to do something with the magic. So he recited one of the two spells he knew and pushed himself gently off from the ground.

A few feet would have done it, used up all the magic and let him float back to earth, but he kept going up and up, past the windows, until he was again level with the roof of the tower. Nearby, the rough stone crenellations shone in the moonlight, bare of any black winged shadow. Slightly disappointed, Kip moved himself over to the tower and sat on the stone, careful to keep the spell going. From there, he looked out and down upon the town of New Cambridge.

Somewhere among the maple trees, his father trudged down the hill toward his shop. Farther still, the lights of the town glittered and danced in the night. The people down there wanted him to leave the school—his people, the Cartwrights and the Morgans and the Porters and the Brocks. Maybe all of them or maybe only some of them. And at least three of the people up here wanted him to leave the school. More than that, but he was only sure of Carmichael, Farley, and Master Patris.

Master Windsor, he reflected, might want him to leave, but it would only be if he failed to apply himself, to live up to his potential. He could respect that; Master Windsor appeared to treat all people with equal disdain, whether they were male or female, human or Calatian. Kip would have preferred a friend, but impartial teacher would do.

The attack from Farley was an unpleasant reminder of what his life had been without Coppy around. If he returned to New Cambridge while Farley remained up here, how long would it be before the boy was back down in the town, using sorcery to throw stone blocks and maybe lift Calatians and drop them? Such things wouldn't be legal, of course, but how many would be hurt before he was stopped? There was the man in Boston who'd killed six Calatians before the police moved to stop him, the one in New York who'd drowned three, and how many more who'd never been caught?

There were plenty of reasons for Kip to stay: the ease with which he'd flown up to the roof with barely more than a thought; the worry over what Farley might do unchecked; the nascent friendships with Emily and Malcolm (and, he added after a hesitation, Adamson). There was only one good reason to leave, and it wasn't the bruises now forming under his fur (Farley was wrong factually but correct in the effect that mattered, which was that Kip's bruises would never be visible). It was that his father might be in trouble. Max had told Kip that everything was fine, but even over the soft lavender scent he favored, Kip had caught the sour tang of worry.

He heaved a sigh. If his father wouldn't confide in him, there was little he could do. Max himself would insist that Kip remain here as long as he was able, so he should concentrate his energies on finding a Master who would Select him. Resting with the stone of the Tower below him, supporting him, he felt slightly hopeful. He had to find a way to talk to Master Vendis.

But for now, he should get back to the basement. After making sure the spell was still active, Kip pushed himself off from the stone and lowered himself to the ground, banishing the spell as he did so. He lifted his nose, in case Farley and Carmichael had snuck back out, but no scents came to him on the breeze. He headed upwind, where he could be sure the wind would help him find enemies, until he reached a point from which he could see the path to the Tower. It lay bare, glossy stone in the dim light, and neither his ears nor nose picked up any movement. Cautiously, he padded beyond the path to the wall of the Tower, almost to the place he'd touched it before.

He hesitated, and then for confidence, placed a paw on the wall. No voice came, no surge of magic, but Kip felt warmth and strength. He belonged here, with the Tower, and no Farley nor Carmichael nor even Patris was going to drive him out. He kept a paw on the stone, sliding all the way to the corner and then listening for thirty seconds until he was sure there was no activity, not even breathing, around the side. Irrationally, he felt as though the Tower would warn him if he were in danger.

Whether that were true or not, he stepped around to find the lawn and path in front of the main doors bare. Only when he had entered the Great Hall and said goodnight to the elementals did he truly feel safe. He hurried down the stairs as quickly as he could without jarring the bruises on his back, opened the basement door, and fell back against it as it closed.

"What did the raven want?" Coppy asked. Emily's door was closed, and the otter read by the light of the sconces, which had not yet gone out.

"My father was here," Kip said, "but listen to this." He told the otter about the attack.

Coppy's whiskers lowered and he touched Kip's chest. "I'll go after Farley for that. Any harm done?"

"I'll be sore. Otherwise I'm fine. I feel…good about it, in a way. I mean, they might have killed me, but I did scare them off." He met the otter's eyes. "Don't go after Farley. I'll be able to take care of him."

"Until they learn magic as well."

"Well then," Kip said, lying back on his bedroll. "I'll have to learn more."

CHAPTER 9: MASTERS

One unexpected consequence of the fight was that Kip got to speak to Master Vendis. His chance came on Saturday evening as Kip, Emily, and Coppy were waiting for Malcolm in the Great Hall before dinner. The phosphorus elementals were restless, and Kip was not helping by inviting them down to the basement. "We need the heat and there's much more room than in this old fireplace."

The lizard-creatures clambered over each other, sending waves of warmth over Kip's fur. Emily and Coppy came up behind him as the elementals started talking. Two new ones had been added to the fire, brighter than the three old ones, and their activity seemed to spur the others to be active and talkative as well.

"Love to come."

"Can't."

"Leave off with the pushing, Ern."

"Only pushing your leg out of my snout."

"Can't go past the edge there." Robby, Kip thought his name was, stared mournfully down at the edge of the fireplace. His tongue reached out and then stopped at an invisible wall.

"Awful crowded in here."

"I'd help if I could," Kip said. "There was a cold snap and it was terribly chilly down there."

"Yes." Emily didn't usually pay attention to Kip's conversations with the lizards, but she was still rubbing her arms, standing near their warmth. "I have told the fox that he had better provide me with some heat or I'll be forced to violate some of Master Patris's precious propriety in order to keep from freezing to death."

"Pro-Pry-Etty?"

"What'sat?"

Kip was attempting to explain that unlike phosphorus elementals, people generally did not sleep all piled atop one another, when his name was called across the hall. He turned and saw a sorcerer whose black robes trailed across the floor, with reddish-brown hair and a goatee. His heart leapt and he turned from the fire. "Master Vendis?"

The sorcerer beckoned him with one hand. "A word, Penfold."

Malcolm had come down the stairs right behind Vendis, and crossed paths with Kip on his way to join Emily and Coppy by the fire. "I'll be there in a moment," Kip said.

The other fireplace in the room lay cold and bare. Vendis stood beside it, hands clasped together in front of him. Kip glanced down at the hem of his robe, and then up at the sorcerer's eyes. "Sir?"

"You made two mistakes last night, Kip."

Master Vendis was the only sorcerer to call Kip by his first name, likely because Vendis worked with Max so much. "Last night?"

The sorcerer held up a finger. "One: you did not gather magic immediately upon perceiving a threat."

Kip's ears lowered as he frowned. His back still ached from the attack. "You were *watching*?"

"Two: you did not tell Master Patris about the incident."

The fox shook his head. His whiskers were tingling and he had that peppermint sting in his nose again. "Why didn't you do something, if you were watching?"

"You handled the fight well enough except for that one mistake. You didn't injure either of the boys, but you showed enough magic to make them back off."

"What if they'd hit my head with a rock? Would you have done something then?" He realized his tone was sharp, and so added a belated, "Sir."

Vendis smiled and shook his head. "The students at this school are watched over. But there are worse things than physical injuries. Those can be mended. You did well to assert your position here. I fear it will be an eternal struggle for you, even should you be Selected."

The weight of that last word silenced Kip for a moment. Vendis turned to leave, but Kip stopped him. "Sir? How do we go about being Selected? I mean—" He searched for a tactful way to ask the question. "Do you need an apprentice?"

Vendis reached up to brush a lock of hair out of his eyes. He regarded Kip with some sadness. "I may be allowed to choose one, but I would not choose you. My relationship with your father is more important than the three years I would have with you."

The stones seemed to shift under Kip's feet; his knees gave way and he had to brace himself against the wall next to the fireplace, the bruises on his arm protesting as he did. His tail curled in and around his legs, and the chill of the dead fireplace seeped through his fur. "How do I...who will take me? We only see Windsor, Patris, and Argent, and the first two hate me and Master Argent's got his eye on—elsewhere." Tact rescued him in the nick of time from saying something about Emily.

There was no help in Vendis's eyes. "I do not know," he said. "You must do your best, and hope that some of the few remaining masters may look beyond your skin to see your talent."

It was easy enough for the sorcerer to say, but Kip could not see how to accomplish that. Although ravens regularly crowded the Great Hall and the dining tent, they did so silently, watching without speaking (was that what Vendis had meant when he'd said the students were watched over?). Were they to be judged from afar, summarized in their behavior at classes and meals? It seemed unfair, and yet, perhaps that was how things had always been done. For the human students, no doubt that would work. Kip thanked Master Vendis and walked back to rejoin his friends.

The other consequence of the fight was that at dinner that evening, Malcolm declared that Kip and Coppy should not go anywhere alone. "With each other if nobody else is around," he said, "but always wi' one of us if we can."

"We don't need chaperones." Kip's fur bristled.

"But we're delighted for the company." Coppy countered his sour remark with a smile.

So on Sunday, when Coppy wanted to walk down to church, Kip and Emily and Malcolm all came down with him. A group of the other students walked down—Farley not among them, though Adamson was—some ways ahead of them, and entered the church for the humans' service. Kip had not talked to Adamson since the attack, mostly out of an obscure sense that Farley would be pleased if Kip complained about it and the growing certainty that it would not change anything.

The day was one of those pleasant fall days in which the clouds drift lazily across the sky and humans and Calatians are equally comfortable in the cool air. The scent of maple trees surrounded Kip on the walk down, and as they approached the Founders Rest, the smells of the town intruded and overwhelmed the maple. Kip breathed in the familiar air of ale and barrels from the inn, bread and people and wood, horses and dirt and manure, all the things he hadn't realized he'd missed on the hill. They greeted Old John, leaning in the doorway of his inn, and John raised a hand gravely in response.

"Doesn't he go to church?" Emily asked.

"He says the Calatians and godless need refreshment as well, and he can feel God's blessing from where he stands." Kip smiled, leading them around the corner of the inn.

"This is our church," Coppy said, mostly to Malcolm as Emily had seen it before. Clouds dimmed the glow on the golden cross above the steeple, but the church still stood proudly above the town.

Kip and Coppy made for the small group of Calatians below a spreading oak tree some ways from the church. Squirrels and dormice sat on the benches, and there were the Cartwrights, a group of red-furred foxes standing apart on the brown and green of the dying lawn. Kip looked for his parents, but did not see or smell them.

"Aren't you going in?" Kip asked Malcolm and Emily when they lingered with him and Coppy.

They shook their heads at the same time. "Rather go to church with our own, even if they aren't our own," Malcolm said.

"Elegantly phrased." Emily smiled at Kip. "Church is about family and friends."

That was also what Kip had learned, but looking around the small leaf-strewn area, he did not see many people anxious to come greet him. Only Adam's mother and younger brother came over to congratulate him and talk to him, and as more Calatians arrived in anticipation of the service, a few came to talk to him and Coppy. But many of them, many of the cubs he'd attended school with and parents who'd helped look after him, stayed a short ways away, and talked in tones meant to remain hidden from fox ears. Even the Cartwrights only greeted him perfunctorily, though Alice gave him the same big smile she usually did and looked cross when dragged away.

"Is it because we're here with you?" Emily asked Kip while Malcolm and Coppy were comparing the technique of magic gathering to the practice of meditation.

Kip shook his head. "Maybe a small amount. I think from what my father's said…many of the people here feel that it's hubris for me to attempt to become a sorcerer."

"Hubris? To try to reach your potential?"

"I'll let him explain." Kip gestured behind Emily, where Max and Ada were approaching with a pair of hedgehogs: the Morgans. Bryce was the unofficial Calatian mayor, his wife the town's best seamstress. They spotted Kip, parted ways quickly with his parents, and walked off to greet another group.

"We didn't expect to see you here." Max embraced his son and Coppy, while Ada smiled and told Emily how lovely it was to see her again. Kip introduced Malcolm.

"Do you think they can come in to our service?" he asked.

His father regarded Malcolm and Emily. "I would welcome you, but it might be prudent to wait. Or to go in now, while the other humans are hearing theirs."

"We'd rather go with you," Emily said.

"Or stand outside." Malcolm lifted his eyes to the steeple. "In my experience, God doesn't much fuss about where you worship Him so long as you do it with your heart."

"Doesn't feel right if it ain't in church," Coppy said.

"To each his own," Malcolm agreed amiably. He blinked as the sun came out again, and shaded his eyes. "'Tis a lovely church, I'll say that much. In New York—"

"They're far more grand?" Emily asked acerbically.

He smiled back. "Some are, aye, but I was going to say they're beset with buildings on all sides and none have the quiet dignity to stand apart as this one does."

Singing came from the church faintly through the closed doors. Emily turned from Ada to Max. "If it will cause problems, Malcolm and I will wait outside."

Max turned to Kip and Coppy. "What do you two think?"

The otter said, "I'd have them in, but I'm not from here and don't have to live here. Kip?"

Kip looked at his friends' faces, and then at his parents. He wanted Emily and Malcolm with him, but it would make life difficult for his parents, worse than he was already making it. It wasn't fair that he had to keep making these decisions, he thought, and yet he couldn't put them off onto anyone else.

"Let's stay outside," Malcolm said. "It's a lovely day, and as me ma used to say, sure, didn't the Lord make the sun and trees and grass just as surely as He made the church and pews and glass?"

"Quite." Emily nodded to Kip. "It will likely be one of the last nice days we'll see. We shall enjoy it while you attend your services."

"Thank you," Kip said. "I'm sorry that the town feels this way."

And as comforting as it felt to kneel in the warm embrace of the church and breathe in the scents of his fellow Calatians in the large open space, present without being oppressive, he could not stop thinking about his friends waiting outside for him and Coppy to have their services separately. His mind returned to a question he had often pondered with Saul, and later with Coppy: if God had indeed made humans, and humans had made Calatians, did that mean that God loved the Calatians less? The Church's position was that because the Calatians were made from humans, they possessed human souls, and God loved all souls equally. But the churches did not seem to follow God's rule in that case, and the New Cambridge church had always offered separate services.

Even so, the words that washed over him from the human preacher gave him comfort. He'd never felt excluded from God's love, and Father Gregory had always made sure to assure him and the other Calatian cubs that they were part of His kingdom. If he listened to the words and let Farley and Patris and the other Calatians slide away from him, they gave him a warm comfort that felt elusive in other parts of his life.

When they left the church, Kip stood with his parents on the lawn. Malcolm and Emily came over to join them. Around them, the business of the town proceeded, Calatians chattering merrily together, but the six of them stood alone.

"I've never been in such a group," Malcolm said, looking around. "Feels a bit unsettling, to be honest."

"You've nothing to fear," Kip said.

"I meant no offense. Only that I haven't been somewhere where I was so aware that I don't belong." He rubbed his forehead. "Save for Penny Lawrence's bedroom, but that was entirely another matter, and there were excellent reasons for being there."

"Charming," Emily said. "We belong here as much as Kip belongs in the college. Fur or skin, what difference?"

"You're enlightened indeed." Max smiled. "Sadly, there aren't many who share your view. And because you can go where you like while we cannot, your presence here may be seen as intrusive."

"Oh, dear." Emily's face fell. "I hadn't thought of that."

"Were they all standing apart like this last week?" Kip asked.

His father hesitated, but his mother spoke up. "No," she said. "Not everyone came to talk, but some did."

"We should probably leave." Emily sighed. "I didn't mean to cause trouble. It's only that since Kip was attacked, we've wanted to—"

Kip flattened his ears. Both his parents stared at him, and his father broke into Emily's sentence. "Attacked? By whom?"

"Whom do you think?" He told them the story briefly, leaving out his conversation with Master Vendis. "I'll be more ready next time."

Coppy stepped up beside him. "And he'll have company. We all will."

"I wager," Malcolm said with a toothy grin, "that they like Irishmen about as little as Calatians. And Miss Carswell might face different kinds of attacks."

"I am perfectly capable of handling myself," Emily said.

Max surveyed the four of them with upright ears and a smile. "I'm pleased you're all in this together. It will take more than one of you to succeed."

And if he didn't succeed, Kip thought, looking around at the town he'd once been a part of, what did he have to come back to? His eye strayed to the Cartwrights, walking away with Alice without even having said goodbye. Would he have a chance to start a family here, even if he wanted to? He saw himself coming to church with his family every Sunday, alone, isolated from the rest of the town for years; he saw himself married to Alice and the rest of the town arrayed against the foxes; he saw the Cartwrights break the engagement, leaving him and his family alone.

Saving his parents, there was nobody in town who meant as much to him as Coppy did, as Emily and Malcolm had come to after only two short weeks. But more than that, he did not think he could bear to return to the town, to live again in the shadow of the Tower after having lived within its walls.

CHAPTER 10: FIRST SPELL

On Monday, they were taught their first spell: a basic levitation spell, the other one Kip already knew. He chafed at the slow pace, at the small wooden blocks they were given to practice with, but when Coppy reminded him that he'd said his magic gathering was better after last week, he forced himself to practice at the same pace as the other students.

His prior knowledge of the spell allowed him to spend some of his practice time watching the others in the class. Most of them were having difficulty gathering magic still, and spoke the spell while their hands were not glowing. Coppy and Emily did quite well, and Malcolm faltered but appeared to be learning quickly. Farley and Jacob Quarrel, a tall, thin student, did the best of the others, which surprised Kip. Farley had not done very well at gathering magic at first, though he'd gotten his hands to glow a steady lime-green by the end of the week. Here he was reciting a spell—out of a book, but still—and his wooden block rose, wobbled, and fell. Yet that was more than most of the others were able to do.

And then there was Victor Adamson.

Victor alone had not managed any kind of glow to his hands the previous week. Now he sat reading the spell book, and though Kip could not see his expression from behind, the boy's head was bowed, his shoulders bent, his whole frame turned inward in concentration. He sat in the front row, directly before Master Patris, and though the old sorcerer strode through the class berating students for their failures, Adamson was as ignored as the Calatians, though his wooden cube never so much as budged an inch from his desk.

When Cobb sat back in his chair, his cube stubbornly unmoved, Patris suggested he revisit the methods of gathering magic. When Quarrel managed to lift his cube and then drop it with a clatter, Patris told him to practice his focus and concentration. But though Kip and Coppy kept their cubes aloft, they were never recognized; though Emily's and Malcolm's wobbled, they were never given instruction; though Adamson's never moved save when he picked it up with his fingers, he was never reproved.

Kip wanted to ask him about his studies, but that afternoon, the questions of Adamson and Farley were driven from his mind. Master Argent took them up to the library.

For the other students, the staircase up was nothing new; they all lived up those stairs, and talked all the way up them about spells or letters they'd gotten from home. But for Kip, simply getting to see another part of the tower kept his senses alert, his ears perked and whiskers twitching at every motion. He looked at the stones, at the nicks and marks left by knives and hands, and wondered if Saul had left any trace of his short time here. If he had even been up this stair; the students had previously stayed in one of the outside buildings, one of the ones that was now a pile of rubble in a shattered foundation.

But yes, of course Saul would have come up these stairs to the library Kip was being shown to now. They passed the second floor, where Master Argent pointed out Master Splint's quarters. "In case you suffer any injuries during your time here," the sorcerer said, and looked back toward Kip and Coppy. Kip's back still ached, but it would be fine in another day, and it would be more awkward to tell someone about the attack now, four days later. He kept his lips shut and his eyes forward, even when Coppy looked up at him.

Then another set of stairs, another set of marks and lines in the wall, and the scents of sorcerers gave way to the scent of paper and cloth, leather and age, similar to the scent in the basement in the way that the smell of a freshly opened bottle of cider was similar to the scent of week-old spilt beer. Kip flared his nostrils and drank it in. Here, at last, was the heart of the Tower, the spirit of the College, all the collected wisdom of sorcery, finally open to him. In his mind he saw himself ensconced in the library for hours on end, learning spells faster than the masters could keep up with him, earning his Selection in the scant two months allowed to him...

"Here is the library." Master Argent had stepped several feet into the third floor hallway and stopped at an ornate wooden door with the terse word "LIBRARY" over it. Carved into the face of the door were enough decorations to render the label superfluous: books, men reading books, and three verses in gold leaf one of which Kip recognized from the introduction to his first book of spells.

"Since you have begun your education in the art of spellcasting, you will be granted access to the library to increase your knowledge. But be warned that only the first set of shelves inside the door is open to you at this time. The books that sit farther inside are still beyond your mastery."

Well, Kip thought, even the first bookshelf was bound to be interesting.

"Just inside the door, you will find two stacks of books. Take one from each. These are to be your spellbooks for the second month of your courses, but if you would like to read ahead," and here his eyes definitely settled on Kip, "you may get started now." That was more promising. Two more books of spells, and ones he could take to the basement and study. "The other books in the library are not to be removed, but you may read them under the supervision of the librarian."

As if the person inside had been listening, the library door creaked open. A gaunt man dressed not in a sorcerer's robe but in a black suit and white shirt with mother-of-pearl buttons stared out at them from deeply shadowed eyes. "This is Florian," Master Argent said. "He maintains the library."

"Hello, students." The man's voice sounded exactly as deep and hollow as Kip would have expected from his appearance, but with a lilt akin to Malcolm's Irish. "It will be my pleasure to assist you in using our library. Provided you treat the books with the respect their age demands."

Florian's hair stuck out white in a fringe around his balding head, and his eyes were a very normal brown. Wrinkles creased the lines around his downturned mouth, and his mottled skin hung in folds around his chin and throat. His eyes lingered on Kip and Coppy, but otherwise he showed no sign that he'd even noticed two Calatians in the group. "Many students in the past have attempted to deface books, or play pranks," and this word was spoken with deliberate slow contempt, "and have discovered that a library is not a place to be..." He drew out the last word as his head swiveled to take in the entire group of students. "Enjoyed."

He looked very human, and yet the moment he'd opened the door, Kip's nose had tingled with that magical feeling. He searched Florian's appearance for anything that would suggest a demonic nature, but found nothing. Still, his nose stung enough that he rubbed it. Coppy didn't seem to have noticed anything.

"If you are ready to proceed," Florian said, "you all may enter."

Only Kip and Adamson, and possibly Emily, seemed honestly pleased to be entering the library. Most of the students made directly for the stack of spell books and picked up their two, and then stood looking at them. Kip and Adamson walked past, straight for the large bookshelf that faced them and the dozens of books on it.

Kip picked one book out at random while Adamson scanned the titles before selecting one. Kip's was *A Specific History Of The Persian Empire, With Particular Detail On The Use Of Sorcery In Colonization.*

He stared at the title and then looked up at the rest of the shelf. They were all history books. Turning to Adamson, he saw the boy holding a book titled *Roads of the Roman Empire.*

"Is this all history?" he said.

"Yes," a deep voice at his shoulder replied. He jumped and turned to meet Florian's eyes. The other strange thing about Florian was that even up close, he didn't have a human scent about him. He smelled of old words and dust, of wood and earth—very much like the library itself.

"Are there other spell books we can read?" Kip asked.

"After your Selection, perhaps." Florian pointed back to the stack of books. "Those should occupy you sufficiently until then."

Kip and Adamson turned to see four books left on the small polished desk. They walked over to it, and Adamson picked up both books from the stack nearest him, handing one to Kip. "Both too eager, I suppose," he said with a rueful smile.

"We'll just have to be Selected." Kip took the book Adamson was holding out and picked up one from the pile remaining on the table to hand it to the blond boy. "Still, there's much to be learned from history."

Adamson took the book and met Kip's eyes. "Indeed there is."

Kip felt that Adamson was trying to communicate something to him that he'd missed, but he didn't have the chance to pursue it, because in his excitement he had let his tail hang down to the floor, and Farley took that chance to tread firmly on the tip.

The two books were the ones that had been present in their examinations: *A Foundation of Translocational Sorcery* and *Altering the Fundamental.* He, Coppy, and Emily paged through them in the basement that night, Emily wrapped in a thick blanket she'd bought in the town.

The first book explained the theories and dangers of translocational magic for pages and pages before getting to any spells. Kip was two pages into the theory when Emily thrust one of her books at him. "Here," she said. "Fire-fox. Learn this one."

The book was *Altering the Fundamental,* and the page she was holding out to him was a spell titled, "Simple Fire." Kip glanced down and then back up at her. "Fire-fox?"

"Your story had fire in it, that one you told me. So isn't it something you have an affinity for, or however it was Master Argent said it?"

"Maybe." He set down his book, picked up hers, and studied the short spell. Something seemed familiar about the words. He bent his head, cupped his ears forward, and murmured the syllables. They rang with familiarity, as though they had been sung to him as a lullaby long ago, or taught to him in a long-ago lesson. He read the first part of the spell, and each syllable seemed to fall into place for him, though he could swear he'd never seen it before. As he read, he thought about fire, about the smell not only of the smoke but of the burning itself, the way it changed the character of the air around it.

His finger traced one of the notes around the spell, which said, *Although spontaneous fire generation is common in children with magical ability, in fact an affinity for fire in the mature sorcerer is quite rare. Unbound magic manifests often with chaotic results and combustible energy, but few sorcerers have the patience and discipline to control such chaos beyond bringing a Flame into existence.* He skipped ahead to the text above the spell itself and read aloud. "This will create a Pure Flame which the Sorcerer must feed with his mind. It will create neither smoke nor ash but requires great will to maintain. It may be used to create a Non-Magical Fire."

"Let's have some heat down here," Emily said.

Kip looked around at the piles of old paper. "You want to start a fire? In here? Where will the smoke go?"

"We'll clear out a spot. And you can make a fire. Go on, Kip, it's below freezing. Even Coppy's shivering."

The otter was not, but he smiled obligingly. "I'll help clear paper if you want to practice the spell."

"I'm not casting fire if Master Windsor's not here." Though in his head, he saw Farley and Carmichael again, outside, saw a simple spell and fire raging around them. That would be a show of force they could not ignore.

"Oh, what's the worst that could happen?" Emily stood, keeping the blankets around her torso, and kicked papers out of the way as she walked to the far wall. "Here. We'll make a clear space here."

"And why am I the one learning the spell? We could all learn it."

"We've not mastered physical spells yet." Emily began shoving paper away and sweeping the stone beneath with her foot. "Eugh, insects again. You're the most advanced, and you made fire that one time, therefore you learn the fire spell."

"Fine." Kip bent over the spell again, reading the syllables to himself and memorizing them. By the time he'd gotten to sleep that night, Emily and Coppy had cleared a small area against the wall, and he could recite the spell to himself with his eyes shut and his paw resting in the otter's warm grip.

Despite the restrictions, Kip and Emily spent a good deal of time in the library that week, Kip because it smelled better than the basement, Emily because it was warmer. Kip could not stay for long; after an hour, the tingle in his nose brought water to his eyes. But he insisted on keeping

Emily company, and in the meantime, Malcolm and Coppy went out to the practice tents to work on their physical magic.

Kip read much of *Altering the Fundamental* that week, though he was not yet ready to try casting any of the spells. Each one was accompanied by a lengthy and often convoluted description of the mental component, and warned that if the spell were not imagined properly, the consequence could be not only failure of the spell, but some irreversible transformation.

All the spells were interesting, but the fire one nagged at Kip, and sometimes he found himself reciting the syllables of the spell in a sing-song undertone without realizing he was doing it until he'd sung it twice through. Once, deeply engaged in reading about the condensation spell he'd attempted during the examination, he actually began to gather magic, only stopping himself when his paws began to glow. Patris had begun to teach them to dispel magic without casting a spell, but the compulsion left him wary of actually casting the spell.

And yet he and Emily and Coppy were casting about desperately for something to distinguish them from the other students, something to bring them to the attention of a sorcerer in search of an apprentice. None of the other students could cast a fire spell, and Kip could not shake the feeling that perhaps he was suppressing his only chance to succeed, especially if sorcerers with a fire affinity such as he thought he felt were as rare as the notes had stated.

Master Windsor, after a week of neglect, began visiting them in the evenings after dinner, and they had asked him whether he would be taking an apprentice. "If one of the students impresses me sufficiently," he said, "which I will be unable to judge until another month has passed." When they asked what they could do to impress him in a month, his lip curled, and he said, "More than you are doing now."

"Not much hope there," Coppy said once the sorcerer had left. "Mostly I'm worried for you two. If I learn to build roads and walls, I'll be happy. I can go back to London and work on the Isle. Not as if our roads and walls are falling down, but they can always use a little help, eh?"

"You're not going back to work on roads." Kip held *Altering the Fundamental* open to the water spell. "You must have some affinity with water, right? Think how much more help you'll be if you can cast water spells."

The otter's whiskers drooped slightly. "Would be nice to get fresh water from the air," he said. "But I've not even mastered the physical magicks yet. How am I supposed to learn that one?"

"With practice." Kip bent over his own book.

Malcolm had taken inventory of the other sorcerers, between his own research and what he'd heard from the boys in his room, and he reported to them later that week as they crowded around the fire in the Great Hall.

"Patris and Master Sharpe work with physical magic. Not too fancy, but Patris is some kind of political marvel, that's why he's Headmaster. There's Master Vendis, he works with translocational magic."

"He's done a lot of exploring westward for the Empire," Kip said. Emily's eyes lit up at that.

"Aye." Malcolm ticked off on his fingers. "There's Master Warrington, he specializes in defensive magic, best I can tell. Sort of alchemical-translocational cancelling out of spells thing."

"Sounds useful," Coppy said.

"Masters Campbell, Waldo, and Odden, they're alchemical sorcerers. Odden works more with demons, Waldo with elementals. Master Argent is translocational but works a lot with demons as well, and Master Brown is another translocational sorcerer. Master Splint is the healer, we saw him the other day."

"Here's hoping we won't have to see him often." Kip exchanged looks with Coppy.

"Then there's the spiritual magic sorcerers." Malcolm spread his hands. "Don't know aught but the names. Masters Jaeger and Barrett. They keep to themselves."

"They all keep to themselves," Emily said. "How are we to impress any of them?"

Coppy indicated the long perches two-thirds of the way up the wall, now bare of hunched black birds. "The ones who're interested send ravens to watch."

Kip thought of the raven who'd met him atop the tower, and wondered again how he might find out which sorcerer that had been. Perhaps he would be willing to take on a Calatian as an apprentice. He certainly had seemed friendly enough, and amenable to Kip's cause. He still wasn't ready to share that with the others, not until he knew more, so he voiced the other thought he'd had while Malcolm went through his list. "So there's someone for all the disciplines."

Malcolm nodded. "It sounds like the best in each one lived in the Tower. Lucky, that."

Flashes of memory: a rumble, a dark night, the tension of fear of what would come next. Coppy leaned against Kip and said, "Aye," sounding tired, and Kip knew that Coppy, like himself, was remembering the night of the attack. They'd avoided talking about it even though everyone else had wanted to at first, and for the most part the others had respected their silence.

The memories must have been visible in their eyes, since humans couldn't ordinarily read their faces, or else Emily had gotten better at reading them. And they knew each other well enough now that she dared to ask again. "Was it very bad, that night?" she asked quietly.

"Not at first," Coppy said.

The noise had come like thunder, but longer, and there was no smell of lightning. Kip and Coppy, in the small attic room, woke side by side and sought each other's eyes shining in the dark.

"Just thunder," Coppy said without believing it.

"It doesn't smell right," Kip replied, nose lifted. He swung his legs out of his narrow bed and checked for the precious spell book beneath it before padding to the window. The new moon offered no light, and clouds hid the stars, so even Kip's eyes could not pick out the shape of the White Tower atop the hill. His fur prickled and rose on his neck and shoulders; there was electricity in the air, but of a different sort. The chill spring air held little scent of flowers, many closed for the night, but the smell of wood and pitch, of stone and earth, and the lingering scents of the people (furred and non) of the town held no trace of menace. And yet, something was different.

He stared through the night until Coppy called out, "Whatever it is, it's over."

Kip's tail flicked anxiously, not believing it. "I'm going outside."

"Why?"

"Just to see."

"Don't climb the hill."

It bothered and reassured him that Coppy knew him that well. "Just far enough to see."

"Whatever it is," Coppy said, "if it's to do with the College, they'll handle it, and Master Vendis will tell your father, and he'll tell us."

Kip flexed his paws, itching to gather magic into them, to do something. He had not heard from Saul since the Feast of Calatus, and wondered if his friend would be able to get word to him if he were in trouble.

Other noises, softer, disturbed the night. He angled his ears toward the open window to catch them. People were stirring: not the Brocks next door, but his parents downstairs were talking, and farther along the street, he heard a door open, footsteps on the cobblestones. "I can't go back to sleep."

"Suit yourself." Coppy yawned. "I've slept through worse than this. The night Napoleon surrendered? Fireworks and singing all night."

Kip scrambled down the ladder and found his father awake in the living room, waiting. "Did you hear it?" Kip asked, excited.

Max nodded. "It doesn't feel right to me. Shall we walk?"

They stepped out into the street, and the sense of wrongness grew. Kip had no idea what time it was, but there was no dawn showing in the east, and the street should have been deserted. Instead, he heard low speech and footfalls all around, scattered but still present, like a gathering of thieves setting a plan in motion.

Bryce Morgan hailed them from down the street with a hissed, "Penfolds!"

The hedgehog stood with the Coopers, a family of dormice, and the Branches, red squirrels. "Thunder," Morgan said, "and yet my spines don't tell me there's rain. I don't like it. Cooper, Penfold, any word from the College?"

Both the dormouse and fox shook their heads. Morgan's brow creased over his small, dark eyes. "That College will be the death of us."

Normally, Max would step in to remind Morgan of the benefits they gained from the sorcerers' protection, but when Kip turned, anticipating the reply, he saw his father gazing up the hill, silent.

"If they want us, they'll send for us," the elder Cooper said.

"A walk up the hill might not be amiss," Max said, and Kip's heart leapt.

"I'll go along," Kip said. "I mean, I think many of us should go. Just in case."

Max laid a paw on his shoulder. "Only Cooper and myself, for now. But I'll have Master Vendis send Brightbeak if you can be of assistance."

Morgan scowled. "Unnatural ravens. Less I see of them in town, the better."

"They serve a purpose," Max said mildly.

"As you do?" Uncertainty made Morgan's words sharp and bitter.

They were interrupted by a hoarse croak, far away, and the hedgehog glowered up with the rest of them. Kip strained to see toward the sound, and eventually five small shapes detached themselves from the blackness of Founder's Hill, speeding toward the town. Wings outstretched, the ravens reached the Inn at the base of the hill and sped along Half-Moon Street, and when they spotted people below them, their croaks became words, and the words they spoke would echo forever in Kip's mind.

"The College is gone!"

"Only it wasn't, not entirely," Kip said unnecessarily. The phosphorus elementals in the fireplace had arrayed themselves at the front of it, remaining quiet as Kip told his story.

"Half the Masters and all the apprentices dead." Coppy, more sober than usual, looked down at the stone and traced a claw along it. The carpet in the Great Hall did not extend all the way to the fireplace, because often the lizards grew rambunctious and sent sparks drifting a foot or two from the edge.

"More than half. And all those tents? Used to be two-story buildings." Kip thought again of Saul's smile. *They put the students in the new buildings and keep the drafty, cold Tower for themselves*, his friend had said, laughing. *They're welcome to it.* Kip had protested that he would give anything to live in the Tower, and Saul had patted his shoulder and said it didn't matter for Kip anyway, because he would only be coming to visit. "When we got here, they were nothing but piles of rubble."

"But the Tower stood." Emily touched the stone as Coppy was doing, looking down at it.

"The Tower stood." Kip's tail flicked across the warm stone. "We didn't know it would last the night."

"Didn't know if any of us would," Coppy said softly. "But there were no more attacks. Not here."

"Any of you here for it?" Malcolm looked into the red glow of the fireplace at the elementals.

"Us?"

"Nay."

"None of us been here longer than a day."

"A month, you mean."

"It's two months, properly."

Kip smiled at the lizards, who now stirred and pushed at each other as they talked. "These three have been here since we arrived, but they're getting more restless and I think they'll be sent back soon. Hodge," he indicated the lizard that had a pattern like a four-leafed clover on the top of its head, "has been summoned several times, and he says they get sent back when their glow fades. Ern and Julienne are newer and you can see their glow is brighter."

"All seem pretty glowy to me." Coppy leaned forward.

"Less than they were two weeks ago," Kip said.

"Too right that," one of the lizards replied.

"Fair faint from chill."

"Missing the Flower."

Emily touched Kip's tail to get his attention, and he flicked it away from her hand. "Sorry," she said. "Do you know all their names?"

He nodded, pointing. "There's Hodge, that's Ern, and Robby's on the left. Chez is the big one, and the one up here at the front is Julienne."

"Are there boys and girls, then?"

Kip laughed. "You try asking them that. I think they just take names the sorcerers give them, if they haven't had one before, or can't remember what they had before, or do and didn't like it."

"Names don't matter," the lizard he'd called Julienne said. "We're all part of the Flower. The names is for you lot."

"I think Julienne got a girl's name because she has a higher voice." Kip reached into the pocket of his trousers and came out with a creased paper. He crumpled it in one paw and tossed it toward Julienne. The elemental lifted her head to watch the paper as it descended, right up until it hit her between the eyes. It fell to the floor, already glowing in parts, and she casually grabbed it in her jaws. Another elemental, Ern, bit at the other part of the paper, causing it to explode in a burst of flame that sent ash spraying out of the fireplace.

"You carry around paper to burn?" Malcolm arched an eyebrow at Kip.

"I bring it up from downstairs sometimes." The fox gazed into the fire.

Coppy drew his knees up and chuckled. "Don't know why you ain't tried the fire spell yet. Seems you're halfway to casting it already."

Kip started to protest and then realized he'd been humming that very spell under his breath. "Anyway," he said, "we all came up the hill, and the Tower was still here. We could only see the top—there was some magical darkness cast around it. Dad said the sorcerers here had done that for protection. So we didn't see anything until much later."

"Did they let people in to clean up?" Emily, too, drew up her knees and rested her chin on them. "I can't imagine how horrible that must have been."

Coppy shook his head. "Offered, we did, but nah. Sorcerers kept much to themselves after that."

"Master Vendis used to come down to the shop. Now he sends a raven."

"If we solve this mystery, aye, that'd get us a Selection, wouldn't it?" Malcolm grinned around at them. "Figure out who destroyed most of this college and all of Prince Philip's down south?"

"I'm certain you're right." Emily brushed a hair back from her eyes. "I'm also certain we could be Selected if we manage to bind a major demon to our bidding. To my mind, that seems more likely to happen in two months."

"We've got resources the other sorcerers haven't."

"Really."

"Aye." Malcolm's grin broadened. "Why, there's not a single woman among them."

Emily's stern expression softened almost into a smile. "Nor a Calatian."

"Well, they have calyxes," Coppy said.

"Not that they'd listen to them."

"Master Vendis does listen to Dad," Kip said.

Coppy inclined his head. "Though he has said that that is an exception and is a result of their being together for ten years."

"Ten years." Emily laughed. "It's like a marriage."

Malcolm chuckled, but the fox and otter remained silent. "I'm sorry," Emily said, touching Kip's tail again. "I didn't mean to offend."

Kip nodded. "My mother used to say the same thing. I think she's jealous."

"Jealous? Whyever..." Emily frowned. "What do the sorcerers do with their calyxes?"

"I think..." Kip hesitated. "I think it involves blood. But it wasn't that. It was a question of loyalty and..."

All three watched him. Emily spoke after some silent seconds. "Your father wouldn't choose the sorcerer over your mother, would he?"

"Well," Malcolm said slowly when Kip remained silent, "and what if he was needed for the defense of the Empire? What if his sacrifice would mean the difference between victory and defeat? Sure, aren't we learning about history and the great battles, the way a single action can turn the tide of a war?"

"That—it wouldn't come to that." Emily turned to Kip. "Would it?"

He thought about what Master Windsor had said in the admission meeting, about history being greater than one person. "Not for any of ours, here." He, in turn, looked at Coppy.

The otter stared down at the stone. "In the month before Napoleon's defeat, there were some on the Isle who went up to the King's and never returned. We put up a plaque at the entrance to the Isle recognizing them for their service."

The four of them let these words die away into the crackle of the fire. One of the elementals still listening to them spoke up. "An' who's going to recognize us for *our* service, that's what I'd like to know."

Whether Farley was occupied with studying spells or discouraged by Kip and Coppy going about in pairs, there were no more attacks that week. At lunch and dinner, the bowls and plates of Kip and his friends sometimes wobbled and lifted from the table, but they soon discovered that hiding them from sight prevented these attacks, and so Emily and Coppy sat in such a way as to block Farley's view of the table, and they ate in peace. On Thursday, their bench rose with them on it, but Coppy gathered magic himself and slammed it back down, for which Emily was grateful once she had, as she put it, gotten her teeth back in their proper places.

They argued about whether to retaliate. Between Kip and Emily and Coppy, they could certainly upend Farley's table and all the benches; Malcolm was in favor of this, but Kip and Coppy did not want to be quite so aggressive.

"If we fight back, they come at us harder," Kip said.

Coppy nodded. "Best to deflect their attacks, show we don't care. Unless they come at us face to face."

"You boys don't have much history with fights, do you?" They were in the Great Hall again, crowded around the fireplace, keeping their voices low, but Malcolm raised his at this point.

"There's no need to snap," Emily said. She sat on the far side, next to Coppy. Kip sat on Coppy's other side, and Malcolm leaned in from the other end of the half-circle, gesturing urgently at Emily.

"I'm not snapping! I'm telling them, if they don't fight back—if we don't fight back, we'll be targets for as long as we're here. Fight back, and we stop this once and for all. And best to do it now, before they get any better at sorcery."

Kip kept his voice soft. "If we fight back, they'll throw us out. Calatians attacking humans? We'd go to jail, or owe them money the rest of our lives."

Malcolm scowled at the fox. "Leave the exaggerations to an Irishman."

"Those things happened to friends of my father. Anyway, if we escalate things, one of us might get hurt." His father's words, but he'd repeated them often enough to make them his own.

"Or one of them might."

"Oh, stop it, both of you." Emily slapped the stone in front of them, her voice low and urgent. "We needn't fight back and we needn't accept it. What we should be doing is changing their attitudes."

"That's what Adamson is trying to do," Kip said.

"So he says." Malcolm lowered his brow.

Coppy leaned back, his thick tail providing support. "To chip down a brick wall like Broadside, it takes longer than three weeks."

"On behalf of brick walls everywhere, I demand you retract those words," Malcolm said.

"The point is," Emily cut across their discussion, "that if we really want to change things, we should be talking to the other students. You," she pointed at Malcolm, "should be telling them that we're regular students just as they are. I'm certain it doesn't help that we're shut in the basement like trolls."

"Which is why Patris did it, I'm sure," Kip said.

Emily nodded. "Regardless of why, it's not a bad place; it only looks bad from the outside. It's private and large."

"Perhaps we should throw a basement-warming party," Malcolm said. "Without ale or wine."

"I am leaving the basement warming to Kip," Emily said, "and you needn't adopt that tone."

"And you needn't adopt that one," the Irishman replied, straightening his back.

Worried that Malcolm was about to leave, Kip put his paws out in a calming gesture. "It isn't a bad idea," he said. "Not the party, I mean, but talking to the other students. Some of them are hostile, but not all of them, and we all go off to our rooms and study on our own. Why not offer to help some of them with their studying?"

"The Masters do that," Malcolm said. "Aye, we're the best in the class— and aye, I'm allowing myself in that group though I'm the least of us—but what have we to offer?"

What had any of them to offer? That was a question they would have to answer, not only for the other students, but also for the masters, if they were to continue studying at the college.

A flutter of wings interrupted the reverie that question plunged them into, and a raven alit on one of the perches above the fireplace. "Kip," it said. "Your father is outside."

The fox rose and stretched. "I'll be back in a moment," he said.

Coppy got to his feet as well. "I'm going with you. I've not spoken to your father since church and I'd like to."

"Another fox?" Chez, the elemental currently paying closest attention to their conversations, spoke up in a scratchy, low voice. "Bring him in. Love to say hi."

The other elementals joined in. "Aye, bring him." "We love foxes, we do." "Maybe he'd bring more paper?"

Kip laughed and drew the last piece of paper from his pocket. He tossed it to the fireplace and said, "Someday, perhaps. I'm not sure how he gets into and out of the Tower; we've never seen him come through the Hall here."

"A back door to the Tower?" Malcolm rubbed his chin. "I'll investigate."

"And I will study." Emily took the translocational magic book from her side and opened it. "I like these spells. They make sense to me."

"That's a good sign." Kip raised a paw, and then turned and walked out, Coppy at his side.

Evening had gripped the world. The autumn night was clear and cold, with stars shining down and a crescent moon overhead that illuminated the stone path and dying grass more than enough for Kip and Coppy to see by. Kip lifted his nose to the air, but the only scent that came to him was the calming fragrance of the trees. He swept the dim line of the forest that surrounded the lawn of the college for any hiding figures, but nothing moved. Toward the orchard, there was a dim white shape that drew his eye, but it didn't move nor appear alive at all.

He pointed it out to Coppy. The otter squinted. "Don't look like aught to worry about."

"Not Farley under a sheet?"

"Never seen Farley stay still so long."

"Aye," Kip said. He stared, but still the thing didn't move.

"Probably a cover they put down over some plants." Coppy began to walk. "I'll keep an eye in that direction."

"I suppose." Kip's breath gathered in front of him as he exhaled, and then dissipated slowly. He walked behind the otter, glancing at the shape until they turned the corner.

His father waited outside the dining tent, as before, and greeted Kip with an embrace, rubbing his muzzle alongside his son's. "You're doing well?" he asked, and turned to embrace Coppy as well.

Kip nodded. "We got new spell books and new spells to learn."

"Which ones?"

Coppy grinned. "Kip likes the fire spell, but hasn't dared cast it yet."

Kip's tail flicked, and he lowered his ears. "It's dangerous. I want to be sure before I try."

"Don't wait too long." His father patted his shoulder, but the older fox's muzzle creased in a smile.

"Did Master Vendis say anything about us being Selected?"

Max hesitated. "He said that it was too early for any of the masters to make up their minds." His ears lowered. "He also said he would not take you or Coppy. I offered to leave his service until your apprenticeship would be over, but he thought his sorcery would suffer in the meantime. I'm sorry, boys."

"We'll have to impress someone else," Coppy said, and patted Kip on the arm. "Eh, fox?"

"Aye." Kip smiled with more confidence than he felt. "How's the town?"

"Oh, things go well enough." His father spoke casually, but Kip saw the flick of his ears, the way his eyes slid to the side. "I let Johnny take some days off so he can work with his mother as well."

"Is he not learning the business quickly enough?"

Max shook his head. "It isn't that," he said. "Johnny's bright. He has other things to occupy his time, that's all."

"And you're able to manage the store by yourself?"

"I get by."

Kip frowned. "Is business doing well?"

His father nodded. "Good enough." He rubbed his paws down the front of his shirt, smoothing the fabric, and then tugged at one of the laces near the collar. "Your mother has some relatives in Peachtree, and they say they need help rebuilding if Prince Philip's is to be restored. We might take a vacation to go down there."

"Down to Georgia?" Kip frowned. "I don't remember hearing about relatives there."

"There's a fox family named Shanton." The older fox lifted his paws to his muzzle and blew on them, then dropped them to his sides. "They're descended from your great-grandfather's brother, who came over to America with him last century. After the attacks, your mother reached out to the town and found them."

"Oh." It seemed strange and sudden, these relatives out of nowhere, but it made sense that his mother would have been reaching out to help those in need, and after all, the Calatians of Peachtree were now a community without sorcerers to defend them. He glanced at Coppy, who seemed unaware that anything about this might be strange. "When would you go?"

"We haven't decided. The next boat from England is due in a month, so perhaps another month after that. There are usually slow times between boat shipments."

The slow times were when his father liked to work with perfumes, sometimes go out on day hikes for plants and other ingredients. "Are there other plants you could bring back from Georgia?"

"I'm reading up." Max smiled. "I'm going to go to Forman's in Boston—you remember them?"

The grand perfume shop, the bright glass windows and marble flooring, the elegantly dressed clerks and the jovial shopkeeper. Kip had not been allowed to walk alone on the streets of Boston, but had brought bottles and boxes down from the shelves that his father had sniffed before consulting with the tall, taciturn Mr. Forman. Kip nodded, and his father went on. "George said I might consult his library if I wished. I shall see what his books know about Georgia herbs and florals."

"All right." Kip felt a tingle in his whiskers that had nothing to do with cold or magic, a feeling he remembered from the night of the attacks, a feeling that something was wrong behind a shroud of darkness he could not penetrate. But his father's easy manner was as effective a barrier as the magical darkness on the hill had been, and so he did not resist the change in subject when his father asked how he was getting along.

He wanted to mimic his father's casual ease, to hide his trouble with Farley behind a similar curtain, but Coppy spoke before he could. "Farley's Farley," he said. "Those kind never change. He threw rocks at Kip, but Kip handled it well."

And then Kip had to recount the incident, sparing the details of the kicks he'd received so as not to worry his father overmuch. Coppy went on to say, "Malcolm wants to have it out, but Kip won't do that."

"Good," Max said. "This fight isn't with Farley. You know that."

Kip did, sort of, but he inclined his head and cupped his ears forward, letting his father explain. "It isn't a case where you've wounded him personally."

"It is, rather," Coppy put in.

"With Farley, yes, but the issues underlying it are different." Max straightened. "If it were only that you'd stolen a chicken from his farm…"

"Dad!"

Max smiled. "Among ourselves, we can laugh at the jokes. The point is, if it were a mundane matter, eventually a fight would settle it. But the tension between you two is not so simple. If he drives you out, he'd turn his malice on Coppy. If you were both gone, he would find another target. And likewise, if you drive him out, there will be others waiting to take up his arms. The only way in which you can win this fight is to strike at its cause."

"How do we do that?"

"If I could tell you, we would already have done it. Look to the agitators in Boston who seek to change Massachusetts Bay's status in the Empire, not with a war of force, but with a war of words."

"The ones who are in jail, you mean?" Kip couldn't help asking.

"Not all are in jail, and the ones in jail are not dead. John Adams takes advantage of his standing with the Crown to remain free and vocal." His father shook his head. "What those agitators are trying to do is change attitudes. They seek to make people believe that Massachusetts Bay—that all these colonies—should be free and independent, willing partners with the Empire rather than subjects of it. Most people will not follow them; why should they? The Empire is all they have known. So Adams and his friends try to change the beliefs of those here, to show them the benefits of freedom.

"There is no blueprint for what you two are trying to do. You must show the sorcerers the benefits of accepting you. You two must change their conceptions that Calatians cannot do some things. Farley is not the enemy."

"He's *an* enemy," Kip growled.

"He throws a mean rock," Coppy said. "An' he's learning sorcery now."

"Defend yourself, but do not allow this fight to become your priority. You can also lose your status at the college if you fight too often, and Farley doesn't lose as much as you do if he's also expelled."

Kip folded his arms. "I won't get thrown out."

His father gestured toward the tents. "This is a large, faceless enemy you fight, and it will take a long time to win even a small battle. It is capable of swift, devastating attacks, and you must always be on your guard."

The thunder, the darkness, the rubble…Kip swallowed and nodded. His father's scent on the air held no fear, only assurance and a small amount of worry. "I'll try."

"Aye," Coppy said, as serious as Kip had ever seen the otter.

"I wouldn't be telling you this," Max said, "if I did not believe you were capable of succeeding."

Though he looked at Coppy as well, his eyes came to rest on Kip, and the fox knew that he bore the weight of his father's hopes and expectations. If Coppy succeeded while Kip was sent home, they would be happy for him, of course, but Kip would still feel a failure. He was the one who had mastered more spells, he was the one who led their class after nearly two weeks of study, he was his father's son.

"Kip," Coppy said, and the change in tone was audible even if Kip hadn't noticed the otter's tightened shoulders, his whiskers flaring outward, his attention fixed on something at the corner of the Tower.

"Go on, Dad." Kip embraced him quickly. "Coppy's got an eye on them."

His father looked past him. "Is that Farley?"

"Yes. We're outside the Tower, alone—you should go."

"I'll fight with you."

Kip shook his head violently. "He knows sorcery now. Coppy and I can handle him."

"He's not doing anything," Coppy said. "Not yet."

Max nodded quickly, and then held up a finger. "Remember what I told you."

Kip still had not seen the shadows behind him, and the breeze was wrong for him to smell anyone, but he felt them at his back. "I will, I will. Go!"

His father turned and hurried toward the gates. Kip spun to face the direction Coppy was looking, already gathering magic and cursing himself for not doing it earlier. He saw the lime-green glow of Farley's magic, saw Coppy's turquoise beside him, but nothing was flying through the air at him, nothing approaching from—

He whirled around, expecting something from behind him, but perhaps that was giving Farley too much credit. No rock shot at them from out of the darkness. No movement at all, in fact, save for his father walking toward the gate, pulling it open...

"Kip!" Coppy called, and in that moment Kip was distracted. He turned his head, saw out of the corner of his eye the green-glowing arms pointed straight at him—and then on his other side, quick motion, a thud, another thud, and the clang of iron on iron.

He spun back and faced the closed iron gates, a form lying prone beyond them. "Dad!" he yelled, and ran for the gates.

Now his nostrils burned with cold, tingled with magic. He reached the gates and pulled, but they would not shift. Desperate, he rattled off the spell, seized them, and pulled back, but still they would not open. Behind him, he heard more noises, but all he cared about was on the other side of that iron. "Let me out!" he cried.

"Steady on," a voice said beside him. "You'd only to ask."

The gates released. Kip forced himself through as soon as there was room between them, and ran to his father.

The older fox lay on his side, breathing, but unresponsive when Kip touched him and called his name. He gripped Max's upper arm and then saw the awkward angle of his father's forearm, a bend in the fur where there was no joint. He turned his muzzle back to the gates and saw the demon who'd greeted them on that first day watching him through the bars.

"Get Master Splint!" Kip called.

"Get him yourself." The demon mocked his tone. "I owe you nothing, nor him either."

"Coppy!" Kip did not want to leave his father. He stared past the demon, searching for Coppy's turquoise glow, but saw nothing. At least Farley's lime-green was gone as well; probably the spell to slam the gates on his father was all Farley'd managed before Coppy had taken care of him.

Kip leaned down to his father. "Dad," he hissed. "I gotta go."

But he hesitated. The demon watched both foxes with cold eyes, and Kip had initially thought his father would be safe with the demon keeping watch. But the demon had let Farley come in with a wild fox and gut it, and had just said he owed Kip nothing. And his father lay outside the gates. If Carmichael were waiting somewhere for Kip to go get help...no, he could not leave.

But he remembered then that someone was watching him. "Master Vendis!" he called.

No raven came down out of the night. Kip called again, while the demon watched him with a smile. Coppy did not answer either; the otter must be occupied with Farley. Kip had heard the start of a fight, perhaps, but now the night was silent when he was not calling out into it.

He stamped the dry ground, his breath a fog in front of his nose. If only he could summon a raven without leaving his father's side—

His eyes traveled up the Tower. And then he cursed himself and held out his arms, gathering magic into him again.

Lifting himself was trickier with his father in his arms. The spell bore the brunt of the weight, but holding the older fox was still awkward. Legs and arms spilled out, and while Kip was careful to keep the injured arm still, he didn't know what other injuries his father might have suffered.

He floated them through the gates under the eyes of the demon, who closed them after him, and down over the lawn. Up close to his father, he stared down at the closed eyes and slack jaw, and almost flew them into the corner of the Tower because he wasn't paying close attention. His eyes blurred; he wanted to wipe them, but couldn't with his father in his arms.

Coppy was coming out the front door as Kip rounded the corner. The otter looked up and gasped. "What happened?"

"The gates." Kip swallowed. "Farley slammed the gates into him. We were prepared, so he attacked Dad."

Coppy gaped, and then his paws clenched into fists. "The filthy beggar ran away before I could do anything. I came back, but he'd run upstairs. I'll go find him now, that's for certain."

"No. Hold the door, please." Kip maneuvered himself and his father carefully to the stoop and through the great double doors.

"No magic allowed in the Tower," Coppy said, and Kip glared at him until the otter dropped his eyes.

"Don't want you to get in trouble," he muttered.

Emily and Malcolm had looked up from the fire and now ran over to Kip, asking the same questions. "Someone get Master Splint," he said urgently over them, and Coppy ran across the Hall carpet, away to the stair.

He didn't let go of the spell for fear that he would have to take his father upstairs. Emily helped guide him over the carpet and Kip lowered him nearly to the ground while he told them what had happened outside."

"I told you," Malcolm said tightly. "You've got to speak a language he understands. Me da used to say, a well-placed fist can be worth a year of trouble."

"It can also cause a year of trouble." Emily bent over Max. "He's still breathing, at least."

Focused on the spell, Kip didn't want to say any more. He stared at the back corner of the hall and waited.

An eternity later, Coppy returned, the scarecrow-like red-haired sorcerer behind him. Though the otter hurried across the room, Master Splint walked deliberately. "What's been going on?"

"We were attacked," Kip said. "He was attacked."

Splint, closer now, knelt beside Max. "Is there sorcery in use here?"

"Er, yes," Kip said, but a voice interrupted him.

"Aye, a physical spell upon the two foxes, cast by Penfold."

The four students looked around, startled. Master Splint did not seem disturbed. "Thank you, Burkle," he said. "Penfold, you may release the spell."

Kip let go, and watched his father sag to the carpet. He sat down himself, partly to be nearer his father, partly because all of his energy had vanished with the spell. The sense of urgency had passed now that the healer was here to take care of his father, and his fear and weariness overtook him. Anger was there, too, below the surface; it would keep until later.

The four students remained so quiet while Master Splint examined Max that Kip heard the soft brush of Master Vendis's long black robe arriving behind Master Splint, but Kip did not look up. "What has happened here?"

Kip waited for someone else, anyone else, to respond to the high voice. But Coppy only said, "Farley attacked him..." The silence pressed in on Kip's ears; even Master Splint was no longer murmuring, his hands still on Kip's father. Kip folded his ears down, stared down at his father's closed eyes.

"Did anyone witness it?"

"I did." His voice scraped against his throat. He pressed fingers to his eyes, squeezed them shut, opened them again and looked up. "Dad...Max was leaving. Farley cast a spell and slammed the gate into him."

Master Vendis's face did not register the astonishment or fury that Kip might have hoped. His brow lowered, and so did his voice. "Why?"

"Because of me, I suppose." Kip thought about his father's words, how the fight was not only between the two of them, but he'd been wrong. The fight was between him and Farley, and the attack on his father was an attack on him. He could see it as clearly as though it were a spell written down. Just as the fox in his tent had not been an attack on the fox, this attack was designed to hurt him in ways that physical magic could not. His fists tightened. Maybe it would not be the best course to eliminate Farley. But at this moment, that was all he wanted to do.

Max stirred, then, and opened his eyes. He frowned, looking up, and struggled to get up. Master Splint held him down. "Lie still," he said shortly. "I've not quite finished."

"What happened? I remember..." His eyes met Kip's. "We were talking. I thought I turned to leave..."

"You did. You got hit by an iron gate."

Master Vendis said, sharply, "You are certain it was Broadside?"

"Yes," Coppy jumped in before Kip could speak.

Kip echoed him. "I saw the glow of his magic."

The sorcerer rubbed his goatee. "I will attend to this," he said. "Max, you are well?"

"I feel well." Kip's father looked up at Master Splint. "Am I?"

"Your arm is mended, and your head is healed. There was something in the tail that did not feel right to me—a muscle pull, perhaps."

The fox's long tail curled and uncurled against the floor. "Yes. Thank you."

"Welcome." Splint got to his feet. "You've provided service to the Tower and been assaulted in the course of that service. A small amount of relief seems warranted."

"Very well." Master Vendis held down a hand, which Kip's father grasped as he got to his feet. "I shall escort you out myself."

Kip scrambled to his feet as well. "I'll go—"

"No." Vendis held up his other hand. "I think it best that you remain here, if indeed your presence is making a target of your father."

"But you'll be with him." Emily had gotten to her feet as well.

"It's fine." Kip reached out to grasp his father's arm. "I'm glad you're well."

"No ill effects." His father leaned forward, his nose an inch from Kip's. "Remember what I told you."

Kip nodded. Master Vendis had said he was going to take care of things, and all Kip felt now was weariness, a desire to go downstairs and fall into his bedroll and sleep.

"We're glad too."

The foxes, and all the others, looked down at the fireplace. Two of the lizards, sparking orange, stared up with eyes like embers. "Hate to see someone go cold."

"Especially someone you like."

"Looks like you, he does."

"Glad we got the chance to see him."

"Even if we didn't meet properly."

"Next time, aye."

Curiosity stirred in Kip; was 'going cold' like death for the phosphorus elementals? But he couldn't bring himself to ask the questions. His father and Master Vendis headed for the door, Master Splint turned toward the stairs, and Coppy's paw gripped his elbow. So he followed the otter and his friends to the basement stairs, still numb.

"I told you, best thing is to take the fight to him," Malcolm said. "Drop one of those lovely wooden benches on his head. Even after Splint heals him up, he'll think twice before he comes for you again."

Kip shook his head slowly. His heart agreed with Malcolm, but his father's words bound his anger tightly, and fatigue dragged his feet and his spirit. He stumbled down the stairs, letting his friends' concerns and advice wash over him, and kicked his way through the grime of the basement to his bedroll.

Lying back while Coppy, Emily, and Malcolm discussed the evening in tones they probably thought he couldn't hear, he stared at the stone of the ceiling. The idea of becoming a sorcerer seemed laughable to him now. Did he think he would be able to succeed at no cost to anyone? Already the town had turned against his parents because of his dreams, and now his father had been injured, possibly almost killed. He had heard of people losing parts of their memory, but hearing his father say that he remembered nothing after turning away from Kip, not the walk to the gates nor the iron swinging shut on him…it chilled Kip even more than the stone that lay below his thin bed.

He turned his head slightly and his eyes caught a flash of red. The small book, the journal he'd found. His paw reached up and snagged the edge of it, bringing it tumbling free. He caught it deftly and opened it to a page. The narrow script blurred before him, but he blinked once and it became clear.

to lift the stones and keep them aloft.

December 8

I have come to understand that I must needs demonstrate my value beyond simply learning what we are taught. If I am to continue my education and become a Master, not simply a bricklayer, then I must not only excel in the classroom; I must reach farther. Master de Lassen has reminded me that I need not convince all the Masters, nor yet half of them, but merely one, and while it is true that Master Fitch detests me and would like nothing more than to see me cast out into the street, it would take but a single word from one of his colleagues to assure me of a place.

And so I search for the Master whose interests run parallel to the course that most intrigues me. It is difficult, for this course of study is not one that is encouraged much in the College, but there are six Masters who engage with it, and there I must focus my attentions.

Master de Lassen, a foreigner himself, sympathizes with me, though the French people are not as hated as mine. Should I follow his course of study, I might well take the place of his current apprentice, but alchemical magic, especially of the variety he practices, does not call to me. Master Cork is engaged in the study of demonic spirits that might be summoned to channel great power, but his work is quite popular and he is certain to choose one of the attractive, popular boys when the time comes, though my talent matches theirs.

And yet, I would say that the difficulty of spiritual magic is a point in my favor. Should I master it, there will be little anyone might say against me. Even were I to show simple affinity for it, that is rare enough to be worthwhile.

Kip turned the page, then set the book down as Coppy entered their little sanctum and lay down next to him. With a scrape, Emily's door closed, and though he could hear her moving about if he concentrated, he could also ignore the sounds out of politeness. "How you feeling now?" the otter asked softly.

"Fine." Kip waved a paw at the journal. "Reading a book I found. The journal of Peter something. He was an apprentice two hundred years ago."

"Oh." Coppy was silent a moment. "What do you suppose Master Vendis will do about Farley?"

"I don't know." Kip was torn between irritation that Coppy wasn't more interested in the journal and relief that the otter hadn't asked more. He was thinking about the advice Peter had gotten, which was similar to the advice Kip had worked out with his friends: they had only to impress one master. And Kip had an affinity, that was certain. So he had to start casting the fire spell, and impress someone with it. That would seem to be his only hope for remaining in the College.

And, a voice whispered in the back of his head, it would certainly sort out Farley, wouldn't it? And it would protect his father, keep him and the other calyxes—and Calatians—safe from harm. An old memory of flames leaping up, dancing around him, came to mind, and Farley was yelling and running, and though Kip in the memory was terrified, Kip in the present closed his eyes, leaned against the otter in the next bedroll, and smiled.

CHAPTER 11: FIRE

The next day, before class, Master Patris made an announcement. Kip, refreshed after sleeping through the night, curled his tail excitedly and sat straight up to listen. Coppy, too, smiled, and even Emily seemed optimistic. Only Malcolm, sitting next to them, said, "He won't do nothing. Wait and see."

Patris began the speech with a vague reference to the attack on Kip's father, referring to it as an "unfortunate incident," and explained that the calyxes were valuable to the College and the sorcerers, and that no further attacks on them would be tolerated.

"Valuable," Coppy muttered, "like paper or ink."

"More like washerwomen," Malcolm said.

"To that end," Patris said, "while I hardly feel we need to reiterate the injunction against harming any others with our magic, because of the current situation and tensions in this class, I feel we must take additional measures. Therefore, all calyxes will be transported to and from the Tower by secure means for the remainder of this year. I hope all of you will think more clearly before you engage in activities that will create more work for the Masters of this College. We have too much work as it is for the small number of us remaining."

He was looking at Kip as he said that, and Kip's heart raced. For a moment, he had trouble parsing the words. Was Patris blaming *him* for the attack on his father? His paw shot into the air before he could stop it, and Patris saw it. He opened his mouth, but Kip began talking before the sorcerer could.

"What about the person who attacked the calyx, sir?" he said. "Is he going to be punished?"

Several of the students turned to look at him. Behind him, Coppy hissed, "Shh," but Kip's eyes remained fixed on Patris.

"The discipline of other students is not your concern, Penfold."

"Because it sounds like you're blaming me and my father for the attack on him."

Patris's bushy eyebrows lowered. "If you are concerned about student discipline, Penfold, keep talking and you will experience it firsthand."

"Kip," Coppy hissed, "shut up!"

Kip clamped his muzzle shut, but continued glaring at Master Patris. The sorcerer returned his glare with equal amounts of contempt, and Kip felt a surprising relief. *Good,* he thought, *at least we are both clear on where we stand with each other.* The next moment, he felt shocked; had he really confronted the Head of the College so boldly, after all his father had warned him about?

"Take your books out," Patris said, "and practice raising your cubes again."

Kip opened his book to the spell, but didn't look at the page. He gathered magic and recited the spell, lifting the cube into the air. *Lifting cubes,* he thought, *yes, I can do that. And you'll be surprised when you see what else I can do.* As his cube rose, his eyes slid over to the fireplace where the lizards sprawled happily.

That night, he took *Altering the Fundamental* out to the practice tent, though he did not think he needed the book. The fire spell, once he concentrated on it, ran through his head constantly now.

"Hurry up and try it." Emily had come along with him, as had Coppy. Her voice shook with the cold. "I'm f-freezing."

Out in the practice tents, they did not need a sorcerer to supervise, but of course none of the other students were out in the tent that night; the past two nights had brought frost and even their basement was warmer than the tents atop the hill, which did not completely keep out the night wind that often scoured the College.

Kip set the book down and prepared to cast the spell, but then looked around at the canvas of the tent. "What if it gets out of control? I don't want to burn the tent down. Not with you inside."

"I'll wait outside, then."

She made as if to leave, but Kip said, "No. Imagine what Patris would say if I burned the tent down. I'd better do it outside."

"Wherever you like," Emily said, "only quickly, please."

They hurried outside, and here Kip had no more excuses. He gathered magic, raised his purple-glowing arms, and then recited the words. Five seconds passed. Then ten.

"How long do you think it should take?" Emily asked, politely.

"It didn't work. I can still feel the magic." It buzzed inside him, uncomfortably, demanding to be used. "At least we finally learned how to dispel it."

Coppy rubbed his paws together. "Maybe you got the words wrong."

"No." But Kip looked at the book this time, which he could read in the light of the purple glow. He said the words again, trying to remember how he'd fit magic to the words of the physical magic spell. All he recalled was one day reciting the words and feeling the magic click into place. But that had been after trying every day for a month.

There was no click this time. The ground remained cold and dark. His throat tightened for a moment and the sense of unfairness that always lingered at the edges of his mind overwhelmed everything. That Farley had learned to slam iron gates in a week while Kip's progress remained as slow as ever felt like nature obeying the laws of man. Maybe Calatians learned too slowly to become sorcerers, even the most gifted among them.

Or maybe Kip simply was not one of the most gifted. "Well," Kip sighed, swallowing the bitterness at the back of his tongue, "at least I can practice dispelling magic."

Patris had taught them relaxation, letting go of the magic and returning it to the earth, and while it still felt strange to Kip, at least that he could manage. "How," Emily asked, "did you get rid of magic before you learned to cast your first spell?"

"I didn't." Kip lowered his arms and tried not to let his shoulders slump. "I studied the spell first and the first time I gathered magic, I cast it, only I wasn't good at focusing, so a lot of it bled away, I think? I'm not sure how it works exactly. But that first physical magic spell was easy; it was gathering magic that was harder."

"Don't tell the class that." Emily sounded very pleased with herself.

"Maybe Master Windsor can tell you what you're doing wrong." Coppy hurried to keep up with them.

They walked the next several steps in silence over the cold hard stone. "I'm certain he could," Emily said finally. "If he wished."

Kip glanced to one side and mimicked the sour master's voice. "What you're doing wrong is not casting the spell," he intoned.

Coppy snorted, and Emily let out a surprised laugh. "You'd best not be doing that inside the Tower," she said, holding the door for him.

"Or even outside. There might be demons or ravens about."

Kip shook his head. "No demons. Ravens, probably."

"How can you know there are no demons?" Coppy asked as he followed Kip inside.

"They—well, I think they make my nose tingle."

The woman and otter both stared at him as the great doors swung shut. "You can *smell demons?*"

Kip shifted his feet. "Maybe. I'm not sure. But I noticed it when sorcerers were about, only not all the time. Every time demons are about, though...I think it comes from them."

Emily gestured about them. "Are there demons in the Great Hall now?"

"I don't know. Probably?" But he turned his head and then shook it. "No. I don't think so."

Certainly there were no other people in the Hall; judging from the sounds, or lack thereof, everyone had retired to their rooms for the night. Kip greeted the elementals in the fireplace and they replied with their usual enthusiasm in breath that smelled of ash with the acrid odor of phosphorus amid the smoky warmth of the fire. He closed his eyes but still saw the brightness, still felt the fire near him through more than the heat. It was the smells that meant the most to him, so he sorted through them: phosphorus, so strong that it overpowered whatever individuality the elementals had; wood, which the lizards ate or sprawled on; the ash the wood burned down to; and a smell behind all of those, a hazy tang that Kip thought might be the fire itself.

"Maybe this is what I was missing," he murmured, though he didn't really believe it.

"I'll go get Master Windsor." Coppy winked at Kip. "At the very least, it'll put him out and that's worth it."

He turned to go. Following his steps, Kip's attention landed on the empty, cold fireplace on the other side of the hall. "I'm going over there. If I try to cast a fire in here, I don't know if I could tell whether it worked."

Emily exhaled and pressed her hands to her face in the Great Hall. "I'll wait here," she said, sitting by the active fireplace. "Tell me when you're about to cast the spell and I'll turn around."

The phosphorus elementals protested, but Kip turned from them and crossed the hall. There was no tingle of magic in his nose, and the hall was quiet once Coppy walked up the stairs. Kip sat before the disused fireplace, cross-legged on the stone, and swept his tail around his legs. He looked into the dark, cold space, at the ashes on the floor of it, and inhaled.

Here he could imagine fire, here he could see it licking at the wood logs whose imprints lay in the pattern of fallen ash. He could envision it dancing, glowing, burning, and more, he could see himself controlling it. He could smell it, the ash and the heated air, and out of all his senses, it was the smell that made it the most real. He closed his eyes and folded his ears down, shutting out sound and light and believing in the reality of the fire before him. *I need this*, he thought. This would be something he could proudly show off to a Master, this fire he had created out of his mind; this would be something that would distinguish him, something that would assure him of a Selection…

His paws stretched out before him, and his body tingled with the gathering of magic, though he didn't recall having triggered it. Purple gathered around his fingers and ran down his arms in bright streaks that joined like streams into rivers and then dazzling suns. Behind him, Emily's voice echoed, but the rush of power dancing through him drowned out her words; the scent and reality of the fire in front of him consumed his awareness. He spoke words as familiar as his own name, poured his power into the spell and molded it with his vision, and with all the strength of his will and the force of his need, he called the fire into being.

It blazed forth in the hearth, with an explosion of light and heat that would have startled him had he not been holding it in his mind a moment before. Though he was barely two feet from the licking flames, close enough that his whiskers curled back from it, he didn't flinch. The fire was his, and he was a part of it.

Then a hand wrenched him back and he became aware of the world again. "For God's sake, put it out!" Emily hissed at him. "Before Windsor comes down!"

Behind her burbled the appreciative words of the phosphorus elementals, and in his euphoric state, he gave them more weight than Emily's "It's not hurting anyone," he said, reaching out as though to caress the flame with his fingers. "I've got it under control."

"Wonderful," Emily said. "Lovely. Then put it out and start it again in a moment. You'll be punished otherwise."

Punished? For bringing this flame into being? Kip struggled to understand, as her grim expression battered its way through his triumph. "I suppose you're right," he said, and reached out to loose the spell. But he hated to do it, to let go of this fire he'd created, as though it were a friend he'd only just met and now had to bid farewell to.

Footsteps sounded above. "Kip!" Emily hissed.

He sighed, the euphoria completely gone now. In fact, he was starting to wonder how he'd been so incautious as to cast the spell without waiting five minutes for Master Windsor…though the fire *was* lovely. At least he still had a chance to escape without punishment. With a twist of thought, he broke the spell.

And the fire blazed on.

"Kip!" Emily wasn't bothering to keep her voice low now.

"I tried!" He reached out with arms bereft of any magical glow, cast about for a spell that no longer existed. "I broke the spell!"

"Well—" Emily stared at him, then turned to the fire. "Reverse it! Or something. I don't know, you're the one who knows it."

Reverse it? He had no idea how to do that, but it was better than sitting around staring at a fire that was only growing, now threatening the edge of the carpet. He took a breath, and the tingle of magic now exploded into his nose. Despite that, his concentration was good enough to have his paws glowing purple again just as a familiar voice rang out in the hall.

"What is going on here?"

Master Windsor strode from the stair to the fireplace, Coppy hurrying behind him. Kip stepped back from the fire as the man drew alongside him, his sour face furious.

"There's a magical fire in the second hearth," a voice said behind Kip.

"Thank you, Burkle, for stating the obvious." Windsor's cold eyes never left Kip's, and the even ice of his voice was more frightening than if he'd yelled. "Am I to presume from your proximity to the hearth and the glow of magic about you that this is your doing? Or did you stumble across it and were about to attempt to put it out?"

For a half-second, Kip thought he could make that story work. But that was what Windsor was baiting him to do. "No," he said, letting magic drain away from him. "I started it. I was trying to put it out."

"I thought Patris had taught you basic spell cessation." Windsor gestured with one hand, and then his expression went from anger to confusion. "Penfold, exactly what spell did you cast?"

Kip recited the spell without pushing magic into it, and Windsor stopped him before he'd gotten halfway through. "Yes, yes, I know that one." He narrowed his eyes and turned toward the fire, which was now licking up the sides of the stone walls. "Burkle," he said, "fetch Master Odden."

Odden, a rotund, bearded master, was not one Kip had spoken to yet. But the footsteps that came a moment later on the stair were too light and too soon to be his. Windsor turned with a frown that became a sigh, and leaned in close to Kip. "Do not speak," he said. "I will handle this."

Master Patris burst forth from the stair, robe askew, hair disheveled. "Who's burning down the Tower?" he cried, and skidded to a halt when he saw the fire. "Windsor—Penfold." He pronounced Kip's name with all the usual distaste, and a small addition of fear. "Windsor, what are you allowing him to play at? Look at that fire! It's growing!"

"I was not present when the spell was cast," Windsor said, and Kip's heart, which had for a moment entertained the possibility that he might escape punishment, sank again. "But both Penfold and I have attempted to banish the fire, without success. I have sent for Odden, but there appears to be no immediate threat."

"No threat? No threat?" The white-haired sorcerer gestured, and the carpet edge flew back from the fire against Kip and Windsor's ankles. He gestured again, and his eyes widened. "A fire that our magic cannot extinguish? How is this not a threat? Even stone can be made to burn, and if this fire grows—"

"What fire?" Odden levered his bulk down the stairs and into the Great Hall. His eyes skimmed Windsor and Patris and came to rest on Kip. "Windsor?"

"Penfold has cast a fire, and none of us can extinguish it. We were not here when he cast it."

"And it keeps growing!" Patris snapped. The waves of fear coming off him made Kip's nose wrinkle.

A breeze against the fox's tail pushed back both the scent of the Head's fear and the flames, at least for the moment. Kip didn't dare look away from Odden while the sorcerer was staring at him. "Well?" the bearded man said. "What did you do, Penfold?"

"I cast the fire spell from Altering the Fundamental," Kip said quickly. "Exactly as it was in the book. I tried it outside and it didn't work there. I just…I can't stop thinking about it and I knew Master Windsor was on the way, so I cast it in a fireplace. I didn't think there'd be any harm."

"You broke the spell?"

"Yes." Kip gained a small bit of confidence at Odden's calmness and belief in him.

"Hm. Allow me to try as well. I know a few tricks with fire."

The large sorcerer turned his attention from Kip to the flames for a moment. However he was gathering magic or casting spells, Kip didn't know, but after a few seconds, his frown deepened. After another few, he reached up to scratch his beard. "Whoever is pushing air at the fire, stop it. It isn't helping."

"It's the only thing keeping it back," Patris said.

"You are feeding the fire," Odden replied equably, "and it is more likely to explode that way. You could pull air away from it, but it is a magical fire, and there is no guarantee that would work. Have you tried Blackstone's Uunraveling?"

"Of course not." Patris's face reddened as the breeze died away. "The creature has barely had a month of instruction; he's not likely to have added bindings to his spell."

Kip's fists clenched, but before he could say or do anything, Emily laid a hand on his arm and squeezed, and that allowed Odden time to answer. "We are all of us God's creatures, Patris. That this *student* has introduced an unexpected and ultimately harmless element—"

"Harmless!"

Windsor interposed. "While I would not characterize the action as completely harmless, it certainly seems unlikely to become an inferno engulfing the Tower. Now, Odden, if you…"

His words trailed off as Odden murmured a series of syllables, at the end of which the fire vanished.

The air around them chilled instantly. Kip almost cried out at the loss of the fire, at the cold, dead ashes that replaced it, and indeed behind him he heard the phosphorus lizards lamenting its banishment. But Emily's grip on his arm relaxed, and Coppy, beside him, exhaled. Even the tension among the sorcerers lessened. "There," Odden said.

"There remains the question of how this—how he managed to bind his spell." Patris ran a hand through his hair in a vain attempt to subdue it; it remained bristled out rather like Kip's tail when he'd been scared.

"I didn't cast a binding," he spoke up as the sorcerers turned to him. "I cast the fire spell just like it was in the book."

"Burkle, can you verify this?" Odden asked.

Burkle's voice piped up, thin and high. "Aye, sir. Wasn't paying much attention, and it's been an age since I cast a fire spell—"

"Well." The large, bearded master waved a hand to quiet the demon, and examined Kip. "Cast it again."

"What?" Patris actually took a step toward Odden before stopping himself. "Have you gone mad?"

"I was about to suggest the same." Windsor's sour tone sounded aggrieved that Odden had beaten him to it. "There are three of us here, and we have demonstrated that we can control the fire. What harm is there in it?"

"There are two of you here." Patris swept his robe around himself and then glared at Kip. "And one student who will bring food up from the Inn for the next week as punishment for casting spells in the Tower without supervision. See Master Sharpe in the morning before class. And you, Windsor, you're responsible for anything that happens."

With that, he stalked away and up the staircase. Windsor and Odden exchanged looks in which Kip thought he saw a small measure of frustration, but the only words spoken were by Odden. "Go on, Penfold," he said.

Emily released Kip's arm. He cleared his mind of the worry of how he was supposed to bring food up the hill and called magic to him. The words of the fire spell returned to his mind even as the purple glow began to wreathe his paws, and he sent all of his magic into it, hungering to see the flame again. But again, nothing happened; his arms remained glowing and purple and the hearth remained cold and dark.

"Certainly—" Master Windsor began.

Kip interrupted him without thinking. "No, I'm sorry, I know what I did wrong."

Again he cast the spell and this time he let the scent of the fire fill his head. Magic sang inside him and the spell came out with ash and flame around every syllable.

The fire exploded to life with a fierceness that made all of them flinch, all of them but Kip, who had expected it and reveled in it. The elementals across the room cooed in delight.

"Very nicely done." Odden looked pleased. "Now, extinguish it."

Kip found it easier this time to break the spell. Whatever pleasure he'd gotten from casting it the first time, whatever pride he'd taken in the fire, both were muted by the situation and by the repetition. If he could indeed call this fire whenever he wished, then breaking the spell wasn't banishing it forever. He released the spell, and the hearth lay cold and grey again.

"Fascinating." Odden stared at the ash.

"I dislike mysteries," Windsor said. "Penfold, you spoke it exactly the same way?"

"Yes," Kip said. "It's stuck in my head. I couldn't not."

The sorcerer turned on Emily. "I don't suppose you have the perspicacity to recall the previous spell as compared to this one?"

"I don't suppose perspicacity has anything to do with it," she retorted. "But as far as my limited training allows, they sounded the same to me. Would this binding spell make it longer?"

"Aye," Odden said. "Though it can be prepared ahead and then activated."

"I was with him for a good bit of time previous, and I don't believe he prepared anything." Emily folded her arms.

"I didn't," Kip put in.

"The spell and extra power must have come from somewhere." Odden rubbed his beard. "Even beyond your clear affinity for fire."

Windsor's head snapped up at those words, but Kip spoke before Windsor could. "Sir," he said, "I have felt a burst of extra power here, back when I first arrived."

Briefly, he explained what he'd felt the first time he'd touched the Tower. Odden turned to Windsor and said, "Why have we not been told about this?"

"Ask Patris or Argent," Windsor said. "I'd not heard it myself." He stared at Kip keenly. "Did you feel a similar sensation tonight?"

"No, but I was feeling very…very excited about the fire, otherwise I certainly would have waited to cast it. I was carried away, I suppose, and I might have missed something else happening." There had also been no voice this time, but as he hadn't told anyone about the voice the last time, he felt that was not a critical component.

"This is an interesting problem." Odden regarded Kip for a moment longer, then turned to Windsor. "Delighted to have it resolved. Feel free to call upon me again should any more questions of fire arise."

He turned to leave. Kip watched him with some regret; it had felt good to hear another master praise his abilities, and now he didn't know whether he would be able to see Odden again. An idea sprang to his mind. "Master Odden?"

The portly man turned. Kip had been about to ask whether he needed an apprentice, but his mind supplied a better question even as he opened his mouth. "Would you have the free time to instruct me on the uses of fire? Only it seems quite dangerous for me to experiment on my own, and I would not want to trouble Master Windsor for more of his time than he is already generously allowing us."

Odden raised a hand to his beard and stroked it. "In the King's College, you know there is a workshop devoted to fire spells for just that reason." His eyes met Windsor's and Kip thought there was something there he didn't want to give voice to. "I suppose if Master Windsor has no objection, then—"

He hadn't even finished the sentence before Windsor was gesturing with a pale hand. "By all means. It will allow me to focus more attention on those who need it." With a stare in Coppy's direction, the tall sorcerer strode out of the hall.

Odden didn't spare any attention for Windsor's departure, nor did he seem to notice Coppy's expression or Emily's hand on his shoulder. "Very well, Penfold. Shall we say Tuesday evening for our first session?"

"Yes, sir." Kip let his tail hang free to wag behind him, a rare luxury when he was sure Farley wasn't about. Even though he had to serve a punishment, he still felt the whole evening had gone rather well.

Emily and Coppy were inclined to agree, and Malcolm when they told him. "Food comes up Monday and Thursday, so you've got to take a morning walk twice," the Irishman said. "If you care for company, I'd go along."

"And me," Coppy said.

"I'll stay in bed, thank you." Emily smiled at them. "Not that I wouldn't enjoy the company, but I see you gents quite enough as it is."

"Boys' morning out it is." Malcolm clapped Kip on the shoulder. "We'll show Patris."

"I wouldn't put it past him to forbid me from enjoying the experience," Kip said.

"Oh," Emily said, "And Kip in a very by-the-way sort of manner has told us that he can smell demons."

"Potent gift." Malcolm whistled and turned to Coppy. "Can you as well?"

The otter shook his head. "But I can't smell half the things he can that aren't magic."

"If I ask you if there are demons about," Malcolm turned back to Kip, "will you tell me?"

"Of course." Kip grinned. "We're in this together, aren't we?"

"For sure and we are." Malcolm reached out and clasped the fox's paw.

When Kip visited Master Sharpe in the morning, he was told that although most food did come up only twice a week, milk and bread came up daily. Still, a week of morning walks did not seem as harsh a punishment as Patris had perhaps thought it was, especially with company. The conversation with the sneering, condescending Master Sharpe, who spent a good deal of time on the value of the food and on instructions so unnecessarily detailed that Kip felt as though he'd already spilled the milk twice, might actually be the worst of the punishment. Kip did learn from it, though, that Farley had been tasked with fetching the food the prior week as punishment for his attack on Kip's father. He couldn't help but think that attacking someone with intent to harm was far worse than experimenting with sorcery, and shouldn't incur the same punishment, but Sharpe was unlikely to be sympathetic to his complaints, so he kept them to himself.

At the Inn, Old John's son Gabriel greeted Kip, Malcolm, and Coppy, and showed them to an irregular pile of twelve crates. "Usually it just up and vanishes," Gabriel said. He squinted at Kip. "You been magicking it up?"

"No." Kip raised his paws. "That's translocational magic. All I can do is levitate."

"And start fires," Malcolm murmured, and Coppy elbowed him before Kip could.

"I'm serving a sort of punishment." Kip tried to keep Gabriel's attention.

"Ah." The tall young man, a few years Kip's elder, leaned against one of the crates. "Hope it's all worth it. There was another fight yesterday. Marshal Winters brought 'em in here to sort 'em out."

Kip's ears folded down and his heart pounded even as his chest went cold. "A fight about me?"

"Aye." Gabriel warmed to his story. "The dormice, two of them, plus that squirrel they're always with…"

"The Coopers," Coppy said. Technically David, the red squirrel, was a Branch, but he had been living with the Coopers for so long that people included him with the family name now.

"Aye, and the Porters. The other mice. They was going on even when they was in here about the College bein' a corruption in the town and how you was makin' everything worse." He kept his eyes on Kip, neutral. "But the Coopers, they said you wasn't doing this for yourself but for all the Calatians, and it was a good thing. The Coopers, they go up there, don't they?"

Kip nodded. "Tom and Amelia are calyxes, yes."

"Ah." Gabriel nodded in satisfaction. "So that's what the other mice meant by calling them 'traitor.' That's when the squirrel threw a punch."

The fox's stomach turned, though he hadn't eaten anything yet that day. Coppy, too, remained silent, and finally Malcolm rescued them. "It's a fine time we're spending here and sure, I'm never one to refuse a story, but as the fox said, we're serving a punishment and so much though we regret it, we'd best be moving along. Kip?"

"Aye." Kip pulled in magic and tried to think about how he was going to manage twelve objects of different sizes. "Do you think you two can take some of the boxes? I don't want to stack them…"

His two friends eyed the stack, and then Coppy turned to Gabriel. "Have you got a table we could borrow?"

Gabriel seemed as confused by the question as Kip. "Borrow? Aye, we've a table with a broken leg I'm to mend today, but…"

"Stack the crates on the table, then lift the table," Coppy said. "All you need do then is keep it level."

"Smart," Malcolm said, and Kip squeezed Coppy's shoulder gratefully.

"By the by," Gabriel said as he helped them stack boxes onto the table Kip had levitated, "what happened to that woman who was to be boarding here from the College? Did she go home?"

"She's boarding with us," Coppy said.

"In a separate room," Kip added quickly.

"Oh, aye." Gabriel dropped a box and lifted the last one to join it. "We didn't hear a word from the College and we didn't keep the room, of course."

"And why should you?" Malcolm asked. "If they've not the courtesy to notify you it's not needed, you needn't have the courtesy to notify them it's not available."

Gabriel wiped his mouth and then looked at the three of them. "So you're sharing quarters with the young woman?"

"Only these two," Malcolm said.

"And she has a separate room," Kip repeated.

Gabriel didn't react to that. "Aye, well," he said, "if she's trying to be a sorcerer, I suppose she'll be judged by the Lord God right enough."

"As will we all." Malcolm started toward the youth, even though Gabriel had the advantage of four inches and probably thirty pounds.

Kip held Malcolm back. "The young lady is a friend of ours, and we are all of us trying to learn sorcery for the betterment of the Empire and New Cambridge, so last May's attack will never be repeated."

That got to Gabriel; his face went dark and he met Kip's eyes. "If you can do that," he said, "I'll not hear a word said against you."

"We've done it so far," Coppy said with a big smile, and after a moment, Gabriel returned the smile.

Levitating the table up the hill was harder than it sounded, until Kip figured out halfway up that he could also sit atop the table. So he sat at the edge, tail hanging off and flowing in the chill autumn breeze, and then Coppy and Malcolm said they were tired of walking, so they squeezed up beside him, and the three of them rode all the way up to the gates, where Kip made them all jump down so it wouldn't seem like they were having fun.

At lunch that day, Adamson approached Kip and asked in a low voice if he might have a private word outside the tent. The fox made sure that Farley and Carmichael were both still quite occupied with their meal (a loaf of bread), and nodded once.

"There have been rumors about the school," the young man said once the tent flap had fallen shut behind them, "that you started a fire that it took three masters to extinguish."

His eyes searched Kip's, and the fox resisted the urge to boast. "Only one master," he said. "But he was the third to try."

Victor rubbed his chin and scratched where it looked like he hadn't shaved in two days. "Odden." When Kip nodded, he went on. "It was a clever trick, however you managed it."

Kip began to protest that he hadn't managed it, that it had been an accident, and then he caught something, perhaps a light scent or a glitter in the other's eyes, and he decided that he didn't have to tell Victor everything. "I—well, to tell the truth, Master Odden thought much the same thing. He's beginning private lessons with me tomorrow."

"We've not even begun alchemical magic, much less defensive magic. Would you perhaps be willing to sit down with me and walk through what happened? I am most interested in the science of sorcery, and you are the only student capable of having a satisfying discussion about it, save perhaps Jacob Quarrel."

Even though you can't even gather magic yourself, Kip thought, and then felt ashamed of himself. "Why don't I have a few lessons with Master Odden first," he said, to put off the decision, "and then I will discuss what I've learned with you."

Victor nodded and pushed back his hair. "I shall look forward to it." He gave Kip a smile, and the words and the smile brought back again a memory of Saul. But Saul wouldn't have left Kip to spend time with Farley. They'd been friends, the two of them, at least as close as a human and Calatian could be.

Or was that true? Emily and Malcolm treated him as an equal, and that did not remind him of Saul as much as Adamson's insistence that he could remedy things between Kip and Farley without any tangible evidence of doing so.

It didn't matter, anyhow. Saul was dead, his body probably still lying beneath the rubble of one of these tents, perhaps even the dining tent they were standing outside. There was no benefit to be gained from stirring up those memories. He had Coppy, Emily, and Malcolm, and he found that he cared less and less whether Victor Adamson was able to control Farley Broadside.

Tuesday evening, on the way to his lesson with Master Odden, Kip passed Master Windsor on the stairs. The dark-haired sorcerer, lost in his own thoughts, barely even moved to make room for the fox. Kip, only too glad not to engage him in conversation, hurried up and crossed the Great Hall in high spirits.

It wasn't until he'd put a paw to Master Odden's door that he caught the scents inside and remembered which students were housed in Odden's chambers. Not that it mattered; even if Napoleon himself waited beyond that door, Kip would pass him to get to his private lesson. He opened the door.

Three pairs of eyes turned to him from two desks and a bed. The students unfortunate enough to share quarters with Farley were hunched at their desks and looked pale and skittish, like rabbits when an eagle passes overhead. Farley, by contrast, lay on his bed on the other side of the room.

"Ey," he said, stirring as Kip came through the door. "Humans only. Get out before we skin you."

The rote threat was delivered in a bored tone. Only when Kip stepped farther into the room did the youth stir his bulk and sit up. "Not joking," he said, and stuck out a leg, which Kip easily avoided. "This is our quarters. Get your filthy flea-ridden hide out, you damned animal."

The smell that arose from Farley's bed as he moved invited a retort, but Kip bit his lip. "I'm here for a lesson with Master Odden," he said.

"Like hell." Farley hit the floor with a thump behind Kip, and despite himself, the fox hurried his steps to the Master's door.

"It's Kip Penfold, sir," he called, knocking. "I'm here for the lesson."

Farley's odor filled the air behind him, but at that moment the door opened with a waft of peppermint tingle. Kip stepped through, turning to allow himself the satisfaction of seeing the gaping jaw of Farley disappear as the door swung shut behind him. Then he lifted his muzzle and stood as respectfully as he could, taking in every detail of the room he'd entered.

The first Master's office he'd ever set foot in lived up entirely to his expectations. Around the walls rose bookshelves crammed with thick leather books and papers, interrupted only by a long oak desk at which Master Odden now sat, covered with more papers and a small copper pot. Near the back of the room, a raised platform had been cleared of everything save a small pile of kindling, and Kip's pulse quickened when he saw it.

A burst of heat from Kip's left drew his attention to a small brazier, and when he looked down at it, he saw a sleek glowing phosphorus elemental looking back at him. "Good evening," he said.

"Oo, I like this one," the elemental said. "Got manners. What's yer name, love?"

"Kip Penfold," he said.

"Penny is rather new," Master Odden said, setting down the paper he held, "and I doubt that your fame has reached her ears, even if she were capable of remembering it."

"I'll remember his name, see if I don't," the lizard hissed.

"Now," the sorcerer said, as though Penny hadn't spoken, "come over by the kindling, Penfold. You may sit if you like."

There was no chair near the platform, so Kip remained on his feet, tail curled around one leg, attentive. Odden gestured to the kindling. "We shall begin with the basic fire spell, and once you have cast it, see if you can break it."

The spell no longer dominated Kip's mind as it had two days ago, but the words remained familiar. He gathered magic and breathed in the scent of wood. His mind turned the dry wood scent to crackling ash as he recited the spell; the hot crackle of fire bloomed in his mind.

Heat brushed his fur. Fire burned merrily around the kindling, and Kip reached out to it, though his fingers became uncomfortably hot when they were a foot away. Behind him, scrabbling against the copper brazier evinced Penny's interest, but she didn't make a sound.

"Now," Odden said, "extinguish it."

Kip hesitated a moment, then broke the spell. The fire went out, leaving the room darker and colder.

"Hah." The sorcerer leaned back in his chair and stroked his beard. "Again."

Again Kip brought forth fire, and again extinguished it. Master Odden made him repeat the practice once more, and then said, "Enough."

Kip turned his attention to the desk and the sorcerer. Penny took advantage of the silence to say, "Could do with a bit more of that kind of magic about," but again Odden ignored her. Kip, though, turned to meet her eye and smiled, and to his surprise, she winked at him.

"Cast your mind back," Odden said. "Something must have happened differently, and while its cause might not be in you or the words you spoke, you might have borne witness to it. What was different about that first time?"

Kip closed his eyes and tried to remember. "I was excited to cast the spell," he said. "I'd never done it before, and it was—I felt driven to do it. Coppy had gone to fetch Master Windsor to supervise, but I couldn't even wait that long."

"And you've not felt that way since."

"No. I still love the fire…" He breathed in the smoky reek that normally grated on his nose; now it felt encouraging and uplifting. "But it doesn't… possess me as it did then."

"Interesting choice of words. There was no other difference that you can recall?" Kip shook his head. "Very well. Then we must conclude that either your emotion and excitement added some binding to the spell, which was broken by an ordinary unraveling, or that some outside agency influenced both your emotions and the fire. While you are certainly not the usual student, and the effect of the magical blood in your body must be taken into account, I do not believe that your emotional state has the power to affect a spell thusly. It is not unheard of, of course. It is told that the Great Feat of the Rolling Rocks came about when the chief of the people who became the Visigoths faced the destruction of his entire tribe, and that he poured his desperation into them. But that is a rare example, and besides, he was an accomplished sorcerer. The others I know of all resulted similarly from extreme duress under external forces. Notably absent in your case. So I lean toward the second explanation, of an outside agent that affected both your mood and the spell. Demon or sorcerer, that's the question here."

"I don't believe it was a demon, sir," Kip said, and then stopped, because he wasn't certain about being able to smell demons and didn't want to reveal this ability.

Odden smiled. "Of course we would like to believe that our actions are all our own, but one can never be sure. In any event, Burkle keeps an eye out for demons and did not report any, so I will cautiously agree with you. And that leaves sorcerers. None of the current apprentices have that level of ability—well, unless—hmm."

He drifted off in thought, staring past Kip to the wall of bookshelves. "Tell me," he said, "did you come up from the basement to cast your spell, or in from outdoors?"

"In from outdoors, sir."

"Did you encounter a figure in a white robe?"

Kip frowned. "No, I don't believe so." His mind flicked back to a white shape in the orchard, but that had been days previous.

The sorcerer nodded slowly. "I believe I have learned enough to make my own inquiries. Thank you, Penfold."

The words had a note of dismissal, and Odden began to turn his bulk back to the desk. Kip cleared his throat. "Sir?"

"Eh? Hm?" Odden answered without looking back.

"I was—that is, I understood that there were to be further lessons?"

"Of course, if you like. Tuesday and Thursday, we said?"

"Yes, sir." Kip exhaled. "And one more question, if I might?"

Odden didn't move, but didn't say no, so Kip went on. "Are you in need of an apprentice?"

Now the sorcerer did turn, and Kip thought he saw the beginning of a smile. "Are you offering yourself?"

"If you would have me."

"Hmm. Hmm." Odden regarded him up and down. "Well, Penfold, look here." He held out a hand. Three seconds, and fire blossomed in his palm. His eyes met Kip's over the fire.

The fox reached out, meeting heat as real as the fire he'd created. "Touch it with your mind if you like," Odden said. "Know it."

With his mind? Kip frowned, started to gather magic, but as soon as purple flickers appeared over the black fur of his paws, Odden said, "Not with magic. Like magic."

Like magic. Kip drew magic from the earth, he knew. Did Odden mean…?

He raised his eyes to the sorcerer's, dark behind the dancing reflection of the flames. The bearded face gave him the barest of encouraging nods.

So…what if he focused that attention on the fire? Tried to draw magic from it as he did the earth? He stared and reached out tentatively and found—

—a welcoming hunger, a drive to consume but not a malicious one, simply the nature of devouring as magic was the nature of change—

—and he drew in a warm breath and looked up to Master Odden's eyes. The bearded sorcerer smiled. "Ah, I thought as much," he said, and the flame went out. "Penfold, you have begun to know fire. Sorcerers with a true affinity for fire are rare and precious, but there are sorcerers who simply like to burn things, which is not the same. If you can learn fire enough to hold it in your hand…" He waved his fingers, which showed no ill effects from being in close contact with the fire. "Paw, what have you. Hold it for as long as I did just now, and I will certainly Select you, no matter what Patris wishes."

Kip nodded. "I will practice it."

He walked out past Farley's increasingly agitated taunts, ignoring them as effectively as if they had burst into flame moments after leaving the young man's mouth. He barely felt the stone beneath his paws, all the way down the stairs and to his bed.

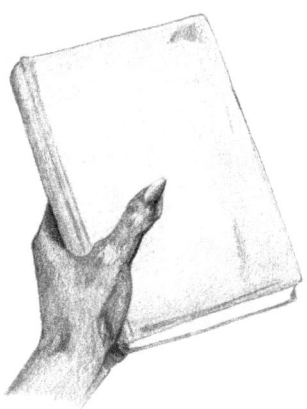

CHAPTER 12: WOMAN'S TOUCH

Two days later, as Kip returned from his second lesson, Emily surprised them all with some news of her own. "Master Argent says he is inclined to Select me," she said with a smile, tossing her hair.

They all gaped, Kip and Coppy and Malcolm. The Irishman was the first to recover his tongue. "He told you this, did he? And how did this happen? Simply walked up and asked you to be his apprentice?"

"Not exactly." Her smile took on a faint smugness. "I have been talking to him about how interested I am in sorcery and how impressive it all is and how much I am in awe of what he's doing and if perhaps I slip in the odd compliment about how attractive he is, well..."

"Aye, 'well.'" Malcolm folded his arms.

Emily did pause, but her smile lost none of its smugness. "Today I showed him some of the strides I have made in learning translocational magic. And he said that I had shown quite enough aptitude to be an excellent apprentice."

"That's not all you showed him, I'll wager," Malcolm said with a glance at her neckline.

"It's wonderful." Kip reached out to clasp Emily's hand in his paw, beaming. "See, there's two of us with hope, and nearly a month still for the other two."

"In view of the rest of the class, I'm not terribly worried." Malcolm's expression didn't change. "For myself, I mean."

"No, of course not for yourself, but if you'd failed to notice, the rest of us aren't exactly the kind of student a Master is accustomed to taking on." Emily's smile did disappear now. "So perhaps you could have a little sympathy."

"That's not what I meant," Malcolm responded, just as sharply. "And besides, as me ma used to say, 'tis better to be garbage than Irish in New York, for at least if you're garbage, someone will pick you up out of the gutter."

"Please," Coppy said. "We all want to get chosen. I'll work hard and maybe I'll have a water affinity or something like Kip's fire…maybe some master will want me."

"You're a sight better than everyone save Quarrel, Carmichael, and, well, Broadside, though I hate to say it. The brute's got a talent for throwing things around." Malcolm grimaced, his attention off Emily, and perhaps that was Coppy's intention, because the otter relaxed and leaned back on his tail.

Emily went to bed early that night, walking a little stiffly, and Kip pointed that out to Malcolm as they sat under one of the sconces while Coppy studied on his bedroll. "Maybe she snapped at you because she's having her monthlies?"

"Is she?"

Kip nodded. "I think so. She's wearing perfume but I caught a hint of blood. She bathed yesterday and today."

The Irishman grimaced. "Friend, I wondered that myself when I first met her. But with many weeks more since then and no change in her sharp tongue or wit, I'm forced to conclude that that is merely her nature. And knowing Emily, I wouldn't expect her to use her monthlies as an excuse for anything she said, so even if it is true, I'll shoulder the blame. I shouldn't have spoken so about her and Argent. Even if that's true as well."

"If one of the Masters had a great liking for Calatians," Kip said, "I wouldn't hesitate to use that to my advantage."

"Even if he wanted to do to you what Argent no doubt wishes to do to Emily?" Malcolm kept his voice low.

Kip glanced in Coppy's direction, but the otter didn't make any sign he'd heard. "Why not? For one thing, I don't believe Argent will ever actually get to do to Emily what he wants. And for another…if it's the only way I'd get to study sorcery, of course I'd do it."

Malcolm nodded. "Aye. I believe you would. And for what it's worth, I believe I would as well. Sadly, there's as little hope of a Master swooning over an Irishman as a Calatian."

When Malcolm went up to bed, Kip fell onto his bedroll, but he was not quite tired enough to sleep. Coppy lay in his bed with *Introduction to*

Sorcery and Kip didn't want to disturb him. Restless, he reached up for the red journal again, wondering if Peter Cadno had any experience that might help Coppy with his selection.

> *struck my fingers with such force that I have not been able to write in this book for two days. And yet he was met with only mild reprimand, whereas my every transgression, however slight, is punished and ridiculed. There are days when the practice of sorcery is a joy to my heart that shields it from every sling and arrow; there are days when black clouds fill my sky and I know that no matter what I do it will never, never suffice.*

> *January 28*

> *I have recovered some of my good spirits thanks to Master Primus. For several days the attack on me rendered me dispirited enough to forego my attempts to speak to the Masters on the topics of their research. But today I sought out Master Primus, who has always been kind to me, and I spoke about the attraction of his work in spiritual magic. There was some connivance to it, but also risk, for Primus is not well liked at the College, and gaining his favour might mark me forever outcast. But I do not delude myself into thinking that I do not already bear that mark, or that I could ever shed it, and Primus has no apprentice, nor is likely to find another in the present group of students. I was careful not to imply that he and I were of a kind, only that the same thoughts appealed to us both. In truth, I find his research implausible and distasteful, but it is no more than I would do to be allowed to study sorcery.*

> *January 30*

> *My mother tried to bring me a basket of bread and apple wine today but was turned away at the door. I was told of it only this evening or I should have gone to prevent it, even risking that they might not allow me to return. I had not realized until I heard the news what a powerful feeling her presence inspires in me and how much I miss her—and indeed any of my family. Our home*

There the page ended, and Kip closed the book, thinking on the January 28 entry. Aloud, he said, "Which sorcerers have we not met?"

Coppy looked up from his book. "Jaeger, Barrett, Sharpe."

"I've met Sharpe." Kip grimaced. "Who else?"

"Ah...Warrington, Campbell, Waldo, Brown." The otter's eyes gleamed. "Did I miss any?"

"I don't think so, but we can ask Malcolm tomorrow."

"Why?"

Kip tapped the red journal. "Peter seems to have tried talking to a sorcerer nobody liked who was doing distasteful research. It was spiritual, though."

"I don't even know what the sorcerers we have met are researching. And I'll never get spiritual magic, never. I can't even make fire, Kip."

"Neither can Emily," Kip said reasonably.

"Speaking of, she was making more remarks about the chill down here. Have you any ideas?"

Kip shook his head. "I can make a fire but I have to sustain the magic ones, and the non-magic ones smoke."

"What about just heat? Can we get heat from somewhere?"

"I'll ask Master Odden." Kip set the book aside. Again, Coppy hadn't even asked who Peter was. "In the meantime, let's think of ways to find out what everyone is researching and maybe if there's someone nobody likes."

Friday morning, though, before he could put any of the plan into effect, Kip had to serve the last day of his punishment. Malcolm and Coppy did not accompany him this time, though they did walk him to the gate in case Farley was about. Friday was a light bread and milk day, and Kip could handle it easily on his own.

Old John himself pointed Kip to the boxes and added, as he did, "Tell your father I've an order going to New York next week should you need to send a message there. It'd be no trouble."

"Thank you," Kip said automatically, and then flicked his ears. "A message? Why would Dad need to send a message to New York?"

"Potter told me he'd sent to Boston already, so I guessed he might appreciate a message to New York as well." John raised a hand and made to leave.

"One moment." Kip stepped toward the heavyset man. "I mean, why would he send a message?"

"To the Calatians there." The old man's forehead creased. "To the other fox families. Surely your father...I mean, I heard two days ago..." John read his confusion, and the lines in his forehead vanished, replaced by pity. "You've not been told. I'm sorry, I shouldn't be the one..."

Kip's chest chilled so much that the words of the fire spell raced through his mind. "Tell me, please."

"Well..." The man spoke slowly. "I have heard that the Cartwrights have broken off the engagement of their daughter to you."

"Oh." Kip didn't need to ask why.

After a moment, John put a thick hand on Kip's shoulder. "Sorry, lad, but there are other foxes, you know. Ones who will take pride in what you're doing."

Slowly, the fox shook his head. "If they can't take pride here, with the College as our neighbours…" He bit his lip and resisted the urge to run to the Cartwrights' house that moment. "Thank you for telling me, John."

"I'm sorry," the innkeeper said again. "And do tell your father about the message."

"Aye," Kip said. "Thank you for that as well."

He brooded all the way up the hill. At times like this, he felt he knew what Peter meant about despair. Even if he won the regard of the sorcerers, it seemed it must come at the expense of his ties to New Cambridge and the community he'd grown up with. As he trudged up past the maple trees whose leaves were edging from gold into brown, his first thoughts were angry: if the town didn't want him, then he didn't need the town. Once he had learned sorcery, he would be able to travel the world and find a wife anywhere who would be happy to bear his cubs and continue his name. It was exactly the familiarity with the sorcerers that made his fellows here so wary of them.

But the greater the distance between him and the town, as the slope of Founders Hill eased up to the gates of the College, the more his thoughts turned to repairing what he'd done. The thought of confronting the town was overwhelming, but he could not just sever ties, not when his father and mother still lived here and would continue to do so, not when any wife he did find, be it in New York or London or Calcutta, would most likely return here to live.

He told only Coppy about the news, and laid out his dilemma: to abandon the town and focus on his studies, or to devote significant energy to changing the minds of the people of New Cambridge.

The otter rubbed his whiskers and grinned. "Aye, well, changing the mind of a town is no easy thing. But who says you must change all the minds? Seems to me the most urgent need is with one family. Just as we search for one sorcerer to take us on here at the college, you know?"

Kip stared and then laughed. "Coppy, you're a genius," he said. "I'll send a message to the Cartwrights today."

And yet, Coppy's genius did not manifest itself in other areas. Under Master Windsor's glare, he continued to struggle with control of physical spells. Malcolm had been right when he'd said Coppy was a better sorcerer than ten of the students, but unfortunately, he practiced with three of the six who surpassed him, and Master Windsor never failed to remind him of it.

"Three seconds," he said after Coppy's levitated marble dipped and wobbled. "As I recall, Miss Carswell had surpassed three seconds of stability the first week of spellcasting, and Penfold has never held one for less than, what was it, Penfold, twelve?"

Neither Kip nor Emily answered; the one time Kip had pointed out that Coppy could hold a rock for ten seconds when Windsor wasn't present, the sorcerer's sharp nose had whipped around, and his dark eyes had fixed Kip like an insect with a pin. "Well, then," he said, "I shall remand Lutris to the class of students destined to be sorcerers who cast their spells only under ideal conditions. I believe they study on a tropical island paradise, attended by young maidens and fed ripe fruit whenever they desire. If that sounds like the sort of school Lutris should be attending, then by all means I will not prevent his leaving Prince George's to seek it out."

Emily had tried once to soften Master Windsor's attitude, as Kip imagined she'd talked to Master Argent. "Must you be so cruel?" she asked softly, leaning in after Windsor had scolded Coppy again.

The sorcerer turned to meet her eyes. "Miss Carswell, I assure you that I am quite competent as an instructor and evaluator of students. There is no need either to protest Lutris's competence or to push your own under my nose. Master Argent and I have quite different tastes."

Indeed, Windsor was hardly less sarcastic with Kip and Emily, but as they began practicing new disciplines, his cutting remarks had complimentary edges to them. Like: "Your fine control over your fire is as underdeveloped as your mastery of the basics is impressive." Or: "Miss Carswell, based on your quick mastery of the basics of translocation, I would have expected you to at least be able to start a fire by now."

Outside in the tent, Kip and Emily both worked to keep up Coppy's confidence, but as November drew nearer, the otter resisted even those forays outside. "It's freezing out," he said, "and I'll be good enough to become a road-layer in three weeks. Patris will be glad to be quit of me."

"But we won't." Kip felt the twin aches of losing Coppy and the otter's indifference to their separation. If only he were cleverer, he was sure that a solution would manifest itself.

"You've got plenty to worry yourself with, what with holding fire and heating the basement, not to mention the classes." Coppy smiled. "Once you're as good at translocational magic as Emily, you can come visit me."

"I will," Kip said, but that alone did not satisfy him.

The Tuesday after Kip had finished his punishment, he entered Odden's study with burns on his paw and a question. Farley had spit on his tail as he'd passed, and he'd kicked one of Farley's books across the floor, but the exchanged attacks felt formulaic and did not weigh on his mind.

"Penfold," Penny crackled as he came in. "See, I remember."

Master Odden turned from his desk as Kip greeted the lizard with a small fire spell in the brazier, something he had thought of on Sunday. Penny's eyes brightened as the magical flames licked about her, and she crawled up to the edge of the copper bowl. "Oh, too kind, too kind! The air is so cold and that feels like a warm breeze, it does."

"If you've finished play," Odden intoned, "I thought we might work on fine control tonight." He gestured to the platform, where single branches lay side by side.

"A question first, if I may, sir." Kip clasped his paws together.

"You may have Splint see to those burns." Odden raised an eyebrow. "Still no luck?"

Kip shook his head. "But my question is about how to bring heat to the basement. Are there any heat spells? Perhaps one that is not so draining as fire?"

Odden shook his head slowly. "Fire brings heat, and heat is tied to fire."

"I know, sir. I was thinking perhaps about opening a doorway to a fireplace that would allow heat to come through."

Penny poked her head up. "Oi, you should just call a skipper."

"A what?" Kip grinned; the lizard looked like she might overbalance the brazier.

"A skipper. Like me."

Odden waved a hand. "Summoning an elemental is too advanced. It requires a sense of the home of the elementals, a summoning ritual, and a binding spell."

"Can't I just cast a binding on a magical fire? Like whatever happened that time in the Great Hall?"

Again the sorcerer shook his head, but more slowly, as he did whenever Kip brought up the Great Hall fire. "The binding holds the spell, but you must still feed the fire with your will. When an elemental is bound, it supplies the will, and the binding is much easier to hold."

Kip nodded. "Can you teach me the summoning and binding spells?"

The sorcerer examined him for several seconds, then shrugged. "You have two and a half weeks to Selection. If you wish to spend them on summoning rituals, I will not prevent you. But neither will I waste my own time. I will give you the spells, and you may practice them under Windsor's eye or, as I would recommend, out of doors."

"Aye," Kip said. "I'd not wish to set one of these 'skippers' free in our room full of paper."

Later, he would wonder whether the door to Odden's office had been open a crack, but as he returned to the basement that night, his mind was full of spells to learn and faint hope. Master Windsor impressed upon him that under no circumstances was he to attempt to summon an elemental without a Master present, and instructed Coppy and Emily to physically hold his muzzle shut should he go into the sort of trance that had led to the Great Hall fire.

"No fear," Kip said, and the others agreed.

He spent the remainder of the night reading the spells and memorizing them, and when the lights were turned out, he lay in bed and recited as much as he could remember in his mind. How would he find a scent to associate with summoning? Would the tingle of magic be enough, or would he need to hold the rich phosphorus scent of an elemental? What about the binding? The problem so held his attention that he did not hear the creak of the door, not until Coppy sat up and said, "What was that?"

"What was—?" Kip's concentration broke as a bright flare appeared at the doorway. He only caught a glimpse of it through the shelves, and then it fell out of sight, but not for long. Footsteps hurried up the stairs, and firelight flickered off the walls, growing brighter quickly. A moment later, the smell of burning tickled his nose.

"Fire!" Coppy scrambled from his bed, and Kip hurried to follow.

What had begun as probably a single match was now a fireplace-sized fire. The dry paper burned quick as tinder, and the flames did not finish consuming one before reaching for the next. Kip and Coppy stared across a sea of fuel at the flames, and then almost without thinking, Kip reached out into the fire. *Hello, heat, hello hunger*, he said, and when he closed his eyes, he saw the fire even more clearly. Its raw power snapped at him, beckoned him to join. For a moment he reveled in the connection, and then realized he had to put the fire out. How? Was it as simple as turning off a spell?

No, he found. Emily cried out behind him, and he heard Coppy hold her back. More desperate, he started to reach for magic, and as its power gathered in him, he felt more confident, stronger, and his connection with the fire grew firm. He felt as though he could talk to it and it would understand.

Not here, not now, he told it, and drew the fire back from the paper, back from the air, understanding its hunger and taking it into himself. It burned in him and then he set it free.

The room grew colder and darker, though the smell of smoke lingered. "Strewth," Coppy breathed.

"What happened?" Emily asked behind them. "Who put the fire out?"

"Kip did. I think?"

Kip nodded. "Master Odden has been teaching me to understand fire. I simply told it…to go away."

"Fantastic," Emily said. "I should think Odden would Select you right away if you can show him that. But how did it start?"

"Three guesses," Coppy said. "Kip, want to sniff around to be sure?"

They both went to the stair, where even Emily was able to smell Farley's odor. To Kip it hung in the air like a miasma. "Ten to one he doesn't even get punished for it," Kip said grimly.

"Oh, he'll pay," Emily said. "Have no fear of that."

And the next day at lunch, every piece of food Farley put on his plate vanished to reappear in front of Emily. It took him half the lunch to figure out what was happening, and when he did he glared at them across the tent and tried to levitate the food back to him, only to be stopped by Coppy. Farley swore at them and crammed bread and cheese from his neighbours' plates into his mouth without stopping to put them on his plate, and Emily did not feel sure enough in her control of the spell to translocate material from within his fingers. Even so, his friends hurriedly finished their food and Farley had substantially less for lunch than he normally would.

"I'll do you for that," he said as they left.

"Think twice before you play with fire," Emily responded coolly. "You're lucky I didn't let Kip return the favor."

"More than one way to make a fire." Farley grinned sourly and stomped away.

Adamson came up behind them, trailing Farley. Kip expected another lecture on the feud, but Victor remained silent while Malcolm said, "I tell you, y'ought to set him ablaze. Sure, there'd be the smell to deal with, but it'd be worth it and then some. After all, he did try to murder you."

"He says he only meant to smoke you out, that there would be no real danger," Adamson spoke up then.

"He lit the fire in front of the doorway," Emily said. "And stop apologizing for him, unless you had something to do with it."

"I do admire your restraint," Adamson said to Kip. "Especially with as far as you've progressed in the study of fire in such a short time. Surely control is no longer a worry."

"Only where Farley's concerned." Kip deliberately walked slowly so Farley would be in the Great Hall before they rounded the corner of the Tower, and he wouldn't have to look at him. "There's so much history there."

"Indeed." Adamson stared ahead. "Congratulations on your progress, by the way. I would still like to hear more about it, when you have the time."

"Perhaps after Selection," Kip said.

"I would prefer before, but you may have good reason to be confident." Adamson raised a hand. "And well done to you, too, Miss Carswell."

"I know it was," she replied. "I don't need you to tell me."

He raised an eyebrow, and then quickened his pace, walking hurriedly ahead of them. All four of them slowed by mutual consent, letting Adamson step into the Great Hall and out of earshot before affirming that they did not like him much. Only Kip kept silent. He couldn't argue with the others, but he felt there was more to Adamson than they were seeing.

CHAPTER 13: FLOWERS

The following Saturday, Kip paid a visit to the Cartwrights. He had sent a message and received a formally polite reply, which might as well have plainly stated, *We broke the engagement, we at least owe you this.* Dressed in his best clothes, wearing nothing that would remind them that he was studying sorcery, he knocked promptly at noon.

Laurel Cartwright opened the door and looked past him. "You've not brought your family?"

"No," Kip said. "I'm here on my own behalf. I don't need my father or mother to speak for me."

"Of course." Her ears dipped and she brought her muzzle forward to exchange sniffs with Kip. "Please come in."

"The house smells lovely." Kip followed her inside and let the door close behind him. The smells of the soup she'd made for lunch and of the bread fresh from the oven wafted over him.

In the small dining room, Thomas Cartwright and Alice rose from the table. As was polite, Kip waited for Mr. Cartwright to broach the reason for his visit, but the older fox simply said, "Let's eat."

When enough compliments had been lavished upon Mrs. Cartwright's chicken and dumpling soup and nothing was left of the bread but crumbs, the smiling mother took her daughter into the other room and left Thomas and Kip alone in the dining room. Kip took a breath and waited for the older fox to speak.

"Well," Thomas said after a moment. "Shall I list the reasons for our desire to break the engagement, or are they understood?"

"I thought there was but one." Kip set his arms on the table and leaned forward.

Thomas inclined his head. "At the core of it, I suppose that is true."

"It would do me good to hear it." Kip deliberately raised his ears.

Silence held for three clicks of the clock, and then the older fox exhaled. "What sort of life does the wife of a sorcerer have to look forward to? Brief visits, the burden of raising cubs entirely on her shoulders, scorn from the town..."

He paused there, and Kip took the chance to jump in. "You think there will always be scorn?"

Thomas nodded once, then said, "Perhaps not always as it is now. Familiarity and time may help. But there will always be those who feel that you are taking a dangerous course and pulling the rest of us behind you without regard for our wishes."

"And do you count yourself among those?" Kip asked, challenging the other in a way he'd never dared before.

Surprise flattened the older fox's ears. He frowned. "I—I do not believe that is pertinent."

"I think it is." Kip leaned forward. "If you thought I was engaged in a noble pursuit, to become one of the first Calatian sorcerers, you'd be proud for Alice to marry me. You'd offer to help raise the cubs. Instead, you construct excuses that would not be excuses if you believed in what I'm doing."

"All right." Thomas lay his paws face down on the table and met Kip's stare. "Yes, I believe it is foolish, because it leads the sorcerers to believe that all Calatians aspire to more than we have. Look around." He gestured to his house. "There was a time, and it was not so long ago as you might think, when we would not be permitted to have a house such as this, even if we built it with our own paws. We would be required to turn it over to a needy human family. There are areas of New York, Boston, Philadelphia, where Calatians can own homes and live freely. Now we are treated as people; strange people, true, but we are people, and by and large we are left alone."

"Left alone," Kip broke in, "as long as we make no pretense of owning land, of voting or participating in politics, of attending the same churches or entering certain trades like the law. As long as we don't ask to live in certain other areas of New York, Philadelphia, Boston. As long as we accept that we are no more than they believe us to be."

"And what if we are no more than that?"

"Then we should discover that for ourselves." The answer shot out of

Kip with the speed of thought.

Thomas sat back and rubbed his whiskers. "The colonies are in a similar situation. We are granted a certain amount of self-governance and freedom, and we give up a certain amount to live under the protection of the more powerful Empire. These people who talk of revolution ignore certain truths: how would we defend ourselves against a foe? How would we build roads and cities when the best road-layers work for the Empire? We would have to hire them—"

"We pay taxes to hire them now." Kip would not have broken in had Thomas not stopped himself, seeming to realize the flaw in his argument. "But the Empire decides where they go."

"But we are part of the Empire." The older fox frowned. "Are you in sympathy with the revolutionaries?"

"No!" Kip barked. "No, I love the Empire, but your analogy does not quite work. Within the Empire we are allowed more rights than Calatians are allowed as compared to humans."

"I feel that you accept one because it suits you, and the other because you have not thought about it enough," Thomas said.

"Which is which?" Kip raised an eyebrow.

"I am not playing games, Kip. My daughter's future is at stake."

"I understand that. And I did not come here to play games, either." Kip took a breath. "I care for your daughter. I have seen her grow and gotten to know her over the last four years, and I promised when we made the engagement to provide a good home for her. I still mean to do so."

The older fox folded his arms. "What has become of the sorcerers' wives who were not killed in the attack?"

Kip kept his ears upright, though they threatened to fold down at the reminder of the danger of being a sorcerer's wife. "They currently reside in Boston. Sorcerers are able to travel expediently to see them, and Boston is safer than the College. But I believe New Cambridge itself to be safer than either."

At that, Thomas did smile, very slightly. Kip pressed on. " And do you not think that a sorcerer would be better able to protect Alice than any other husband? Would you like to see what I can do?"

He'd not thought out that statement, and regretted it as soon as he uttered it, because the other fox jerked back in a flash of panic. Kip held up a paw. "Nothing dangerous,' he said. "And I have won respect even from human sorcerers for my progress."

Curiosity now crept into Thomas's features. His ears, which had gone flat, came up again. This was more encouraging. Kip knew that all of his family were possessed of a strong curiosity, and Alice, at least, had shown similar tendencies, so perhaps it was a trait of foxes. "If it is not dangerous," the older fox said.

"Not at all." Kip held out his left paw, palm up. Purple flickers grew around both of them, and then he called a small flame into being on his paw.

So far he had only been able to hold it for three seconds before the pain grew too intense, and that was enough in this case. Thomas stared at the small bright flower until it vanished, and then shook his head as though from a dream. As Kip rubbed his paw, Thomas sniffed, becoming alert again. "Would you like some butter for that?"

Kip shook his head. "It's been burned many times. That's a challenge one of the sorcerers set me. He can hold the fire without burning himself and I'm to work out how he does it."

"I thought you said it wasn't dangerous."

"I meant to you."

There was something comfortable in staring into amber slit-pupiled eyes so like his father's. Kip relaxed into the silence, and eventually Thomas extended his paw. "I'm not decided in your favor, but we will not write to other families about matching Alice just yet. There may be more to the situation than I had seen."

Kip took the paw and clasped it firmly. "I would appreciate every consideration you can give me."

"It means a lot that you came. We were wondering whether you would."

"Of course."

They walked into the yard to say good-bye to mother and daughter, and then Thomas escorted Kip out to the front gate. "Tell me," he said in a low voice pitched for Kip's ears, "do they treat you poorly up there?"

"Some do. Some respect what I can do."

"Mm. And you judge it worthwhile, what you're doing?"

Again, Kip held those amber eyes, reflections of his own. "More than anything I have ever done."

The older fox nodded. "Godspeed, then."

Kip felt that there was more he could have said, but he wasn't sure what. He stopped to see his parents and told them about his visit, but they had no other insights. So he tried to let the matter go for the moment, which proved easier than he'd thought it would be, because there had been frost overnight and the day remained cold, with winds picking up in the afternoon. His furred ears grew numb enough that he thought for a moment about constructing a pair of torches to hold by them and keep them warm, and that returned his thoughts to the problem of heating the basement.

With the Selection just two weeks away, all the students redoubled their efforts to impress the Masters, mostly to little overall effect. Jacob Quarrel, the most advanced after Kip, created a small floating orrery of his marbles in class one day, attracting the attention of the ravens who'd come to watch. Joshua Carmichael attempted to outdo him using his own marbles plus Farley's, but Farley took his marbles easily back and Carmichael's clattered to the stone floor, several breaking. The noise distracted Quarrel enough that he lost control of his orrery, though he managed to catch several marbles in his hands and then sat looking ashamed. After that, Master Patris instructed the class to limit themselves to the exercises he set them, and Kip did not get to see any more student attempts to impress Masters, though he heard his classmates talking about them enough to know they continued to happen.

Kip had memorized the summoning and binding spells, but his attempts to bind a magical fire had failed until he'd convinced Master Windsor to bind one for him. He'd leaned in close, studied the fire, tried to smell the difference between it and an unbound fire. He tried all that night but did not succeed, and then the next night he thought about the smell of an old fire, one that had been burning a long time, and with that in mind, he cast the binding spell well enough that Windsor accused him of having also cast the binding spell on the Great Hall fire, which Kip took for a compliment.

It was figuring out where to reach for the elementals that puzzled him. He had asked Odden, who had repeated that he didn't want to waste his time on that spell, and Windsor had told Kip he was mistaken if he thought elementals as easy to bind as fire.

That afternoon, though, hurrying into the Great Hall rubbing his paws together, he stopped by the fireplace to warm up and said hello to the elementals, and the solution presented itself, so simple he wondered he hadn't thought of it before.

"Say, fellows," he said, staring down into gold-bright eyes, "I don't suppose you'd care to tell me a little about where you come from."

The seams in their skin glowed brightly, and the lizards that had hung back now crowded up to the front, speaking in a babble of voices that Kip could not sort out.

"Home? Oh, it's lovely."

"Aye, home, well, it's much like this—"

"—a hundred times this—"

"—with skippers far as you can reach—"

"—and darkflies—"

"—horrid things—"

"—but the Flower is there—"

"—wouldn't be home if the Flower wasn't—"

"—home *is* the Flower—"

"Truer words never spoken, Ern."

"But what does it *feel* like?" Kip asked.

"Feel?"

"Hot," many of them said at once.

"Delightful."

"Bright."

"Alive."

"Oh, alive, good one."

"Always moving."

"Like the inside of a fire."

"But more so."

"And different."

"Very different."

"But not that different."

"No, no."

"Except for the Flower."

Whenever the Flower was mentioned, the level of chatter rose as each of the lizards pushed its opinion into the mix.

"—Flower's not *different*—"

"—it's more—"

"—more, that's the perfect word—"

Kip broke in again. "What is the Flower?"

This stymied the lizards for a moment. Then they broke into their chaotic babble again.

"Flower's the center—"

"It's the start—"

"It's our home."

"But," Kip asked, "does it look like a flower? What kind of flower?"

They laughed. "Course the Flower looks like a flower."

"Elsewise we wouldn't call it the Flower."

"We'd call it the Scuttle if it looked like a scuttle."

"Besides, the Flower don't look like—"

"It just is—"

"And we gathers round it—"

"And dance—"

"I was gettin' to that!"

"An' it's like—"

"Well, you can't know—"

"Fine fellow, you are, but—"

"Not made of fire, are you?"

At this, they fell silent and contemplated this inescapable flaw in Kip. He bowed to them. "You have been most helpful," he said, and hoped he was right. He had as much information as he could have hoped for from one conversation, and an idea of what to look for: a dimension of fire and hunger, magical fire living without consuming, a bright-hot Flower at its center.

Master Windsor arrived late that evening, and he had not even completed half a sentence of his customary greeting before his eyes fell on the large half-circle of cleared floor against the right-hand wall. His gaze turned slowly to Kip and Coppy, both covered with dust. "What," he said slowly, and then realization dawned as he looked at Kip.

"We didn't use magic to clear it," Kip said, dust rising from his tail as he curled it against him.

"Obviously. Where is Miss Carswell?"

"Bathing." Coppy brushed some dust from his fur. "We said we'd wait for you and she said she hoped the place would be warm when she returned."

The sorcerer stared at Kip. "You believe you can perform the summoning and binding?"

"I believe so, sir."

"You realize that if you meet this task with the carelessness that has characterized much of your spellcasting that you risk starting an inferno in this room?"

Kip gritted his teeth. "Aye, sir. I will be precise." As I always am, he added silently.

"An' Kip can deal with fire anyway. He put out that one that Broadside started," Coppy chimed in.

Windsor turned his attention to the otter. "Lutris. You will be prepared to levitate into the air any creature that escapes the binding. Away from the paper, it will be relatively harmless until I manage to banish or confine it. Which," he added, "I will be prepared for the necessity of doing in the three seconds you will be able to hold it."

"Yes, sir." Coppy closed his eyes, and a turquoise glow spread up his arms from his fingers.

"Penfold. Where have you been researching the elemental planes? Did Florian give you Loudermilk's treatise?"

Kip blinked. "I asked the elementals upstairs." When Windsor frowned at him, Kip added, "They were very helpful. They told me about the Flower, and I think with my understanding of fire, I'll be able to..."

The sorcerer shook his head slowly. "At the very least, I suppose this will be an exercise in how much energy is wasted when spells are cast without the proper research. Proceed, then."

He seemed to relax and didn't even ask Kip about the binding spell. Kip flicked his ears down but didn't allow them to stay down. He pulled magic to him and held the summoning spell in his head. He would have to speak the binding spell as soon as the summoning was done, but he knew the form and was confident he could do it.

The syllables of the summoning spell came to him as he closed his eyes and reached out as he'd done to the fire in Odden's office. Here, there was no actual fire, and he faltered at first, missing a point in space to hold on to. Then he felt a clear note of understanding: the fire was all around him because the potential for fire was all around. He could build the world in his mind and then go questing into it, into a place of thick phosphorus scent around dancing glowing lizards, of unquenchable hunger and dark spots like flies around them and in the center of it all...

The Flower unfolded before him, a magnificent pillar made up of the hearts of a thousand fires. It consumed hunger, burned flame, and gave off the heat of a sun. Kip's body would have fallen to ash had he approached the Flower with it, but his mind simply admired it from a safe distance, watched the cavorting of the lizards around it, and wondered if he might be seeing an aspect of God.

Moments passed, and he felt himself slipping back and out of the world as the strength of the spell faded. He reached out to the lizards dancing around the Flower and drew their attention. Their eyes burned bright as the Flower itself, here in their home, all turned to him. "Come," he said, and readied the binding spell as he felt the weight of one of the lizards on his spell. It was heavier than he would have expected, but it came back with him all the same.

With a snap, he fell backwards into a pile of paper, but he continued to speak the binding spell even as a burst of heat and an acrid wave of phosphorus odor washed over him. He reached out and caught the lizard with his spell, closing it in the clear half-circle they'd prepared, and he was just congratulating himself when he heard Windsor cursing.

Kip's lizard stood in front of him, skittering back and forth in front of the piles of paper. To his right, Windsor had both hands out facing *two more* elementals, one floating in the air and kicking its feet and tail out, the other lunging toward the stacks of paper.

With a snap, the one on the floor disappeared. Papers fluttered in its wake. Windsor exhaled and turned a fearsome eye on Kip. "Penfold," he said in a low growl worthy of any Calatian, "see if you have also mastered the banishment spell."

He gestured to the floating elemental, which was now calling out, "Lemme down! Not fair!" in a high-pitched voice.

When Kip did nothing, Windsor snapped, "Quickly, now, before Lutris lets it fall into the paper."

"I..." Kip swallowed. "I haven't prepared the banishment spell, sir. I didn't think there would be need..."

Windsor nodded grimly and waved his hand. The elemental in the air vanished with another snap, and the air of its passing ruffled Kip's whiskers lightly. "And yet there was need. And you were unprepared. Without myself and Lutris here, you might well now be in the center of a conflagration. Work on your focus; there was no need to bring back three elementals. And always be prepared for any eventuality your spell may bring about. Is that clear?"

"Yes." Kip nodded.

"Very well." He turned to Coppy. "Lutris, it appears you can now command the levitation of a single object. Let us work on multiple objects tonight."

And without even a word of praise for Kip, the sorcerer began instructing Coppy on the movement and suspension of multiple objects at once.

The fox lay back on his elbows and then lowered his head to meet the glowing eyes of the lizard he'd summoned, patiently watching him Or maybe it was looking past him at the mounds of paper. He hoped that was why it licked its lips.

"Hi," he said. "I'm Kip Penfold. What's your name?"

"Penfold," it said in a low voice. "Pleasure t'meet you. I'm Neddy."

"Welcome to our room, Neddy. We're pleased to have you."

"I like it very much here," Neddy said, and his gaze shifted beyond Kip to the paper again.

Kip grinned, reached out, and crumpled an old paper in his paw He lofted it to Neddy, who tracked it, moved with surprising speed, and nabbed it in his mouth. It vanished in a puff of spark and flame, and the lizard brightened. "Another?" it said.

"Maybe later." Kip lay back on the paper, because he was already filthy, closed his eyes, and basked in the warmth.

If Windsor had been disappointingly reserved in his praise, Emily more than made up for it. Though she was as clean as Kip was dirty, she hugged him and kissed his muzzle before the startled fox could react. "Oh, you clever man," she said. "I knew you could do it. Why, this place is almost livable now. Can you feel the difference?" Before he could answer, she hurried back to her small room and then out again, standing before Neddy and shaking out her wet hair. "Well, it's still frigid in *there*, but I suppose it will warm up in time."

"We could create another binding spot just outside your room, there." Kip pointed, his tail wagging from Emily's delight. "Then he could warm your room and our bedrolls both."

"It's fine as it is for the moment." Emily's smile was as bright as Neddy's eyes. "Thank you, Kip."

Master Windsor cleared his throat. "Miss Carswell," he said, "there is half an hour of my time remaining here, and although I am certain that the bath was of the utmost importance *and* that Master Argent has made it clear that sorcery is not a requirement for you to continue your studies here, should you wish to practice some of *those* talents, it would be best to begin now."

She fixed him with an eye. "Wouldn't it be more pleasant to *not* be horrid all the time?" she asked. "For you, I mean. For those around you, it goes without saying."

"Undoubtedly it would be quite pleasant to cheerfully permit my students' incompetence," Windsor replied without hesitation. "It would be rather less pleasant to have to suffer from the consequences of that incompetence in many coming years. Consider my attitude a prophylactic to future misery."

"But we're not incompetent." Warmth had evidently stoked Emily's fire as well. Kip wanted to tell her to stop, but also wanted to see how far she would go.

Coppy dropped the three marbles he'd been levitating. Windsor didn't notice, his attention focused on Emily. "No," he said. "You three are among the least incompetent of the current group of students. That is true. And yet," he said as she opened her mouth to retort, "simply rising to competence is the mark of a sorcerer who will work on roads his whole life. The ease with which you master spells, even Lutris, speaks to a potential that you have barely begun to tap. If I can impart to you discipline and if I can train your minds properly, you may reach a good deal more of that potential. That is my goal. That is why I do not allow you to rest after a triumph, or excuse a small mistake. In the world of sorcery, a small mistake may," he gestured to Neddy, "burn up your entire living quarters, or may result in the destruction of your king. So yes, I am less pleasant than many other Masters. But my students have always excelled."

The silence following this speech filled the room. Even Neddy stopped his rustling around and watched with glowing eyes, understanding the feelings, if not all of the words. None of them spoke until Windsor turned to Coppy and said, "Again."

When Master Odden heard of Kip's achievement, he did not react as stoically as Windsor had. "Three?" he said, with more enthusiasm than anything he'd said to Kip in the past. "I will resist the temptation to have you reproduce that feat here, but that is well done. A better test than holding fire in your paw, I daresay."

His eyes twinkled a challenge, and Kip quelled the discomfort he felt at being reminded that he had not accomplished that. After all, Odden had said that what he had accomplished was more impressive. "Does that mean I can stop trying to do that?"

"No, no, I would still like to see you master it. But I see that what I had intended to be a somewhat easier path to respectability was not necessary."

Easier? Kip felt as though there was something he was missing, but he didn't dwell on it. Instead, he shifted his line of inquiry. "Is it required that every student perform some impressive feat before a Master will consider Selecting them?"

"Not at all." Master Odden looked him up and down. And then, just as Kip's spirits had risen slightly with some hope for Coppy, Odden went on. "In your case, however, Patris is so resistant to the idea of your apprenticeship that without that feat, it would be difficult for any Master to argue your case. I will tell you honestly that I might not be equal to the task, and that the reward for a few years of working with an exceptional student might not be worth the difficulty of living with Patris for those years."

Left unspoken was the truth that although Patris did have a special dislike for Kip, he would hardly be generously inclined toward Coppy. So as they proceeded with Kip's lesson, his concentration on the narrow focus of the fire spell was not at its best. He wanted to ask Master Odden what he thought Coppy might be able to do, while knowing full well that he could as easily answer that question himself. More easily, for he knew what Coppy had been studying and where he might impress a Master.

"Just look through the whole book," he told Coppy that evening, pushing the otter's copy of *Altering the Fundamental* toward him, "and see if any of the spells appeal to you. And try it with your translocation book as well."

"I appreciate what you're doin'," the otter grinned. "And I'll be sorry to leave you and the others. But if road-building is what God planned, then I'd be a fool to run counter to His word, would I not?"

"What if it's not what He has planned?" Kip gestured to the books. "What if His plan lies in these pages and you fail to discover it because—"

He had been about to say, *because you gave up*, and then stopped himself. Coppy seemed to read his words, and the otter's smile dimmed slightly. "I work as hard as you do," he said.

"I know you do." Kip reached out and grasped Coppy's arm. "But you have this opportunity only for another week and a half. Why leave any path unexplored?"

"I suppose you make sense." The otter's whiskers twitched as his smile returned. "Give us the books, then. I'll read until Windsor comes to make me lift dust again."

"Add this one to the pile." Malcolm had entered during the conversation and now held out a book that Kip hadn't seen before. The title, *Protection and Forbiddance*, gleamed gold in the light of the torches.

"Where did you get that?" Kip demanded. He reached out reflexively, eager to see the book himself, then pulled his arm back and watched Coppy accept it.

Malcolm's smile grew. "Ah, now, our Emily isn't the only one with gifts to take her 'round the normal course of things."

"I *beg* your pardon?" Emily put her hands on her hips.

Kip gauged Malcolm with more interest. "Which Master is interested in your gifts?"

The Irishman stared between the two of them. "I meant simply that my people may not have been blessed with a fair countenance, but with the gift of the gab, we call it."

"Aye, that we've noticed," Emily said.

Coppy held up the book. "You talked Florian into giving you this?"

Malcolm focused on the Calatians, perhaps giving Emily up as a lost cause. "In a manner of speaking. I spoke to Master Splint—the healer, aye?—and informed him of Farley's little game with fire. I pointed out to him the benefits of allowing us to defend ourselves, the most pertinent one being that we should trouble him much less, and described the great benefits that could be obtained from such simple spells as the sealing of doors and the blocking of physical spells. I asked if he could make an exception on my behalf to allow me the use of one book of his choosing in the library."

"He didn't mind that you don't live in the basement?" Kip asked.

"I was merely looking out for my dear friends, who are all preoccupied with their own Selection trials. He did ask whether this could wait two weeks, and I said gravely that there were many students quite desperate to see that a Calatian not be chosen as an apprentice, and that the next two weeks might well be our most perilous."

Emily made a small "hmph" noise. "Did you actually say 'perilous'?"

"Your living quarters were nearly immolated," Malcolm said. "Would you *not* say 'perilous'?"

She regarded him a moment and then said, "Gift of the gab indeed," and picked up her spellbook, apparently uninterested in the rest of the story.

"So he was well convinced," Malcolm went on, "and accompanied me to the library, where we procured the book from good Mr. Florian, and here we are."

"Have you studied any of it?" Kip asked as Coppy flipped through the book.

"I went the night after the fire and been studying and working every spare hour since. D'you think I would have come to show you the book before I'd mastered one spell? Funny how it just seems to make sense, and then it's easier once you understand what it's doing." Malcolm turned behind him and gathered magic. He pulled the door closed with a physical spell Kip recognized, and then uttered one more spell that Kip didn't. "Go on," the Irishman gestured. "Try to open it."

Kip stepped across the paper on the floor and unlatched the door, then pushed. It wouldn't budge. He tried again, and then gathered power and tried with a spell, but nothing could budge it. "Master Splint recommended that's one of the easiest sort," Malcolm said. "Cast a binding and it should last the night, you think?"

"You know how to use bindings?" Kip asked.

Malcolm shook his head, and the door came free in Kip's paw. "I thought I might trade one spell for another."

Coppy, to Kip's delight, was most taken with the door-locking spell, but he did not practice it when Windsor came to supervise their exercises. "I'd rather not until I can do it properly," he said when Kip asked.

Kip didn't know when Coppy was going to practice otherwise, because the tents didn't have doors, and he wasn't allowed to cast unsupervised magic inside the Tower. He went back to his bedroll and paced back and forth, tail curled tightly behind him. Unless he crept up to the upper floors of the Tower to ask all the reclusive masters if they would take an otter apprentice, his options for saving Coppy from a life of laying roads were fast running out. He stopped facing the bookshelves and espied the bright red leather of Peter Cadno's journal. With nowhere else to turn, he reached out and let it fall open.

Master Windsor came while Kip was reading, and did not remind Kip to practice sorcery. Nor did any of the others come tell Kip to open his spell books. When he put the journal down without having found anything of use, his frustration doubled when he saw the others practicing.

"You might have called me over," he said, picking up some papers for fuel and walking past Emily to the cleared-away area they had begun to call the fireplace, where Neddy paced back and forth.

She blinked. "Oh, hallo," she said. "Where have you been?"

"I've been right over there, reading." He pointed to his bedroll.

"Better get to practicing before Master Windsor sees you," she said.

"That's what I'm doing." But Kip hesitated. "Why didn't you come get me, or at least call me?"

"Oh…" She cast the spell she was working on, and the paper in front of her disappeared. "Didn't think of it, I suppose. Sorry, Kip."

It was odd, but not remarkably so. He waited to ask Coppy until the lights had gone out and they lay side by side on their bedrolls. Then he did ask, "Coppy? When Master Windsor came down, did you see me over here?"

"I suppose," Coppy said.

"Did you not think to tell me?"

"Well…" The otter seemed confused. "You can see Master Windsor well enough, aye? And you've as much as secured your Selection, so if you've no need to practice, then…"

"But we always warn each other. If Windsor catches us wasting his precious time simply reading a book, he gives us one of his speeches."

"He didn't, though." Coppy yawned. "So why are you so stirred up?"

"I don't know," Kip said, and lay his head back. "It's odd. It's like you and Emily—and Windsor, too—forgot about me for a time."

"That's silly. We wouldn't forget about you."

"Not normally," Kip said. "Only when I'm reading that book."

But Coppy didn't respond, and a moment later, his even breathing told Kip the otter had fallen asleep.

"If you're going to impress a master," Malcolm reasoned as they sat down to a lunch of apples and cheese, "you'll have to do it here."

They looked up at the ravens, five of them today. "You'll never impress Windsor enough," the Irishman continued, "and there's no other master going to take you aside and look for a reason. So it has to be here."

"I suppose," Coppy said.

"How are those defensive spells coming?" Emily asked.

"Fair enough, without much practice."

Kip watched the otter and kept quiet, crunching a sweet Westfield apple. He knew Coppy as a bold spirit, and this reluctance to try spells worried him. Was Coppy afraid of failure? The otter had come all the way from London to Massachusetts on his own, had worked his passage on a boat and then taken a job with a perfume shop. He was a quick study and had a bright wit about him, and he knew that. Was it Windsor's harping that was having this effect on him?

When Coppy looked to him for support, Kip smiled and said, "I know you can do it. If not the first time, then the next."

He didn't know what else to say without saying, "Forget bloody Windsor," and because the ravens could hear, he wouldn't say anything like that. But Coppy knew Kip well too, and the fox thought his intention was clear enough, because the otter smiled. "Right, then. One of you want to attack me?"

Emily volunteered to do it on the theory that she would most easily get out of trouble if any occurred. Kip kept an eye on Farley and his table, but the stout boy did not appear to be sparing them any attention today. Adamson was engaging him, and while Victor did look Kip's way from time to time, he had Farley and Carmichael well in check.

Quarrel, at the other table, watched them with some interest, but the rest of the tent ignored them. The crunch and smell of apples filled the air along with the sharp tang of cheese, and conversation formed a low background noise.

"All right," Emily said. "Ready? I'm going to—"

"Don't tell me." Coppy waved at her with a turquoise-glowing paw as he gathered his magic. "I don't want to be expecting it."

"For the first time," she started, but he waved her down again and she shrugged. "All right."

You couldn't gather magic and cast the spell all in the time it would take to notice something whizzing at your head; ducking was preferable and easier. But if you were in a fight and had magic ready, and wanted to re-aim the missile, then the deflection spell would allow you to take control of the magically animated object.

Emily held her hands in her lap. Kip, beside her, saw the glow of magic against the wood of the table. Then Coppy's apple core shot upward from his plate.

The otter muttered the spell under his breath, but faltered midway through, and the core hung in the air at the apex of its arc, then dropped unimpeded to smack him between his ears.

A loud "Haw!" from the opposite corner told them that Farley had been watching after all. Carmichael, too, snickered, but Adamson just looked thoughtful. A moment later, they returned their attention to their lunch, with a considerably more jovial air.

"Let's try again," Emily said.

Coppy shook his head. "Let's not. I need to practice more."

"And where are you going to do that? It's a simple spell, the shield," Malcolm said. "Come on, give it another go."

"Now you sound like Master Windsor." Kip spoke before he could censor himself.

"'Ere," Malcolm said sharply. "Take that back."

"No, he's right," Emily put in. "Don't talk about how simple the spell is. If he doesn't want to practice, he needn't. Let's finish our lunch."

Malcolm stared at her, then slid around the table and very deliberately, very softly, spoke into Kip's ear. "Selection's in a week and a few days. When will he practice, if not now?"

"No secrets," Emily snapped.

"It's all right." Kip put his paw on Malcolm's arm. "I know you want to see the best for him. I do too."

It wasn't helping Coppy to have people talking about him behind his back. The otter lowered his head and finished his meal, then hurried out of the tent to sit in the classroom without waiting for the others.

They remained behind a bit anyway to talk about him. "We've got to build up his confidence," Emily said.

"If words could lift stones, every house in Ireland would be a castle."

"Words can lift stones, or haven't you been paying attention the last month?" Emily asked.

Malcolm ignored her and leaned in. "Kip, you know him best. What can we do?"

"I've been trying to figure that out." Kip shook his head. "If we could only find the thing he has an affinity for, we could convince someone it's worth keeping him here to study."

"If we could get him with someone other than Windsor," Emily said, "he'd improve dramatically. There's nothing so frustrating as someone whose expectations always exceed your abilities."

"Windsor has a point, though," Kip said, looking up nervously. The ravens had all left with the rest of the students. "I mean, he's tough, but he's helped all of us, hasn't he? I wouldn't be able to gather magic so quickly if he hadn't pushed me to do it. Emily, you're much better with your precision in the translocational spells because he wouldn't let you get away with 'good enough.'"

"Aye, but will Coppy have enough time to improve?" Malcolm tapped the table.

"He'll have to—"

Kip broke off mid-sentence, staring at the tent flap. Malcolm turned, and the three of them watched as a slender white-robed figure stepped inside with the careful grace of a white-tailed deer. He saw them, but didn't stop, only crossed to the table opposite them and picked up a lump of cheese.

"Who is that?" Malcolm whispered. "Why's his robe stained?"

In the diffuse tent light, Kip only saw white cloth, but the young man's odor and the dirt that clung to him came clearly to his nose. The tanned features and unruly shock of blond hair atop them made him think that someone had taken Victor Adamson and abandoned him in the woods for months. But this youth's nose was short and round, and anyway, Kip was sure that even abandoned in the woods, Adamson would somehow emerge confident and perfectly coiffed. "I think," he said slowly, "I saw him in the orchard. We thought he was a ghost."

"Ho!" Malcolm called across the tent, so loudly that Kip jumped. "You! White Robe. Are you a ghost?"

The blond youth continued chewing, ignoring them. "Maybe he's a ghost and can't hear us," Kip said.

"A ghost that eats cheese?" Emily scoffed. "He's someone who wishes to be left alone."

"Is he one of our mysterious masters, then? Jaeger or Barrett?"

Kip shook his head. "They eat in the Tower."

"He's not in our class." Malcolm stood. "I'm going to talk to him."

The Irishman got up and crossed the tent. Kip and Emily exchanged glances and then hurried to flank him as he approached the white-robed youth. "Ho," he said, standing right in front of the weathered face. The youth's eyes were grey and distant as the sky, and still he didn't acknowledge Malcolm, but ate the last of his cheese.

"Can you hear me at all? Are you a student or a master?"

The youth stood. Grey eyes turned on Malcolm, seeming to struggle to focus. "No," he whispered, and then he walked quickly around them and out of the tent.

They followed, but only in time to see him walking directly to the orchard through the frosting of snow on the grass. "Caretaker, maybe. Gardener." Malcolm crossed his arms.

"Odd fellow," Kip said.

"Damaged in the head." Emily tapped the side of her head. "We'd get them in Boston. They could spread fertilizer and some of them could weed, but more often than not they would pull up your dahlias with your dandelions."

"They're so particular about who they let into the college, is the thing," the fox replied, still watching the white shape drift across the lawn.

"And where's he live? Built a shack by the orchard?" Malcolm rubbed his hands together.

"No, there's nothing like that there that I can see," Emily said. "Let's go inside and worry about it later."

Kip followed them, but he cast another glance toward the orchard as he stepped through the door into the Great Hall. He'd expected the mysteries of the Tower to be more like old books, spells he could decipher and learn, or records of ancient magicks cast. He hadn't expected voices in his head, or books that made his friends forget about him, or an unsettling wild man who lived on the college's lawn.

Malcolm was right, though: Selection was just over a week away. There would be plenty of time to think about all the other things after that, or else they would not be in a position to worry about it.

CHAPTER 14: LAST RESORTS

They practiced all their spells most of the day Saturday and Sunday. The four of them held a short prayer session Sunday morning, as they'd grown accustomed to, and then suffered through a cold, clear day in the practice tent. Kip had to remind Emily several times that he could not bring Neddy out to the tent even if he wanted to risk sending the whole canvas and wood structure up in flames. She and Malcolm ran back to the Great Hall fireplace periodically, but Kip and Coppy stayed out in the tent, warm enough when out of the wind.

In classes, meanwhile, they were learning physical magic and the theory of alchemical magic. Had they only learned the spells they were taught, they would have no chance of being Selected, Malcolm pointed out as they sat in a semicircle before their fireplace Monday evening, waiting for Master Windsor. Neddy lay peacefully stretched out across the stone, watching the four of them in turn, and occasionally asked for a piece of paper to eat. "Like half the class," he said. "They're struggling just to keep up."

"Lucky we're so talented," Emily said.

"Luck helps," he replied, "I don't deny it. But in our case, 'tis more than that. We share a common passion, a need to prove ourselves. Me da always said, hire an Englishman and you get a reliable worker; hire an Irishman and you get someone who works twice as hard to prove you wrong about him."

Kip expected a sharp retort from Emily, but she only nodded and said, "You may have the right of it there."

"Maybe that's why I'm lagging behind." Coppy stared at the phosphorus elemental's shimmering form.

"Give us a page?" Neddy asked, and Coppy reached behind him, picked up an accounting sheet from a hundred years ago, and threw it to the lizard.

Kip watched the play of the firelight over Coppy's sleek brown fur. "What do you mean?"

"I mean…" Coppy spoke slowly. "I never much cared what people thought of me. Growin' up on the Isle, you know, it becomes your world and you make the best of it. It don't matter if someone's right or wrong about you. Matters what you do, and what you are inside."

"Matters if the fellow wanting to hire you thinks you'll spend all your money on drink," Malcolm said.

"Or will run off to pursue quilting," Emily put in.

Kip curled his tail back to lie over Coppy's thicker one. "Or can't be trusted because you have fur."

"But see," Coppy said, "on the Isle, it was all Calatians. We knew what the outsiders thought and we didn't care. Much. We did for ourselves. So in the end, I don't really care if Patris or Windsor doesn't think I can do sorcery. I know I'm doing my best."

"I really think Windsor is trying to help," Kip said, just as the door opened and the dour sorcerer stepped through. The fox's ears went down, but Windsor did not appear to have overheard their conversation.

By unanimous agreement, Kip, Emily, and Malcolm told Master Windsor that he should spend all the study time with Coppy, and though the otter did not enjoy that announcement, he didn't protest it. Master Windsor, in his usual backhanded way, said that it was their prerogative to waste his time with the candidate least likely to be Selected, and when Emily pointed out that he could be using his time more productively by telling Coppy what to do to get Selected, he turned an icy eye on her and said, "The gap between knowing and doing is not mine to bridge."

"If he performed a difficult spell," Kip said, but Windsor cut him off.

"The likelihood of that, as faint and remote as it is, grows ever smaller the longer you delay the beginning of his practice."

Coppy did not like being talked about anyway, so Kip shut up and went to sit near Neddy and practice his control of fire, while Malcolm looked over his defensive spells and Emily moved papers to the dining tent, the practice tent, and the fireplace upstairs—she hoped.

In only two months, Kip reflected, he had already become used to this company, to practicing sorcery in the evenings and taking classes in the day, to being on alert for Farley—well, that last had been a fixture of his life and was unlikely to change. It was a pleasant change, though, to have Farley too occupied to harass Kip every day, even if Kip had the uneasy feeling that Farley was only applying himself to his studies in order to perfect new and more deadly attacks. As much as Adamson might wish to take credit for restraining the bully, Kip thought that either Adamson was not doing as complete a job as he claimed, or overestimated his power.

When Master Windsor left, his final words to Coppy were, "Perhaps your future is not entirely hopeless."

"That's as near as he'll get to a compliment," Emily said when the door had closed.

"What did you do?" Kip stood and walked over to Coppy.

The otter smiled around at them. "Kept my focus though he was berating me. I kept the rocks in the air for fifteen seconds, didn't wobble a bit. Unlike me knees."

"There you go." Malcolm clapped Coppy on the back from the other side, while Kip clasped his paw. "Knew you had it in you."

"It's only one step," the otter protested, but they would not let him downplay the achievement and encouraged him to give the deflection spell another try. He asked whether something more visible might be better, but Malcolm pointed out that when Coppy was expecting an attack, he was quite good at casting the deflection. Even when he wasn't, he got it to work about half the time.

"Tomorrow," Kip said, "you'll try that spell again at lunch."

The next day, Kip and Emily spent the morning trying not to let on how nervous they were. When Coppy got up for a break during class, the fox and woman met each other's eyes and saw their worry reflected. "He'll do fine," Kip said.

"He'd best." Emily brought one of her bangs around and twisted it around a finger. "He's not got much time left."

At lunchtime, they hurried out to the tent, noting six ravens crowded onto the perch above them. At their usual table, the four of them ate slowly, and as they finished the simple meal of bread and cheese, all of them gathered magic. The ravens above, perhaps noticing the glowing hands and paws, paid them close attention.

The silence in the tent felt unusual to Kip. He didn't want to take his attention from Coppy, but he risked a look over at Farley. The large boy was chewing on a piece of bread—Kip knew it was bread because a crust protruded from his wide red lips. Both of his hands were under the table, which was suspicious enough without seeing whether they were glowing, but the quiet focus with which everyone at that table ate made Kip's fur prickle. Of course, he thought, they would be as anxious to prove their worth for

Selection, and would have arrived at the same conclusion as he and his friends about when to do so.

They were a little more than halfway done with their food when a piece of cheese rind rose from Emily's plate into the air over Coppy's head. Kip turned his attention to Coppy and as a result, nearly missed the gleam of the knife that came arrowing through the air at him.

He had magic gathered and a short levitation spell at hand, second nature now. He seized his plate and lifted it as he ducked. The knife hit the plate with a clatter, but sharp pain lanced through his shoulder.

"Kip!" Emily cried as his plate fell to the table.

"I'm fine," he yelped automatically. This scenario was familiar and his reactions almost as scripted as a spell: let your friends know how badly you're hurt (his shoulder did hurt but he could still move it), identify whether they are in danger (he stared toward Farley's table, where like a winter storm, an array of forks and plates were rising), then decide whether to fight or run.

With a quick reapplication of the spell, he yanked Farley's table upward, catching many of the intended missiles. At the other tables, students dove for cover under their tables; above, the ravens muttered among themselves. Kip had an eye on two forks and a tankard that were headed their way, but in seconds, the tankard winked out of existence, one fork dropped to the floor, and the other halted in mid-air.

Emily, Malcolm, and Coppy had all focused their attention on the projectiles, and then Coppy turned to Kip, but only managed to get the fox's name out before the tent flap burst open. The white-robed stranger entered, robes billowing about him, and Kip felt the hissing of wind all around. He tried to speak, but the words caught in his throat as though something were pushing them back down.

"Stop!" the young man cried, unnecessarily, because everything in the room had already frozen. Kip tried to keep his grip on the table, but it was pulled downward despite his spell. The air had grown thick, making it hard for the fox to breathe.

"No…no *fighting*!" The young man's voice was high, desperate as a child witnessing his parents coming to blows. "The branches of…a great tree… must sway together."

He appeared to have trouble breathing as well. In the silences between his words, Kip caught not only the rustle of a breeze, but also the faintest sounds of a conversation going on just beyond his hearing. He stared up at the ravens, but they appeared as transfixed as everyone else.

The youth's eyes met Kip's, grey so pale they were almost white, blond hair still unkempt and dotted with leaves and twigs. He smelled rank, as though he hadn't bathed in months, but also earthy, and the smells came and went in a manner that gave Kip a headache: one moment they were there, the next they weren't. He couldn't even smell the blood from his shoulder one second, and the next its odor filled his nose and he wanted to sneeze. There was no order to it, no design; by turns he smelled cheese and students and nothing and Emily and Coppy and ravens and nothing again, as though his nose were under the effect of some sort of spell.

And still nobody spoke. Kip sat cautiously upright, and the youth's eyes dropped to his shoulder. "You are bleeding," he said.

Kip nodded slowly.

"Go."

As Kip stood, air rushed past his ears. Emily's hair rustled and she looked startled, and then the heaviness was gone and Kip's nose worked again.

He made his way to the front of the tent as the young man reached over to a table and grabbed a piece of bread. Kip had reached the tent flap, the cold outside air on his paw, when a voice above said, "That was unnecessary, Forrest."

It was the voice of the raven who'd spoken to him atop the Tower. Kip whirled, but the six ravens looked all alike, none with a beak open.

"They were fighting," Forrest—if that was the young man's name—said.

Kip waited, but the ravens did not speak again. Emily made a shooing gesture at him, and with reluctance, he went off to see the healer.

He passed time talking to the elementals in the Great Hall when Splint had healed him, keeping an eye on the doors. When Emily and Coppy arrived, he fairly pounced them with questions. They told him nothing further of interest had happened; Forrest had eaten and then left and scarcely another word had been spoken by anyone else. "Is your shoulder better?" Coppy asked.

"Good as new." He beckoned them closer. "I asked Master Splint who Forrest is, and he told me he's Master Jaeger's apprentice. Only apprentice to survive the attack, but he's lived in the orchard since then and nobody can get sense out of him." This information had also told Kip which master had been speaking to him through a raven, a fact he'd filed away for himself.

"Poor fellow," Emily said. "I want to go see to him now. Make sure he's warm and has enough food."

"He comes to the dining tent to eat," Kip pointed out.

"Did it hurt?" Coppy asked, laying a paw on Kip's shoulder. "When Splint mended it, I mean."

Kip shook his head. "It was warm and then the aching stopped. Did none of the ravens comment on your spell?"

"Nay." Coppy quieted after that, making Kip's ears fall, not only because the otter's spell had gone unnoticed—twice—but because he'd reminded his friend of that fact. He turned to his desk, staring at the small marble cubes there. This afternoon, more boring Physical magic exercises, when he wanted nothing more than to speed through time to his lesson with Master Odden the next day.

At the end of the afternoon's lesson, Master Patris called Kip aside. "Penfold," he said. "For your role in the fight at lunch, you will fetch the day's food from the Inn tomorrow morning."

"*My* role?" Kip yelped, and then controlled himself as two of the nearest students looked up from gathering their books. "Sir, Farley threw a knife at me. He wounded my shoulder."

"And had you not imposed your presence on the other students here, there would have been no fight. Can you deny that?" He glared while Kip stood mute, furious. "The punishment of other students is not your domain. If you would like to continue arguing, you may leave the school altogether. Believe me, if I did not feel certain you will be gone within the month anyway, I'd be delighted to send you on your way."

Snickers greeted this pronouncement from those students still listening. Kip snapped his muzzle and sense of injustice shut and carried the words he wanted to shout back down to the basement, where he kicked papers at Neddy and stomped about until Emily told him to leave off raising dust.

He breathed, coughed, and thought of the rushing air. Forrest had been able to control the wind somehow; another advanced magic, another secret that Kip would not be able to discover if Patris stopped his Selection the way he was threatening to. Fire he could control, but what good was fire in the face of people determined to stop him from learning? He reached out fluidly, brought magic and flame to the air, wondering for a moment whether dust in the air was the answer to holding fire in his paw, but the dust particles snapped and popped like little falling stars and then went out, leaving filaments of smoke in their wake.

"Kip!" Emily stomped over to him.

His ears lowered; he turned away and stared at Neddy. "Sorry."

"First off," she said, up close to him, "if you use magic here unsupervised again, you'll get in further trouble."

"I know." Past her shoulder, he saw Coppy staring at him.

"Second, if you just start casting fire spells—"

"I *know*. I'm sorry." He raised his paws. "I was frustrated. Patris—"

"Would expel you in a moment if he had reason to."

He curled his paws into fists. To one side, Neddy said, "Does 'expel' mean he'd send you back to the fox world?"

The lizard had his head raised inquisitively, ember eyes glowing bright. "Sort of," Kip said, and stalked back to the bedroll. He knew one way to make everyone leave him alone, and indeed, as he picked up the little red-bound leather book, Emily paused in her walk across the room and then asked Coppy if any Masters had commented on his defensive spell casting after their lesson.

Kip listened to their conversation; apparently he didn't need to be reading Peter's journal to disappear from everyone else's awareness. Coppy said that nobody had talked to him, and he and Emily discussed whether they should try another demonstration.

Don't bother, he wanted to yell at them. Even if by some miracle Master Odden decided to brave Patris's displeasure and take on Kip as an apprentice, nobody would take that risk with Coppy. He needed more time, and nobody would give it to him.

The fox sat down and curled his tail around his legs. The white tip rested down against his black-furred ankles, and drew his attention. Magic had given him this appearance; he owed his life to it. The Festival of Calatus, the Acceptance, the calyxes, all of those were reminders to every Calatian that magic was part of their heritage, part of *them*. Of all the people here at the College, he and Coppy had more *right* to magic than anything else.

His claws dug into the cover of the book. The give of the leather made him look down, where four indentations remained when he pulled his claws out. Breathing, forcing himself to relax, he flipped the book open.

> *days when I most despaire here are more frequent. Master Smythe has indeed made his position quite clear on the subject of my apprenticeship. Not a one of my fellow students allows me much chance save for Edwin, who shews sympathy for me when no others can see. I have told him to make no public display, for I would not have him shunned as I am. It is not only by the students that I fear he would lose standing, but he might indeed place his own Selection into peril.*

> *And yet he persists in small acts of kindnesse, as tonight, when he, knowing well that the vile Oliver had trodden hard pon my tayle, brought a water-bottle that did ease the pain.*

Kip stared at the book. "*Tayle*"?

He looked up to see Master Windsor working with Coppy, Emily concentrating on something with great focus and determination. His paws gripped the book, wanting desperately to share this discovery, knowing he would never be able to due to the magic on it. Anytime he mentioned Peter's name, Coppy and Emily's attention slid away, and he didn't dare speak in front of Windsor for fear that that master's attention would not.

But *Peter Cadno was a Calatian*. The snippets of the diary Kip had read previously came into focus now and he turned the book back again to look at the front page.

> *Being the Journal of Peter Cadno, Apprentice to the King's College of Sorcery, London, England, 1614.*

There had been a Calatian apprentice over two hundred years ago, and Kip had never known about him. Nor, in fact, had anyone else. Perhaps the spell of memory on this book was only part of a larger spell, one that someone like Patris had worked to ensure that nobody ever knew there had been a Calatian apprentice. A sorcerer, even?

Kip tapped the book. Perhaps Peter had become a sorcerer, had become embroiled in a fight with another sorcerer due to his heritage. Or perhaps he'd never been Selected.

He could verify that. He flipped forward through the book and found the entry for Selection Day.

May 15, 1615

Today it is difficult for me to write, my paws shake with so much joy. Master Primus did indeed defy Master Fitch and Selected me to be his apprentice.

Kip read through the rest of the entry, where Peter described the scene: a hall full of apprentices, his tail kept curled neatly beneath his robes, the apprehension he felt as his classmates were assigned to the roads, to the army, and still his name was not called. And at the last, his joy in walking up to stand beside Master Primus on the stage, registering the scowls below though his heart soared far above them.

If only he could be sure that the same would be his fate, and Coppy's. The book felt warm between his fingers. "Emily," he said.

She looked up from her practice, squinting as though looking through a fog. He glanced at Master Windsor, absorbed in working with Coppy, and then back at Emily, but she had already turned back to her own spells. "Emily," he said, more insistently.

This time she looked up vaguely and then frowned. "Kip?"

When he didn't reply, she turned back to her spells again. He would talk to them later, when Master Windsor wasn't around, and he would put the book aside so they could focus attention on him.

He turned to the last page of the journal, but it was blank. He flipped back until he found the last entry:

January 22, 1620

It is colder here than it ever was at home. Fortunately my fur keeps me warm and I have no need of the thick coats worn by all the masters. Today we undertake the spell I have worked so hard to create. I am of course very worried, but I have worked on it with him and so I am prepared for it. What I fear most is not the loss of my own life, but that such a momentous spell may never be known or remembered. If this fails, I will be <styorfa>, but if it succeeds…I will be <ansmæk>.

No more appeared after that. Kip stared at the last sentence, specifically the two words written in Greek letters. He'd never seen the words written out, and the letters only approximated the pronunciation, but he was sure those were fox-scent words, and that Peter had been not only a Calatian, but a fox. Writing out those words had to have been a way for him to signal his species to other foxes; anyone else would assume the words were some ancient Greek that they didn't know. But "styorfa" was <storf>, he was sure, the scent of someone newly-dead, and "ansmæk" had to be <ansmek>, scentless. It was a strange word to associate with a person, never used that way any more than you would say a person was "jagged." It was more something you would say about a piece of metal or…

He trailed his fingers across the floor, across the cold stone.

The voice that had echoed in his head when he'd first touched the stone of the Tower had said, "*Fox?*"

He lifted his head from the book and stared out at Master Windsor instructing Coppy. Was it possible that a spirit could be bound into the very stone of the Tower? And that spirit, if it could still communicate with people, could protect the Tower against an attack that had felled lesser buildings? Spiritual magic remained a distant mystery to Kip, but he could think of no reason why that would not be possible.

Excited, he flipped back through the journal. The College had been founded in 1618, and indeed, when he found the entries from 1617, he found references to a sea voyage, to a "new world." Peter talked of walking with Lord Primus "up a hill," and though he didn't refer to the college by name, he did refer to the small window of peace he would have before more students arrived.

Peter, a fox-Calatian who had been accepted as a sorcerer, had walked these very stones. And then had been…killed? His spirit bound to the White Tower? And then he had been forgotten so completely that not even his journal could be read by any but another fox.

If Kip became a sorcerer, then he could find out why that was. And could those same forces erase Kip and Coppy? He closed the book with a firm slap that did not even stir the attention of anyone else in the room. They would not, he vowed. He would die first.

CHAPTER 15: TRIAL BY FIRE

All the way down the hill in the early morning fog, Kip kicked at the earth and brooded over the unfairness of being punished, when he was the one who'd been injured. And yet it was no worse than he'd been used to down in the town when he'd ventured out of the Calatian neighborhood, and the punishment was not so severe. Patris's threat to expel him was. He was going to have to keep a tight rein on his temper at least until the Selection, and probably beyond. A branch caught his foot, and for practice he picked it up and set it alight, then extinguished and relit the flame.

The information from Peter's journal rattled around in his head as well. In the light of morning, the idea that a fox had been made a sorcerer and then bound as a ghost felt far less reasonable. Ghosts, Kip knew, did not exist; at least, that was what everyone had told him. And yet, how else to explain the journal? He wanted to ask someone about it, but if he told them that a ghost was protecting the Tower, they might think he was taking leave of his senses, which could mean the difference between being a sorcerer and being a bricklayer. Moreover, whatever or whoever had spoken to him from the Tower clearly chose to remain silent most of the time, and maybe being hidden was part of its defense. He didn't want to destroy that secrecy without understanding it better.

Movement stirred inside the Inn, but Kip stayed outside, tail swishing, still restless, so he took a short detour to see if his parents were awake yet.

He felt the need to complain to them about his treatment and simply to see them again; his father had not written him since the last attack, and while he understood the lack of communication and had himself been quite busy, he now found that he wanted to breathe in their scent, hear their voices and reassuring words.

Half-Moon Street hummed with activity, the fog already dissipated here. Mr. Scort had loaves out, their familiar smell sweet on the morning air. Horses and mules clopped from door to door, some carrying carts, others saddlebags full for selling or empty for shopping. Kip hadn't missed their thick animal smell up at the college, and here he dodged around one and came to his father's store.

The door should have stood open at this time of the morning, breathing flower and spice into the street, but the shop was dark and the wooden door firmly shut. A small piece of paper had been fastened to the door, and his fur prickled as he made out the letters on it. "Penfold's Perfumes will be closed indefinitely. Thank you for your patronage. We hope to return one day."

He ran around to the back of the house, whose silence now felt unnatural, and came to the back gate of the garden. Impatient, he vaulted the gate, ran to the back door, and grabbed at the handle, only to find it latched. He rapped sharply on the wood and then pressed his ear to it.

Voices and then movement inside. He stepped back and waited, and when his mother answered the door, he threw his arms around her. "Mom!" he cried, and nuzzled her. "What happened? Why's the shop closed?"

"Oh." She stepped back and kissed his nose. "We were going to wait—"

Kip couldn't keep from interrupting. "What happened to the parlor?" The pictures had all been taken down from the walls, and the shelves were clear of the small ornaments he'd grown up with. The bookcase stood mostly empty, and the whole room smelled <jeng>, full of recent scents of things now absent. Through the door into the kitchen he saw two large trunks, one open in which his mother's cooking pots were visible. "You're leaving?"

"We're going to Georgia. Just for a short time. Your father received an offer…we have family there, relatives of mine, and there's no perfume shop. The owners of the last one fled after the attack. We've been offered a house, but we haven't made any decisions yet…"

"What about Master Vendis? He said his relationship with Dad was too important for him to Select me as an apprentice!"

"Yes, well." His mother turned her muzzle toward the kitchen, and in the silence, Kip caught the noises of someone coming down the stairs. His mother lowered her voice. "They're rebuilding the sorcerer's school. There's a Master Huxley in charge there, and he thought it would be good to have an experienced calyx to help that side of the school rebuild. Not that he'll be doing much of that work anymore. One in the family is enough."

"I'm not going to be a calyx, Mom. I..." Kip exhaled, staring around the room again. This felt like a bad dream, but he couldn't deny the reality of it. "You were going to leave without telling me?"

His father walked into the kitchen, then out to join them in the parlor. "Of course not," he said, ears flicking back. "We're sending most of the luggage down tomorrow, and we'll be leaving in a week."

"You're sending luggage. So you've already decided to live there!"

"We wanted to wait until after your Selection so our decision doesn't influence you." His father came over to put a paw on his arm. "What you're doing is important, and our situation doesn't mean you should abandon your pursuit."

In his mother's flattened ears, Kip saw a different opinion, but he didn't care. "You don't have to leave. Where do I go—where will Coppy go—" He gestured around with a paw, wildly. "This is my home!"

"You'll have a new home in Georgia. Master Vendis will be coming to see me on occasion, and if you ask, I'm sure he will bring you." His father's paw remained steady on his arm. "Listen, Kip. Most boys your age in this town are married and taking charge of their own acres or their own property. You can survive on your own."

"Most boys in this town have parents a stone's throw away," Kip retorted.

"Most boys in this town haven't access to translocational magic," Max said equably. "Once you start learning that, or Coppy does, you can come down and visit whenever you like. It won't be so far away."

"It'll be different. It'll smell different." Kip folded his arms. "And what if I don't get Selected? You act like you know it's going to happen." His ears came up. "Do you—did Master Vendis say something?"

Max shook his head. "I'm afraid not. I haven't asked. But I know you, and I believe in you. If there's a way, you'll find it."

Kip looked around again at the bare walls, the empty shelves, the trunks in the kitchen. "You'll come see me before you go?"

Both his parents smiled. "We wouldn't leave without saying good-bye," his mother said.

"We'll come to celebrate your Selection." His father squeezed his arm.

It wasn't much, but Kip clung to it and tried to keep his spirits up. He told them of his success with fire, and of Coppy's progress and the uncertainty around his Selection. He told them about Forrest and his master Jaeger, but Max didn't know Jaeger and so Kip didn't mention that Jaeger had spoken to him. Finally, the story of Farley's attack and Kip's punishment made his mother gasp and his father's ears flatten. "It's to be expected," Max said with a heavy sigh. "People like Patris are everywhere, and unfortunately often in highly influential places. But you don't need everyone at the school to be an ally, and you do have at least a few of them."

"A few," Kip said.

"Pray God let it be enough." His mother's voice shook. "A *knife* flung at you?"

"I've had knives drawn on me before," Kip said roughly. "Down here, without magic. At least up there I can defend myself."

"And well, too." Max squeezed his shoulder. "But you'd best be getting on with your punishment now. Don't give Patris more cause to find fault."

"If I quenched a fire in the Great Hall, he'd scold me for getting the carpet wet." Kip growled and then willed his hackles to go down. "I'll cope. I wish you'd be closer, but…I understand."

"Good." His father hugged him again, and then his mother, and they gave him a piece of bread with honey to send him on his way.

Levitating the day's stores as he walked up the hill, Kip turned over the visit in his mind. Their business had been suffering for a while, and though neither his parents nor he had brought it up, he knew it was because of his enrolment in the College. Humans bought the expensive perfumes, but Calatians bought basic scents in greater numbers and his father's shop survived on both trades. It was the Calatians who'd abandoned them, he was sure, angry that he was stepping out of his place, fearful that he would bring ruination on them. He turned and looked over his shoulder at the town, at the streets he knew were mostly Calatian-owned, and wished he could see which ones had driven his family away. If only he could visit them all as he had the Cartwrights…but he hadn't the time nor the skill to do that. He had the time and skill to light fires, and if threats could have kept his family in their home, he would have used them gladly. But this was not a time for threats. The town already feared what he was doing; making them more fearful would accomplish nothing.

And yet, the feeling of impotence gnawed at him. He had come to the College to learn magic, to unlock doors and solutions to problems, and here was a problem that none of his magic could solve. But his father had said that what he was doing was important, and he had a sense that he was unlocking doors not only for himself, but for others who might follow after. At this moment, though, he took little comfort in that.

He could come back down to the town, announce that he was finished with sorcery, and then perhaps business would return to his father's shop and his parents could stay. Or was it too late for such a grand gesture? No, it couldn't be. He could talk to the Morgans, ask them to spread the word to end the unofficial boycott of Penfold's Perfumes. It might take a little while, but with him working at the store again and perhaps doing odd magic jobs on the side, they could build their family's reputation and income back up to what they had been.

In front of him, the crate of milk and bread floated, reminding him of what had just a few months ago been so difficult for him and now was so easy he barely had to think about it. What then, if he restored his family to their standing in New Cambridge? Everything would go on as before, as far as everyone was concerned. But not for him. Ahead of him the Tower rose, the great and powerful structure he'd grown up admiring, that had withstood a magical attack by means unknown even to the sorcerers within it. It would no longer be the symbol to Kip of the mysteries to be explored; it would instead represent the potential of all the things he might have had, had he the good fortune to have been born without fur and tail.

No, if he failed his Selection, better to leave New Cambridge altogether, fiancée or no, parents or no. He could go live with his parents in Georgia, at least until the new school got under way. Or Coppy's Isle of Calatians sounded like a place he might enjoy living, again in the shadow of an academy, but amidst different people in a different town.

On the other hand, what if he succeeded? What if he were Selected by Master Odden despite Patris's threats and rose to the rank of sorcerer? If his parents lived far away in Georgia and the Cartwrights decided to withdraw their daughter from the engagement then what was left for him? What purpose was his pursuit of sorcery if not the betterment of his friends and family?

There were those beyond himself, as his father had intimated. Maybe his work could not benefit his family directly; maybe he would lose his wife and his family line would end (his chest tightened at the thought of that), but maybe there was a Calatian cub in New Cambridge or in London even now who was moving objects with his mind, calling water, calling wind (how had that white-robed stranger done that?), who with the right training could be a master one day. If Kip failed as Peter had failed, it might be another two hundred years before circumstances allowed for another Calatian to be admitted to a college. The earth did not discriminate; it dispensed magic equally to Calatian, woman, and Irishman alike, so far as he could tell. So Kip had to believe that the laws of nature viewed his kind as equal to man, and that they were not so under the laws of mankind meant that there was a wrong for him to set right.

If forced to face himself honestly, the reason he wanted to continue at the College was his own curiosity, that hunger for power and personal justice, the ability to deflect a thrown knife with a plate and meet the full force of hatred from Farley and others with a might of his own. But it was not even the power to fight back. At the core of it, sorcery called to him. When he was pulling magic from the earth and using it, he felt alive in a way he rarely had before. And fire especially tugged at something deep inside him. When he pulled it out of the air…

He held his paw out and called fire onto it. The flame blossomed, one, two seconds, and then Kip snuffed it out and rubbed his paws together. Maybe the trick was to sear away any sensation in his pads so that the fire could burn there for ten seconds without affecting him.

There were so many things he didn't know, so many things he ached to explore. If he had to do so without his parents, then…then so be it. He set his jaw and walked the last few steps to the gates. His nose detected no peppermint tingle, and he wondered briefly where the demon who guarded the gates had gone, but was too deep in his own thoughts to spend much time on that question.

It wasn't until he caught Farley's scent and automatically snapped to attention that he saw the stout boy standing in front of the practice tent, his attention focused on Kip, hands glowing lime green. Kip let the crate drop and gathered magic, but nothing came at him from Farley—or Carmichael, out of sight but still detectable to Kip's nose even over Farley's stink.

"Now we'll have some fun." Farley's voice floated across the dead grass of the lawn. "Gonna show you what happens to pelts what try to take the place of honest God-fearing men."

Kip followed Farley's gaze up and saw the shape suspended in the air, struggling against bonds Kip's eyes couldn't make out. But he could see the stubby muzzle and the long, thick tail, and there was no doubt as to whom Farley had kidnapped.

He formed the spell and tried to wrest Coppy away, but whatever force was holding him up—Farley—was stronger. Kip barely got the otter to dip at all.

"Not so strong as y'think, are you?" Farley sneered. "Look." And he jerked Coppy up and down in the air like a child's toy. "I can do whatever I like. Just like old times, before he got here. An' I'll keep doin' them until you're both gone, one way or another."

How had Farley gotten so strong? Maybe Kip had ignored how good his tormentor was at throwing knives and other projectiles in the tent because that seemed easy. Farley could have been practicing his control and his strength, just as Kip had been practicing fire, without any of the other students noticing. Well, Kip could throw things, too. He lifted a bottle of milk from the crate and sent it hurtling at Farley, preparing to catch Coppy when the boy let go to intercept the missile.

The milk stopped in mid-air, then turned and flew directly back at Kip. He gaped at it and barely got his defensive spell up in time, seizing the bottle in the air a foot away from him. The cap dislodged, the milk sprayed out over him, but he held his concentration. Carmichael, it must be; Farley couldn't be controlling Coppy and also casting a defensive spell to intercept missiles. That Kip could wrest control of the milk bottle away didn't necessarily mean that the caster wasn't Farley; they were different spells and he doubted Farley had put as much effort into defensive magic. But he'd smelled Carmichael, and now, as he shook milk from his clothes, the taller boy stepped out from behind the tent. "Can't do that neither," he said.

"Two on one," Kip said. "Quite the sports, you are."

"Two on two, I see." Farley sent Coppy flying another twenty feet up, let him drop, stopped him again. The otter's muffled cries now came to Kip, and the fox lay his ears back. Coppy of course must have his mouth bound or be somehow incapable of casting his own spells.

"Let him go. Your fight's with me."

Farley laughed. "Want you both out of this human school. Get out, take yer brutish friend with you, don't ever come back."

"No."

The bully shrugged. "Figured you'd take some convincing." He smiled at Kip as Coppy flew as straight and true as the milk bottle into the side of the Tower.

The otter managed to kick out with a leg and mute the impact, but Kip still heard it and he winced. Where were the masters? Where were the ravens who were all over the dining tent? He hurried to the side of the Tower, looking up, but then Farley brought Coppy back over the tent and called out. "Want me to play some more? Only paid back three of the blows he landed on me so far."

"Do it," Carmichael urged. "He won't bend after one. Maybe when some blood drops…"

"You two will be gone as well," Kip said tightly. "When the masters hear of this…"

"Oh, Patris will likely be upset over the damage to the stones of our great Tower, but a word from me an' he'll likely let it slide. Seein' how you'll be gone and all." Farley sneered.

"I'm not going anywhere except inside the Tower to find Master Argent." Kip started walking. Milk had soaked through some of his clothes and the cool breeze became chilly.

"Go on ahead," Farley called. "We'll have fun with the river rat out here. Might drop 'im on the gates a few times, see how he likes that. Probably he'll be alive enough for the healer to mend when you get back."

Kip was reasonably sure that Farley wouldn't kill Coppy, but neither did he want his friend to suffer. He cursed himself and the school for not teaching him more spells to communicate, so he could call Emily or Malcolm within the Tower, or Master Argent. He could levitate a stone and bang it against the main doors of the Tower, but if nobody were in the Great Hall, that would be little use. And then he saw something beside Farley that made him start. A small flame licked up the edge of the canvas of the tent, bright and unmistakable.

Of course. He'd been so stupid. He could set Farley's clothes on fire, burn the bully until he dropped Coppy. He could probably do Carmichael at the same time if his control was good enough now. He gathered magic again, feeling the fire surge inside him demanding to be let out, demanding justice for Coppy's injuries and Kip's injuries and their humiliation and all the years behind the two of them.

The flame at the tent flickered, serving as a key, and Kip sought out its hunger, ignoring Farley's continued taunts. The smell of fire and ash filled his nose and the spell took shape...

And then he stopped, held back the inferno inside him screaming to get out. The rational part of him, overwhelmed though it was, struggled out with a question: Where did that other fire come from? There was a third party inside the tent, waiting there only to...set it on fire? Some ally of his reminding him what his strongest spell was?

The side of the tent was blackening, the flames as tall as Farley himself, and yet the bully seemed completely unaware or unconcerned. He was so close, he had to be feeling the heat. But no reaction, nothing but continued invective hurled at Kip.

Burn him! screamed the fire inside him. But Kip was in control now, his will dominating the burning need to exact revenge on Farley. He thought he knew who was inside the tent and what this whole scenario was designed to do. If only he could find a master, someone to put a halt to this, even if they blamed him or Coppy for it, just to put an end to things. With the power he'd gathered, he reached out and pulled the life from the flame, and abruptly the tent was nothing but charred cloth. That Farley did notice, snapping his head around and jumping forward. Kip took another step toward the Tower, then hesitated. If he let Coppy out of his sight...

Kip's tail brushed the wall of the Tower behind him and almost without thinking, he put his paw back. *Help,* he thought, *if the voice is there or anyone is there, help me, give me the strength to pull Coppy away from Farley.*

Cold stone met his fingers and nothing more. He pressed, pleading again, but no voice answered, no surge of power poured through him. "Well?" Farley demanded. "Shall I count to three?"

"Can you?" Kip retorted, his mind working furiously, and then he remembered the morning he'd heard the voice and felt the power, and the first time he'd talked to Master Jaeger's raven. Desperate, he launched himself into the air again.

Below, Farley and Carmichael yelled up at him and made threatening motions. Smoke curled up from the tent where the fire had gone out, but it had been relit: flames licked up through the roof of the tent now. Kip ignored them, keeping his eyes on Coppy as Farley moved the otter farther away. That was all right; Kip wasn't intending to fly over and untie his friend. He pushed himself to the top of the Tower; halfway up he felt some resistance, but he overcame it. In seconds he stood on one of the crenellations, looking around the bare stone and empty roof. "Hey!" he yelled. "You said you'd be here! Where are you?"

He whirled around, his magic still holding him up so he had no fear of falling. "I need you!" he yelled, turning to keep an eye on Coppy floating now a little below him.

For a moment, nothing happened. The confused cries of Farley and Carmichael were the only sounds that came to his ears; the next time he turned and saw Coppy, the otter's eyes reflected the sky's light back at him, watching him. "I'm trying to help you," he said to his friend, even though he doubted Coppy could hear him.

If the raven didn't reappear, if Kip were truly alone, then what? He could pretend to leave, agree to go, but Farley—and Adamson, whom Kip was now sure was inside the tent and behind this whole scenario, would have some kind of setup, perhaps calling Patris as a witness, perhaps something else Kip couldn't bother to think of. If he even pretended to give in just to save Coppy, it would make everything more difficult. But what else could he do?

As he watched, Coppy came hurtling at the Tower again as Farley yelled up, "Come down here, pelt!"

Desperate, Kip dropped himself onto the roof and put all his power into stopping Coppy from hitting the wall. The otter slowed, and Kip felt the force of Farley's power against his. But this time, for some reason, he was equal to it. He fought to pull Coppy to the roof, and slowly the otter rose. Kip saw clearly now the gag tied securely around his friend's head, the ropes binding his paws behind his back, the pleading eyes. He reached out, fingers straining toward the gag, and Coppy stretched his neck toward Kip's paw. But a moment later, another force joined Farley's—Carmichael, no doubt— and pulled Coppy away again. Kip's control lessened the farther Coppy got from him, and as he stared down he realized his precarious position on the roof. Once they no longer needed both spells to control Coppy, one of them could easily give Kip a push.

The fox stepped back onto the roof and wove a levitation spell around himself again. He turned and came face to face with a large raven.

For a second, they stared at each other in silence, Kip unsure if what he were seeing was real, and then the raven said, "What's going on?"

The voice spurred him to action. "That! There!" he pointed at Coppy. "My friend is being tormented by two of our fellow students. *Three* of our fellow students."

"You can't get him away from them?" The raven hopped to the edge of the roof and looked down.

Kip followed. Farley and Carmichael had gone silent, while behind them, the tent roof crackled with flame. "I've tried," the fox said. "I can't force Coppy down against his spell."

"Have you tried moving closer?" The raven angled its head up to stare at Kip. "From this distance your power is less."

"I don't want lessons!" Kip shouted. "I want you to save my friend!"

"Tch." The raven clicked its beak and turned back down to the scene. "Master Windsor and Master Patris will be out in a moment. In the meantime, might I advise you to turn your attention to that fire?"

The fire on top of the tent had spread, and large patches of the roof had fallen in. "Can't you do it?" Kip asked even as he reached out to the fire. He felt it burning, knew it, embraced it. To quench it he would have to drop his levitation spell, but behind the parapet of the roof he felt safe enough to do that.

"No," the raven said. "Fire is not my specialty and I have no particular affinity to it."

The fire flared and then went out as Kip pulled the power from it. "Really?" he asked, amazed even in the heat of the moment that there was something he could do that an accomplished master could not.

"Really."

The creak of the doors at the hall alerted Kip. A moment later, two black-robed figures strode across the lawn. Coppy dropped out of the air, and Kip let out all his breath in one long exhale.

His knees did not seem to want to support him anymore, so sat down on the roof, leaning back against one of the crenellations. "Can you teach me to talk to other people at long distances?" he asked the raven, who hadn't moved.

"Not yet. Maybe in two years or so. If you are Selected."

"Can you not Select me? I mean, if Master Odden doesn't."

"Odden is under great pressure from Patris to Select no apprentice this year. As for me, I already have an apprentice and would not be permitted another."

"Does Forrest even count, though?" Kip asked the question without thinking, and regret washed over him. "Sorry."

"I understand your desperation. There are not many masters who will risk alienating the Headmaster. He has ways of making life difficult for people who do not follow his wishes."

"Who would risk it?" Kip closed his eyes. Despite everything he'd done today, the idea that Farley would win felt unbearable.

The raven considered. "There are perhaps two or three. Master Windsor, certainly. Myself."

Kip was about to ask about Master Odden, but at that moment a voice spoke into his head. *You have more allies than you know.*

The last time a voice had spoken into his head, it had been in one short burst that had gone almost before he was aware of it. This sentence, the complete thought of someone else entering his head, made his fur prickle and set him to shivering. He stared at the raven, whose head turned from side to side. Had the raven spoken silently to him so as not to be overheard by others? Or had it been some other being, perhaps the one who'd spoken through the Tower so long ago? Cautiously he said, "Thank you," and pushed himself to his feet.

It was a simple matter to re-cast the levitation spell and lower himself gently to the ground. Patris and Windsor became recognizable the closer he got to them; when they spotted him, they argued for a moment and then Windsor came to meet Kip while Patris continued on toward Farley and Carmichael. Kip glanced down but for the most part kept his eyes on Coppy, now being lowered to the ground, and he directed his own downward flight to follow the otter's.

When he landed, he dismissed the spell and ran forward, only to be stopped a moment later by Master Windsor's grip on his arm. "You fool," he said. "Had you no heed for the history here before you set *fire* to the *school*?"

"I didn't!" Kip tried to twist away, but the old sorcerer's grip was too strong, and the way he was holding Kip's arm threatened to break it if Kip pulled too hard. Windsor's face had lost none of its stoicism except in the eyes, which burned intensely and made Kip stammer. "I—it just caught—I thought about it but I *didn't*."

Now he caught the tingle of peppermint as Coppy reached the ground some thirty feet in front of him. He strained again, and this time Windsor came with him to Coppy's side. "You'd best have a witness, if so," the sorcerer growled.

The ropes and gag were coming undone by an invisible hand. "Burkle," Windsor said as he and Kip approached, "did you witness any of this?"

The little satyr-demon winked into visibility beside Coppy. "Nay," he said as the otter threw the ropes away and stood shakily on his feet.

Kip ran to embrace him, and Coppy leaned into the fox's arms before smiling. "I'm all right," he said. "A bit shook up is all. Had worse falls."

"Corimea!" Windsor called.

Burkle shook his head. "Not here," he said.

"You sure?" Kip asked Coppy. "I saw you hit the wall…"

"I'm tough." The otter punched his own arm and smiled. "Not all glass like you foxes. Bit bruised maybe, not even worth bothering Master Splint about."

"Where is he, then?" Master Windsor demanded of the satyr.

Burkle shook his head again and then went invisible. Windsor folded his arms and turned his still-fierce eyes back on Kip. "The remaining witnesses are not likely to testify in your favor," he said.

"There was someone else in the tent." Kip snapped his jaw shut before he said the name. "Someone else started the fire."

"Set fire to a tent they were inside?" Windsor raised his eyebrows.

"And then probably snuck out the back."

Patris had corralled Farley and Carmichael and his shouts carried across the lawn. Kip perked an ear toward them. Patris actually seemed to be angry at Farley; the phrases "never be Selected" and "unconscionable behavior" floated to Kip, and while he couldn't find it in himself to smile, he did feel warm in his chest. Gone from the college he might be, but at least Farley wouldn't be remaining here learning sorcery while Kip suffered exile alone.

"You'll excuse me if I find that somewhat unbelievable," Windsor said. "Lutris, can you support this story?"

"I only saw the tent catch fire."

"Did you see the fire go out?" Kip asked. "Because that's what I did. Twice! They set fire to the tent flap there, and then to the roof. I put it out both times. The raven!" he said, pointing to the top of the Tower. "I talked to Master Jaeger up there! He summoned the two of you. He knows I didn't set the fires."

The old sorcerer's eyes lost their intensity for a moment. He looked up at the Tower, then frowned in concentration. Finally he lowered his head, reached up with one hand, and scratched his short black hair. "I will have to ask him when we return to the Tower. And speaking of returning, you should do it now before Patris arrives here." The white-maned sorcerer, dragging Farley and Carmichael behind him (figuratively, not with a spell), was indeed storming their way.

"No," Kip said. "I'll stay. I should face him on my own."

"You stand to gain nothing by it," Windsor said. "This battle is not worth—"

But it was too late already, as Patris roared, "Penfold! Pack your things and be gone from the school by sunset!"

"Watch your temper," Windsor muttered to Kip. "If you truly did not set a fire on that tent, do not start one here either." Coppy came up behind Kip and put a paw on his shoulder.

Kip nodded shortly and breathed in, then out, a long plume of white breath. The fire still burned in his chest, but he knew how to hold it in and the support from Coppy and even Windsor bolstered him. He ignored Farley's smirk and met Patris's eyes with as much sang-froid as he could muster. "I did not set that fire," he said. "I took no action save trying to rescue my friend from the people who abducted him, tied him up, suspended him in the air…" His voice began to shake, and he got it under control. "I put the fires on the tent out. Twice. I don't know how they started."

"Who else in this Tower has that ability with fire?"

"Master Odden," Kip replied promptly, and saw the mistake as soon as he'd spoken.

"Oh," Patris sneered. "So Master Odden attempted to immolate two of our students? Is that your story?"

"Fire can be set by other means," Kip said calmly. "Someone concealed in the tent could have taken a piece of wood from the Great Hall fireplace and set fires in the tent so that I would be blamed for it. Or there might be a phosphorus elemental—but there wasn't. I would have smelled it."

"It seems all very complicated." Patris folded his arms. "Are you suggesting that Broadside or Carmichael here concocted a scheme to get you expelled from the school a mere week before you will fail to be Selected?"

"No," Kip said. "I don't think it was either of them. I think it was someone who was afraid I might be Selected." He tilted his head. "You seem very sure that I will not be. Have you expressed doubts about that to anyone? Someone who might be friendly with Broadside or Carmichael?"

"Of course not." But the dark eyes slid away from Kip's for a moment as he spoke.

"And…" Kip made another connection in his head. "Where is Corimea? Isn't he under your control? Why wasn't he watching the gate, witnessing this?"

Windsor winced; Patris turned his furious gaze back on Kip. "What do you mean by that? Are you accusing me of helping plan this?"

"Of course not, sir." Kip lowered his head. Coppy squeezed his arm, and Kip flicked his tail back in response. "It is unfortunate that the demon who is always here by the gates wasn't watching, that's all. Luckily for me, a sorcerer did appear to witness my part in it."

"What? Who?"

Windsor stepped forward. "Penfold claims that Jaeger was present and can verify his claim that he did not set the fires."

"Who else would've set the fire?" Farley cried, pointing at Kip. "He tried to burn us!"

"Jaeger." Patris scoffed, ignoring the outburst. "Since when has he taken an interest in anything outside the Tower?"

"You may ask him that yourself," Windsor said, "but until that moment, I suggest we move indoors. There we can take roll of the students and see if perhaps one is missing." He met Kip's eyes.

"Yes, yes, fine." Patris looked murder at Kip one more time and then swept past him, bringing Farley and Carmichael in his wake. Kip stepped back as the two bullies passed by, and then waited for Master Windsor to follow before he and Coppy brought up the rear. But Windsor stayed in step with the two of them. "What happened, Lutris?" he asked.

"I was asleep…" Coppy hesitated. "I don't know how they got in."

"I didn't lock the door behind me when I left." Kip cursed. "I'm sorry, Coppy. It's my fault."

"They had the gag in and I couldn't cast any magic."

Master Windsor kept striding straight ahead. "Spellcasting without vocalizing is an advanced technique."

"Maybe we should learn it sooner," Kip said.

The sorcerer glanced sideways at him. "In a week, we will see whether that question will be relevant at all. Given the difficulty in mastering even the vocalized version—"

"Oh, leave me alone!" Coppy cried. "I've done my best for weeks, and I was just attacked and hung in the air and smashed into a Tower and I'm sorry if I wasn't able to levitate a few rocks. It doesn't seem like that would've helped me very much fifty feet in the air, thank you!"

Master Windsor stopped dead in his tracks while Patris and the others kept going. Coppy's white breath dissipated in the wintry air between all three of them. Kip swallowed and bit his lip, both he and Coppy watching Windsor. The sorcerer's face had a shocked cast, and he opened his mouth, but then closed it again without saying anything and inclined his head.

Coppy, as surprised as Kip and Windsor by his speech, spoke again cautiously, in his normal tone. "I don't know why they didn't just keep beating me against the Tower."

"I think they were waiting for me. They wanted me to burn the tent." Kip felt again the flush of shame, that all of what had befallen Coppy this morning had been because of him, that he'd gotten his friend injured and almost more severely hurt.

The otter patted Kip on the shoulder. "It looks that way, but I still don't understand how Farley restrained himself."

"Because someone was telling him to." Kip looked back at the lawn and the still-smoking practice tent as they approached the great wooden doors of the Tower. "I suppose we'll find out who in a moment."

In the Great Hall, Patris turned to the five of them. "Wait here," he said tersely, and then, "Burkle! Gather all the students in this Hall in five minutes. Tell me immediately if anyone is not present."

"Yes, sir," came the demon's disembodied voice, and the peppermint tingle disappeared from Kip's nose.

He rubbed it and went over to the fireplace to talk to the elementals. They'd roused themselves and were watching the activity eagerly. "What's the do?" one asked Kip as Coppy came up behind him.

Quickly, he told them, and they shuffled around happily. "Fire, eh?" "Did you start it?" "Was it big?" "Was it hot?"

"Not so big or hot, and no, I didn't start it." Kip hushed them as students stumbled down the stairs, watching each one for the familiar blond hair, knowing he wouldn't see it. Eleven students assembled in the Hall, Adamson nowhere among them, and then Emily joined them from the basement, going to stand next to Malcolm with a questioning glance at Kip and Coppy. The Calatians looked back at their friends and the other students standing where the desks normally appeared for their classes.

Patris counted them, then smoothed down his unruly mane of hair. "Ahem," he said. "We have had an incident…"

And then one more set of footsteps clattered down the stairs. Victor Adamson hurried into the Hall, smoothing his hair back in a motion very similar to the Headmaster's. Kip gaped as he took his place with the other students. "Sorry to be late," he said.

When the fox turned back to the front of the room, Patris's worry was gone. "Please be punctual in the future, Adamson," he said. "Now as I was saying, we had an incident this morning in which four of your classmates fought using sorcery. While the level of skill displayed was indeed impressive, the conduct displayed during the fight was not at all what we wish to see from our future sorcerers. As you are taught more dangerous spells, the ability to do serious damage to each other will come in line with the temptation to use it, especially where certain elements are present in the school." His eyes lit on Kip, and the fox's fur bristled. Of course, he thought bitterly, Patris would be of the mind that the entire fight was his fault simply for existing. "But," Patris went on, "the tests of restraint and judicious conduct you face will be as important as the tests you are given in this room. I am sorry to say that the four students involved in this fight have all failed that test today. With the Selection so close, I will levy no punishment other than the full report of their conduct to the body of sorcerers here, so that their character is made plain to everyone who might be considering Selecting them as apprentices."

Kip opened his mouth to ask how Coppy had failed an examination of restraint by allowing himself to be tied up and flung about, but he caught Master Windsor's eye as his mouth opened, and the glare from the sorcerer stopped him cold. He balled his paws into fists and looked instead at Victor Adamson as the boy rubbed at his forehead. Adamson was not looking at him, but at Patris, maintaining a composed, almost vacant expression.

"The thirteen of you," Patris went on, "should not be too pleased, ever, if you think this improves your own chances of Selection. Any of you might be in the same situation. If you have the good fortune to be Selected as apprentices, your behavior will be held to still higher standards."

Coppy put a paw on Kip's shoulder. The fox tried to relax at the friendly touch, but couldn't keep his mind from leaping ahead. Would Odden still Select him? Would Patris's lies be enough to convince the sorcerer Kip had thought of as his salvation that the fox would be too much trouble? He looked again at Adamson, and again felt the fire in his chest, stronger even than the blaze at his back. This boy had ruined—or at least severely damaged—Kip's chances to study sorcery. It didn't matter that he'd done everything right. Patris needed only the tiniest shred of an excuse to dismiss him, as his father had warned him, and Adamson knew that. And now it was all for naught. His parents' ruined business, his failed engagement, all of it had come to nothing because of Adamson, Farley, and Patris, three people out of thirty who hated him only because of his fur. At least, he knew that of Patris and Farley. Adamson he could only guess at.

When Patris dismissed them, Kip strode quickly along the carpet, ignoring Malcolm and Emily, and caught Adamson by the elbow. "A word, if you would?" he said tightly. He could still smell the drying milk on his clothes and in his fur, so strongly that he was sure everyone else could, too.

Victor did not so much as wrinkle his nose. "Of course," he murmured, and followed Kip to the back corner of the hall. Coppy, Malcolm, and Emily followed, but at a distance, hanging back when Kip warned them off with a shake of his head.

"I was afraid things might come to this," Adamson said when he and Kip reached the wall. "Farley has been talking—"

Kip interrupted him, his eyes fixed on the shiny red mark below the blond hair. The scent of ash and smoke hung all around Adamson, as clear to him as the straw-blond hair or the ice blue eyes. "That's an unfortunate burn," he said. "Piece of the tent fall on your head, did it?"

Adamson's eyes narrowed. "Last night, I was—"

"The mark's fresh," Kip said, "and you stink of fire. How did you get back into the Tower?"

Behind Adamson, Coppy stood up straighter, then whispered explanations to Malcolm and Emily. Good. At least they would be able to hear. Adamson either didn't see them or didn't care. If anything, his slight smile curved upward. "I'm surprised you have to ask, since you should be intimately familiar with it."

Stung, the fox asked himself, how would one get into the Tower without anyone else seeing—and then he realized. "The calyx's entrance."

"Ironic that I should have to use it." The boy rubbed at his forehead.

"So all your talk of restraining Farley, of building understanding…"

"Oh, don't be juvenile." Adamson leaned against the wall. "I mean you no harm. Though you may not see it, I am doing you a favor."

"A *favor*? By trying to get me expelled?" Kip held up a paw as Malcolm started forward.

For the first time Adamson took note of the others. He glanced their way, then back at Kip, but as he spoke, he shot sideways glances at Kip's friends. "Yes, a favor. You know that progress comes in fits and starts, not all in one grand gesture. Sorcery is all well and good, but there's no spell that will accustom people to a Calatian sorcerer. You've done quite well in your studies here and you've proven to several sorcerers that there is no reason a Calatian can't cast spells. But to earn the rank of full-fledged sorcerer?" He shook his head. "The forces arrayed against you will be vast and merciless. You have not heard the conversations I've heard among the sorcerers here, the shocking sentiments some of them have expressed. You think Farley is bad only because he wears his hatred like a tunic for all to see, but I tell you there are people in the school who feel twice as strongly and have ten times the power he does. If you leave now, you will be able to serve as a very valuable calyx to any—"

"I'll never be a calyx," Kip said. "Never."

"Whatever path you choose, you've opened a door for others to walk through. In a generation, perhaps another Calatian will come along with a truly extraordinary talent and your short stay at this college will inspire him. The sorcerers will remember you and the otter and will say, maybe this time one of them will succeed. More will rally to support him, and he may even be Selected."

"I could've been Selected if not for your interference."

Adamson reached out to Kip's shoulder, but the fox brushed his hand away. The blond boy let it fall to his side. "Perhaps you could have, but history is not kind to the pioneers, the trailblazers. Look at those who squawk of revolution in Boston now. Do you think John Adams would dare to be so vocal if not for his late cousin's words of thirty years ago?"

"I hardly think that his cousin's execution eased his path."

"It inspired him. Kip, I like you. Why else would I have given you the chance to get rid of your hated enemy?"

Kip stared. "You wanted me to kill Farley? Your friend?"

Adamson's expression remained neutral. "The opportunity was there. You'd be leaving the school either way."

"I'd be tried for murder!"

"It's a moot point now." Adamson spread his hands. "It's over, Kip. Let another Calatian bear the next burden. You've done enough."

Kip stared back into the blue eyes. He was no dab at reading people's faces, but he knew enough to tell the difference between the genuine friendship Emily and Malcolm held for him and the calculated words of this intellectual. "Not yet," he said, and stomped across the hall to fetch Master Windsor.

Windsor did admit that Adamson smelled of smoke, waving away the boy's objections and silencing him more effectively than anyone else Kip had seen attempt that feat. "It proves nothing save that he might have been there," he said. "But Master Jaeger did indeed testify in your favor to Fatris, for all the good that will do."

"How much good will it do?" Kip asked bitterly.

Emily, Coppy and Malcolm came up around him, standing close as if the smell of milk didn't bother them. "He didn't start any fires," Emily protested before Windsor could respond. "Coppy was attacked and Kip reported the attack to a Master! What else could they have done?"

"Not been Calatian," Malcolm said.

Emily rounded on him and began furiously, "If you're not going to help—"

"He has the right of it." Windsor interrupted. "Perhaps it is not yet the time for a Calatian sorcerer."

"I can't accept that." Emily looked Windsor in the eye. "There's no rules, no institutions deciding it. There are always going to be people who hate them for what they are. If now is not the time, then when? When they've been kept under heel for another hundred years? A thousand years? Who decides when it's time if not them?"

"Times are made by people," the master replied. "If you've learned nothing else from my history lessons then I hope you have at least learned that. For great change to occur, great sacrifice is required, and in addition a measure of luck and timing and all the right people as well. There will always be those who fight against change, and when there are enough fighting for it to overcome those fighting against it, then the time is right. But not before."

"I think there are enough here," Emily said.

"Today's events would appear to prove you wrong," Windsor said. "I am sorry."

"If you think we have potential," Kip said, "then you can…"

But he trailed off as Windsor shook his head. "That I am sorry for your departure does not mean that I am fighting on your side. I hope that we may maintain our acquaintance following your departure. I will see you in history class this afternoon." With that reminder that today was a school day and classes were to start soon—unnecessary, as Burkle was arranging desks behind them and Patris had taken his place at the lectern—he turned and left them.

"It isn't fair." Emily almost had tears in her eyes. "I thought at least that Kip and I—I'm sorry, Coppy, I didn't mean—"

"No, you're right." The otter put a paw on her shoulder. "I'd no expectation of being Selected. Fight or no, I've not the makings of a sorcerer, not like the fox here, nor either of you even. But I can at least help build roads and houses, and maybe I'll be allowed to help with those things back on the Isle."

Kip, who had been brooding about great sacrifices being required and trying not to be angry about losing his family, possibly his engagement, and his town all for nothing, looked up at this. "Why would you not be allowed to? We repair our homes without any trouble or permission from anyone."

"Aye, but it's the use of magic, with the Academy so close." Coppy's eyes turned up as if looking at the buildings of King's College. "Course, no Calatian ever was able before, so we've no idea how they'll see it."

"If they don't find out," Malcolm said, and shook his head, patting Kip on the shoulder. "What about you? Anyplace needing fires lit and put out? Signal fires, maybe?"

"I might go to Georgia with my family." Kip walked toward his desk, unwilling to spend too much time speculating about what he would do after the last week.

Emily took her place beside him and leaned over. "I still think you'll be Selected," she whispered. "Because otherwise I'll be left here on my own, and I won't stand for that."

That, of all things, made Kip smile. "I'd like to believe you have the will to make it happen," he whispered back.

Patris was about to start his class, but just before he did, Emily turned to Kip. "I believe *you* do," she said.

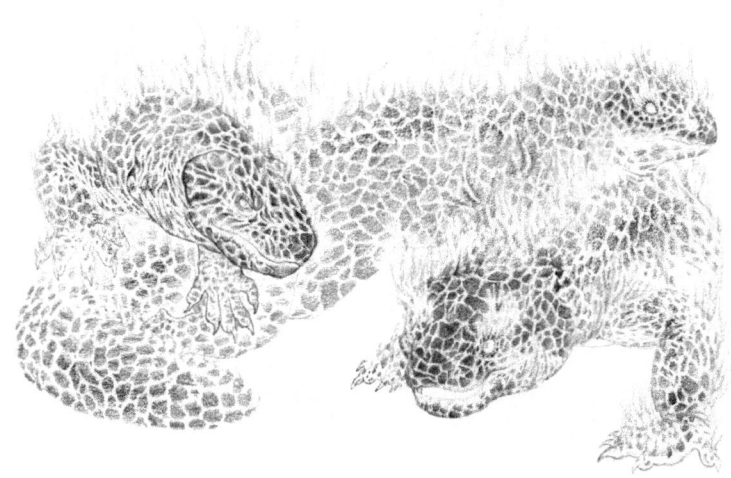

CHAPTER 16: BARGAIN

That evening, Kip went up to Master Odden's chambers. He ignored Farley's taunts and the chilly silence of the other boys and rapped on the wooden door. When the sorcerer opened it, his face was resigned. "Broadside, hold your tongue," he said to Farley. "If I hear you once more you'll be sent back home immediately." Then his eyes met Kip's.

"If I could speak to you for five minutes in private," Kip said quickly.

Odden sighed and then nodded quickly. "Come in."

He closed the door, mindful of the fox's tail, and that small courtesy heartened Kip. But Odden's words returned him to desperation. "I know what you are here to ask," the master said, sitting down at his desk. "You must understand how difficult Patris is making it. That you have a rare talent only makes him more desperate still to, well, 'keep you in your place,' as he puts it. He wants Calatians at the side of sorcerers, not standing in their robes."

"I won't become a calyx," Kip said.

Odden linked his hands over his stomach and nodded. "No, I should think not. Yet there are many who will, and your success or failure here will mean little to them."

"Master…" Kip gestured toward the dais where he'd practiced many times. "I can promise you that I will work harder than any other apprentice."

Malcolm's words about Irishmen came back to him. "Because I know Patris is watching me, and I must work twice as hard for half the reward. I know that. I—I accept that. But not to be given the chance at all is unfair, and I think you know that."

"What I know matters very little in this case." Odden heaved a sigh.

"I didn't do anything wrong in the fight this morning," Kip said. He let his tail hang down, flicking back and forth, and stood upright. "I came up the hill and Farley and Carmichael and Adamson had captured Coppy and were torturing him, using him to bait me into starting a fire. When I didn't, they started one that I was to be blamed for. If not for Master Jaeger, everyone would believe I had."

"Master Jaeger is no longer Head of this school," Odden replied tiredly. He leaned an elbow on his desk and rested his head against it. "I have no wish to spend the next three years fighting with Patris, being given the worst of the duties…"

"You wouldn't be alone," Kip said quickly. "There are other masters who favor my case. Master Argent, Master Vendis, Master Windsor—" He faltered, remembering Windsor's words. *I am not fighting on your side.* But the master, despite his ill humor, did believe in Kip. He'd said that Kip and Emily had a great deal of potential.

Odden shook his head. "I will speak to some of the others, but in your place, I would prepare for a life outside the college. I am sorry. It would be best if you did not come and speak with me again before the Selection. I have heard your case, and believe me, I am sympathetic."

He didn't have to add the "but"; Kip could hear it very well in his head. He left the office, walked briskly through the outer room where the students worked, ignoring Farley, and mechanically down the stairs to the Great Hall, his mind blank. Only when he reached the hall did he hesitate, starting to think about his life after Selection—or after a failed Selection. As much as just that morning he'd been thinking that he couldn't bear to live near a magic school, he thought he might be able to go with his parents to Georgia, to help rebuild the magic school. Maybe one of those masters would give him another chance. Or he could go to the Isle with Coppy, the two of them working to improve the lives of the Calatians there. As a life, that seemed more worthwhile, even if the chance of furthering his education was far more remote there than it would be in Georgia. As of this moment, he felt that if Master Odden didn't choose him as an apprentice, all his other chances of becoming a sorcerer fell to as close to zero as made no difference, so a slim chance versus a slimmer chance was not a distinction that mattered much to him.

The elementals in the fireplace greeted him with chuffs of smoke and activity.

"Hello, fox."

"Penfold."

"Hello, you all." Kip leaned against the edge of the fireplace. "I might not be here to see you much longer."

They brightened. "That's wonderful!"

"Ah, good f'you."

"Going home at last."

"Blessed Flower."

"I'll miss all of you." The words spilled out, sincere and unexpected. He would miss the magical fireplaces, the elementals with their strange habits and languages, the mysterious book, and all the things besides the education itself.

"Aye, it's been a pleasure to talk to you," Chez, the largest said. "I reckon I'll go home m'self before too long. Been feeling a bit cool."

"Lucky." Julienne bit him on the leg, and a short scuffle ensued.

Kip smiled and raised a paw. "I've another week, at least. I'll see you all."

"Aye!" they chorused, and went back to their tussle.

"Hey," Hodge, Kip thought it was, said. "Don't be so down about goin' home. Don't you want to see home again?"

"It's not that," Kip said. "I just don't know if it's there anymore."

"How could it not be there?" Hodge asked, but Kip didn't have an answer. He waved to the lizards and trudged across the hall to the earthy smells of the basement.

Master Windsor's voice greeted Kip as he descended the stairs. "Lutris, it is not that you are unable to perform the spells. It's that you are unable to perform them *consistently*."

Kip's eyes widened. Why was Windsor even here? He braced himself and opened the door as the old sorcerer went on. "I know you can do it once because I have seen it. I do not know that you can do it every time, and until I know that—"

Windsor turned to meet the fox's eyes as Kip closed the door behind him. "At this point," he went on, still talking to the otter but watching the fox, "a lesser sorcerer would have given up. But you are still a student here, and I am still your Master, so you will continue to practice under my instruction until you leave this college."

Kip walked past the two of them to sit in front of Neddy, who faced cheerfully back and forth at the front of the fireplace. He called up fire for the elemental to play in until Emily came to sit beside him. "At least you still have family," she said. "I'll be left here alone."

"You'll have Malcolm," Kip replied, and she made a face.

"I'd sooner go to Georgia with you."

The thought made him happy and immediately guilty as well. "You could," he said before he could stop himself. "I mean…you know sorcery as well. We could…"

"I'll consider it for certain." She smiled and put a hand on his leg, and he appreciated the touch and the response even though he knew it to be a lie. "The world is always arrayed against us; you know that as well as I. If only you had something they wanted enough to keep you here."

"I might." Kip's eyes flicked over to Peter's journal. He'd thought a lot about what was in it. "But I don't know if it's enough."

"If there's anything…" Emily lowered her voice. "Anything at all. Then what harm can it do to try it?"

There was still a faint chance that Odden would select him. Kip wouldn't go spouting his theories about ghosts to him. But Master Windsor…

He turned to look at the sorcerer, still instructing Coppy. His fingers rested on the stone, but no voice came to offer him guidance. All right, he thought, and got up.

"Master Windsor? Might I have a moment?" Kip gestured toward the door.

The sorcerer paused, and then looked down at Coppy. "Five more times, Lutris, while I attend to Penfold here." He swept his robes around him and met Kip on the landing outside the door.

Kip let the door close behind them before he started talking. "I know Selection is very near," he said. Out here, away from Neddy's heat, his breath showed white in the air.

Master Windsor held up a hand. "I have done all I dare on your behalf."

"Dare" or "care," Kip wondered, but he let it go. He took a breath. "Sir, I might have…I may have come across some information that explains why the Tower was spared in the attack."

Windsor's gaze sharpened. "You know who was behind the attack?"

"No." Kip pressed his paws together. "And this theory is…well, it sounds a little crazy."

"You have only been at the College for two months." Windsor's mouth twitched, almost smiling. "Allow me to judge what is crazy. What did you find?"

Kip took a breath and looked the master in the eye. "I believe I'm the only one who can properly research this information. And it would take me a while longer, with access to the College. More than is granted a calyx."

The sorcerer's dark eyes flickered and his brow lowered. "I can call Master Barrett or Master Jaeger here to pry the information from your mind. It will be considerably more pleasant if you tell me."

"They're the ones I would need to speak to," Kip said. "I can't explain, but I promise you, if Coppy and I are Selected and can remain here, I will tell you everything." He forced himself to stand tall and maintain eye contact even though his instincts screamed at him to tell Windsor what he suspected. His tail curled between his legs, but he kept his ears upright and his paws still in front of him.

For the space of three breaths, the cold stone staircase was still. Windsor folded his arms, studying Kip. "You will tell me now," he said, "and if I judge your idea has merit, I will make one more exertion on your behalf." When Kip hesitated, the old sorcerer said, "Surely you must know how ridiculous you sound. A magical secret to which only you and Lutris have access?"

Windsor had misunderstood him and thought Coppy also could study it; that was fine. Kip did not correct him. "Very well." He wrung his paws together and then let them drop to his sides. If he didn't tell Windsor, the old sorcerer would walk away. "I think," he said, taking a breath, "I think that a—a human spirit might have been bound to the Tower. For protection."

"Really." Windsor's lined face did crack a smile now. "Penfold, I expected better of you. You know that human spirits cannot be bound. You think we have not scanned the Tower for any demon or elemental? And why would you think that only you can investigate this theory?"

Kip was about to tell him about Peter's book when he saw another, more elegant explanation. "Because it talked to me," he said.

The old sorcerer's smile vanished like ice under Neddy's paws. "It *talked* to you?"

Slowly, Kip nodded. "When I first arrived. Not since then. Maybe once more, I don't know. I didn't understand at first. I thought I might be hallucinating. But I was reading some books from the library about spirits—demons, I mean—and I thought, well, what if…?"

"What if indeed." Windsor's eyes gazed past Kip for a moment, and one hand came up to rub his chin. After a few more breaths, he put that hand on the door. "Penfold, I can promise nothing, but I will at least tell you that I see some value in your thought, which is not something I expected to say when you made your proposal. You have surprised me today, and that is not a feat to take lightly. Patris is stubborn and the hill you have to climb is taller than the one you stand on, but…hm. Hm. You have extended the range of what I dare to do."

Again, Kip heard "care" for "dare," but he followed Windsor back into the basement with his heart leaping with hope for the first time in days.

CHAPTER 17: SELECTION

During the following weekend, Kip stayed at the College the entire time, despite the urge to visit his parents again. They wouldn't leave without saying good-bye to him, and he had to do all he could to show that he was an exemplary student, to keep alive any faint hope he had of being Selected. He and Coppy both did the best they could when Master Windsor came down to supervise their sessions; the practice tent was off limits until it had been rebuilt, and anyway the weather was getting too cold for even the Calatians to stay out more than an hour. But Master Windsor conducted the sessions as if nothing had happened, as if he expected them to go on forever, and he made no more mention to Kip of the conversation they'd had, even when Kip asked him. Like a small flame, Kip kept his hope burning, but it burned lower with each day of no news. He couldn't even bring himself to tell his friends about it, for fear of kindling too great a hope in them.

Their last week of classes before the Selection, too, felt maddeningly normal. Masters Patris, Windsor, and Argent all spoke of what would be covered the following week as though they all would be there for it. Only Patris twice said, "Though not everyone will have those lessons."

The second time, Farley said, "If we won't be here, then can we skip the lesson?"

Patris turned a cold eye on him. "If you wish to return home and quit the school now, you are free to do so."

Farley began to get up, but Adamson, next to him, put a hand on his arm, and the stout boy sat back down. Adamson reclined back in his chair and returned his attention to Patris.

The blond boy still confused Kip. They hadn't spoken since the Friday of the fight, but beyond that…Adamson had yet to demonstrate a single act of sorcery. He hadn't even been able to gather magic the way the rest of them all could (though some only managed flickers of light). And yet he retained an air of perfect confidence, and Patris praised his studies constantly.

Once during the week, Malcolm had asked if they thought Adamson had any chance of being chosen, and Kip said, "Patris would Select him to keep his father's money coming in," and the subject had dropped, because none of them wanted to think of the injustice of magic-less Adamson as an apprentice while the two Calatians were sent home.

Peter's journal occupied much of Kip's spare time that week, but he discovered nothing new about either Peter himself or the ritual that, successful or not, had ended his journal. Peter wrote extensively about some of his lessons and troubles with the other students, but about his Selection he wrote only that "Master Primus did Select me this morning. Many of the other students did cause a clamour, but Primus told me to ignore them and keep my ears upright. The other Masters, though less vocal, did also express their displeasure with the choice, but Primus paid them no heed and so I did not either."

Kip's own ears stood when he read that. This other fox, two hundred years before him, when Calatians had been newly granted personhood by the church, had been brave enough to stand alone because he wanted to learn magic. Kip pressed his paw to the floor and whispered, "Peter?" No voice answered him, and doubt crept into his mind. Windsor had gone to Master Jaeger or Master Barrett, had asked about Kip's theory, and the spiritual master had laughed. Windsor had joined in, laughing at the stupid, desperate Calatian. And yet, Master Windsor came down to work with them every night with the same stoic demeanor, and would not discuss Kip's idea nor the possibility of Selection with him.

The day before their Selection, Kip took the journal down again but did not open it. Even when he simply held the journal in his paws, he found, his friends forgot to talk to him, almost forgot that he was there. If he carried the journal with him always, could he live in the Tower with nobody noticing, like a ghost? He could tell Emily about it and she could bring him food; he could continue to attend classes and practice his sorcery.

But that would hardly be a satisfying life, skulking in the shadows, relying on a spell he didn't understand to keep him hidden. He had seen it work on Master Windsor, but what if some of the other sorcerers could see through it? Master Jaeger, for example, could talk into people's minds and see into them as well. Kip had still not met a quarter of the masters remaining in the College, unless you counted talking through a raven as meeting Master Jaeger. If he tried to stay behind and was discovered, that could end badly for him. Nonetheless, he kept it in his mind as a remote possibility.

To the others, he talked again about either going to Georgia with his parents or to London with Coppy, who was quite pleased with the idea and told him he'd be welcome. Kip hoped privately that he might convince Coppy to come to Georgia with him, but that could wait until they knew their fates. Malcolm thought Kip and Coppy were prime candidates for the military, as sorcerers to one of the Calatian units. Kip hadn't thought of that, but was sure Patris would love to see them facing combat.

Emily, assured of her Selection, grumbled that she was going to learn to translocate herself to wherever they were so that she would have some pleasant company if they all left. Malcolm thought he would either go to the military or as an apprentice; he'd talked to Master Vendis about his defensive spellwork, shown him the two spells he'd mastered, and Vendis had said he was impressed. When Malcolm had pressed for a confirmation of his Selection, Vendis had said that the issue was "tricky," and that he would have to "put some thought into it."

"I've no idea why they feel they must keep to themselves," the Irishman said. The four of them sat on the floor with Neddy close by for warmth. "Surely by now he knows whether or not he'll Select me, just as Odden knows whether he'll Select you."

"Master Argent's told me he will Select me," Emily said. "And I heard that Master Waldo has promised Jacob a Selection, and Master Warrington the same for Matthew."

"It's because you're friends with us." Kip curled his tail around his knees and picked up a paper. In the light of the torches and the phosphorus elemental, he made out a scrawl of letters detailing a purchase of linens from 1733. He crumpled it in his paw and tossed it over to Neddy, who scurried forward and devoured it. "It's because he has to be sure Patris won't make his life miserable for three years for daring to associate with someone who of his own volition associates with Calatians."

"And your father is his calyx," Coppy added.

"Maybe not for much longer." Kip folded his arms across his knees and rested his head on them. He didn't know what would happen when his father moved to Georgia, but he suspected that Vendis would want to find a calyx closer to home. The thought flitted across his mind that Vendis might be waiting to see if someone else Selected him so that if not, Vendis could take him as a calyx, which might make it difficult to have Malcolm as his apprentice. If that was the case, then Kip was going to disappoint his father's master; he wasn't going to be any nearer New Cambridge than his father was, and maybe farther.

Monday morning when the Selection was to take place, Kip and his friends arrived from the basement and found the desks arranged in the Great Hall as if for class, in neat rows on the carpet. They took their accustomed seats as the other students filtered down the stairs and did the same, though no master waited at the front of the room.

"How long you suppose they plan to make us wait?" Malcolm asked the moment he slid into his seat beside Emily.

Kip's ears caught footsteps on the stairs. "They're coming," he said.

Malcolm frowned, but as the footsteps grew louder, he slouched back, affecting disinterest. Under the desk, where only the students behind him—Kip and Coppy—could see, he wrung his hands together in visible display of turmoil much like that in Kip's own stomach. The fox kept his tail and paws still as the footsteps quelled the rest of the muttering among the students.

Ten masters in their formal black robes lined with crimson velvet and gold stitching walked single file into the Great Hall. Patris, at the head of the formation, stood behind the podium, while the other nine arrayed themselves behind him. Kip could name almost all the Masters present: from left to right behind Patris, he saw Windsor, Vendis, a tall red-headed portly man he assumed was Warrington, Brown, Splint, Odden, Sharpe, Waldo, and last, Argent. He assumed that the missing sorcerers, Campbell, Jaeger, and Barrett, remained in their rooms.

Patris launched into his speech without so much as a "good morning." "The Selection is a time-honored ritual at the College, and before that at the King's Academy since its founding, by which method the current sorcerers choose the young men…" He paused, staring down at his podium; beside Kip, Emily sat up straighter and folded her arms. "Who will make up the next generation of sorcerers," Patris finished. "The work you have done these past months will determine what path you take from this day forward. Because of the dire straits in which the school finds itself now, the sorcerers have chosen to evaluate your talents over two months rather than over a year, as is customary. It may strike some of you as unfair to have such a short period in which to prove your worth, but I assure you that in our discussions over the past week, we have taken pains to consider every aspect of your education. In fact, we have spent far more time than usual in meetings to finish our evaluations."

"What does he want, a medal of honor?" muttered Malcolm over his shoulder. Emily covered her mouth with her hand, and Kip and Coppy exchanged tight, tense smiles.

Patris launched into a short history of Selections and the various colleges of sorcery that Kip lost interest in quickly. Some of the sorcerers also looked bored; Waldo and Argent leaned in close to each other, whispering. Odden and Sharpe fidgeted, Warrington examined his fingernails, and Splint stared up at the ceiling. Master Windsor stayed standing at attention, and though he didn't appear to be following the speech at all, neither would he meet Kip's eyes.

"…long and storied history of which some of you will now be a part," Patris concluded some ten minutes later. He looked out at the class as though checking to see that they were all paying attention. Kip couldn't stop his fur from bristling up on his neck and tail, but at least that wasn't visible. Neither could he keep his paws still any longer, so he focused on keeping them on his legs where their tapping would be silent.

"You know that some of you will be assigned to the Royal Civil Corps, there to help build the roads and buildings that will make the Colonies the jewel in the Empire's crown. There is a great frontier to the West waiting to be developed and claimed, and your work will be integral in securing it. Some will go to His Majesty's Army or Navy, to fight for the Empire against those who would tear it down. All your skill and learning will be needed to help our forces defeat the Spaniards. And some will be chosen as apprentices to sorcerers here in the Tower. This last is a great honor, not bestowed lightly, and we expect that those of you so chosen will live up to the responsibility of being not only exceptional sorcerers, but exceptional men as well." This time he did not hesitate over the word "men." Emily gave a small sniff, and Kip bit his lip, but neither of them said anything aloud.

"A few of you will not hear your names called at all," Patris said. "You have demonstrated no talent for sorcery, and we will not recommend you to any other work."

Kip glanced at Coppy, but the otter stared straight ahead. Of course he would prefer not to be recommended, to be allowed to go home and work on the Isle for himself and his people. If he were sent to a civil corps, much less the military, they would dictate where he was to be posted and what work he had to do.

Patris shuffled the papers on the podium and brought one to the front. "The students recommended to the civil corps are: Cobb. Cooper. Smith."

Two rows ahead of Kip, Mark Smith slumped in his desk. Kip's eyes were on Farley's back. He would have guessed that Farley's talent lay in the military, but he'd rather hoped to see his nemesis building roads for a living. He had noticed that Patris had said that those chosen for the military would go to the military, no choice, and so he swallowed and prayed he would not hear his own name in the next round.

Coppy, by contrast, looked bright-eyed at the omission of his name. "Military," he whispered to Kip. "Never woulda thought it!"

Maybe, Kip thought, some of the Calatian units had heard of them and requested Calatian sorcerers. Maybe he and Coppy would be assigned together. That wouldn't be so bad. Travel to exotic places, good pay, and sorcerers usually fought from a distance and were well protected, or else were kept behind the lines to move supplies.

"The student recommended to His Majesty's Army and Navy is Carmichael."

That was all. Kip sank back into his seat and looked up at Master Odden, trying to read the expression behind the bushy black beard. But the sorcerer remained impassive as Patris went on, and it was from Patris himself that Kip got his only indication of what his fate might be.

"Students selected to apprentice to a Master are to be commended, for an apprenticeship is awarded not solely because of talent in sorcery. Hard work and proper comportment are also key to being Selected. This year, despite the paucity of apprentices in the College, we Masters refused to relax our standards. We are delighted to Select the following students for their apprenticeships in Prince George's College of Sorcery. As I call your names, please come up to stand beside the Master who chose you."

He didn't look delighted; he looked as though he'd bitten into an apple and found multiple worms there. Kip's ears came up. Though Odden remained impassive, hope blossomed in the fox that he would become an apprentice.

"As my apprentice," Patris began, "I select Victor Adamson."

Kip's good mood evaporated. Adamson? The one who couldn't cast a single spell? Announced first, as though he were head of the class, and apprenticed to the headmaster, to boot? In front of him, Emily hissed, but he couldn't look up to meet her gaze for fear that he'd burst out yelling at the unfairness of it all. What was Adamson going to do as an apprentice? Bring a whole lot of the senior Adamson's money to the College, he reminded himself bitterly.

"Swot," Emily muttered beside Kip, and that broke his tension, allowing him to relax in his seat. He flashed her a tight smile.

Adamson had walked up to stand beside Patris. The white-haired sorcerer brushed hair out of his eyes and continued. "The apprentice to Master Waldo will be Jacob Quarrel."

Quarrel, a lanky young man with a mop of black hair and a scruffy beard, stepped up quickly as Master Waldo came forward to greet him. The two exchanged words briefly and then stepped back into line, Quarrel a step behind his Master.

"At least he can actually perform sorcery," Kip muttered to Emily.

"Nice to know they take that into account," she replied.

"The apprentice to Master Vendis will be Malcolm O'Brien." Patris read it quickly, without inflection.

Malcolm turned and flashed a wide smile to Kip, Emily, and Coppy, then marched quickly up to the front. Master Vendis shuffled his feet beneath the folds of his robes and made space for Malcolm, but did not speak to him.

"The apprentice to Master Warrington will be Matthew Chesterton." There was less hostility there, but still no enjoyment, none of the pleasure Patris had shown in reading out Adamson's name. Perhaps it was merely that he saved that emotion for his own apprentice. Kip thought there was likely another reason. Not that Matthew Chesterton had done anything particularly offensive to Patris, but he was the last name Patris was going to read before he got to the distasteful ones.

The red-haired boy had barely gotten to the podium before Patris read the next Selection, quickly. "The apprentice to Master Argent will be Emily Carswell."

Emily took her time getting to her feet, returning Kip's and Coppy's smiles, and stepped carefully up to the front of the Hall, clearly prolonging the moment to antagonize the Head. He ignored her, and as she reached the podium, he said, "Master Odden selects Philip Penfold."

For a moment, Kip couldn't breathe or move. He stared up at the front, his ears straight up, his brain still buzzing with the words. Odden had done it somehow, had overcome Patris's objections and had saved Kip's…life, perhaps. The relief of not having to think about military service, or Georgia, or the Isle overwhelmed him, and it wasn't until Coppy hissed, "Kip!" at him that he got to his feet, nearly knocking down his chair in the process. It caught his tail, so he had to extricate himself before hurrying up to the front.

"Don't take much to be an apprentice," Farley sneered as Kip passed, looking entirely unconcerned about his own standing.

But behind him, the elementals had figured out that Kip was going to stay, and from the fireplace came a small chorus of cheers. "Hooray for Penfold!" "Good on yer, fox." And up on stage, Emily beamed and Malcolm barely restrained himself from jumping up and down, fidgeting until Master Vendis turned and spoke sharply to him. Kip wished his father could be here to see, wished he could tell him right away rather than having to wait hours, maybe even a day. He wanted to thank his father for all he'd done, all he'd given up, so that Kip could have this chance, and Kip wanted him to see that all that work hadn't been wasted.

When he reached his place beside Master Odden, the sorcerer turned and said softly, "We will discuss the implications of this presently."

Kip nodded, his throat still feeling tight and unusable, and stared out at the Great Hall. Farley and five other students remained at the front, most of them looking down at their desks or playing with quills, and Coppy sat alone in the back. The otter was smiling up at Kip, and Kip felt an ache in his heart at not even having considered his friend's state. He'd assumed that whatever happened to him and Coppy would happen together, good or bad, and that he would have the choice of remaining with the otter if he wanted. But Coppy's smile held not a trace of sadness or jealousy; he was genuinely delighted for Kip and proud of his friend. He opened his mouth to whisper to Master Odden, to plead with him to take on Coppy as well, but Odden turned to him as though reading his thoughts and shook his head slowly. Kip closed his mouth and lowered his head.

"The rest of you," Patris began, but Master Windsor stepped forward.

"Clement," he said, softly, but Kip's ears caught the word.

"I will not permit it," Patris hissed back. "You said last night that—"

"I have changed my mind." Windsor spoke in soft steel.

The other sorcerers looked at each other. Splint and Brown whispered, but Kip was focused on Windsor and Patris and missed what the others were saying. He hardly dared hope, but there could only be one thing they were talking about, one person left whose Selection would enrage Patris. Windsor was taking a chance on Coppy; Kip's desperate bargain had saved his friend.

"No," Patris said. "He is not ready."

"The potential is there, and you cannot prevent my decision."

"Announce it yourself, then." The Head turned to the class. "Those of you not chosen, good luck with the rest of your lives. You must be off the College grounds by sunset today." He grabbed the sleeve of Adamson's robe and marched him around the side, past the empty fireplace and to the stairs.

Master Windsor stepped up to the podium. "The apprentice to Master Windsor will be Copper Lutris," he said without ceremony. "Lutris, join me in the basement, if you please."

The other sorcerers muttered among themselves, clearly as surprised as Kip himself was. "Bloody hell," muttered Jacob Quarrel, just down from Kip. Coppy, for his part, looked more shocked than happy. He'd stood but hadn't taken a step toward the front yet, and as he looked at Kip, the fox tried to give him an encouraging smile, tried to put all the happiness bursting in his chest into that expression. But Coppy only smiled weakly in return, then scrambled to follow Master Windsor to the basement stairs.

Malcolm leaned back to grin at Kip, bouncing again, until Master Vendis reached out to restrain him. And then Master Odden turned to face him, looking up from under his bushy eyebrows. "All right, Penfold," he said. All around them, sorcerers were talking to their new apprentices. "Come on."

They mounted the stairs, Kip's tail lashing with excitement all the way through the smell of Farley in the room outside Master Odden's office and into the office itself, still thick with phosphorus and smoke. Master Odden shut the door and gestured to the chair behind his desk. "Have a seat."

There was no other chair in the office. Kip looked to the sorcerer for confirmation, got a nod, and shakily seated himself in the large wooden chair, curling his tail around his hips rather than threading it through the back. Still giddy from having made the bargain to keep Coppy with him at the college, he folded his paws in his lap and looked up, willing himself to concentrate.

Odden paced to the dais and back to the door, then faced Kip. "You know the difficulties that lie ahead of us both, though perhaps not so much those that I am facing." He held up a hand. "Let me finish. Patris is understandably concerned about your temperament, and even setting his biases aside, the issues he raises have merit. One," he counted on his fingers, "your presence here attracts unwelcome attention and puts you in situations in which your temper will be sorely tested. Two, your presence here may unsettle the balance between sorcerers and their calyxes. Three, there is the rather serious question of what use you will make of your powers. The revolutionary elements in Boston have been discussed often inside these walls, and now that you are to be an apprentice, I may tell you that the Crown has advised us to be prepared to use our powers against our fellow Americans within the next five years, and that the revolutionaries have approached many of our number to sniff out our loyalties. One of the reasons your class is being rushed into apprenticeships is to increase the sorcerers available to us as soon as possible. Rather than the general rounding of spells you would expect to receive in your first year, you will each be asked to focus on your chosen discipline. Patris's concern is that the revolutionaries will promise liberties to the Calatians—this has already been mentioned—and that you will turn your powers to that cause. As it seems very likely at this point that you are a fire sorcerer, a rare and powerful commodity, this is greatly worrisome, and his preference was that you not be trained at all rather than risk you becoming a weapon that might turn on us."

Rare and powerful. Kip filed that information away for future review. "Sir," he said, "do you think the attack on the College came from revolutionaries and not from the Spanish?"

The sorcerer rubbed his beard. "I cannot say. I would not dismiss it as a possibility. Windsor is the one studying the attack through the lens of history and he seems to think that if Spain had launched an attack so successful, they would have followed it with another by now. But perhaps the survival of the Tower has confused them and delayed their next attack."

"And maybe they're working with the revolutionaries."

"Yes." Odden peered at him. "Sharp, you are."

"I hadn't thought the revolutionaries were anything but talkers," Kip said. "People with ideas. They don't seem to have done anything yet."

"No, but they would hardly move openly, not while their influence is still so weak. But this is all for a future discussion. I feel Windsor might enjoy participating as well."

Kip drew his shoulders in and nodded. "Perhaps I will ask him," he said, knowing that he would have to have at least one conversation with Windsor before too long.

Odden linked his hands behind his back, his broad stomach protruding, and paced back and forth again. "My response to Patris's points, in inverse order, is as follows: I believe that the third is unprovable. You have shown no revolutionary bent, and your admittedly iconoclastic attitude seems solely aimed at improving the lot of yourself and your fellows. Someone willing to fight for his people is just the kind of sorcerer we want, if only you will recognize that the sorcerers here at the College are now your people. Do you?"

His bushy eyebrows rose, and Kip nodded. "The Calatians—the town drove my father out of business. I don't owe them anything." Even as he said the words, his chest fluttered, but he sat up straight and didn't let the flutter touch his voice.

"Good." Odden stopped pacing. "I believe that with a small amount of further study, you may be ready to spend time studying with Master Cott at King's, which would further cement your loyalties and address Patris's worries on that score. On the second point, that the calyxes might revolt upon seeing what you have achieved? I feel it is as likely that they may revolt if you are prevented from achieving your potential. In any event, that is beyond your capacity to influence. I do not see that it should have a strong bearing on whether you are allowed to pursue an education.

"But the first point, that one troubled me the most. I believe you have the best of intentions in your pursuit of sorcery. Left to your own devices, there would likely be no problem."

"Farley Broadside won't be continuing," Kip put in. "So I think that will reduce the problems still further."

"Yes." Odden inclined his head. "But Victor Adamson remains, and Patris himself, not to mention the people of New Cambridge. You've told me they drove your father out of business. As you master fire and learn to summon demons and other destructive magics, the damage you will be able to do with a single impulse will be greatly increased. So from you I need a promise that in addition to studying sorcery, you will study self-control, that you will never use your abilities against another person except to save your life, and then only as much as is needed, no more. Can you promise me that?"

That was what he had done to save Coppy, he'd thought, and wouldn't any sorcerer need to promise that? But what was needed here was agreement, not argument. "Yes, sir," he said.

"Good. Now, to the less pleasant parts of our talk." Odden leaned back against the wall next to his door. "You can imagine that Patris was not inclined to agree to your apprenticeship, even given my rebuttal to his points. So you will be taking over one of his duties, as his own apprentice is not suited to do so."

The flare of anger at Adamson rose again; Kip suppressed it. "Which duty, sir?"

"Scanning the ruins of the attacked buildings for remains and other clues."

Kip kept his voice steady and nodded, trying not to picture Saul's twisted, shattered body. "Yes, sir. How do I do that?"

"You will be told when you are ready to start. I have to teach you some basic mastery and summoning of demons, but I believe your facility in summoning elementals indicates you will not take long to learn it." Odden rubbed his hands together and met Kip's eye. "You have a rare talent, Penfold. I would not see it wasted, and that is why I have taken a great risk to help you foster it. I hope you remember that."

"Yes, sir. I'm very grateful. I promise you I will do the best I can."

"I know you will." Odden reached across his desk to clap a hand on Kip's shoulder. "There is the matter of having you work with a calyx, which will be rather awkward, I'm afraid, but I feel certain you can manage that as well."

"I can," Kip said, though he felt less certain about that than about anything else he'd agreed to in the past hour.

"All right, then. I'm sure your friends will want to celebrate with you. No classes today, but tomorrow they will start again, except that Tuesday and Thursday mornings, instead of Patris's class, you'll come have a private class with me." Odden clasped Kip's paw in his hand as the fox rose to his feet. "Ah, and if you wish, you may move to the outer quarters there. They'll be vacated by tomorrow, and it's traditional. All the apprentices are moving to their masters' outer quarters."

"Must I?"

Odden raised his eyebrows. "I thought you'd be pleased to escape the basement. Of course you may continue to live there if you wish. I don't believe Windsor will have Lutris up at his quarters, and if the two of you would prefer to remain together…"

Kip had been thinking more that Emily would not want to live with Master Argent and would want company, but he nodded as though that had been his main concern. "We will discuss our situation," he said.

The sorcerer opened his door. Outside, Farley was nowhere to be seen (though his smell lingered, another reason for Kip to choose the basement), but the other two students were packing up their clothes. Kip stepped through, and Odden called out as he left.

"I look forward to being quite proud of you, apprentice," he said.

"I'll do the best I can." Kip held his head up and walked out.

Coppy had finished with Master Windsor by that point, so with the day free, Kip asked if he would come to say good-bye to Kip's parents. Emily asked if they would come back for dinner—"We plan to have a celebration, and maybe you can burn Broadside's stench off the bench in the dining tent," she said with a sparkle in her eye.

"I'll be sorry to miss it," Kip said, "but if my parents want us to stay for dinner, we will."

So he and Coppy left the gates, passing Corimea who was present again, and walked down the hill. Coppy remained silent, so Kip tried to nudge him into conversation. "Master Odden is going to be pretty strict," he said. "Told me I'd best not put my nose out of line or he and I would both be in trouble with old Patris." Still Coppy didn't respond. Kip cleared his throat. "How was Windsor?"

The otter walked with him a few more paces, then shrugged. "Same as always. Told me I'd got a long way to go. Said I'd better show more work than I had the last two months. Said I could be kicked out at the end of the year as easily as now."

"You will work hard, though," Kip said. "And it'll be easier without so much distraction. Now you've learned a little, we can work with some other spells. I bet you'd do well with water."

"I don't understand why he chose me!" The words burst out of Coppy, and then he ducked his head.

Kip set a paw on his friend's shoulder. "You're not unhappy he Selected you, are you? We get to stay together and learn together and all."

"Oh, Kip, I'm not sad about that." Coppy stepped closer to him, their tails touching and hips almost bumping, and then he stepped away again. "But I don't understand it. I never thought Windsor saw any value in me and of all the Masters, I never thought he would want to work more with me. He's always so angry and he makes me nervous like nobody else. Why would he want to torture me more? He gets no joy of it."

The outburst caught Kip by surprise. He almost confessed his role in it, but what would happen to Coppy's confidence if he knew Windsor had only Selected him at Kip's request? "I don't know," he said. "Maybe he sees something in you…"

"He sees someone he can bully," Coppy said. "I don't know. If it weren't for you, I'd likely say 'good day' and go back to the Isle. I could be useful there, and there'd be nobody to yell at me for not lifting something as fast or as steady as everyone else can do it. There'd be nobody else."

"You'd be arrested."

"Not if nobody knew about it. My people wouldn't tell. I'd be discreet." The otter rested a paw on Kip's arm. "We were discreet before coming here."

"But…" That all felt wrong to Kip. He tried to put his finger on why. "But if there's nobody to challenge you, you'll never get better. Think of it, Coppy, think of what you *could* do. More than just lifting rocks, you could, you could maybe get fresh water to flow. Or you could learn to translocate, or you could be a healer like Master Splint."

"Aye…" Coppy exhaled. "Sorry. I know I should want to do more. But sometimes I want to leave it all behind. You won't need me around to protect you no more, and I can't help you with your studying, so what good am I?"

"What good are you?" Kip wrapped an arm around the otter's shoulders. "What *good* are you? You're my best friend."

"Aye." Coppy smiled brightly. "I reckon there is that."

They reached Kip's house a little after noon. Kip heard one person moving around inside and opened the door with a sharp knock to alert them.

His mother dropped the apple she was holding and ran to wrap her arms around him. "We didn't know when to expect you," she said against his cheek ruff, and then kissed him. "Your father is off making sure of the carriage. It's for the first thing in the morning."

Their trunks stood against the wall of the kitchen, and beyond the kitchen door, the parlor furniture was stacked and wrapped in burlap cloths. All of Kip's life up until two and a half months ago lay here in these rooms, wrapped to be sent a thousand miles south. He turned away from it as his mother moved to embrace Coppy as well. "What's the news?" she asked, stepping back, her eyes fluttering between the two of them.

"We're both apprentices," Kip told her, his tail wagging.

She couldn't hide the flicker of disappointment in her whiskers before masking it with joy. "I'm so delighted for you," she said, and embraced them again. "Your father will be so proud. Two apprentice sorcerers in our family!"

"The first two Calatian apprentices," Kip said, with a guilty flick of the ear as he remembered Peter Cadno. "And Emily's the first woman to be an apprentice."

"And all here in New Cambridge. It's history in the making." His mother picked up the apple and set it with the plate of simple cheese she'd been preparing, her tail swishing back and forth. "Would you like to have lunch with us? We'd be quite happy for your company."

The amount of food was about what Kip and Coppy were each accustomed to eating by themselves at lunch. They looked at each other and then Coppy said, "We already ate, but thank you."

"Mom." Kip stepped forward and took her paw. "It's a good thing, it really is. They'll hear about us in London. Calatians down in the Bronx and in Boston and Philadelphia and down in Georgia will know that if they show magic, they can be considered as students."

She squeezed his paw back. "I know that," she said. "I am proud of you, really I am. But it's hearing about you that worries me. The good people will hear about you, and the bad ones, too."

"Coppy and I can defend ourselves." Kip started to call magic, to show her that he could make a fire in the stove, but she waved him down before he got very far.

"I know you can," she said. "But every mother wants an easy life for her cubs. You know how I admire those bluestockings in Boston and Miss Clotilde here, running her own farm, all those women trying to make it easier for the rest of us."

"But that's what I'm doing, too."

"Yes, but Kip, all those women are making their lives harder for themselves. And on top of that, you're in the College, and…oh, I know it's a good thing, a very good thing, but if you could find a less dangerous way of doing good, something that might not end with you killed…"

Coppy had turned to see Kip's reaction, and now chuckled. "It's little use, Mrs. Penfold. You know Kip better than I do. When his mind is set on a thing, there's no shifting it. But we'll stick together, we two, and two have it easier than one."

"We're four if you count Emily and Malcolm, and I do," Kip added. "We've got friends among the sorcerers, too, Mom. We won't be in more danger than anyone else."

Her ears slid back, and she lowered her voice. "I had nightmares the past two months. I woke up with that noise in my ears again, that awful thunder, and I knew for certain it was you under the rubble. I couldn't stand it, Kip. I'm sorry."

"Oh, Mom." He hugged her again. "There's nothing to be sorry about."

She kissed his cheek and pulled back. "Don't give me anything to be sorry about."

Steps sounded outside. A moment later Max came through the door, his mouth creasing into a smile when he saw Kip and Coppy. "Good news?"

"Good news." Kip ran to his father and hugged him, and his father returned the embrace powerfully, patting Kip on the back. "Good news for us both!"

"Ah, that's wonderful. Oh, son." Max pulled his head back, his nose an inch from Kip's, his eyes shining already. "I'm so bloody proud of you."

"Max!" Ada said.

The older fox laughed and moved to hug Coppy as well. "There's a time for profanity, and this is quite definitely it. You realize what our son and our adopted son have accomplished? What they've shown the world?"

"Yes," she said. "We were just talking about it."

Kip gave them more details about the Selection, about Master Windsor's surprise Selection of Coppy and the argument with Patris, about Vendis taking Malcolm. "Are you going to continue to be his calyx?" Kip asked his father.

"No," Max said. "I'm done with that once we move. I've set him up with Johnny Lapelli."

"And you're leaving in the morning?" Coppy asked.

"First thing." Max smiled and shook his head. "I am not looking forward to this trip. The better part of a month, some wild roads…but we've the company of two other families from Boston headed south for the climate, and we've pooled our money to hire a guard—a human guard. So we'll be in less danger than you will, I daresay."

"Max!"

"I'm joking." He reached out to take Ada's paw, and leaned over to kiss her. "I'm sure we'll be in *terrible* danger."

"I don't want any of us to be in danger," she said, but she smiled and leaned into his kiss.

Kip and Coppy stayed through lunch, and then Kip pointed out that they could load the carriage much more quickly and easily than his parents could, so Max brought the cart around and the two apprentices (Kip got a thrill out of thinking of them that way) floated all the luggage and furniture into the cart bed.

"Perhaps it's not so terrible, this sorcery," his mother said. "If only it was available to us more often.'

Kip set his ears back, feeling guilty that he wouldn't be going with his parents. His father saw it and took him by the arm. "I'm going to talk to Kip for a moment," he said. "Excuse us."

They walked through the house, to the bolted door that led to the closed shop. His father unbolted it and gestured for Kip to go through.

The smell of dust and neglect hit him first, and then the sight of the empty shelves, bare wood where there had been bottles he'd run his fingers over countless times, sniffed the stoppers of, catalogued and counted and wrapped for customers. A thin layer of dust coated the counter that had seen him grow up; it had been nose height, then neck height, then chest height. Now it came to his stomach and he rested a paw on it, trying to focus on his father and not on the silent, empty space that had once been a thriving shop.

"Your mother wasn't asking you to come along," Max said. "In a way, she was telling you how proud she is. You're bringing sorcery to the Calatians of New Cambridge. We have been afforded certain protections because of our association with the college, but the sorcerers still do not offer us services as they do the humans. Master Splint, for example, will come down for certain extreme cases—of humans. Never of Calatians."

"He healed me once." Kip remembered again the teeth of the steel trap on his foot.

"As a favor to me. My relationship with Master Vendis allowed for certain privileges. I tried not to abuse them, but only used them when you needed them." Max shook his head. "I'm pleased for Emily, too. Like Calatians, women have never had an outlet to develop any magical abilities. Think about what your life would have been like had you never entered the College, and then think of hundreds or thousands of women around the Empire who face the same fate. Emily is doing for them what you are doing for your people."

"My people." Kip looked around the empty shop. "How can you say that after what they've done to you? They're not my people. They don't care about me or my family."

Max reached out and gripped Kip's arm tightly. "They are always your people. Don't forget that. Not all the Calatians in New Cambridge ruined this business. Some humans did too, and many Calatians came to support me. Many spoke well of you but could not afford to support the business. Humans may borrow money, but not so much us." He released Kip's arm and sighed. "Those are matters I hope you will never have to concern yourself with. Suffice to say that if you must be angry—and it serves you little purpose, and I would counsel you against it—then be angry at the persons who have taken action. Don't reject the town. Don't reject your people." He rubbed claws through the fur on the back of one paw.

"Master Odden said I'm part of the College now." Kip folded his arms. "I'll look out for other Calatians, but this town doesn't deserve my help." He couldn't keep his eyes from the empty shelves, and every breath of neglect made him angry all over again.

His father looked around, too. "I won't say I won't miss it. Or that sometimes, at night, I don't get a bit angry myself. I wish things could have been different. But I think that your situation right now is more than I'd dared dream for you. And so all this…" He waved his paw at the store. "Is worth it."

The weight of the moment kept Kip silent. He curled his tail behind him and then let it relax. He wanted to be a sorcerer on his own merits, not have to have his father sacrifice for him, or Odden make deals with Patris, or have to be vigilant every day lest he give anyone an excuse to upend his life. "I wish you could stay here," he said, because it was easier than articulating the turmoil in his head, and because it was true. "At least for the Feast."

"Well." Max lowered his voice and stepped close to Kip, speaking in a whisper. "That's what I brought you here to tell you. Master Vendis will continue to summon me, via magic this time rather than raven, and so I will be at the College for brief occasions over at least the next year. Don't tell your mother. She thinks my association with the College is ended, and it would cause her too much worry to know that I'll be going back. Johnny Lapelli will be taking my place, but I'll be helping him get used to his duties."

"Will you be able to come see me?" Kip asked. "I won't tell Mom."

Max nodded. "I think I will, since you'll be an apprentice. I'll ask Vendis—Master Vendis, now that he knows you'll be staying on. And we'll try to come back for the Feast, but no promises. There's a Calatian community down there too, and even if we plan to return here, we should spend some time forging bonds with them."

"Good." Kip hugged his father. "I'm going to miss you."

"You'll see me about as often as you would have anyway." Max smiled. "Now, can you and Coppy stay for dinner?"

Kip had seen what his parents were having for dinner, and he'd feel guilty taking half of it for him and Coppy, even though his stomach was growling from having missed lunch. "We'll stay a bit longer, but we get fed at the College."

"All right." Max stepped back, setting his paws on Kip's upper arms. "But remember what I've told you here. Your life is your own to plot, and no-one else's, so think about these choices. And help Coppy when he needs it, too."

Again the weight felt too much for him, but he stood and bore it. "I will, Dad. I promise."

They returned to the parlor, joined Coppy and Ada, and passed another pleasant hour before the daylight began to fade, and Max insisted they return to the College while Coppy could still see well. They embraced, and Ada cried a little and said she would write often, and Kip didn't want to take that first step out the door, because while he still stood inside, his home still existed and he was part of it.

But the moon was rising, and the sun just one long night behind it, and his parents had to leave, and he had classes to attend. So he and Coppy said their good-byes one last time and then walked out into the garden, through the alley, and into the street. Twilight had enveloped the town, but Kip could see easily as long as he looked away from the windows where fires and candles burned. In the night, the town felt restful, not the sort of place that would force his parents out and attempt to force him to stop his studies.

They remained silent as they passed the church and the Founders Inn, and then Coppy said, "They'll be all right. I'm sure of it."

"Aye," Kip said.

"And we will, too."

Kip nodded, tail swishing behind him. He walked three more steps, then turned and looked down at the town.

There were Calatians and humans down there; there were those who wished him well or ill; a few who loved him and a few who hated him. Up at the Tower, which rose in the other direction, there were Calatians and humans, some who wished him well or ill, a few who loved him and a few who hated him. For now, his home was there, on top of the hill, in the ancient White Tower, and he was a sorcerer, though also a Calatian, a balance he hadn't struck in his head quite yet. Again he wondered whether Peter Cadno also still lived in the Tower, the only other person in the world who'd had to strike the same balance. Perhaps in the coming months, Kip would discover the truth of it.

"Wonder if they've had dinner yet," Coppy said a few steps later as the gates came in sight.

Kip put a paw to his own stomach and smiled. "Let's go see," he said, and together they walked through the gates, past a bowing Corimea, and into the College.

EPILOGUE

Dinner was in fact over, but Kip smelled food and heard conversation in the dining tent, so he held the flap open for Coppy. The tent was mostly empty, but Emily and Malcolm still sat at their table over crusts of bread. The rest of the tables showed little sign of being used, but the smells of roast fowl lingered along with cheese and the smells of a few students amid the strong phosphorus scent that was so familiar to Kip now that he easily filtered the other scents through it. He waved to the phosphorus elemental in the closest brazier as he came in, then smiled at Emily and Malcolm, talking alone at their table. "Come sit down," Emily said, gesturing to the bench across from them. "It was a glorious meal. There was no Farley he went down to the Inn with Adamson and the others. Oh, and the ones who weren't chosen for anything had to have some spell done to them by some ancient master we'd never seen. Malcolm believes it was one of the spiritual sorcerers making them unable to cast spells or tell the college's secrets."

Malcolm smiled widely. "I asked Master Vendis and he told me the college 'takes precautions,' though he'd not tell me what exactly."

"It was the best meal I've had here," Emily went on. "Peace and quiet and even no ravens. It was heaven."

"We didn't even get to eat." Kip explained his parents' situation quickly. "And I think they spent all their money on the trip."

"Oh." Emily looked about. "I'm sorry. The demons have cleared away all the leftover food."

A peppermint tingle lingered in Kip's nose. He raised his voice and looked toward the empty center of the tent. "Hey. Can we have some food?"

Malcolm raised his eyebrows. "Got a demon in here watching us?"

"Aye," Kip said, then turned back to the empty space. "I know you're here. If you're going to spy on us, you might as well bring us food."

The peppermint tingle disappeared. Kip rubbed his nose and turned to the others. "It's gone," he said. "Maybe it'll be back with food."

"If not," Coppy said, "we can go down to the Inn."

"Rather not." Kip smiled and looked around the tent. "Not while there's such fine company here."

The demon did return with food, refusing to become visible but slamming down a tray of bread and roast fowl. The fowl was cool, but still delicious. "Ho," Kip said to the peppermint tingle in the air, "can you bring some food down to my parents in New Cambridge?"

His answer was a loud raspberry blown in the air, and the disappearance of the tingle. Coppy looked down at the tray, at the half chicken and three slices of bread. "We could take this down," he said wistfully.

"They'd want us to eat," Kip said. "Besides, we've said our good-byes now." He picked up a piece of the chicken, sniffed at it, and bit.

They told Emily and Malcolm about their day, and as Kip was talking about his instruction from Master Odden, he asked Emily what she knew about the revolutionaries in Boston. "Not very much," she said. "A bunch of blowhards, Thomas said, so I expect they have some good solid standing."

"Master Odden seemed to think they were serious." Kip wasn't sure how much to say.

"He might know. I read that Mr. Adams' articles from time to time, and he made sense to me, but I don't know how he plans to do the things he talks about, and I'm not sure he does either. He's just talking." Emily twisted a lock of hair around her finger and lowered her voice. "Not that it wouldn't be nice, you know, being in charge of our own country. I don't trust a bunch of men across the ocean to know what we need here."

"We can't talk like that," Kip said with alarm. "Not if we're going to study here."

"We're talking, that's all," Emily protested. "Like your Mr. Adams. Oh, very well. I won't say more about it."

Coppy's eyes had widened, and Malcolm looked between Emily and Kip with interest, but both stayed quiet. Kip rubbed his whiskers, feeling foolish and relieved both. "How was your day once you were done with your masters?"

"We sat with the students who were leaving and talked about where they were going," Emily said. "Michael Cooper was going back to his father's farm, and Peter Davies was going to try to attend William and Mary University. Carmichael pouted the whole day; he wanted to stay here, but no Master would take him. They said he'll be receiving orders to report to a ship, but nobody knows where."

"I thought it'd be somewhere off the Canary Islands," Malcolm said with relish. "Lots of good battles there."

"Don't wish him dead." Coppy said softly.

"You of all people should, if anyone does." Malcolm leaned his elbows on the table.

The otter shook his head. "Even Farley I wouldn't wish dead. I'd like to see him suffer some for what he's done. Carmichael, though, he was only caught up with Farley and trying to impress him. You know, Kip, the way Thomas was for a while, and then when his father forbad him spending time with Farley he wasn't nearly as bad."

"You're right," Kip said, "but he still did some terrible things."

"Aye, well." Coppy shrugged. "I suppose we'll see his true colors after some time of his service, should he ever come back."

"I hope he doesn't," Emily snapped. "Let him discover his true self somewhere else. We'll have enough to worry about with Patris and Sharpe, not to mention Coppy working with Windsor. What?"

Coppy had lowered his head, and Kip held up a paw, too late. "Oh, Coppy's worried about that too," he said.

Emily reached across the table and set her white hand on his brown paw. "Don't you worry," she said "If he mistreats you, you come tell us and we'll get you through it just like we've done this year. With all we've accomplished, we're not going to stop now, nor leave anyone out."

Malcolm set his hand on hers, and Kip lay his paw on top. "Not a chance," the fox said. "We're in this together."

At that moment, the tent flap moved aside, and the white-robed apprentice walked in. He sat down at a table, and within moments the peppermint tingle returned to Kip's nose and food appeared in front of the vacant-eyed blond young man. He ate peacefully as the four of them watched.

Emily stood. "Let's leave him to his dinner," she said.

Malcolm followed suit with the rest of them, but started toward the young man's table. Emily grabbed him by the arm. "What are you doing?"

"Talking to him."

"If he wanted to talk to you, he'd talk to you. We'll be here for years. There'll be plenty of time. Come on."

"But—yes, yes, all right." He hurried after Emily, but she didn't let go of his arm until they were outside the tent. Then they stood in the chill night air, looking toward the Tower. "Time for us to get some sleep, you figure?"

"Just about. First day with our masters tomorrow." Emily rubbed her hands together. "And it's chilly out here."

They had set along the path to the Tower when the creak of the gates stopped them. "Who's coming back so late at night?" Emily asked, but the answer came in the form of two people walking toward them along the path, one taller with blond hair that glowed in the moon's light, and one shorter and stouter. The evening breeze brought his odor to Kip's nose, raising the hackles on the fox's neck.

"Hey," Kip shouted before he could stop himself. "Aren't you supposed to be gone?"

Farley brayed a laugh and elbowed the boy at his side. "Tell it, Vic."

Victor Adamson cleared his throat. "My father had offered to pay full tuition for one more student to go on as an apprentice. Since I and you," he inclined his head toward Kip, "were chosen, I offered Mr. Broadside the favor, and he has accepted. Master Patris has already approved it."

The words iced Kip's chest. Malcolm reacted first. "Ah, you can't do that," he cried. "We only just got the smell out of the upper hall."

"You want to watch your mouth, Mickey," Farley sneered. "I'll be happy to relieve you of a few teeth if you like."

"Sure, and you could use a few extra," Malcolm retorted.

"All right." Emily put her arms out. "We're just getting some air. Go on back in."

The four of them stood against the wall of the Tower, well away from the path as Farley and Adamson walked past them. Kip couldn't resist calling after Adamson, "So now we know where you stand, I suppose."

Adamson turned and raised an eyebrow. "I told you my intentions," he said, and then came closer. "Broadside can be useful," he said in a low whisper. "And I intend to make use of him. There's no need for you to interfere, nor be interfered with."

"If you make use of him to get me kicked out, there is," Kip hissed back.

"You're secure in the College now," Adamson said mildly. "And you've proven capable of defending yourself against Farley. I shouldn't even be worried, if I were you."

"What are you using Farley for, then? To be your magical muscle because you haven't any?"

Adamson's eyes looked silver in the moonlight. His expression flickered with annoyance and then set back to neutral. "Sorcery is not the only power in the world, Kip, nor even the strongest. You'd do well to learn that." With that, he turned and accompanied Farley down the path, around the corner, and back to the Tower.

Coppy came over to Kip's side. "That's put rather a damper on the day, hasn't it?"

Kip shook his head. The moon's light now seemed stark and bare rather than silvery, and the Tower loomed over them. Kip put a paw to the wall behind him, but felt only cold stone. The days ahead now felt more difficult than ever, but he tried to think of what his father would say. "There's good and bad in everything," he said. "Let's go inside and do our part for the good."

ACKNOWLEDGMENTS

Over the seven years this novel has been in the works, a number of people have read drafts and provided valuable feedback. Ryan Campbell, David Cowan, Malcolm Cross, Kevin Frane, Watts Martin, Jim Worrad, and Becky Wright in particular helped out. Malcolm and Mark Brown encouraged me to rewrite the inital draft, and Kij Johnson's novel workshop provided invaluable assistance in figuring out what to change.

In bringing this novel to publication, I have to thank Mark and Grant of Argyll for their patience and belief in the book, and Laura Garabedian for the beautiful artwork.

And as ever, my thanks to Mark and Jack and Kobalt, the best family a writer could ask for.

ABOUT THE AUTHOR

Tim Susman started a novel in college and didn't finish one until almost twenty years later. In that time, he earned a degree in Zoology, worked with Jane Goodall, co-founded Sofawolf Press, and moved to California. Since finishing Common and Precious, he has attended Clarion in 2011 (arcoo to my Narwolves!) and published short stories in Apex, Lightspeed, and ROAR, among others. Under the name Kyell Gold, he has published multiple novels and won several awards for his furry fiction. You can find out more about his stories at *timsusman.wordpress.com* and *www.kyellgold.com*.

ABOUT THE ARTIST

Laura is an illustrator of weird and whimsical work primarily of a fantastical bent. Her weapons of choice when assaulting her canvas include watercolors, ink, oil, or pencil, and her subject matter is as widely varied as walking trees, bleeding flowers, or dancing gryphons.

The niece of an illustrator, Laura grew up knowing that art was in her blood and took every opportunity to decorate her schoolwork, clothes, and skin with drawings, but was torn between Veterinary school or a career in the arts. Laura's current work often attempts to bridge that gap, incorporating her love of animals and anatomy into every piece that she creates.

Nestled near the Rocky Mountains, Laura draws inspiration from the inspiring vistas, her goofy noodle-dragons, Isis and Baku, the small plot of land that she is curating for vegetables, and the local wildlife.